Herbert Kastle was born  as
been an English teacher, a t
he now devotes his time of
many successful novels s-
Country, Hit Squad, Di d's
War.

'A thrilling novel set in Bay Island, an exclusive resort on the
coast of Miami. Bucky Prince . . . plans a return, the object being
an incredible robbery of the eleven members of the Super-Rich
who live on Bay Island. Herbert Kastle sustains the tension right
through to a shattering climax.'
Bucks. Standard

'Penniless Bucky (welcomed by long-resident families who have
known him since so-high) plus gang of hired help, has plan to
leave no stone unturned (diamonds for preference) not to say
lifted, on the island. If these are the hazards, who'd be rich?!'
Evening News

'A taut story full of suspense.'
Nottingham Guardian Journal

The Amber Road

A Warrior of Rome Novel

DR HARRY SIDEBOTTOM

PENGUIN BOOKS

PENGUIN BOOKS

Published by the Penguin Group
Penguin Books Ltd, 80 Strand, London WC2R ORL, England
Penguin Group (USA) Inc., 375 Hudson Street, New York, New York 10014, USA
Penguin Group (Canada), 90 Eglinton Avenue East, Suite 700, Toronto, Ontario, Canada M4P 2Y3
(a division of Pearson Penguin Canada Inc.)
Penguin Ireland, 25 St Stephen's Green, Dublin 2, Ireland (a division of Penguin Books Ltd)
Penguin Group (Australia), 707 Collins Street, Melbourne, Victoria 3008, Australia
(a division of Pearson Australia Group Pty Ltd)
Penguin Books India Pvt Ltd, 11 Community Centre, Panchsheel Park, New Delhi – 110 017, India
Penguin Group (NZ), 67 Apollo Drive, Rosedale, Auckland 0632, New Zealand
(a division of Pearson New Zealand Ltd)
Penguin Books (South Africa) (Pty) Ltd, Block D, Rosebank Office Park, 181 Jan Smuts Avenue,
Parktown North, Gauteng 2193, South Africa

Penguin Books Ltd, Registered Offices: 80 Strand, London WC2R ORL, England

www.penguin.com

First published by Michael Joseph 2013
Published in Penguin Books 2014

001

Copyright © Ballista Warrior of Rome Ltd, 2013
All rights reserved

The moral right of the author has been asserted

Set in Dante MT 11/13pt by Palimpsest Book Production Ltd, Falkirk, Stirlingshire
Printed in Great Britain by Clays Ltd, St Ives plc

ISBN: 978-1-405-93285-1

www.greenpenguin.co.uk

HERBERT KASTLE

Millionaires

GRAFTON BOOKS
A Division of the Collins Publishing Group

LONDON GLASGOW
TORONTO SYDNEY AUCKLAND

Grafton Books
A Division of the Collins Publishing Group
8 Grafton Street, London W1X 3LA

Published by Grafton Books 1973
Reprinted 1973, 1974, 1976, 1982, 1984, 1985

First published in Great Britain by
W. H. Allen & Co Ltd 1972

Copyright © Herbert Kastle 1972

ISBN 0-583-12078-4

Printed and bound in Great Britain by
Collins, Glasgow

Set in Linotype Times

For Butchie

'He heapeth up riches, and knoweth not who shall gather them.'

Old Testament, Psalms

FEBRUARY 26, 1966

The phone in the guard booth rang; not the usual brief spasms but a clangorous unceasing alarm. The emergency signal.

It was the first time in nearly two years of service here that the big man in the blue and white of Miami Beach's police department had heard the signal, and he didn't quite believe it. He glanced left toward the General Causeway and its heavy in-season traffic scoring the night with headlights and tail-lights some hundred feet back along the fill-in road, then looked over the narrow, three-hundred-foot bridge to Bay Island immediately on his right. Everything seemed normal.

But as he turned to enter the booth, he saw flashlights converging on the island end of the bridge. The private cops were running around over there.

He lifted the phone. 'Beaufort,' he said, pronouncing it Byuferd in the Southern fashion.

'Mayday!' the voice masked by shrill excitement shouted. 'Code B!'

The big officer's face was pockmarked from forehead to chin. It wasn't the kind of face that expressed the gentler emotions at the best of times. Wesley Beaufort (and lived there a man who dared call him Wesley when he expressly requested Beaufort?) had been given this cushy assignment after eleven years of exemplary service, two wounds in the line of duty and three citations for bravery. Now the hard face softened ... with contempt.

'All right,' Beaufort said. 'How many, and are they coming this way?'

The shrill voice said something off-phone, and then, 'Get reinforcements!'

Beaufort began to repeat his question. The line clicked. He cursed the fool with his Maydays and Code B's in a cool murmur that belied the venomous obscenities. Someone on Bay Island had been robbed. So the thieves, unless they were insane, would use a speedboat for the getaway instead of trying to come over this two-lane bridge where they'd have to run first past the gaggle of island security men and then past Beau-

7

fort's post. It was up to the private bay patrol and whatever city water police could reach the area in time. Still, in the manner of a cop who never overlooks a bet, he loosened his ·38 in its holster as he dialed the 93rd Street station.

He didn't complete the dialing. He heard something, and put the phone down gently. He stood with head cocked, listening hard, then walked quietly from the booth, under the lowered crossing gate and off the bridge. He reached the whitewashed stone-and-concrete fence that ran along both sides of the bridge, and stopped to listen again. He smiled, not a reassuring sight, and moved to the end of the fence and around it to the grassy slope leading down to the waters of Biscayne Bay. He saw the dark shape struggling along the bridge's metal underpinnings. His right hand drew his revolver, his left took the flashlight from the clip on his belt. He aimed the flashlight as he would a gun, and slid the button forward. The man whose legs were caught in its beam froze. Beaufort pinned him squarely in the light and said, 'C'mon along now,' his eyes already moving beyond to look for others.

There was a splash. The man had dropped something. Beaufort's thumb pulled back the hammer of his revolver. 'You heard what I said, didn't you?'

'Yes, but wait ...' The voice was a youthful croak, and Beaufort realized he had a boy here. 'Wait ... I have to ...'

Beaufort saw the shotgun then, slung over the boy's back and somehow being swiveled into position to fire. He wasn't worried. The boy was bracing himself with one hand and trying to aim and fire with the other. Beaufort said, 'Well that's too bad,' and with precision and no reluctance whatsoever shot the boy in the stomach. There was a choking scream, the shotgun fell, the boy twisted and bent, turning in on himself in agony, but despite this he managed to hold to the bridge. Beaufort shot him again, and yet again as the boy fell into shallow water.

Beaufort waited a while, looking for others. He heard voices and saw flashlights coming across the bridge. He almost hoped there *were* others with the boy, because it would be a field day potting those fools on the bridge.

But there were no others. Turned out it was this one dumb eighteen-year-old who got onto the island somehow, maybe hiding in back of a delivery van, and had held up the Vener place for considerable jewelry and cash. 'Mayday, Code B,'

Beaufort murmured to the three khaki-clad private guards who helped him drag the boy onto shore and retrieve a pillowcase full of loot. In return, one young guard rolled the body over and said, 'Two in the stomach wasn't enough for this public enemy. That third slug in the back, now that one was *really* necessary.'

Beaufort said, 'Yes,' and went into knee-deep water to bring out the shotgun. He looked it over; a customized Browning Automatic-5, about the best you could buy, its tooled stock and part of the barrel hack-sawed off. No fifty-dollar piece of junk but a beautiful weapon, a true work of gunsmith's art, butchered . . .

Upset, he dropped the gun and went back to the bridge. He called Captain Rainer at home and explained the situation, concluding with: 'The newspapers don't have to know, do they, seeing as that's how the Bay Islanders want it?' The captain said he'd make a few phone calls and be down in a while to handle things personally. When Beaufort hung up, there were several more people outside. One was Jack Ebbing, head of island security, not too old a man but fat and pale and, so Beaufort had heard, sick in the kidneys. 'You always do a job, Byuferd,' Ebbing said. 'We going to have any publicity?'

Beaufort said not if he and Captain Rainer could help it. Mr. Mortonson, who had the house on the west end of the island, the *entire* west end, and was worth so many millions Beaufort felt a little scared just to look at him, Mr. Mortonson was there and he said, 'Come to see me on Monday, Byuferd. We've been talking about you for quite a while. There are better things for a man cut to your rare pattern of loyalty and ability than a city policeman's job.'

Beaufort paled with pleasure and said yes-sir-he-would-sir, then glanced at Ebbing. Ebbing was turning away, but he gave Beaufort a nod and Beaufort knew Ebbing was through at Bay Island and would boost Beaufort into his job. The job paid real well. And more than that, there was the stone cottage with office and living quarters, right on the island.

Later, he talked to Wally Jeckle, his midnight relief, and Jeckle said he didn't understand why more thieves hadn't tried to make this scene. 'Imagine, twelve millionaires, and I mean *rich* ones, all together on this bitty island two, three months each winter, with all that ice and cash and whatnot. It's a *natural*, right, Byuferd?'

'Not right, Wally. The only way to rob this place and get away with it is from the inside. And I don't mean a chauffeur or cook or nigra maid. I mean one of the millionaires who can case out each home and know what things are worth and then know where to sell such things for close to actual value. And millionaires hardly have motive, do they, Wally?'

Wally said he didn't see as how they could, since money was the motive and they had more than they could count.

Beaufort said. 'That's the first time you've been right all year, Wally.'

Wally made himself laugh, then struck back with: 'But this thing you got for rich people, Byuferd. They's rich bastards as well as poor ones, the way I see it.'

Beaufort lit a cigarette. 'That might be the way you see it, Wally, but that's not the way it is. To be as rich as *these* folk, you've either got to be born from the best—which means you build on the best to get better—or you did it all yourself, and that's *proof* you're the best. To be as rich as *these* folk, you've got to be close to perfect.'

'C'mon now, Byuferd...'

'What do words like "bastard" coming from people like *you* have to do with *them*? Words like "good" and "bad"...' he made a laughing-snorting sound ... 'what can they mean coming from me and you about *them*?'

Wally began to answer with some heat. 'I figure as Americans we got the right to opinions...'

'These folk,' Beaufort interrupted coldly, 'are what America's all about. Everyone in America wants to be where they're at. Where they're at is the top. So they're the best America's got. Anyone who don't believe that can't be much of an American. And that's the way *I* see it, Wally.'

Wally watched him walk to the patrol car on the sandy shoulder, limping just a little. He figured Sergeant Corbet was right when he said the real reason they'd put Wesley Beaufort on the Bay Island Bridge wasn't because of that bad hip—smashed by a stick-up man's lucky shot—but to get him and his mean face and his acid tongue away from the Beach and the tourists ... and maybe even the lawbreakers.

Book I

TODAY . . .

MONDAY, JANUARY 20

It was one of those springlike January days: Clear sun and a few high, white clouds, and speedboats frothing across the blue-green surface of Biscayne Bay. All very pretty, if Miami was your bag. All rather exciting, if you hadn't seen it before.

Miami wasn't Walter Danforth Prince's bag, and he'd seen it all before. Seen it as a boy three Christmas vacations running, aged nine to twelve, when visiting his grandfather right across the water there on Bay Island. Old Cleve had known how to make money, using the family mining company for starters and taking off into stock and futures, but, like all Princes since great-grandfather Daniel, he hadn't known how to *hold* it.

Bucky, as he'd been called since prep school, switched to the left-hand lane as he approached the turnoff marked 'BAY ISLAND—*Private*', down-shifting by stages from fifth all the way into first, playing with the Carrera-type gearbox. A pause to find a hole in traffic, and he rocketed across the General Causeway's westbound lanes and onto the blacktop road built atop a crest of fill with bay water lapping close on either side. There were three more signs—'NO SIGHTSEEING', 'NO TRESPASSING' and 'SLOW! *Check Point Ahead!*'

A few feet up on the bridge and to the left was a guard post, a Beach policeman standing outside, leaning on a tall lectern. Walt pulled the dusty green sports car to a stop at the lowered crossing gate. 'Good morning. I'm Walter Prince.' The policeman came up to the window, peering suspiciously and masking it with a smile. 'You're visiting...?'

'Not visiting. Taking possession of my new home.'

'Oh, yes...' The smile became natural, and he returned to the lectern to examine a ledger. 'Just a minute now, Mr. Prince.' He went into the booth and picked up the phone.

Bucky looked across the bridge. He hadn't been here in twenty-two years, yet it seemed the same. Freshly white. Immaculate, as everything *had* to be on Bay Island.

From where he sat he could see on his right the east end of the island with its small, blue yacht-club (small because each home had its own cottage that Grandfather had referred to as 'the penitentiary', and behind that, almost hidden by pines, a water tower which was part of the private fire-fighting unit manned by the security forces. The rest of the island stretched westward, a slender finger of heavily vegetated and heavily valued land lying in the northern section of Biscayne Bay, pointing from Miami Beach to mainland Miami. His own house, he knew, was the first west of the bridge, the least desirable in terms of location because it was closest to both entry and causeway. But it had been the only one available during the six months he had tried to buy onto the island, and the price was right. Two hundred and fifty thousand dollars was, as the committee head had written his lawyer, 'practically a giveaway'.

He saw a pale-blue car leave security headquarters. At the same time the officer came out of his booth and pressed a lever fixed to the lectern, raising the crossing gate. Bucky waved his thanks and moved forward sedately, keeping the savage little car under tight control.

Tall and dark, with heavy black hair lightly gray at the temples, loose and rangy behind the wheel, leashed motive power under his foot and leashed emotional power behind his bland smile, he rolled over the bridge and stopped at the second crossing gate. This one was raised immediately and the private guard called, 'If you'd pull over to where that blue car is, Mr. Prince?'

He did, and the man from 'the penitentiary' got out of the Dodge sedan and walked toward him. A big man in a loose fitting, off-the-rack brown suit, white shirt with not-quite-right collar, and stringy dark tie. A wide man with scalp showing through his straight brown hair. A hard man with a face like a battlefield.

'I'm pleased to welcome you to Bay Island, Mr. Prince.'

No hand was offered because this one was a true servant of money, all the way through. Bucky put out his own hand, which was quickly and lightly shaken.

'I'm Byuferd. Maybe I should say welcome *back*, Mr. Prince. I hear your grandfather owned a place here long before my time and you used to visit.'

'Who would remember *that* far into the past?'

'Mrs. Greshen remembers everyone who ever lived here and their families and most of their friends.'

'Not Willa Greshen of Greshen Chemical? I thought she'd ...' No, it was her husband who had died six or seven years ago; Trent, senior brother in the family that was among the ten richest in the nation. 'She must be a very old woman.'

'In her eighties. Lives here all year round now. She said your grandfather was the best dancer on the island, and the best sailor on the east coast.'

Bucky nodded. The Princes had all danced and sailed well ... when dancing and sailing had been important.

'Would you like me to show you around, Mr. Prince? Bring you up to date?'

'Thank you, yes. Hop in.'

Beaufort came around the front of the car, eyes seeming to gauge the interior for room in which to fit his considerable bulk. When he entered, he sat hunched into himself, trying not to take up too much space. 'Left on the road here, Mr. Prince.' His voice also hunched into itself.

'There's more room in this litle car than meets the eye, Byuferd. Relax.'

The big man smiled. 'Porsche. The six. Top of the line, isn't it?'

'You obviously know cars, Byuferd.'

'I watch cars go in and out of here all day, Mr. Prince. It's part of my job. A car like this costs upwards of nine thousand dollars, with air. That's better than most Caddies and Lincolns. I have to know things like that. People sometimes try to come on this island who don't belong. Cars help me spot them. Cars first and then clothes and then the people themselves. I can be fooled by cars and clothes, yes, but not by people. Not very often, Mr. Prince.'

'Makes me feel secure, Byuferd.' He drove sedately along the two-lane blacktop road. 'But that's your job, isn't it, making Bay Islanders feel secure?'

Beaufort smiled and nodded.

'Is it a hard job?'

'Not at all, Mr. Prince. My men and I enjoy our work. No problems. This isn't central Miami, not by a long shot.'

Bucky gave him the laugh he was seeking, and Beaufort said, 'Here's *your* place, Mr. Prince. Your people have been busy.

13

Looks good, doesn't it?'

The house *did* look good. He'd seen only photographs of it until now, though he'd had a vague recollection of it, as he had of all the island homes. It was a two-story colonial, gray with white shutters and trim, set several hundred feet back from the road across a fine green lawn. House and grounds both had generous proportions by anything but Real Society standards, and just last year Bucky would have felt it opulent. But now, moving back into the actuality and, more importantly, the *feel* of his past, he thought of it as adequate.

'Your boat's in back,' Beaufort said. 'The dock still needs painting, but that's to be done this week, from what I gather. Not that it looks bad, Mr. Prince. Everything shipshape.' He said this last with a certain stiffness; a landlubber for sure.

Bucky murmured his pleasure. They drove past a parklike area of stately trees and were at another house, low and long and rustic. 'Number Two,' Beaufort said. 'You remember the addresses? You're Number One Bay Drive and the numbers go up from there, clear around the island.'

'Yes, twelve in all.'

'Well, Number Twelve's been empty for three years. The club committee owns it and they're going to make some sort of theater out of it. It's too close to the services area, so we have eleven addresses on Bay Island as of now.'

Bucky was trying to read the mailbox sign as they passed the gate. 'If you'd give me that refresher course on the residents, Byuferd.'

'Mr. and Mrs. Vener, the beer people.'

Hans Vener Breweries. Not the largest by any means, and split among three brothers. Walt put a fifty-million figure, tops, next to Charles and Karen Vener's names. But they collected Picassos on a grand scale.

'They have a little boy. He was sick last year and they were here almost to the end of May. Now Number Three . . .'

Another colonial, in traditional white with black shutters, much larger than Bucky's, belonging to Avery and Dale Cornwall. A chain of restaurants gave these *arrivistes* in the neighborhood of seventy million.

Number Four was ranch-style, enormous, the third largest house on the island, owned by Brian and Abigail Waters, whose money was old enough to have lost its origins. Investments were Brian's game, his and his married son's and his son-

14

in-law's. Two hundred million was a conservative estimate of their worth.

Number Five was a Federal brick mansion of the McIntyre type on a large, manicured plot; a not too successful attempt to bring old Salem to Florida. Gerard and Selina McKreigh, both active in the McKreigh publishing enterprises, were new–old money ... most of it new. About a hundred million, unless they had given away as much of it as their P.R. people insisted they had.

A soft turn right, and they were driving along the huge Bertram Alvah Mortonson property, which took up almost the complete west end; the second largest house on the island, a rambling Mediterranean villa with red-tile roof. 'Mr. Mortonson is president of the club committee. He and his daughter, Cecily, entertain some of the most important people ... But I guess you know all that, Mr. Prince.'

Bucky did. He also knew that Bert Mortonson, called Allie, and his daughter Ceecee were worth over two hundred fifty million. Mortonson's heavy holdings in California real estate were a variable investment, with the value forever rising.

'We'll cut over to the country club here ...' Beaufort pointed to a tree-lined road, and Walt swung into a shadowy tunnel of old pines so heavy they cut sunlight to a minimum. There was a sudden widening to a parking lot shaded by an enormous banyan tree, and Walt saw the redwood building, the country club, with golf course stretching out beyond.

Beaufort talked while Bucky remembered following his grandfather around the course, being allowed to play occasionally, having lunches in the club, which old Cleve insisted were 'execrable', perhaps his favorite word. (Very good lunches, as Bucky recalled.) Beaufort explained that the golf course, along with the polo field and a new landing strip and heliport, took up a third of the island's center. 'There's been talk of putting in another eighteen holes, since it gets a little crowded when the guest list is heavy. Also, Mr. Mortonson thinks it's much too easy for a good golfer. But nothing's been done as yet. Most people don't want to cut down the palms, pines and banyans.'

'I'm with them,' Bucky murmured; then said he would forgo inspecting the club. They returned along the shaded road to a spot just past the Mortonson home.

Number Seven was the first house on the breezy north side, a

15

son of cans, paper containers and throwaway bottles. A hun-yellow-brick ranch belonging to Lambert and Patricia White-dred million there if a dime, and a chance to be worth half again as much if a recently discussed merger went through.

Number Eight was the smallest home on the island; a concrete block-house affair considered ultramodern in the thirties, built by one of the lesser-known DuPonts and quickly sold and resold. Its current owner was the once famous bandleader–singer, Dick Brandy. Brandy had made more in Southern Florida real estate than he had in show biz and was worth upwards of twenty million. He had suffered a stroke two years ago, had retired and lived here all year around.

Willis and Deborah Miller of oil and natural gas had Number Nine, a beautiful Georgian with formal gardens that were considered the island's best. The Millers were definitely among the centimillionaires, but that wasn't what concerned Bucky as he stopped for a long look. This had been Cleve Prince's home. This was where those three Christmas vacations had been spent. This was where he had dreamed the not-at-all impossible dream of being a great yachtsman, a great businessman, a builder of the Prince fortunes. As he preferred to remember himself, he had been a good little rich boy who had wanted only to become a bigger, better and richer man.

But then again, there had also been the summer he'd run away, and that hardly fit into the mold of good little rich boy. He was fourteen and all set for a 'grand tour of the Continent', or an exclusive Claude Brengen vacation tour for the scions of the rich. Eight boys, three of them classmates of Bucky's at Andover, were to form the congenial group following the classic English tradition of spending several months traveling through France, Germany and Italy, absorbing, via the retired schoolmaster's practiced eye and tongue, the riches of European culture. Brengen preferred members of Real Society, that heavy cream off the top of American wealth, which was a combination of money and established family, but only Bucky and one other boy, an offshoot of the Morgans, were in this category. And, to his disappointment, Professor Brengen lost Walter Bucky Prince.

Bucky had no real resistance to travel, or to doses of European culture administered while traveling. But he did develop considerable resistance to Professor Brengen during two 'in-doctrination and introduction periods' the good professor conducted to make *sure* his group would be a congenial one. There were those warmly humorous statements concerning 'our deodorized masses and their deodorized education', and other, sometimes less warm comments on popular music, popular reading, popular culture in general. Some of the young travelers-to-be seemed to enjoy Brengen's witticisms; others exchanged wry glances, but weren't disturbed—certainly not to the extent of wanting to endanger their parent free vacation. But Bucky Prince was just beginning to experience the joys of his sexuality; a very nubile thirteen-year-old had recently allowed him to draw down her panties and fondle her plump backside, and there was the promise of more to come if he remained somewhere in the vicinity of Southampton. That this girl was daughter to the caretaker of the Prince's summer home and therefore, despite an intelligence that overshadowed Bucky's own, a member of Brengen's despised 'deodorized masses', made Bucky even more determined not to go on the tour.

His father saw it otherwise. His father said, 'You don't fool me, young man. You've got girls on the brain. I don't know who exactly and where exactly, but you want to play house with *some* little bit of stuff. Tad was and is the same.' A smile then. 'I was the same, and so it seems was every Prince of male gender.' End of smile. 'But that can wait a few years. You're going with Brengen, even if he is a toadying old ass. As for his non-democratic talk, as you put it, let's say it's a small and necessary counter influence to the vast amounts of Marxist-Socialist propaganda we've been ingesting since F.D.R....'

Bucky waited until his bags were packed, his good-byes said, then took one small suitcase, two hundred dollars and caught a bus. Grandfather Cleve was in Prouts Neck. Grandfather Cleve listened to Bucky's diatribe against prejudice and entrenched conservatism, and laughed. 'Who is she?'

Bucky didn't tell him.

Grandfather Cleve hid him out until the tour had left, then interceded for him when Father came storming to Prouts Neck.

Bucky ended up sailing, swimming and playing tennis at Southampton. The caretaker's daughter didn't deliver quite as much as she had promised, but Bucky did develop a lifelong predilection for plump buttocks. The girl learned that the hand is quicker than a fourteen-year-old boy's ability to seduce,

17

and of course safer, and used this knowledge to masturbate Bucky regularly. Bucky further developed what some might characterize as a strong appetite, and others a strong weakness, for women in general. And because they *did* talk occasionally and the girl *was* bright, he also further developed certain ideas that were to make him the very first Prince to publicly support political ideas other than those espoused by the Republican Party...

'Your grandfather's old house?' Beaufort interrupted his thoughts.

Bucky nodded.

'Bring back memories?' the security man murmured respectfully.

Bucky said, 'Yes,' and drove on.

Number Ten was a three-story Regency (remarkable how so many of the original islanders had been tied to their northern homesteads even when building in tropical Miami) constructed by one of the Woolworths and sold not too many years ago to a man known for his quiet ways, his impeccable manners and his past as a high officer of the Mafia. Vincent Drang (*né* Drangostine) was clean now, and no one in law enforcement or out had questioned it for ten years. Established as a member of the Bay Island community before his past had leaked, he was tolerated if not really accepted; he and his hotels and stud farms, which gave him a net worth of anywhere from forty to sixty million, depending upon your informants. All Beaufort said about him was. 'Mr. Drang is a well-known horseman.'

Number Eleven was a house Bucky remembered as well as he did his grandfather's. The largest on the island; castlelike, baroque and cluttered, but perfectly maintained. The growth was so heavy, the trees and shrubs so massive (and so designed) that Bucky had to edge into the driveway to get a partial view of it. 'Mrs. Greshen's home,' Beaufort murmured, and Vincent Drang, *né* Drangostine, could have walked on water and not gained such respect.

They drove past the decaying wooden mansion that had been Number Twelve and was too far gone and too close to the services at the east end of the Island to find a tenant. Quickly past the yacht-club, the water tower, the garage housing the island's fire engine and Beaufort's stone cottage, and they were back at the bridge, Beaufort got out of the Porsche. 'If you ever need me, Mr. Prince, dial one three. Thirteen. Any time, day or night. There's a printed form...'

Bucky thanked him, said he was anxious to see his place and pulled away. He was still thinking of Willa Dorcas Greshen, so old and so venerably rich that the inevitable nickname had been lost. (Besides, who could call an *institution* Bunny or Babe or Happy?) Willa Dorcas Greshen who'd had liveried footmen ... and almost fifty million in jewelry. (Did she still own the Light of Stars diamond?) Willa Dorcas Greshen whose personal fortune was half a *billion* dollars.

He turned into the driveway of Number One Bay Drive. The muscular boy clipping a shrub looked up as he went by. He stopped at the imposing entrance and got out. The door was open by the time he mounted the four broad steps. He nodded at the white-jacketed butler and stepped into the cool of air-conditioning.

'Place looks good, Charles.'

'Yessir.' The lean, ferret-faced man walked in front of him and opened a door off the broad foyer. 'I'll get the others.'

Bucky went into a library, looked around and sat down at a green, leather-topped desk. The furniture wasn't bad. It had come with the house. He had let it be known that he would replace it with his own things, later.

His own things. Where were his own things?

He turned in the chair and looked out the window at blue water and the distant causeway and more water beyond. He was tired. He wanted a drink.

He leaned left to see the dock. His boat was there.

'No, not *his* boat. *The Spray* was sold and gone long ago. This boat had been chosen for him, bought for him, by strangers. This boat was a prop, a stage setting...

He pulled at his tie, his collar. He wanted a drink, *now*! He began to rise; then stopped, settled back and adjusted his shirt and made himself neat again, a Prince again. This was inexcusable. And with everything just beginning to take shape.

He looked down at himself. His double-breasted blue jacket and gray trousers fit like skin; fit like the custom-made clothes they were. His shirt too. Everything made expressly for Bucky Prince. And why not? Hadn't it always been this way? Always ... except for two strange years. And then he had decided he need not live other than as a Prince and he'd made his plans and Charles DeVino had walked into his net and through DeVino had come the others and the two strange years, the

19

two lost years, were dismissed and he was here. And he would stay here and in the other places of his caste ... or die. Not jail. If it came to jail, it would come to death.

He took out his cigarettes and lit one, watching his hands ... steady ... and the two strange years were nothing, forgotten, as if they never were.

But then he asked himself if a man could really forget two years of his middle age, two recent years of his life? And he knew that he *hadn't* forgotten, merely refused to review, to dwell upon, those years. And he also knew that those years had made *this* Bucky Prince something other than the Bucky Prince of money and pride.

He smoked and tried to read titles on the wall of books across from him. The bindings were morocco and the room was rich with wood and leather, it reached out to him, comforted him. There was a collection of Robert Louis Stevenson.

'Home is the sailor,' he murmured, 'home from the sea, and the hunter ...'

He remembered then that Stevenson had written it as an epitaph, and the comfort fled and the deep, prophetic chill came.

The door opened and the servants filed in and stood looking at him.

Charles DeVino said, 'This is Mr. Prince.'

Vino's girl, Sandy, cute in the black-and-white of a maid, made a little mock curtsy. Bucky smiled.

The other woman was in her fifties; dark, stringy, dried out. She watched him with shrewd eyes, her mouth sour.

Vino motioned at her. 'Fanny Lescou. Good French Canadian name. Good French Canadian cook.'

'*Bonjour*, Fanny.'

She nodded. The sour expression remained.

'Buddy-Boy Rollins,' Vino said, indicating the muscular youth in earth-stained levis and T-shirt. 'He's older than he looks.'

'He had better be,' Bucky murmured.

Rollins smiled shyly, moved his lips as if to speak, then didn't.

'You know Sandy ...'

'Not like he should,' the saucy blonde cracked.

Bucky felt a momentary twinge, but whether of worry, or desire (or both), he couldn't be sure.

20

'Then there's our mainland man, Bramms. We'll get together first chance.'

'*Brahms?*' He had Vino spell it for him and chuckled and rose. 'That's all for now. We'll talk when there's something to talk about. At the moment, what I want is a gin and tonic, followed by a shower and lunch.'

'So now we get the *beeg* boss...' Fanny Lescou began.

Vino said, 'He *is* the boss and you remember that, Fanny.'

'Or else I'm fired?' She showed her teeth.

'In a way,' Vino murmured. He kept his eyes on her and she shifted her gaze and muttered, 'But why, when we're relaxing, alone?'

'Because if we get bad habits we'll slip in front of someone who'll wonder. Because Mr. Prince is putting up more than half the money and all the *In*. Because a mistake or two might be enough to ruin everything and I know you wouldn't want to ruin five or six million.'

'Or eight or ten or more,' Bucky said. 'Will someone show me to my room?'

Sandy Blake began to play sexy again; then seemed to think better of it. Vino's lectures had obviously taken hold.

Bucky followed the maid. That was how he would think of her; the maid. And of Vino as the butler, and of Lescou as the cook, and of Rollins as the gardener. The maid ... even though on the stairs and out of sight of the others she rolled her full haunches and glanced back at him and said, 'You look good, Mr. Prince. Nice trip down?' He nodded, and she led the way to a large, bright bedroom and stood there, wetting her lips. He could feel her appetite for him, had felt it the first time they'd met six months ago for a brief conference at O'Hare Airport, and his own appetite stirred. She was in her mid-twenties and had a generously curved body and he needed it the way he needed a drink. Bucky Prince had always needed women and a certain amount of liquor. Now, with seven months of frantic preparation behind him and two months of uncertainty ahead of him, those needs seemed to be growing.

'That gin and tonic, please.'

She hesitated, looking directly at him. Her eyes were smoky and he knew she wanted him and he said, '*Please*,' coldly.

She left. He promised himself a woman, any woman, at the very first opportunity.

Later, he stretched out on the bed and drank his second gin

and tonic and considered ringing for a third. But as with Sandy, he exercised control. He had rung too often for a third and a fourth, *ad infinitum, ad nauseam* ... literally. He had drowned too many gray days during the two lost years, and he couldn't afford to do so any more.

He dressed in sailing whites and went down and had lunch on the sun washed patio, attended to by Vino and Sandy, being correct and sending his compliments to Lescou and pulling together all the frayed threads of Bucky Prince's personality.

Soon, he would begin paying his respects to his fellow Bay Islanders.

THURSDAY, JANUARY 23

Even as other people, Curt Bramms felt that monsters stalked the earth. And even as other people, he would have recognized Adolf Eichmann, Lavrenti Beria and similar well-known butchers as prime examples. But unlike other people, Bramms *admired* these monsters. Perhaps because, in his own small way, he was a monster himself.

He didn't look it. A small, thick-set man of forty-seven, his face was round, ruddy, jowly; his eyes weak and uncertain; his hair all but gone. Only the mouth, flat and hard, generally clamped trapdoor shut, gave hint of what went on inside.

What went on inside would have gladdened the heart of the staunchest old-line Nazi. Curt Bramms believed that the way to handle aspiring minorities ('and their damned Jew manipulators') was to exterminate them. 'Wait until they have one riot too many. Wait until their Jew lawyers spring one black bastard looter too many. Then with the *real* Americans ready ... and I mean they're ready now, you don't think all those pistols, rifles and shotguns they've been buying the last ten years have *disintegrated*, do you? When they're ready, *we* riot, in every darktown in America. And in one day, one night, they go from better than twenty million to maybe four or five, and that four or five won't raise its head for another two hundred years. At the same time, an élite corps will eliminate the prime Jew manipulators...'

He was lecturing Charles DeVino this night and Vino was

22

sighing over his whiskey and water. Vino wouldn't have believed it possible that Curt Bramms had been born Louis Abramson, and into an Orthodox Jewish family. Bramms' theory that Jews were unable to perform dangerous sports and feats of courage had led him to become an expert skydiver, skin and scuba diver, skier, horseman and racer of autos and speedboats. Only his present lack of money kept him from practicing these activities and thereby continually strengthening the 'evidence' that he wasn't, *couldn't* be, the legitimate heir of Marvin Abramson.

More conclusive proof of Bramms' right to membership in the monster corps lay in his past, in his *actions* as well as his tirades. But he wasn't fond of advertising in this area. He had stood trial for his life once, skillfully avoided standing trial once before, and mum was the word. (But he thought back often to those two climactic periods with deep satisfaction.)

Bramms and Vino sat in the Pelican Bar in Hollywood Beach, north of Miami. Vino wore tight green slacks and a black turtleneck, Bramms a loose lightweight suit of pale blue.

'About the feint,' Vino said, when Bramms had paused to drink. 'You had any more thoughts?'

'A landing barge is still the best bet, considering the way it'll look to the island security guards—give them the feeling they're really being invaded. I'd prefer an LCVP, the smallest in the line.'

'About like a cabin cruiser?'

Bramms looked amused. 'A cabin cruiser that can hold eighty Marines packed tight for assault.'

'*That's* the smallest? You sure you can handle...?'

'I can handle any LC made. They're flat-bottomed, like rowboats, and just as easy to pilot. I could take one around the world, if the weather was mild and the fuel unlimited. Besides, we wouldn't want anything as small as a cabin cruiser, or as ordinary and unmilitary looking. We need something unusual and threatening and it's got to be big enough so the guards will sweat over possible armaments and how many men might be aboard. That tarp I described to you—it'll cover more than half the interior, including all the modifications...'

'But you never handled one before, did you?'

Bramms' lips compressed tightly. 'You never robbed an island before, did you?'

23

Vino glanced quickly around. 'Take it easy! It's just that Prince might ask you the same question.'

'You mean we're going to meet *before*?'

'In the next few days.'

'Why?'

'It's his setup. He has to stay on top of it.'

'And what if we don't get along?' Bramms asked, smiling a little. 'He returns my money and I walk away?'

'Just make sure you *do* get along,' Vino said flatly. He stared at Bramms, but the squat man didn't take up the challenge. 'Play it cool. No personal talk, or opinions ... like about Jews and Negroes. Just answer his questions about the job and you'll get along fine.'

Bramms drank in silence. Vino said, 'You were telling me about the LC. You found one?'

'According to the manager of a naval surplus outfit near Delray Beach. I made a dozen calls, and he was the only one who had an LCVP. But he wasn't encouraging about its condition.' He drank again. 'I can get an LCM—they carry a tank as well as men. Good condition too. That's up in Daytona.'

'Well?'

'LCM's are kind of big. But that's not what's worrying me.'

'You mean the price? How much will the *smaller* one cost?'

'I don't mean the price. There's not much of a market for used LC's. Anything over their junk value should do it, for the basic cost. But then—if we take the smaller one—we've got to make it seaworthy, even for its one day of use. And there are our modifications: A stand for the rockets, extra tank for emergency fuel ...'

'Won't it hold enough for that one day?'

'Not very likely, since I'll be running the engine from morning until after sundown, according to Prince's basic plan. No change in *that*, is there?'

'Not that I know of. We won't have the complete plan for a while yet, but the way he put it, the sea assault is a constant.'

'All right then. The extra tank; since I can't refuel at a marina and have people looking, asking questions and later remembering. Hooks or cleats along the sides for belaying the canvas's lines. A spotlight. And a big scuttling plug cut into the hull. All that will cost ...' He paused for thought. 'The LCVP in Delray should be around two thousand. The reason I want to use that and not the LCM isn't cost but where they're located. I'd like to avoid a long voyage down the coast.'

'I thought you said you could take it around the world?'

'If I had a few years of perfectly calm weather. An LC in top condition will only make about five knots.' When Vino looked blank, Bramms said, 'A knot is one nautical mile per hour. A nautical mile is about eight hundred feet longer than a land mile. That means a new LC can make five and a fifth land miles per hour. Say our secondhand LC can make five miles an hour. From Daytona, about two hundred forty miles north of our Miami Beach passage into Biscayne, it would take me twenty to twenty-five hours, depending upon weather. That would mean I'd have to take the LC the day before the robbery and we'd be stretching the odds for decent weather ...'

'I got it,' Vino said. 'And from Delray?'

'That's about twenty-five miles north of our entry point. Say five or six hours. Then an hour more to Bay Island. The rest of the time I'll maneuver around off the island.'

'You'll have to go for the one at Delray.'

Bramms finished his drink. 'I intend to, though it's not in Delray proper. Little place on a canal called Berrywood. I'll be up there Monday or Tuesday.'

'And if the weather is bad, no problem from Berrywood?'

'If the weather is *real* bad—a storm—it'll be a problem even crossing the bay. Flat, barge-type thing like an LC ...' He shook his head. 'But whatever the weather, I'll do it. Barring hurricanes, of course.' He grinned at Vino's worried face. 'Want to take over for me?'

Vino smiled sourly.

Bramms finished his drink and raised his hand for another, but Vino stood up. 'I have to get back now. Remember to keep the price down. Fight for every last buck. We're getting close to broke and Prince needs money to play his game.'

Bramms followed him out of the barracks-like bar to the parking lot. 'Fight for every last buck,' he murmured, looking at the Cadillac limousine.

'If I'd known you were going to be so touchy, I'd have brought the Mercedes—it's a little smaller—or the Porsche.'

'Three cars? You mean to tell me a bachelor needs three cars, even on that island?'

Vino smiled. 'You're not dealing with LC's here, baby. Here it's Prince's bag and *he* knows the nautical miles.' He slid behind the wheel. 'Three cars just to get by, just to make ends meet.' He backed up and put his head out the window. 'I'll be in touch soon. Play it cool with Prince and everything will be fine.'

Bramms returned to the bar. He spoke to the bartender, who murmured, 'The one you had last time okay?' Bramms nodded, giving his ritual, 'If I wasn't short of cash, I'd never touch any of them.'

The bartender made a *sotto-voce* call and Bramms had another bourbon and water. He nursed the drink, and a tall Negro girl, quite dark and quite heavy, came to the doorway and caught the bartender's eye. 'Your friend's here,' the bartender said to Bramms, who paid his tab and walked past the girl without a glance.

In the parking lot, Bramms got into his Chevvy and started the engine. The girl hurried after him. She hadn't quite closed the car door when he backed up and screeched out of the lot. They drove onto the A1A.

She said, 'You mad at something, or is it your kick?'

'Take out your tits.'

She stared at him.

'Take out your tits or forget the whole thing!'

'All right, we'll forget the whole thing. You can stop here ...'

He sighed, an exasperated sound, and drove even faster. 'It's my kick, Annie. Only if you make me *say* it ...'

'I'm not so sure,' she muttered, her face strained. 'Twenty bucks isn't enough for your kinda scene. You gonna get rough again?'

'I'll pay thirty. And I didn't really hurt you.'

'You went over your hour last time.'

'Thirty, and I'll get you back in an hour.'

She undid the buttons of her blouse, worked her hand around back to unhook her brassière, then pulled it up over her heavy breasts, letting them hang free. He reached out with his right hand and touched and stroked and, finally, pinched. She grunted but didn't stop him. He cupped one breast and squeezed and only when she said, 'Jesus!' did he let go. 'It's gonna be the same as last time!' she said.

He shook his head. 'No, not the same as last time.' He hadn't really made it last time; he'd faked it last time.

He dropped his hand to her thighs, well exposed by a yellow mini-skirt. He worked around and between them and muttered, 'Like silk, Annie, black silk.'

26

She didn't answer. She watched him from the corner of her eye.

'The pants,' he said hoarsely.

'Listen, man, everything in the car? What're we going to your place for if you ...'

'The goddam pants! Off with your goddam pants!'

She lifted her bottom from the seat and drew off a pair of brightly colored bikinis. As she bent to pull them over her shoes, he jammed his hand between her compressed thighs, worked his fingers into her, said, 'Now you get it! Now ...'

She grunted and got the pants off and straightened, spreading her thighs. Her face remained strained, but he felt the moisture and muttered, 'You like it, you bitch. You know you do. Say you do! Say it!'

She said, 'Oh sure, I'm crazy about it,' but her voice was weak and she leaned back, breathing heavily. 'If anyone looks into this car ...'

'*Say it!*'

Squirming, she muttered, 'I like it.' And then, as he worked frantically at her and drove faster, threading dangerously through traffic, 'I don't know why, but I really like it.' And as they pulled into the darkened parking lot of his motel, 'You goddam honky nut, you turn me on!'

He cut lights and ignition and went at her with both hands, working on breasts and buttocks and groin, bending to suck and kiss and bite. She tried to touch him once, but he pushed her hand from his fly, not wanting her to know he still hadn't attained an erection.

'Let's go ... to your room,' she panted.

'Get my briefcase from the back seat.'

'Your ...?'

'Get it!'

She turned and peered into the back. 'I don't see ...'

'Maybe on the floor. Lean over.'

She got on her knees, bending far over, and he quickly shoved her skirt up above her hips and jammed his face into her backside. She gasped, 'Baby, if someone drives in ...'

He pushed himself into her as far as he could go, face and mouth and tongue as far as they could go. And the flare of headlights came.

'A car!' she whispered, trying to move.

He held her rigid, fingers digging into her fleshy hips. The

27

lights swung by, illuminating them for an instant. And he might have been seen and he cried out his anguish and his penis stiffened.

The car parked further down along the motel building. He pulled her into an embrace and opened his fly and directed her. She manipulated him and used her mouth and he was ready. Quickly, he took her to the room. Quickly, he shoved her onto the bed and got between her thighs. Quickly, he pumped away, mauling her buttocks and breasts. 'My ... kick,' he gasped. 'What I say ...' And then, plunging his head into her breasts, 'Black cunt! Black cunt! Black cunt!'

She convulsed before he was through; then quieted and watched as he slobbered and moaned and quivered in surprisingly weak movement. It looked to her as if he'd barely made it.

She was right. He barely made it with blacks but he no longer made it at all with whites.

When he returned to his second-floor motel room, he changed into pajamas, hoping to get a long night's sleep. But sleep wouldn't come and he got up and dressed in his khaki breeches and riding boots, striding about the room, thick chest bare, back ramrod straight, a Mussolini figure out of time and out of place, looking at himself as he passed and repassed the mirror, slapping the riding crop against his thigh, thinking of his father and how he would punish him. Thinking of his wife and how he had punished her for failing him. Thinking of Barbara and how he had punished that boy who had dared to visit her. Thinking of all the people he would punish ... once he had money again, position again, a base of operations again.

And because he had managed an orgasm (the first in several months), he was strong enough to stop the thoughts there and not go back to beginnings and Lou Abramson, Registered Pharmacist, and the rage and terror experienced at being a Jew at a time when Jews had been fuel for ovens. At being a son without a father, a husband without manhood, a warrior denied a war. At the long list of defeats he had suffered ... and now blamed on his previous state of Jewishness, revealed as a false state in the mind of Curt Bramms.

He thought instead of that island, of all the jewelry on that island, of the bad luck that turned out to be good luck, of being spotted by a girl on the beach when he was trying to steal a

28

stalled and temporarily abandoned speedboat, of meeting Vino and being sounded out on his knowledge of boats and skin diving and his willingness to take chances. Oh, *incredibly* good luck! Louis Abramson would never have had such luck; had never *deserved* such luck!

His was a most important role. He was the invasion force; the one-man landing party that would draw the island's fire and decoy its defenses. And later, he would escape with the loot, almost all of it.

His was the role of greatest courage, greatest danger; exactly what he wanted.

And the rewards would be correspondingly great. He would get a full fifteen per cent share, along with Vino, as compared with Lescou's ten per cent. (Of course, he'd had to put in the last of his money, but how far would twenty-five thousand have carried him anyway? Another miserable two years, rotting away in Hollywood Beach?) Fifteen per cent of six million was nine hundred thousand! And they might get even more.

Al right, say the loss in value suffered when translating stolen jewels to cash would be higher than Prince said it would be. Say they only got *five* million. Make that four. Even with four, his share would be six hundred thousand.

He thought of Prince getting fifty per cent and it bothered him as it had from the beginning. He'd accepted Vino's reasoning that Prince's hundred thousand dollar investment was four times that of the other three major partners, and therefore could be expected to be four times their fifteen per cent ... or *sixty* per cent instead of fifty. And he'd accepted the logic of Prince being the only one who could set up a plan like this and hope to get away with it.

But Prince wasn't going to be involved in the actual stickup. His risks were minimal.

And why did they have to give that boy five per cent? And Vino's girl five per cent? Vino should take care of the girl and Rollins should get a flat fee—fifty thousand was more than enough. Five per cent of four million was two hundred thousand dollars! Two hundred thousand for a dumb kid with muscles!

He had to talk to Vino about that.

He would call Vino tomorrow!

But he couldn't call Vino. That was one of the rules.

Vino had to come to see him! This had to be settled!

And yet he knew, even as he planned what he would say, that Vino couldn't change anything, that the rules of the game were set, that he was stuck with his fifteen per cent.

Unless, of course, something happened to Prince.

No, nothing must happen to Prince. He was their only hope for peddling the jewelry at anything close to actual value.

Quite suddenly, he stopped pacing.

Wouldn't Prince be the most vulnerable of men once everything was over and the money divided up and all of them supposedly scattered to the winds? Wouldn't Prince, remaining on the island, or returning to wherever he came from, wouldn't he be a sitting duck for a little polite blackmail?

Curt Bramms undressed. He relaxed. He smiled to himself as he got into bed. He slept, as peacefully as Curt Bramms ever slept, which was to say with a minimum of twisting and outcry.

'He worries me,' Fanny Lescou said. She, Vino, Sandy and Buddy-Boy Rollins sat around the table in the long kitchen, coffee cups full, a pot on a trivet in the center, sliced pastry on plates before them.

'You only met him once,' Vino said around a mouthful of pastry. 'He'll do his job.'

'But anyone can see he's a sick man ... *un fou*. Mad, not so?'

'He hates colored,' Sandy said. 'Maybe a little too much, but lots of people do. I'm not too wild about them myself.'

'And Jews,' Vino said.

'No Negroes or Jews on this island, are there?' Rollins murmured.

'Maybe a delivery man, a worker, but not anyone *he* has to deal with. I know from what Prince said they wouldn't let a Jew buy a house here even if he was as rich as Rockefeller. As for colored...' He laughed.

'But the way he *talked*,' Lescou said. 'You remember, with the *hate*. I too am not so wild about colored, about Jews. Why should I be? I'm not so wild about my own family.'

Vino and Sandy laughed. Rollins drank coffee.

'But not with so ... so much *anger*. Not even for the *English*. How can a man like that be trusted to do such an important job?'

'He's in the best possible job,' Vino said. 'He'll be *alone* in

30

that boat.'

'I'm Jewish,' Rollins muttered.

'What?'

'*Part* Jewish. Part Scotch, part French ...'

'Ah,' Fanny said, 'the good part.'

'... part German and part Jew.'

'How so many parts?' Lescou asked, smiling.

'You're not mad about the way we were talking?' Vino asked.

'I hear Jews make great husbands,' Sandy said, grinning into Rollins's face. He flushed, his freckles nearly disappearing. 'But I'm not sure about one-quarter Jews. Maybe they lose out to the French and turn into ...'

'My mother was born in Germany. When the Nazis came, she and her mother came to the States because my grandma was Jewish. My grandpa stayed. He was one of those good Germans, the bastard. My father was French and Scotch.'

'And here you are,' Sandy said, still grinning at him. 'A big, beautiful package. Maybe we oughta mix more. Take me and Vino, both Italians. Maybe we oughta split and mix.'

'You mix enough,' Vino said mildly. She smiled at him; a slightly malicious smile. 'And you really give a damn, don't you, Vino?'

He shrugged.

She turned to Rollins. 'What made you tell us? You want Fanny to serve you kosher food?'

Again Rollins flushed. He stared at the table, seemed about to answer, but didn't. He was a young-looking twenty-one, built so compactly, in such perfect proportion, that his size, his strength, didn't show. At the moment, his complexion matched his reddish-brown hair, but normally he was a quick-to-burn pink, this despite his having worked on and off as a gardener since he was sixteen.

Fanny Lescou took the pressure off Rollins. 'You are Italian?' she asked Sandy. 'With a name like Blake?'

'Bianchi,' Sandy said, turning to her coffee and cake.

'Why did you change it? Bianchi is so nice a name.'

'You don't understand. Canada is different. In America everyone wants to become Blake, or something like it.'

Vino began to agree. He was interrupted when Rollins stood up, thick arms corded as if carrying an enormous weight. 'The reason I told you about being part Jew is because I don't like

31

hearing some things. My mother and grandma, they were the only decent ones in the whole damn family. And my mother was *all* Jewish ... I mean the way she felt, what she *wanted* to be. I don't like this guy Bramms. If he ever talks again the way he did the first time we met...' The big hands opened and closed spasmodically.

'Take it easy,' Vino murmured. 'You're not going to have anything to do with him, except for a few hours when we pull the job.'

'Remember you get a couple hundred thousand,' Sandy said, 'like me.'

'And up,' Fanny added.

They all looked at him, worried. When he didn't answer, Fanny said, 'I didn't mean anything when I...'

'No,' Rollins said, voice thick. 'Not you. I know that what you said ... people always say things like that. I don't care about things like that. I can't change it and I don't care. But when they talk like Bramms, about Jews and blacks and killing everyone, I remember what my mother said about Germany and I can't listen. I didn't say anything when we all met at his place to talk because I couldn't see breaking up the meeting and ... I...' He swallowed and turned away. 'But you tell him. Once more. I mean it.'

'Come back and finish your coffee,' Vino said.

Rollins returned to his seat. He was deeply embarrassed and drank his coffee quickly.

Fanny sighed. 'Now take me. I don't like Prince.'

Vino's eyes snapped to her. She quickly added, 'Nothing like Mr. Bramms, understand. I mean, I just don't like working for *le grand Charles* kind of man. The *beeg* boss...'

'You don't like working for *anyone*,' Prince interrupted from the doorway.

It was Fanny Lescou's turn to redden. Walter Prince said, 'I'm the same way. I want to be my own man and not a poor one either. That's why we're here ... all of us, isn't it?'

Fanny muttered, 'Yes, I didn't mean...'

Prince nodded coolly and turned to Vino. 'I meant to tell you, the boat needs work.'

'It's brand new.'

'And beautiful, but it has a wooden hull. Shipworms, teredos, and other borers can eat her up in tropic waters. Also, the sun can burn off her varnish in a week. She has to be hauled

32

once a month and examined for bare wood every ten days. Remember, she's our getaway.' He then murmured good night and left.

Vino leaned across the table. 'Fanny, will you please get the hell off his back! You give him the needle every chance you get!'

'You think he *feels* my needle? The job—that's all he cares about. But us? We're not important to him, not really people to him.

'I don't believe that,' Sandy said, and she said it with some heat.

Vino looked at her. She picked up his pack of cigarettes and shook one out. 'Well?' she muttered, the cigarette hanging from pouting lips. He struck a match for her. She inhaled deeply; he kept looking at her; she refused to meet his eyes. He rose, said good night and walked from the kitchen.

Rollins refilled his cup, expression withdrawn and troubled. Fanny began clearing the table. Sandy sighed and stabbed out her cigarette. She glanced at Rollins; them moved into Vino's chair, next to the big youth, and stroked his arm playfully. 'Hey, baby, bet you're a real swinger back home.'

He surprised her with a straight, open gaze. 'When I think of it, sure.'

'You mean there are times a growing boy *don't* think of it?'

'This boy's stopped growing.'

She looked him up and down, only *half* playfully now. 'Good thing too. You're king-size already.'

Rollins stood up and walked out the door. Sandy caught him in the passageway leading to the foyer. 'What's your room like?' she asked.

'Like yours. A little smaller, since it only holds a single bed.' His eyes moved boldly over her. 'But big enough, in case you're wondering.'

'Hey, you're something else again when it comes to girls, aren't you?'

He kept walking toward his room, which was in the servants' quarters behind the staircase leading to the second floor. She hurried to keep up with his long strides. They went across the foyer, past the staircase and into another narrow passageway. He glanced at the first of the doors, hers and Vino's, and went on. She tried to soften her footsteps. They passed

Fanny's door and reached the last one, Rollins's. He went inside, leaving the door open behind him. She hesitated, glancing back down the hall. When she turned to Rollins's room, she saw he hadn't put on the light. Suddenly timid, she murmured, 'Buddy-Boy? Hey, man, want to talk?' There was no answer but she saw movement near the bed and stepped inside. 'Why don't you put on the light?'

'What for? I'm going to bed.'

'Oh.'

'If you want to stay, close the door. If not, close it when you leave.'

She made herself laugh. 'Play it cool, that's what the big boys said, huh, baby? Show the chicks it isn't important.'

'It *isn't* important,' he said, and the bed sighed.

She waited, certain he would make some sort of pitch. She waited what seemed like a long time and suddenly heard his breathing. It couldn't be, but it sounded like he was falling asleep!

The bastard! First Prince (but he had *wanted*; she knew that) and now this goddam kid! She turned to the door. She had Vino and he really knew what boy–girl was all about, old Vino did. He was more man than she'd ever known; surely more than Rollins (maybe even more than Prince, with all his smooth ways), and there was no reason for her to be catting around.

No reason except the reason that had been with her since puberty—curiosity, the need to know what every (well, *almost* every) man she met was like in bed.

'Good night,' she said, and laughed to show he wasn't fooling her.

'Yeah,' came the muttered, sleep-drugged reply.

She made up her mind. She closed the door and felt her way to the bed and sat down. Her eyes adjusted and she reached out and stroked his face. He cleared his throat. 'You sure it's not gonna be trouble with Vino?'

'Never. You heard us at the table.'

'All right.' He moved over. 'C'mon.'

'With my clothes?' She kissed him and his arms came around her, gentle for such *big* arms. He raised her dress, pulled down her pants and said, 'Don't you worry about your clothes.' And then, voice thickening, 'It's bigger than it looks.'

She got under the blanket. He was nude and ready. In a

34

minute, so was she. He kept playing with her ass, and she murmured, 'You a backdoor man, Buddy?' He cleared his throat twice, trying to answer, but she got rough with her hand and his words were lost in groans. Not that he didn't like it. When she paused, he whispered, 'Go on. Pull. *Pull!*'

His cool was something of the past. She enjoyed bringing him closer and closer to white-hot. And she was right about him. When he couldn't wait any longer, he whispered in her ear, 'Just for a second. Honest. Not to a finish. *Honest.*'

He wasn't too big so she figured what the hell. It wasn't as if she'd never tried it. He had Vaseline in his night table, and after a brief struggle got it up her rear. No real kick for her, but his wildness was fun. Then she flattened out, unsheathing him, and they began again. She played to his taste, again turning backside to him, only this time it went in the right place.

He was a quick come, but without losing steam. He didn't pull out and leave her hanging. He stayed and stayed...

She slipped into his bathroom an hour later, and when she'd finished washing and dressing, he was fast asleep. She smiled, liking him, but her curiosity was satisfied and she didn't know that it would ever happen again. Vino was waiting. She went back up the hall and entered their room. He was in bed, reading a book.

'Detective story?' she asked, going to the closet and kicking off her shoes.

'No. Something Prince got me. On being a butler.'

She laughed. 'Maybe he expects to keep you after the job.'

He didn't answer. She turned, pulling her dress over her head. 'You mad at me?'

He still didn't answer.

'Hey, *paisan*, what goes?'

He put down the book. 'I don't know,' he said, voice low. 'But don't push me tonight.'

She was startled, and showed it.

'Yeah,' he muttered, picking up the book. 'So the thing's changing.'

She was flattered. But then, knowing who and what she was, knowing that it had never been different and she had lost every man who'd wanted her all to himself, she said, 'Please, Vino, don't let it change. No strings, you said. It's been good that way, hasn't it? Why change it?'

He shrugged, hidden behind his book.

35

In bed, she kissed his cheek and turned on her side. His lamp went out. 'You don't have to do that,' she murmured.

He settled himself beside her. She waited. He didn't touch her. Later, when she was almost asleep, he said, 'Who was it? Prince or Rollins? Or did you meet someone outside, like that chauffeur from Number Two?'

So he hadn't heard her footsteps. 'Forget it,' she said. 'I have.'

'Better than me?'

For the first time in their relationship she began to feel impatience. 'No one's better than you, *paisan*.' And it was true and it didn't mean a thing right now because, goddam it, Vino the great was beginning to *beg*!

He went to sleep then. So did she. But toward morning, with light gray in the windows, he woke her and didn't even let her brush her teeth. He was as great as ever ... and while she didn't want it to be so, wouldn't quite admit it was so, it was less than ever. Because of what he said. The gentle whispered things he said. The please-be-faithful things he said.

Walter Prince now ... he would *never* beg.

FRIDAY, JANUARY 24

Mortonson received Prince in a glass-roofed courtyard. There was a fountain and tile flooring and fine patio furniture, all more or less *de rigueur*. The *light*, however, was something special; something that made Walt glance up to check the source. It wasn't lost on Mortonson, a man just shy of six feet with sloping shoulders, a soft, relaxed manner and thick hair worn heavy at the sides and back. That hair was still in the process of turning from blond to gray; a very gentle gray. The face continued the feeling of softness, gentleness; apple-cheeked and wide-eyed and full-lipped. But the voice was crisp and the mannerisms, once he rose and came forward, the very opposite of softness.

'Bucky Prince. I've been looking forward to meeting you since your lawyer's first visit. How *is* Mr. Mondredale?'

'Fine, now that he's back in Philadelphia.'

'You're wondering about the light?'

36

Walt glanced up again, nodding. 'Very effective.'

'Have you ever been in New York's Metropolitan Museum? The main floor, right off the Fifth Avenue lobby? They have— or had; I haven't been there in some years—a re-creation of a Renaissance Italian courtyard, Venetian, I believe. The light there, a cool lime, was what I tried to re-create here. It took considerable effort but I'm pleased with the results. That glass...'

He went on with a description of the workmanship ... and Bucky had a chance to seat himself, to look around while nodding and exclaiming politely.

There were two other people present. One a male servant, Oriental, clearing away the remains of a large breafast. The other a girl, seated at the cluttered table, side turned to him, who had barely glanced his way. She was dressed in white denim shorts cut ragged at mid-thigh, a man's blue shirt with epaulettes, the tails hanging loose and heavy leather sandals. Her hair hung straight, long and dark. She looked a typical teen-ager, but then she crossed her legs—very long, brown legs —and lit a cigarette and he wasn't sure just how old she was. Remembering salient facts from Mortonson's dossier, he knew the man was in his late fifties ... but there was no age listed for his daughter, Cecily.

'... couldn't find a domestic company that would supply the glass I needed, so the order was placed with a German firm. Their first sample was bad, beer-bottle green. The second sample was better, and after I'd paid for a third and a fourth, we had it.' Mortonson turned abruptly. 'Come meet Ceecee.'

So it *was* Allie Mortonson's only child. Bucky followed, the girl looked at him, and he wondered if the light wasn't having an effect here too. He was struck by her face; struck hard. A strange face, large featured—especially the mouth, so very wide, large eyes of an indeterminate blue-gray-green color, and a strong nose. She smiled as her father made the introduction, her teeth were large too and slightly irregular.

Irregular teeth among the rich? Whatever had her dentist been up to?

He reached for her hand, and belatedly she offered it. There was a laziness in her movements. In her smile too. A laziness and a sensuality.

Something stirred in him, and he laughed at himself. Bucky Prince and this ugly child? He *really* needed a night out in

37

Miami Beach! But then he amended that, told himself any interest he showed was part of his plan.

He held the hand. Long cool fingers, a totality both large and delicate. Without planning it, his thumb moved slightly in minute caress.

She withdrew her hand and stood up, no longer looking at him. She was almost as tall as her father, and thin, except that she filled those shorts and shirt . . .

'I hope we'll see you again, Mr. Prince.' Nothing ugly about her voice. A light voice, a sweet and delicate voice.

'Bucky,' Walt said. 'I expect you will, the island being as small as it is.'

She nodded and without further ado left them. And shocked him. She walked with a hip-swing, a haunch-roll that would have done a street-walker proud; a tall, lean girl with fantastic legs and a strange face and he hated to see her leave.

'Ceecee,' Mortonson snapped.

She turned at the archway. 'Yes?'

'I wasn't aware that you had anything important to do.'

'I haven't,' she said, and was gone.

Mortonson sighed. 'Do you have children, Prince?'

'Let's hope not. I'm still single.'

Morton smiled a little. 'A man your age couldn't have this kind of problem anyway. What are you, thirty-five, thirty-six?'

Bucky said thirty-four, and thought that two years ago people had consistently *under*guessed his age by two or three years.

'Cecily will be twenty-one in March. And the older she gets, the less I understand her. The less we understand each other.'

'Generation gap,' Bucky murmured. 'She's a charming girl.'

'Charming? You really think so?'

At first Bucky smiled, thinking Mortonson was indulging in a parental joke. But then he realized the man expected an honest answer of him.

'Yes, not ordinary. Not in looks or, from what I can gather, in personality. But charming, certainly.' And saying it he meant it.

They sat down. Mortonson drew a cigar case from his shirt pocket and Walt accepted a blunt Havana. 'Not that she was *ever* easy to handle,' Mortonson said, puffing his cigar end red. 'Did you notice her teeth?'

Bucky acted as if he didn't know what Mortonson meant.

38

'They're not straight. You think I didn't have a dentist that could straighten them? She wouldn't go. Not for that. For fillings and cleanings and checkups, yes. For wisdom tooth extractions, not a murmur. But not for orthodontia. She didn't want to be *changed*. That's what she said. Imagine.'

'I'm surprised you didn't insist,' Bucky said, smoking and looking at the fountain.

'After her mother died ... I just didn't seem to be able to discipline her properly. And you never knew a girl like Ceecee, believe me. Strong willed? That's not the word for it! You ask some of the boys who dated her.'

'I envy them,' Bucky said, to say something.

'Cecily needs a mature friend. Hell, she needs a friend, *period*. The two or three who've tried to be friendly this season have received absolutely *rotten* treatment. Nothing seems much fun for her lately.'

Again Bucky felt he had to say something. 'A stage, something she'll pass through and leave behind.'

'I hope so.' They smoked a while longer, and Mortonson said, 'How about a drink? I know ten thirty is damned early, but I feel like it. Join me?'

There was no refusing a man who had indulged in such confidences on such short notice. The drink would seal their friendship. Bucky said, 'If it's Irish Coffee.'

Mortonson pressed a button set beneath the edge of the handsome marble table. The Chinese houseboy took their order and left. They smoked and talked. Bucky said he seemed to recall hearing that Mortonson played polo.

'Not since I broke my hip six years ago. I sometimes ride. But mostly it's golf, fishing and boating.'

The Irish Coffee came. It was the first morning-alcohol Bucky had allowed himself in months. He tried not to enjoy it too much. They finished and Mortonson insisted on showing him the estate.

The house was everything a vacation home should be. It was everything a permanent home should be, with the exception of really good paintings and family heirlooms.

They left the house. Mortonson kept a small stable and three horses. 'Nothing I'd care to enter at Saratoga,' he said, smiling and stroking the nose of a sleek reddish mare. 'Besides, the riding's not very good here. Once or twice around and you've had it.'

39

They discussed Hialeah as they walked to the dock and Mortonson's forty-one-foot Hatteras cabin cruiser. 'It's no *Christina*,' he chuckled. 'I have a big boat dry-docked at Southampton, but this is fine for Ceecee and me.' The Hatteras had hot and cold water, shower, electric range, refrigerator, electronic navigational aids, twin screws and the easy maintenance of fiberglass. 'Basic, yes, but still fully seagoing.' He looked at Bucky. 'The Prince family, I hear, hasn't quite accepted engines at sea, except for an emergency auxiliary puttputt.'

Bucky smiled and let the challenge go. He could have said that the stench of gas and diesel engines had already polluted the land and that wind and sail were a better way, a more challenging and skillful way. He could also have said that the Prince family no longer existed, outside of himself.

They strolled through the flower garden, not one of Mortonson's primary loves and therefore not very extensive. They took a flagstone path, passed through a thick wall of evergreen, and were at an enormous amoeba-shaped swimming pool. At the center, a head bobbed and went under.

'I'll leave you now,' Mortonson said, eyes on the pool. 'Say hello to her again, would you, Bucky? I think I inhibit the girl.'

Bucky wasn't prepared for this, began to say he had to be going and found himself alone as Mortonson disappeared through the evergreens. The head came up at the far end, and immediately went under again. He walked to the end of the pool, feeling a strange reluctance. At the same time, he also felt a definite excitement. The old Prince appetite for anything female, he told himself. And why *not* pursue her? It wasn't unusual for a rich bachelor to pursue a rich maiden. And to all the world—with the exception of Chick Aston, now safely dead of a massive coronary, and perhaps a few others, who had lost heavily in Prince Mining speculations, none here or connected with anyone here on Bay Island—to all, Walter Danforth Prince was a rich bachelor. Not as rich as before, some might say, but who would guess at complete disaster? No one, now that he was a Bay Island resident ... not unless they made a very complete investigation. Which was the single most important reason for his not pursuing a rich maiden all the way to the altar, and marrying rather than stealing back his wealth and station. Allie Mortonson, for example, would have wanted to know considerably more than the simple, 'How's business, Bucky?' He'd have wanted to talk specifics and, as the evasions mounted, would have gone into that complete and, eventually, deadly investigation of Walter Danforth Prince. Not that, even then, he would have guessed at the *completeness* of the financial disaster that had overtaken the Prince enterprises. Allie would be certain Bucky Prince had a million or so safely hidden here and abroad, because who didn't put a little away when that wolf howled outside the door? Who in Real Society, that is? A recent example was the bankrupt who had committed suicide in Palm Beach. Within the year, his grieving widow had realized close to five million from real estate and the contents of various safety deposit boxes.

Bucky Prince could play with heiresses, as long as he didn't play too seriously. And this was a rather delectable heiress, if not in the customary mold.

Her head came up on the opposite side of the pool, facing away from him. 'I'm here,' he said.

She turned, brushing hair and water from her eyes. 'So you are.'

'Come out.'

'Is that an order?'

'If you obey orders, it is.'

'I never obey orders,' she said.

'Then it's a request.'

'Abject pleas are more in my line.'

'Sorry. Abject pleas lead to contempt.' He saw her taking a deep breath, and quickly added, 'It's no use going under again. I won't disappear.'

She hesitated. He said, 'Come out, *please.*'

She was near a ladder and climbed out, dripping. She wore an orangey-red bikini and a deep tan. He said, 'Well,' softly. She pushed back her streaming hair as she came around the pool, walking with that incredible hip-roll. She chewed her lower lip as she approached him. 'You're staring, Mr. Prince.'

'Boys stare at you, don't they?'

'Only when they're horny, and you're not a boy.'

He turned to a table with center-pole umbrella. 'I'm so old I can't stand up for more than a minute at a time.' He sat down.

She came to the table and picked up a towel. A quick rub-down of body and hair, and she took the chair furthest from

41

him. He moved into the next chair and pulled it close to hers.

'You *are* a boy,' she said, smilingly. 'Emotionally.'

'Sexually too.'

'That's too bad. Boys are a drag. Men, on the other hand ...' Then she shrugged. 'Dumb talk. What do you do, Mr. Prince?'

'Investments.'

'Everyone here does that. I mean, your bag. Engineering? Law? Physics? Metaphysics ...?'

'It's still investments. I was educated to invest. Business administration and that sort of thing.'

'Then what do you *like* to do? Chess? Pot? Polo? Travel? Cooking? Coitus? What?'

'Oh, all of that, scratching pot and substituting martinis. And add sailing.' He put his hand on her arm. 'And stress coitus.'

She asked for a cigarette. When she leaned forward for a light, he stared at her full breasts. She caught the look. He caught her catching the look, and smiled.

She exhaled words and smoke at the same time. 'Let's get something straight. I'm here to hole up and rest, not to think or do much. I had plenty of action at Skidmore. It didn't make me happy. I'm ... well, empty's as good a word as any.'

'At twenty-one?'

'You might have a point.' She chewed her lip again. 'Would you answer my question, if I ask it seriously this time?'

'What I do? My bag?'

She nodded.

'Why is it important?'

'It isn't. Just interesting.'

He hesitated. 'I'm a rich man, Ceecee.'

She said, 'Ask a silly question,' and rose to go.

He said, 'I mean it. It's what I want, what I care about, what I work at. To be rich ... or rather, richer.' (And yet, it hadn't been entirely true when he'd really been a rich man. There had been boredom, irritation with the 'good matches' people were always trying to arrange, periods of depression ... relieved by days of sailing, and nights of loving.)

She said, 'It doesn't seem enough,' looking at him, looking closely.

'There's sailing,' he said, but was stung into adding, 'and yet my bag, my avocation and vocation both, my truest love, is to build money, any way I can.'

42

'But how much money can a man...?'

And now he had to get out of this, because when he'd had money he hadn't really valued it in the way he was trying to make her believe he valued it. He'd dreamed so long of having money again, he'd forgotten that it had been an ignored constant, an accepted and relatively unimporant part of his life. Only *losing* it had given it its present eminence. He said, 'And women,' once again taking her arm. 'Money and sailing and women.'

'In that order?'

'Not necessarily.'

'Depending on the woman?'

'Depending on the wind.'

She laughed.

'And *your* bag?' he asked.

'But that's the whole point. That's why my father is worried and sicked you on me—don't bother to deny it; he's been doing it with every eligible male on the island. That's why I'm holed up and empty. I haven't found my bag. It should be men, or *a* man. And then marriage and family. Or work ... a career. I'm an honors graduate in English; the modern novel. I could get a fellowship and instruct, and it would be meaningful and rich for most people. A man, or a job, or both; a life for most of my friends. But for some reason, not for me.'

'Not yet, little girl.'

She shrugged. 'Take me out tomorrow?'

He was surprised, but replied without hesitation. 'Honored.'

She smiled. 'What a lovely word. So rare in the modern novel. Nine P.M. for my Saturday night date?'

'Fine.'

She went toward the evergreens with her incredible whorey walk. He watched. Just before she disappeared from sight, she turned and looked back. She didn't smile or wave, simply looked, but his heart began to pound. He knew, quite suddenly, he was going to have her.

Dick Brandy was feeling much stronger. He'd reached the point where he was spending two and three hours a day on his feet, and so he decided that he would get the hell out of the house, off the grounds, and over to the club where he could see someone besides Irena and Claude, his servants.

He took a seat at the bar. The club wasn't exactly booming,

only three of the twenty tables in the beautiful wormwood dining room being occupied. He saw Brian and Abigail Waters and called 'Lad, Nabby, how are you?' The sixtyish couple smiled their pleasure at seeing him here. They'd been regular visitors during his period of immobilization.

At a table near the Waters' sat Patricia Whiteson and a nonresident, a woman younger but not nearly as handsome as Baby Whiteson, at whose coming-out party Dick had played and sung some twenty years ago.

The third occupied table was over in the east corner. The man dining there was a stranger, sitting alone ... and yet he couldn't be a nonresident. The rules plainly stated that non-residents could be served *only* when accompanied by residents.

'Mr. Brandy!' the bartender exclaimed. It was Olaf, as fat and red-faced as ever. 'So nice to see you again! Scotch, isn't it?'

'Yes. Nice to see *you*, Olaf. Half-and-half with soda.'

He sipped his drink, looking at the stranger in the corner. 'Olaf, that gentleman near the windows ...?'

'Walter Prince, sir. His grandfather was an original owner.'

'Prince,' Brandy murmured, trying to remember where he had heard the name. His memory wasn't as good as it had been before the stroke. Still, he'd heard *something*. Four or five years ago, was it? Maybe not that long. Prince ...

'He's bought Number One.'

'What's he in?'

'The family was in mining.'

Something stirred in Dick's mind. Prince Mining. Futures. Heavy speculation. Three years ago; a month before the stroke. A society dance in Philadelphia. Tad Prince. Bucky Prince. The father—Martin? Melvin?—dead of heart disease and some-one passing a remark about him. A fist fight. Then, a week later, an accident which could have been suicide and only one Prince boy was left.

He looked across the room and Walter Prince—yes, Bucky, the younger son—looked up and met his eyes. Dick raised his glass and smiled. Prince raised a beer mug in return. They drank. Prince returned to his food. Dick lit a cigarette and nursed his drink.

Something still bothered him about Prince.

But why should anything *bother* him about one of the crowd? And old money at that.

44

And yet it did. An unpleasantness in the mind. A tickling, annoying sense of something wrong.

His memory wasn't anywhere near what it should have been, but it was getting better, along with the rest of him. In time...

SATURDAY, JANUARY 25

She was so very old. Eighty-seven didn't describe how old she was. Eighty-seven was a number and numbers are dead. The multitude of minor ailments (she was remarkably healthy for one so very old) didn't describe it. Nor did the style of her clothing, frozen fast in the late 1930's. Not her Meyer Davis records. Nor her two liveried footmen (who dreaded their rare excursions into the outside world via the huge Rolls limousine). Nor the rigidity of her social, economic and racial ideals. Nor even the knowledge that she had met Presidents Harrison and McKinley.

In this last, lay the proof of her age. For she had *knowledge* of certain important events in her early life—in her childhood, adolescence and adulthood—but not *memory*. Memory was gone. In its place were vague recollections of people saying she had said and done this and that, been known for this and that. Willa Dorcas Greshen no longer could bring up the scenes, the voices, the emotions of the past.

She realized this. She had reasonably sharp memories of last month and some recollections of last year, but after that it all dimmed out. It didn't bother her. Nothing bothered her. But it saddened her, occasionally.

This was one of her sad days. She sat at the huge bay window in her second-floor bedroom, the sun falling across her hands, her lap, her legs. She faced the gardens, the fountains, the hedging, the tall pines which protected her view on the east from that second oldest thing on this island, the abandoned Belledone home. Soon, she too would be beyond renovation. Soon, she too would fall into death and decay.

She turned slightly, reaching for the pull cord. At one time, servants had been nothing more than extra arms and legs, performing the thousand tasks she as mistress of four large homes had to execute. Of late, however, they were far more important,

45

though she never allowed any of the reduced staff—nine, was it?—to know this. Now that she had outlived everyone she had truly loved, servants were a reason for getting up each morning, moving about, eating and speaking; a reason for living still another day. They expected it of her, and she had always tried to live up to expectations.

Mildred entered, a plump woman with a smiling, foolish face. She wore the long gray dress over white, long-sleeved blouse that had always been maid's attire in the Greshen houses. 'Yes ma'am?'

'I would like you to walk with me to the small parlor.'

Mildred came across to her chair. Willa rose, left leg trembling just a little, and grasped Mildred's arm. Bent as she was, she still stood tall over the maid. Slowly, they walked out of the bedroom and along a wide, paneled hallway that smelled faintly of inner rot, somewhere beyond the reach of constant waxings and polishings. (Willa refused to recognize the smell, because she then would have to set workmen to tramping and banging around the place and it was too much of a nuisance now ... and hidden beneath that mild reason the true one: it was too late for that now; time was too short for that now.)

They entered the second-floor sitting room, twenty-seven by forty feet and small compared with the main drawing room on the ground floor where at one time Willa had entertained seventy guests quite comfortably with the buffet in the adjoining dining room. She said, 'Thank you, Mildred.' The maid was already moving the Gainsborough that Trent's mother had given them on their tenth anniversary.

'Anything else, Mrs. Greshen?'

'Just close the door as you leave, please.'

'Yes, ma'am.'

The maid left. Willa went to the wall safe, exposed when the Gainsborough had swung aside on its door-panel. She had to work the combination three times before it came out right, and she was upset by this. Her hand had trembled badly.

But then she was taking the necklace out of the safe and the sad day became less sad and her upset disappeared. She held the gift of gifts, Trent's 'apology' after that nastiness with the Polish film actress, the forty emerald-cut stones leading to the one-hundred-and-thirty-seven-carat Light of Stars diamond. She had been offered two million dollars for it by that Greek person who visited Miami briefly in his showy yacht, but she had told him that raising his price (as he attempted to do) would be useless. Trent had wanted it to go into a museum and it would. Perhaps the A & P boy's place.

She really should specify *which* museum very soon.

But she hated the thought of assigning the Light of Stars out of her hands. It was not only beautiful, it was an object which triggered the single sharpest memory left to her: Trent pleading for her not to divorce him. Trent explaining what she meant to him and that his taking any other woman, certainly one out of their class, was simply a form of *droit du seigneur*. Trent earning her forgiveness for this and all future transgressions ... though she couldn't recall if there *were* any after that.

She placed the Light of Stars around her neck, arranged it, felt its weight but without discomfort. She stood straighter, a regally tall and slender woman whose aged face still showed traces of previous handsomeness if not beauty. She touched the cold, heavy stone that represented the wealth, the power she had always possessed.

And now nothing.

And now a waiting for shadows to deepen and darkness to come.

'Dear God, be kind and make it happen soon.'

She heard the shaky voice with surprise, and realized it was her own. Enough of such nonsense! Willa Dorcas Greshen was no ordinary woman! People had always said that. The press had always printed that. No ordinary woman, and she would go on.

Still wearing the necklace, she took other boxes from the safe, other items of jewelry from the boxes. She smiled as she examined a pin in the shape of a racehorse, one of many jeweled animals in her collection. Emeralds for eyes and rubies for hoofs and diamonds studded all over the beautiful platinum frame. She had an elephant much like this, somewhere in the safe, and fish and birds. Her toys, given as gifts by Trent each birthday, and by Addy and Marius.

Her daughter and son-in-law. Her loving children.

Why had they flown to Jamaica that summer day and never arrived? Why when they were so very fortunate in each other and everything else?

She tried to remember. The papers said a crash over water. The papers said the bodies hadn't been recovered. And so she

47

didn't read the papers any more, not even the society columns which once had given her pleasure.

Everything had given her pleasure. Then one by one her pleasures had died...

There was a knock at the door. Mildred called, 'A Mr. Prince to see you, Mrs. Greshen.'

Willa turned, mouth opening, heart pounding dangerously. Cleve Prince she was able to remember. Cleve was one of those who had admired her, one of those who had tried (in a very gentlemanly way, of course) to gain her favor.

But then she shook her head. Cleve Prince had sold his estate on the island. And ... hadn't he passed away?

'Tell him to wait a moment, please. And return here for me afterward, Mildred.'

She put away her jewelry. She closed the safe and turned the dial. She went to the cheval glass and touched her upswept white hair and smoothed out her long purple dress.

When she entered the sun room on Mildred's arm, the young man rose and bent his head in a small bow. 'Mrs. Greshen,' he said, and his voice was like Cleve's, rich and warm, but his face, no. 'I'm Walter Prince,' he said.

She moved toward him, hand outstretched, remembering her talk with Mr. Beaufort. 'You've returned to us, Walter. I remember you at your grandfather's house.' It was a lie but not a very large lie since she remembered Cleve and knew he'd had a grandson with him for a while.

They sat down. She had iced tea and biscuits brought. He talked about his grandfather, who had died fourteen years ago, and about his grandfather's racing sloop, the *Wet Baby*, which had won so many regattas despite its disreputable name; and about his home, Number One, a small but comfortable place.

She tried to ask about his father, but somehow he didn't understand and said no, he wasn't married, and she said, 'Not married? A dashing fellow like you? Well, we'll have to put some lovely young thing in your path at the next gala.'

'I'm glad you'll be attending, Mrs. Greshen.'

'Attending? But I always attend.' And then she realized that wasn't quite true. She hadn't attended last season's galas. Not even the costume-ball finale. But last season she'd had that bad hip.

Had she attended the season before?

'If I could escort you?' he asked.

Cleve Prince was still trying ...
Not Cleve!

She was annoyed with herself. She hadn't wandered quite this much before. But annoyed or not, she was pleased at the invitation and smiled a real smile and not just something for the servants to see. Her smile grew and she bent her head a little, raising her hand as if it held a fan and she could hide behind it. 'Why thank you, Mr. Prince. I accept that invitation.'

He talked about a gala he'd been allowed to see, just for half an hour, as a child. A masked costume gala. He remembered her there, her clothes and her jewelry. 'That diamond and your face ... two incredible jewels.'

Yes, she remembered too ... now that he described it. Remembered through his eyes. And then confused it with an earlier gala, when she'd worn the Light of Stars for the very first time and created a sensation. And Cleve Prince; Cleve had taken her outside before the midnight unmasking and for once he hadn't been gentlemanly and she had trembled and almost ...

Walter Prince was leaning forward, asking what was wrong. She was still smiling, yes, but she felt the tears and realized she was also crying. Smiling and crying and Walter Prince leaning forward and oh, she was such an old lady, such a foolish old lady!

She rose, terminating the meeting. 'You mustn't think I'll keep you to your promise, Mr. Prince. I know you were jesting about the gala.'

'But I'll keep you to *your* promise, Mrs. Greshen. And for the biggest and best gala. The season finale.'

He said good-bye and was gone. She sipped her tea and then felt hungry and had a boiled egg and toast, when only an hour ago she'd had milk and graham crackers. Sitting looking out the French doors at the garden and a servant working the flower beds thinking of red-and-white striped tents set up on a lawn and hundreds of people ...

Her party? At Prouts Neck? At Saratoga?

The freckled pattern of sunshine-through-leaves matched a memory pattern buried deep in her brain and she smiled. The smile brought warmth and the warmth made her remember Walter Prince's invitation. Yes, she *would* attend the final gala with him. Her costume would be regal—Marie Antoinette, one of her heroines, and the mask would cover her old, old face.

49

And yes, she *would* wear the Light of Stars diamond. He was a dear boy and she would do it to please him and she might even dance...

Fanny made sure no one was in the hall outside her door, then sat down on the bed and lifted the phone. She asked for Long Distance and placed a collect call to a Toronto number. When the man answered, she said, 'Armand? Are you all right?'

'Of course. What sort of greeting is *this*?'

'You sound tired. You've been getting enough sleep?'

'What else is there for me to do but sleep? And soon I won't wake...'

'Stop that! I told you what the doctor said.'

'Yes, you told me. But when I ask him, his eyes...'

'Trust me.'

'I do, Fanny.' The voice softened. 'I trust you to want to make me happy, to want to protect me.'

She bit her lip. 'Your medicine will make you better.'

'My medicine makes me sleep and forget pain, for a while.'

She covered the phone and fought to control tears; then, briskly: 'Is the woman coming in every morning? Is the food all right?'

'Yes, fine.'

'Is it quiet?'

'There are some girls next door. They have boys visiting and play music half the night.'

'I told you we should look further. Robert Street has too many university students. When I get home we'll move...'

'You misunderstand. I like it. They're full of life, those girls. Their laughter, their talk, it is better than the medicine I take. It makes me remember good things. One girl came to borrow ice the other night. She sat and talked a while. Today she brought me a book.'

'You behave yourself, you old devil.'

They laughed together. She asked about his model planes. He didn't answer her but said, all laughter gone. 'The worst thing is not being able to be with you, to help you.'

'I'll send money next week.'

'No need to. There's plenty left.'

'You're sure?'

'The doctor won't come without payment. The woman neither. And I can't live without them. I *want* to live, Fanny,

50

long enough at least to know that *diable* has suffered.'

'He'll suffer.' She nodded grimly. 'I swear again, he'll suffer.'

'But you must be careful.'

'Yes, so we can sit together and think of his suffering. And we will have money too. So much money we will get the best doctors...'

'You are completely good, Fanny. *A capite ad calcem*, as our little Latin student used to say. You remember?'

Her voice was sepulchral. 'I remember. Now I must say good-bye.'

'Yes, good-bye. It is working out well?'

'Everything. Very well.'

'*Dieu vous garde.*'

When she'd returned his blessing and hung up, she let the tears come. She should be with him. Nothing was more important than being with Armand these last few months. Nothing!

But then she thought again, and she knew she had to do what he would have done had he been able. She washed her face and checked carefully in the mirror and went to the kitchen.

Dinner had been excellent, a *poulet au Brisson* that made Walter Prince reconsider the little French Canadian woman with new respect. Jewel thieves were one thing, but a truly talented cook was something else again, something much rarer. He went out to the Porsche, waiting at the front door, where Rollins had brought it from the garage, thinking he could give a little dinner party without fear of being disgraced.

And yet he hadn't eaten much; not nearly as much as the dish deserved. The excitement he'd felt on watching Ceecee Mortonson walk away from the pool this morning had persisted and grew as evening approached, getting in the way of his appetite for *poulet*. It was a different kind of appetite that had him in its grip right now, a surprisingly strong appetite, this in spite of his trying to place it in proper perspective, of his trying to play it down. After all, what exactly was he going to do? He was going to take out a not-quite-twenty-one-year-old girl. If all went well, there would be a little driving around, a little drinking, a little conversation, and then they'd get to bed. Nothing he hadn't done dozens of times before. And exactly what he needed, in the same way that he often needed a good meal. But, of course, he'd been 'dieting' of late...

51

It had been seven, closer to eight, months since he had said good-bye to Barby at the Ambassador East in Chicago and nodded at her plea that he visit her later that night for a *real* good-bye. But he hadn't kept his word. In the Pump Room, there could be no tears, no recriminations, no further discussion of how he was giving up 'a fantastic career in promotion' for a wild scheme of mining in Honduras. (If she only knew how wild a scheme it really was!) In her apartment, it would have been messy. Besides, he had wanted her to forget Bernard Ergen.

Bernard Ergen had sported a very long hairdo, big mod moustaches, a fast line of chatter for his clients and an awesome reputation for putting away the sauce. Bernard Ergen had been fast with everything but a buck. He had held onto his bucks, at first with only a vague idea of how to use his savings and a hundred eighty thousand dollars left from the Prince debacle (most of it personal life insurance carried by his father). Later, however, the plan had developed and he knew exactly what his money was going to buy...

It was summer when Bucky Prince arrived in Chicago, the facial hair already in its second month of growth. Operating out of his room at the modest Knickerbocker Hotel, he found a comfortable apartment on a street of comfortable apartment houses. (He first was tempted to take a very small place in a very inexpensive house, but found that, despite the need to save money, he was too depressed by the cramped studio apartment. Later, he was to congratulate himself on this decision; the more luxurious one-bedroom flat on Melrose became part of his developing plan.)

Furniture and accessories were purchased in one day of quick and casual shopping; he didn't indulge taste, because given his background that would have been ridiculous in his new circumstances. He bought by price, and that included the large supply of gin, vermouth, Scotch and other potables. Bucky Prince had always liked a drink, and in the three bitter months preceding his removal from Philadelphia and the other places of his life, months filled with such delightful details as burial of father and brother (dead within six weeks of each other), as well as the final stages of bankruptcy proceedings, he indulged this liking to a new and previously unmatched degree.

52

In Chicago, Bernard Ergen prepared for his first day of job-hunting by breakfasting on four cups of coffee heavily laced with rum, and only then opened the want-ad section of the *Tribune*. Logically, Ergen-Prince should have looked for positions under Stockbroker or allied investment listings, but the same reasons that had brought him to Chicago—lack of personal and business contacts there—sent him to Cherner-Steerman Associates, Public Relations, to apply for the position of 'contact and field man to handle top-flight domestic and foreign clients; must be personable to a high degree; salary plus commission...' Bernard Ergen was personable to such a high degree, spoke French and Spanish to a sufficient degree and was insistent on forgoing salary for a straight (and increased) commission, that the job was his that same afternoon. Shortly afterward, the girl who introduced him to the major television, radio and newspaper personalities in the field and responded to his confession of total ignorance of the mechanics of his job by spending evenings with him, was also his. Barby Freeman was his key to competence; his own style, presence and manner were the keys to his meteoric success, giving Mr. Jan Steerman reason to regret the straight commission basis when Ergen's income reached five thousand dollars a month after only five months, and a record seven to eight thousand thereafter (shading Steerman's own income).

Another record, albeit a personal one, was set by Ergen in the consumption of alcohol. He drank considerably throughout the day and more at night, but his heaviest consumption was saved for those late-late hours when, finally through with selling communications people on clients, and through with escorting clients to television and radio shows and newspaper interviews, he could sit down with a bottle and a pack of cigarettes and explore yet another possibility of reviving Prince Mining.

One of the first possibilities considered was marrying into a wealthy family, after allowing a year or more to pass and creating a good cover story for an apparent recouping of fortunes. It was rejected because of the impossibility of any cover story withstanding specific investigation. Nevertheless, it was considered again and again, in desperation, when all other plans seemed impossible. And then there was the night, a little over a year after coming to Chicago, when Bernard Ergen staggered into the bathroom of his apartment and vomited up his day's intake of alcohol and slumped down on the toilet seat as his legs gave way. He stared blearily at the wall before him, and after a while noticed something—a broken tile. And was aware, for the first time in minute detail, of the changes in his life. There had been no broken tiles in Walter Prince's home. There had been no broken tiles in the several homes of the Prince family, or in the homes of Walter Prince's friends. Inconceivable that there be broken tiles there. And the luxury, the cleanliness, the constant catering...

He rose and stumbled into the living room. He stood there, blinking, feeling he was in a good-sized closet. He went to the bedroom, and here he had to cover the feeling of despair with an attempt at humor. 'Walls closing in,' he said, laughing. The words were true; the laughter wasn't.

He went back to the bathroom and washed his face with cold water and when that didn't help he stepped into the shower-bath ... and again felt the walls closing in. Back home, he'd had a room-sized sit-down shower with steam attachments ... though he'd rarely sat and even more rarely used the steam. But he'd had them.

In the kitchen, he drank coffee and nibbled toast and when his brain came out of its alcoholic haze, dawn was slipping gray fingers into Melrose. He could go to sleep if he wished. It was Sunday and he had nothing on until late tonight, when he was escorting a minor producer of minor Hollywood films to the Jack Eigen show. The minor producer had major connections and if *they* decided to promote their products and themselves in Chicago via the *Tribune*, Kup's Show and other TV shows, and set up a promotion campaign of column items and spot ads, it could mean another solid commission. Still, nothing to do until eleven P.M. He could stop running for a while.

He knew quite suddenly, he would soon stop running for good; he would run down and out. There was no joy in his life. He had taken on a new name, a new image, but no new set of values and relationships. All his values were the old ones; all his relationships ghosts of the real thing. Bedding Barby was fine; he could *feel* that, when he wasn't too drunk. But *knowing* Barby was something else again. He was a man marking time, smiling false smiles and speaking lines, waiting to leave the stage and go home and become himself.

'Whatever that is,' he mumbled, heading for the bedroom.

Bernard Ergen was close to some sort of breakdown that morning; he was losing hope of becoming Walter Prince again.

54

Bernard Ergen got his bankbooks from a dresser drawer and counted his money. He now had two hundred and six thousand dollars. At this rate, he would be a millionaire in ten years; about nine years after becoming a confirmed alcoholic. What could he do for Prince Mining then?

He went back to the kitchen and drank more coffee. He swore off martinis ... and knew he'd be on Scotch by tonight.

Bernard Ergen felt panic rolling over him. He grabbed the first piece of reading that came to hand; a *Travel Today* magazine. He flipped pages. He read words without getting the sense of them.

Why couldn't he live forever as Bernard Ergen, without alcohol and with Barby or another pretty girl?

He couldn't. He didn't know why, beyond knowing that he had to get back to where he had been. He could still hear Chick Aston railing at Tad, calling him and Dad and Bucky thieves. He could still see Tad's face. Tad's drunken, disintegrating face ... much like his own must look now. He could still hear the minister intoning nonsense over Tad's bier, praising the 'captain of industry and generous supporter of multiple charities' (standard doubletalk for a man whose major talents lay in wine, women and roulette; who was suspected of running his car deliberately into that stanchion; whose generosity to charities was part of the usual tax-free hand-out of every Real Society family). He wanted to free himself of those images and memories and the only way he could think to do it was by reviving Prince Mining. And he wouldn't be able to do that saving twenty or thirty thousand dollars a year. He had to get a few million to work with, and get them *now*!

He had already considered every aspect of gambling, of putting his stake on the line at high odds, and the chances of winning were just too slim.

He had followed the market, the slipping, sliding, shaky market, and several times had wondered if a dramatic upsurge wasn't coming; and each time had admitted it was as big a gamble as a roll of the dice, and each time the dramatic upsurge had failed to materialize.

He had examined the range of high-risk investments ... and felt that the returns were too uncertain and too slow in coming for his purposes.

He had looked for something new in business, something in which to invest both his money and himself, something that would offer big, fast returns. He didn't find it. The dictum that it takes big money to make big money still held true. About the only way to get big money that he *hadn't* considered was stealing.

He turned the pages of the magazine. He thought about calling Barby and consoling himself with her pert face and beautiful body. He stopped turning pages. He opened a centerfold. No Playmate of the Month. Something far more interesting to Bernard Ergen. A beach. Blue sea. A group of sunbathers, several of whom were familiar to Walter Prince.

He read the headline:

'*Millionaires' Paradise.*'

He read a paragraph:

'Portugal's Estoril on the coast west of Lisbon has everything the Beautiful People desire, and they continue building *quintas* there in ever increasing numbers. Their parties last for days and the guest lists read like special editions of *Who's Who*. Put it on your travel schedule by all means, but don't plan on attending any of these parties unless you're someone very special. Of course, there *is* a way an ordinary person can get to see if not participate in a gala, *if* that person has muscles and some experience in police work. Private officers are much in demand this season, what with the ladies wearing items that offer considerable incentive to jewel thieves. At one recent affair, an insider estimated the worth of the assembled baubles to be in excess of ten million dollars.'

Bernard Ergen closed the magazine. *Ten million dollars.*

He laughed at himself. And then stopped laughing and started thinking.

It was noon before he went to bed. He had the beginnings of a plan. It didn't include Estoril. There was a place closer to home, more familiar, more accessible to Walter Danforth Prince. It too could be called a millionaires' paradise, if one cared to use purple travel-magazine prose. It too had galas at which the women wore their best jewelry ...

Bernard Ergen drank considerably less than usual during the next two weeks. He wanted his mind as clear as possible, as sharp as possible, while he further developed his plan.

He would need dossiers on every resident of Bay Island.

He would need a home there.

He would need servants, but servants unlike any he had ever had before.

Getting the names of residents and information regarding homes for sale or lease was easily accomplished. He wrote the family attorney, Archer Mondredale, saying he was now on his way to re-establishing Prince Mining as a viable financial enterprise and asked him to make certain enquiries ... 'very discreetly at this early stage'.

Finding his staff of 'servants' was something else again; the method eluded him for ten straight days and nights, during which Barby remarked on his preoccupation and the lack of 'fine edge' in his work. And even when he did hit on a way to contact people who might be willing to lend themselves to his robbery scheme, a way which wouldn't leave him wide open to all sorts of pressures and dangers, he couldn't be sure it would actually work ... and if it did, just how long it would *take* to work. But he began setting what he thought of as his 'trap', a trap for a thief.

He changed his life style; no more sitting in his apartment most evenings, drinking himself under. He went walking several nights a week, even though the doorman at his apartment house warned him of the large number of pedestrians who had been robbed recently. He walked down dark side streets and along deserted avenues at two and three in the morning ... but always in good neighborhoods. No use stacking the odds too heavily in favor of his being mugged by drug addicts or teen-aged hoodlums, likely enough in any event. He needed people more professional and trustworthy than that. And always on his person was a compact thirty-two caliber Special, for which he had a license in Philadelphia but which wasn't even registered here. He was no longer concerned with legalities.

As an adjunct to inviting robbery on the street, he left his door unlocked and his lights off when spending time in his apartment. It was rather restful, not being able to read or watch television; simply sitting and drinking, dredging up memories of Grandfather Cleve and Bay Island. A house burglar was the type he really preferred, but he felt his chances were better on the street.

He was approached while walking one night by a trio of young blacks, and quickly flashed his weapon to scare them off. Not that he was prejudiced in his choice of servants. He simply knew what he could and could not use on Bay Island. Another night, he was jumped by a half-crazed addict and was unwilling to use his gun. He returned home with a bruised stomach and sore knuckles, but the addict had forgotten his need, at least for the half-hour he lay unconscious in a doorway. This was the sum total of two months' night-time strolling, and Bernard Ergen began walking less and drinking more. Another month, and the hope that had entered his life dimmed almost to extinction. The next three months saw a return to the patterns of his first year in Chicago—heavy drinking and a thickening of despair. In Gage's East, a slight, balding diner was pointed out to him as a member of the Mafia, highly connected, and Bernard Ergen almost asked for an introduction. Almost, but not quite. He knew that once he went *that* route, he would be owned; whatever he gained on Bay Island, it wouldn't be the old life; whatever he did with Prince Mining, it wouldn't be his.

And still he looked for ways. And after reading a list of things vacationing tenants should *not* do, he taped this note to his door: 'Stan, couldn't contact you. Will be away two weeks. Please water plants. Bernard.' And locked the door. And two nights later Charles DeVino picked the lock and entered and found himself facing a smiling man and a snub-nosed revolver. 'It's certainly taken you long enough,' the smiling man said.

After that, Bernard Ergen worked very, very hard. He swore off martinis and went on Scotch and swore off Scotch and went on bourbon and never did manage to control his drinking ... but he worked on his dossiers and he worked on his plan and he held onto every dollar. And when there was enough for a down payment on a Bay Island house and a few extras, the two lost years drew to a close. He contacted Vino as they had agreed, writing to the New York box number Vino was to check at least once each week: 'It's time for that Florida vacation, my friend, or do you prefer Leavenworth?'

Vino hadn't needed prodding; his answer was prompt. They met briefly at O'Hare, Vino accompanied by his girl-friend and partner; then Vino and Sandy left for Miami to find a 'group'. Bernard Ergen said his good-byes, shocking Barby and his employers and everyone else who felt he was insane to give up seventy thousand a year and, as Barby put it, 'such an exciting rewarding career'. Bernard Ergen felt he was giving up a long nightmare. He shaved his mustache, trimmed his hair, dumped his sharp clothes and flew to Philadelphia, where Walter Danforth Prince reappeared at the offices of his family's lawyers. Prince spoke only to the old man, Archer Mondredale, who was delighted to learn that the Prince fortunes were now definitely on the upgrade and that Bucky was able to afford Bay Island. Certainly he would handle the purchase of a house for the last of the Princes; in fact, he insisted on it. And later, of course, the firm would again handle the Prince mining ventures.

There had been a girl or two in Philadelphia, but nothing steady, which was unique in Bucky Prince's life. Bucky had little inclination toward women while he dried himself out (discovering, in the process, that he had come dangerously close to alcoholism) and waited to get his island home, spoke to Vino once a week and completed his research of the Bay Island residents. He had little real desire while he sweated over his plans and rejected momentary flashes of fear that he was insane to think he could get away with anything as big as this; little time for play while he took two jet 'vacations'—first Switzerland, Holland, France and Belgium, then Saudi Arabia, Lebanon, Kuwait and Taiwan. The European trip was to set up markets for otherwise unmarketable jewelry, these suggested by Vino, who was sure a man of Prince's quality could get top dollar; the near-Eastern and Asiatic trips were to contacts Bucky recalled from hearing his peers talk of how and where to purchase otherwise unpurchasable art objects, only in this case he would be selling, not buying. Both trips were successful. Jewelry could be recut, reset, changed in many ways; art could be sold to those who lived in feudal splendor and power, answerable only to their own laws. Finally, there had been the purchase of Number One Bay Drive, the last call to Vino and the leisurely trip down by car, not because he couldn't have had the Porsche shipped ahead of him, but because he wanted a chance to think everything through one last time; wanted to face those flashes of fear and defeat them, since once he reached Bay Island, there would be no turning back.

He was on Bay Island and there was no turning back. And it was, in a sense, a release, a return to normal, despite what lay ahead. And so women once again became a need. And tonight he would be with Ceecee Mortonson, young and desirable . . .

But mixed with his mounting excitement was another emotion—worry. Ceecee was Real Society ...

And that wasn't it, even though he told himself it could be dangerous if Allie was prone to jump to conclusions and have a prospective son-in-law investigated. It was Ceecee herself or his reaction to Ceecee. Some chemistry working there, to be sought after in the normal course of man–woman business ... but certainly not by Bucky Prince at this critical stage of his life!

Sandy, he now felt, would have been a wiser choice, even with Vino's proprietorship. Sandy would have been quick release and no chance of emotional hangover. She was representative of the women he'd had in his teens and early twenties. She was Verna, the chubby maid at his family's summer home, who had given him his first toss in the hay (literally so, in the barn behind the Bucks County place when he was fifteen). She was Leda or Leah, he couldn't remember exactly, the tall black cook he had hunted assiduously all during his first Christmas vacation from Harvard Business, and made in her bedroom just before returning to school and again and again during the following summer. Then there was that sullen redhead his mother had discharged for being 'impertinent' to a guest, but who hadn't given Bucky much trouble in his Ford convertible and then in a series of motel rooms. And while he'd had his share of coeds and girls of his own class, these three had been uncomplicated sex, and he had always remembered them for the *way* in which he had taken them, the *way* in which they had given themselves, with no need for protestations of love, with no possibility of lasting emotional ties. Because they'd been possessed less by Bucky Prince than by the Prince name and fortune; the Prince family charisma.

Bucky Prince, for whatever the reason, had never met a girl he'd wanted for very long; certainly never one he had wanted for *life*, even though he'd been all but brought to the altar by Elvira Wainer of the Maryland Wainers. He'd been saved there by his father's and brother's deaths and the doubt about the family that had crept into certain circles at the Philadelphia Hunt Club fund-raising ball ... though most people attributed it to Chick Aston's natural (or unnatural) pugnaciousness.

Thinking of Elvira made him smile, because when it had looked as if the match were made she had turned from cool and cautious to fast and furious. They'd had a dozen excellent sessions; the only reason he remembered her with a degree of affection. Elvira, the three servants, the coeds and let us not forget Barby of the thirty-eight-inch superstructure. And all his other women—and there had been many. Thinking of them brought him to the point where his desire for a woman, any woman, climbed high and he sped into the Mortonson road.

She was waiting for him in the tri-partitioned living room, a large affair with different types of furniture in each arched section; sitting in a massive high backed chair of noble Spanish design, listening to rock music that seemed to come from everywhere at once. She wore a mini-dress and sandals of pale yellow and her hair was as straight and simple as it had been at the pool. The maid left and Walt moved up to the chair and shouted over the sound, 'When do we put on the Vladimir Horowitz?' She didn't smile. She went to a cabinet, reached inside and the music stopped. Then she simply walked out of the room, leaving him to follow her.

In the car, she said, 'I want to drive down to Collins Avenue.'

'Certainly.' (He felt her tension.)

'And have a drink in the Fontainebleu; the Boom-Boom Room.'

'Vy not?' (A tension that matched his own.)

'And have a hamburger and fries at a Royal Castle.'

He clutched his stomach, nodding.

'Then I'll pay off.'

She met his gaze squarely and they were on their way.

They stayed only long enough for one drink at the Boom-Boom Room, Ceecee watching the energetic Latin dances with obvious (and irritating) amusement. They drove the length of Collins, fighting horrendous Saturday night traffic all the way, and returned to a Royal Castle near the Carillon Hotel. Ceecee had two hamburgers, a bag of French fries and a shake. He nibbled a few of her fries and thought of the *poulet* and felt like saying that her taste in food matched her taste in music.

Back in the car, she fiddled with the FM radio until she found, surprisingly, jazz. 'You like Parker, Gillespie, Davis?' she asked, and continued without waiting for his answer. 'Miles Davis has become the guru of intellectual jazzmen the world over and yet the American public is practically unaware of his existence. As for the Bird...' She went on and on, until he said: 'You must have talked the boys to death in school.'

She smiled then for the first time. 'Yes. The brains loved me, but I didn't love them. The others couldn't stand me, and some of *them* turned me on. Straight A Ceecee Mortonson never found her place.'

'And still hasn't,' he said, and then was sorry he'd said it. Was he fighting that chemistry; that strong and continuing chemistry? Were they *both* fighting it?

'For someone who prays to J. Paul Getty, you're rather sensitive.'

He told himself *not* to answer, *not* to quarrel this close to bedtime, and said, 'I don't pray, but if I did it would be to Francis Chichester, not Getty.'

'We'd better give up talking, Bucky. We're on different wavelengths.' He glanced at her, ready with a grin, but she was shaking her head, not mockingly but with something like despair.

They reached his room without alerting any of the staff. He closed the door. She was walking around, looking at things. He said, 'Nothing of my own here,' and then was angry at his defensive posture. He came across to where she stood and turned her by the shoulders and kissed her. Quite suddenly she was out of his arms, sitting on the bed and removing her shoes. 'Let's get on with it,' she said, smiling a little but with no true feel of humor. It chilled him.

'Like a drink?' he asked.

She stood up, reaching for the hem of her dress. 'No.' She pulled it over her head and stood in tight yellow panties and bra. 'You know what I'd like.'

The sight of her warmed away the chill. Her tall and lean and seductive body. Her beautiful body. He unbuckled his belt.

'Or *do* you?' she added, turning her back, taking off the panties, presenting him with a round, swelling bottom.

'I don't understand,' he said, continuing to undress. They were on different wavelengths and it could end in an argument and an argument could ruin things.

She was nude now, sitting at the edge of the bed and looking at him. He was down to his underwear. He was aroused and her eyes fixed on his shorts and it aroused him even more. And still he waited for her answer, while hoping it wouldn't come.

'I know you don't understand. That's why we're going to copulate, Bucky. But making love, that's something else again, isn't it?'

'I wouldn't know,' he said, forcing the smile and pulling off

62

his undershirt and walking toward her, bulging through his shorts and raging at what she was thinking about him ... even though it was true. He had never really loved a woman, except for Mother, and she had died when he was eight; never loved anyone except for Tad and, perhaps, Father...

But why was this girl talking of love? What did she expect of a fast make?

She seemed to read his thoughts, or his face. 'Forget it,' she said, laughing. 'I always talk too much, and at the wrong times. I once put down a history professor, while he was *in* me. A funny scene, but he didn't think so.'

He chuckled. She wouldn't put *him* down! She wasn't even twenty-one, and no matter what experience she'd been able to garner it couldn't match his. He would finally shut her mouth, in a variety of ways.

He put his hand on her head, stroking, standing in front of her that way, and said, 'Do *you* understand making love, Ceecee? Have you ever experienced it, as opposed to copulating?'

'No.' Lost little voice.

'Well then, let's enjoy what we have.'

'Yes.' Without his having to tell her, she pulled down his shorts. Without his having to direct her, she took him into her mouth.

He looked down at her. Her eyes were closed. Her mouth worked expertly. He groaned. She increased her tempo. She was trying to bring him to quick orgasm, trying to avoid real sex with him.

That turned him off, *hard*. He lost the luxurious feeling, the ecstatic feeling, and withdrew swiftly from orgasm; and then drew back from her.

She was surprised. Wiping her mouth, she said, 'You must be older than you look.'

He lay down and drew her down beside him. He pulled her head to his chest and pressed his lips to her hair. He closed his eyes and stroked her shoulder, her side. He felt himself going soft, yet he wanted her, wanted to do something for her, wanted to be with her.

She must have seen. She sat up, face tight, and tried to get up. He held onto her. She jerked free, saying, 'Let me *go*!' and ran to the chair and her clothes.

She was humiliated. She didn't understand. Not that he did,

63

fully, himself, but it wasn't what she thought. He could have made love to her for *hours*, if they hadn't talked.

'Not your body,' he whispered, tired of it all and yet unwilling to add to her hurt, this girl who seemed so full of hurt.

She was dressing.

'I got hung up on what you truly want, Ceecee.'

She stopped. She stood there, her back to him, frozen in the act of picking up her dress.

'You talked too much, baby. You reached me, put me down, just as you did that history instructor.' He ventured a laugh.

She turned her head. Her face was sullen, but waiting.

He held out his arms. 'Forget we're in bed. Just be with me. We'll go back to the methods of the generation before mine. We'll work up to it, over a number of dates.'

He moved his fingers, beckoning her. She came back and lay down, wearing her panties and brassière. He felt her trembling, and hugged her and touched her face, the chemistry very, very strong, despite what had happened.

'Why do you hurt so much?' he asked.

'I don't know.' Her mouth was in his chest, her voice foggy.

'You have everything. Allie seems a good sort of father.'

'Yes, I guess so.'

'How did your mother die?'

'Heart attack, but she was so young.'

'Could that be it?'

'I don't know. I don't think so. I was only four.' She paused. 'And *your* mother?'

Why was she questioning *him*? It was Ceecee Mortonson they were discussing. 'Cancer,' he said, 'when I was eight. As with you, too long ago to count now.'

'And yet you do hurt, Bucky. What's *your* reason?'

He began to tense.

She said, 'I'm sorry. I'm not being combative, at least I don't think so. Shall we drop it?'

They had to. He hurt because he was stripped of everything he valued, and was going to get it back in a way no Prince had ever dreamed of. No talking about *that*!

'Tell me about Francis Chichester, Bucky.'

'Chichester? He circled the world alone in his ship, the *Gypsy Moth*, when he was about seventy years old. You can read his book.'

'I know that. I mean, tell me what it meant to *you* when you

64

read his book, or saw him on television.'

He had never really thought about it. He admired the Englishman's accomplishment and envied it. He said that.

'Yes, but would you rather be Chichester than Getty? Rather be Chichester than anyone alive? Rather be Chichester than the President, or a king, or a ruler with unlimited power?'

He laughed at the childish questions; then stopped laughing and thought and said, 'I think so. More than that, I'd rather be a Chichester at seventy than Bucky Prince at thirty-four.'

She raised herself to look at him. 'That's *really* something!' For once he had reached her. 'I wish there was someone I admired like that! I don't think you can hurt too much if you know...'

She was beautiful now, this gangly girl with the wide-eyed excited stare, this long, full-chested, round-assed woman. Her lips were twisted in that strange, near-ugly way and he reached for her mouth with his mouth ... and at the same time the thought she had forced upon him was there. He would rather be a sailor of Chichester's stature than Bucky Prince; even a rich Bucky Prince. Could there be other things...?

It confused him and kissing her ended the thoughts and confusion. He undressed her and his hands went to her breasts, her belly, the nest between her legs. She said, 'I thought we were going to forget ... bed ... Bucky ... Bucky...'

How quickly she spasmed! His fingers stroked the moist entry three, four times and she arched up and grunted, grunted, and fell back. And was at his mouth again, rising toward ecstasy again.

As she kissed him she spoke, pushing her words into his mouth. 'Bucky ... love you ... love you ... Bucky, love you.'

It upset him, even though women, and men too, said such things in the throes of orgasm. He murmured, 'No, just a little, Ceecee, just a little, for now.'

'Yes, a little, for now.' And a moment later, as he kissed her hard breasts, 'Love you, love you, Bucky...'

He raised his head, worried despite her obvious passion. She drew him back to her breasts, smiling, saying, 'A little, yes, just a little, for now.' And he was still worried.

But he was beyond being stopped by anything now.

He was kissing those long legs.

He was kissing those firm thighs.

He was kissing that moist nest.

He was on her and pushing into her. She was very tight, yet soft to enter. She was very, very good. And looking at her, at her face, at her eyes half closing, at her body beginning to arch and pulse again, was very, very good.

He couldn't remember it ever being this good, even in the wildness of adolescence. He gripped her bottom, driving, saying. 'So good! God, so good!'

She smiled at that, but soon her mouth twisted and her body rose and the words of love came and the grunts, three or four of them in quick succession. The tightening of her sheath was excruciating! 'Good! Good!' And he came.

Softly now, his ear against her lips, he heard, 'Love you, love you, Bucky. Yes, just a little, for now.'

She detached herself a moment later and went to the bathroom. He sat up, calling, 'I never thought to stop. Are you all right?' Now that it was over, he feared its consequences, feared her words, her intensity.

'I hope so,' she said from behind the half-closed door. 'I'm just about midway between periods.'

He blanched. 'Why didn't you say something?'

The water ran. She smiled around the door. 'I said plenty.' She kept looking at him, slowly her smile went away and she closed the door.

Why had he started with this girl ! The galas were coming. The final gala was coming. He had to think *only* of that!

Francis Chichester ...

What sort of nonsense game was he playing anyway! If she got pregnant ...

She came out and began to dress. He went into the bathroom and washed. She was putting on her shoes when he finished. 'Can I have a cigarette?' she asked.

He gave her one, lit it and said, 'Did you take care ... ?'

'As best I could.' She didn't look at him. 'I took the pill for eighteen months but stopped two months ago because of weight problems.' She smiled thinly. 'I've heard that a woman is more fertile than usual after stopping.'

He dressed in silence. As soon as he tied his shoelaces, she went to the door. He chuckled. 'It's the man who's supposed to want out after sex.'

'Don't,' she said, voice flat. 'I saw your face.'

'My face?' He knew exactly what she meant. She had seen his fright, his worry. She had seen how quickly he had changed from lover to anxious male. What she couldn't see were his *reasons* for being so worried. Whatever threatened to complicate his life at this point also threatened the plan.

And yet, he wanted to touch her, to tell her ... what?

She walked out. He followed. As he did, he thought he heard footsteps downstairs. But when they reached the entry hall, it was empty.

He drove her home, said good night, received a quick nod in return. Then she was gone.

Lord, what a fool he'd been to start with her! If only she didn't get pregnant!

But worrying about pregnancy was foolish. Married couples sometimes had to try for months before being able to conceive. Who conceived after just *one* bout?

Those who feared pregnancy most, that's who!

He got back in his car, vowing *never again*, no matter how good it had been, no matter how strong the chemistry ... even now trying to reassert itself with memory flashes of their love-making.

He went to bed as soon as he returned home. When he slept, he dreamt. He was an old man. He was sailing his yacht across a vast, empty ocean, free, free of plans and worry and ambition. And somewhere behind him the voice called, promising rewards beyond fortune and passion:

'*Bucky, love you, love you ...*'

Sandy came into the kitchen where Vino, Rollins and Fanny were playing cards. 'Listen,' she said to Vino. 'I want to get off this goddam island.'

They all looked at her. Vino said, 'I thought you were watching television?'

'I got sick of it. You going to take me?'

'It's eleven o'clock,' he said.

'So what?'

'So it'll look funny to the guards if the servants ...'

'I'm no servant and it's Saturday night and I want a few drinks and a few laughs!'

'Two weeks and she's what you call, stir crazy,' Fanny muttered.

'I don't need *your* cracks,' Sandy snapped, eyes blazing. 'You want to rot here, okay. I'm not that old!'

Rollins murmured, 'Hey, take it easy.'

67

She began to answer him. Vino stood up and grasped her forearm. 'What happened?'

'Let go! You're hurting me!'

He pulled her roughly to the door and into the hallway. Voice low, he said, 'What's the matter with you? I've never seen you like this. Of all the times to get buggy...'

'Your fingers ... leggo!'

He shook her. 'I asked what happened! Answer me!'

She was suddenly crying. He let her go. She shook her head. 'I don't know. Just got ... sick of playing maid.'

'But you know the payoff! A few months and we're set for life!'

'I ... I got the shakes, Vino. I'm afraid.' But it was a lie. She had been raging and lost control and now she had to cover up. 'I was thinking and it looked so crazy to me, so wild and crazy, and I got the feeling that we'll never get away with it...' She was in his arms, sobbing.

He stroked her head, murmuring soothing things. She thought of lying on the bed, staring at the TV without really seeing or hearing, thinking of Prince and of how she had never known anyone like him; anyone with his looks and manners; with his *class*. So what if he wasn't a millionaire now. He had always been one and he would soon be one again. You couldn't hold a man like that down for long. She had day-dreamed a little. What if he fell for her? She was pretty enough for most men. If she could get him in the sack, just once, there would be a chance of hooking him good.

She had lain there, sighing, wanting him, wanting what he represented. Her father—dear old drunken Pop—had always called her a tramp, a no-good piece of trash. He had said it so many times she'd been convinced it was true by the time she was fifteen.

Wouldn't he have a fit if she ended up with Walter Danforth Prince! *Marrying* Walter Danforth Prince and being in the society columns! He'd fall off his goddam barstool in the Cozy Hour Tavern. He'd run all over Lake Wyanoth, that stinking upstate New York town where she'd served her first seventeen years before cutting out for the wide, wide world.

God, wouldn't it be something for everyone to know...

At that point, she'd heard a sound on the stairs. It could only be Prince, going to his room. By the time she got up and turned off the TV the door upstairs was closing.

She gave him fifteen, twenty minutes to maybe wash and undress, then stepped into the hallway. She moved silently out to the entry hall and paused. The others were still in the kitchen, playing rummy. She took off her shoes and slowly climbed the stairs. *Why couldn't she hook Prince?* she thought, working up her courage. He had turned her down because he didn't want trouble with Vino. But he might take her on if he felt there'd be worse trouble with *her*.

That thought led to another, and she came to a dead halt. If they made it a few times and he liked it ... if later, after the job, she stuck around and let him know it meant a lot to her ... if she told him it meant enough so that she'd spill everything unless ...

Christ, it could work!

She had gone up the rest of the way and come to his door and put her hand on the knob. And only then realized he had a girl with him. She had listened a while with the rage, the sick rage, burning her insides, and fled.

Vino was holding her closer. '... Miami next week and really have a ball. We have to set up a days-off schedule anyway. So the guards will see the same faces leaving the island on the same days. They expect that. Anything else might make them wonder. But next week for sure.'

He was stroking her back, her rear. 'Want to turn in, baby?'

She said yes. He said he'd finish out his hand and be with her in five minutes. She went to the room and undressed and by the time he came in she had calmed down, had convinced herself that Prince wasn't a lost cause. So what if he'd screwed a rich bitch? When it came to screwing, she could give as good or better! What else did a man want from a woman anyway? And then there was what she knew about him. Once the robbery was done, she would have a beautiful hold on Walter Prince. So even if he didn't *marry* her, she could stick around just as long as she wanted to, years and years, and he'd have to be good to her.

She didn't give Vino the chance to wash or anything. She got it out and said, 'Fly, little bird, fly,' and he said, *'Little?'* But he couldn't even smile, he was so turned on, and he almost gave it to her standing like Pete Chizro in Lake Wyanoth who was her first and her tenth and her hundredth, she guessed, they did it so often that year she went with him and it was a blessing she didn't get knocked up the times he skipped the rubber and now of course the pill was great and no worry...

'*Ah, God, ah!*' It was the best thing on earth and she closed her eyes and made believe it was Prince socking it to her and whispering what Vino was whispering about her being the greatest, the only one for him. 'Ah! Baby ... ahhhhh!' She swallowed the name 'Bucky' the rich bitch had called him but said it inside. 'Ahhh, Bucky—baby, more, *more...*'

Later, she wondered how it was she wanted him so much without their even having touched hands. It had never happened this way before. Could she be *falling*? The real thing? Well, she was twenty-six; time for it to happen. And who better to have it happen *with*?

Vino lit two cigarettes and gave her one and she said, 'You never told me, Vino. How'd you and Prince work up this gig? You didn't go to school together, that's for sure.'

He laughed. 'And we didn't serve time together either ... though who knows, we might yet.'

'Then how? I know you got Rollins from back east.'

'First rap graduate.'

'And Fanny was casing the island on her own when we got here and you recognized her and felt her out. And I spotted Bramms trying to cop that boat on the beach. But Prince?'

Again he didn't tell her; just said it was a trade secret. She acted mad. He said, 'Now come on, baby. A man has to keep *some* secrets.'

She got up and went to her clothing. She said she was going to have a snack. 'Then maybe Rollins'll take me for a walk. I got this up-tight feeling.'

He waited until she was almost dressed, then lit another cigarette and blew a lot of smoke and muttered, 'No use telling you. You won't hardly believe it.'

She shrugged, moving to the door, but she knew she had him. He said, 'It was in his apartment, in Chicago, about a month before I met you. I didn't know he was there.'

'You mean he was a *mark*?'

He nodded.

'And he nailed you?'

'He didn't really nail me,' Vino mumbled. 'It was sort of a stand-off. He pulled a popgun, but I had a thirty-eight in my belt and I wasn't going to let him bust me. Then he said he had a proposition, so we talked.'

'Sure, he talked and you listened, with a gun on you.'

'No, he put down the popgun; took a chance and talked and what he said was Bay Island.'

She shook her head, marveling. 'You're right. I can't hardly believe it.'

She went to the kitchen and brought back the rest of the chicken Fanny had cooked for Prince. It was made with wine and things and she didn't like it much, but Vino did, and they washed it down with cans of Bud. After that, she modeled her tan leather mini outfit with the matching knee-high boots and put on her black wig and he got steamy again. He wanted her to stay dressed, but she was afraid to spoil her outfit. It was wild and foxy. She was going to try it out on Prince.

MONDAY, JANUARY 27

It was what amounted to a combination junkyard and marina on a wide canal north of Berrywood, which wasn't far from Delray Beach. Curt Bramms hunched inside his windbreaker, the thin rain beginning to trickle from his balding head and down his neck. He didn't like Coeman, the manager of Berrywood Naval Corporation. Too smooth-talking; young, tall and with a face that reminded him of the make-out athletes back in college, the big men on campus. And what sort of name was *Coeman* anyway? He glanced sideways, catching the manager in profile. *Maybe a nose job.*

'... not much as it stands, but if you decide to purchase we can rehabilitate. It'll cost a little more, naturally, but for, say, fifteen hundred you can have a working model of an LCVP. You said you wanted it for tie-up use, didn't you? To sit at a dock?'

'I said I wasn't going to use it more than once—about forty nauticals.'

They were at the far end of the canal, having walked over from the office. Here were no gleaming cabin cruisers, no sprightly sailboats. Here, out of sight of the money trade, were various rotting and rusting hulks, lying in stark disarray. It smelled ... sad, dismal.

'And then?' Coeman asked.

Bramms shrugged and stuck a smile on his lips. *'Veir veist?'*

Coeman said, 'What?'

Bramms felt he was *pretending* ignorance of the Yiddish expression, but translated anyway.

'Who knows? Some sort of promotion stunt, my boss says.'

'Well, if you keep it docked, fine. If you try to use it...' He suddenly said, 'Forty nautical miles? You mean *towed*, don't you?'

Bramms moved around the beached, grayish hulk still marked USN with the numbers lost in a patch of orange rust. 'The engine's still in her, right?'

'Well, yes, but it hasn't been used in years.'

'That would be part of the rehabilitation you mentioned, wouldn't it? You can't expect fifteen hundred for a useless hunk of metal.'

Coeman followed him, his tan rain hat dripping as he shook his head. 'I don't know. We'll have to speak to Mr. Armor, our shop foreman. It might not be possible...'

The barge-like craft was resting on an incline, tilted low on the port side. Bramms grasped the rusty top and leaped over, just clearing.

'Careful, Mr. Burns!' Coeman called. 'No one's been aboard her...'

'It's all right,' Bramms said. Walking carefully and at a tilt, he went aft and bent to the engine hatch. The latch was rusted solid. He took the wheel in both hands. It wouldn't move, but that might indicate it was still functional, still attached to the rudder which was touching ground. He walked fore, looking around. Rusty, yes, but no serious hull damage that he could see. If the keel was good and the engine could be made to run...

He reached the gate, thinking of all the newsreels he'd seen of Marines and GI's packed into these craft, hunched and ready, and then the gate flopping down and the men stepping into water, sometimes so deep that the weaker drowned under the weight of their packs and rifles, under the terrible weight of their fear; and others going on to fall and die on the beach; and still others surviving to triumph over the Japs and themselves. Guadalcanal. Okinawa. The bloody Pacific islands where he could have proved his courage once and for all. But the damned Jew doctors (no matter *what* their names, their lies) had kept him out of it, knowing, *sensing* his enmity, using that

72

business in high school with Mr. Weil and the other kid stuff to label him 'mentally unstable' and keep him from triumphing early in his life. They, and his mother, had pushed him into pharmacy school and marriage and all the other mistakes he had made.

But he would prove his courage on another island, have his triumph on Bay Island, and how many of those Marines and GI's would have dared what he was going to dare?

'Are you all right in there, Mr. Burns?'

He said, 'Yes, fine,' and prepared himself for the unpleasantness of talking business. . . .

Bucky had taken *Spray II* out for a trial run that morning. It was rainy, gusty, with occasional heavy swells; perfect weather, in his opinion, to test a new boat. He stayed out almost four hours, quickly checking the obligatory auxiliary engine, then turning to important matters. He was generally pleased with the twenty-nine-foot sloop's performance, jotting down notations for changes in rigging, most of the time simply sailing, allowing the *Spray* to run before the wind, then tacking slowly back up along the Bay Island coast. He went past the Mortonson place four times, once close enough to be seen . . . if anyone had been there to see him.

He had been relieved not to hear from Ceecee Sunday, and when he returned from his sail, there still were no messages. He had lunch and told Vino he was going for a drive—to Vizcaya Museum. At the door, Sandy helped him into his raincoat, murmuring, 'Want some company?' The truth was he *had* wanted company, and the girl looked at him so intently he almost said yes. But Vino appeared and Walt went out alone.

Vizcaya was the ornate, baroque Italian Renaissance villa of James Deering, filled with a multiplicity of *objets d'art*, a profusion of furniture of mixed lineage. It also had an excellent docking area—a stone breakwater in the shape of an Italian barge with a yacht landing at one end. Beyond lay the waters of Biscayne Bay, immediately northward was the Rickenbacker Causeway and farther north, much farther, lay Bay Island. He hadn't quite decided how, or even if, he would use Vizcaya. But the villa was now a museum, and it closed at five P.M., and after that, say in the dark morning hours following a gay party, who would think to look there?

73

He returned to Bay Island, but not to the house. He went instead to the country club.

He was at the bar now, almost alone, sipping a martini on the rocks, talking to the bartender.

'... remember your grandfather.'

'You don't look old enough, Olaf.'

The stout, red-faced man chuckled. 'I was just breaking in as a bus boy, sir. Not many of the originals around any more, owners *or* attendants.'

Olaf was a garrulous man and went on talking about his early days on the island. But Bucky stopped listening and began preparing himself to meet his peers. He was no longer alone. A large party had just entered the club, and among those in it were the Mortonsons. A large, *noisy* party. In a moment he was engulfed, Mortonson introducing him to a good dozen men and women, while Ceecee stood at the far end of the bar to his left, one foot up on the rail, cigarette between her lips, a pants-suited version of Bonnie with a young, blond, oh-so-cool version of Clyde listening as she spoke.

Selina 'Sweets' McKreigh and her husband came by, trailing talk of National Steeplechase and Hunt Association affairs. At sixty-eight, Sweets was beginning to get a leathery, desiccated look despite the inevitable face lifts and body work. But her diamonds were still youthful.

'... collection of over two hundred pornographic paperbacks for his seventieth birthday. And from his own daughter!'

'Well, what else do you get a man who not only *has* everything but *manufactures* everything?'

Bucky didn't recognize more than a third of the people here; too many of them were guests, but guests either in Real Society or so *riche* that the *nouveau* didn't count against them.

'... *divine* party at Marbella, after yachting over from Sardinia. The Baron and Baroness have a simply *incredible* estate...'

'... bought that new health insurance Allie was talking about. Expensive by any standards, but then again organ transplants aren't exactly in the blood transfusion category. At least not yet.'

'I'd rather have a *quinta* in Estoril than all of Jamaica!'

Bucky identified faces, returned nods and hellos ... and found he was beginning to feel a little edgy; up tight the kids

74

would say. Was it that he was too far out of the Real Society game and was envious, or had he simply lost patience with such exotic minutiae?

Or had he *ever* had patience with chatter on this level? For two years he had hungered to be here, and now that he was, he began to remember certain irritations, certain minor hangups.

He had always treated money with respect; the processes of making it, helping it grow and spending it, that is. He had understood very early what money *really* was—power over people—and so even as he went after it, he had wanted to avoid giving it too much power over Bucky Prince. He had not allowed it to intrude on his after business hours and had been progressively more impatient with the talk he ran into at Real Society meeting places. He had wanted to be totally free of its dominance in his private life.

Yet he had *used* it in his private life, with a calculation beyond most of his peers, even when still in school.

There'd been a spring break and a party in Bryn Athyn and a girl who lived in Philadelphia, a very beautiful girl whom he had wanted very badly, but who was a year older than he. She had accepted his invitation only after stalling with call me next Thursday as I'm not sure if I'll be in town, and he'd known she was hoping for another invitation. He had thought how best to appeal to her and on the night of the party, suddenly decided against picking her up himself, as she and everyone else expected he would. She was from a reasonably well to do family but couldn't be classified as wealthy, so instinct and reason got together and worked out a plan of operations.

She knew Bucky Prince was wealthy. That is, she had *information* that he was wealthy. But she hadn't yet *felt* his wealth, experienced it. Therefore she had to feel and experience it.

He had sent the family Rolls and instructed the chauffeur to be *extremely* courteous to his passenger. There was a corsage on the back seat.

At the party later, the girl accepted his excuse that he'd been held up by a sporting event, and laughed about her surprise at the car and chauffeur. She also began to change.

While dancing, she thanked him for the corsage. He simply nodded. She pulled away to glance down at it, saying she was puzzled by the pin which was a safety type and seemed attached to metal; a far more solid mechanism than the usual corsage affair. He smiled and murmured, 'Just don't throw it away.'

That night he kissed her in the Rolls on the way home. The next day she called to say she couldn't accept the jeweled pin concealed in the corsage. He said, 'Why not? Just a little costume thing.' At that she murmured, 'Oh, well . . .' sounding vaguely disappointed. But someone in her family knew the real thing, and two days later she called again. She had to return his gift; it was far too expensive for her to accept from 'a casual acquaintance'.

'Then let's not be so casual.'

He saw her that night, and convinced her that she should keep the three hundred dollar 'costume bit'. They saw each other the following day, and toward evening she became very amorous.

They had quite a relationship during the remainder of his vacation and part of the next summer, until he decided he'd had enough. He had known all along he was buying her, that his money was overcoming an initial resistance, an initial lack of interest if not active dislike. Yet she was far from a whore. She was a nice, well bred Philadelphia deb who was now married into the lower echelons of Real Society. She had responded as most women would to the feel and experience of enormous money. She had given herself to the Prince family fortune more than to Bucky himself, and he had known it and she hadn't.

That was the first time he had used the power of money overtly. But not the last. After college, he had spent a year at the west coast offices of Prince Mining and the same principle, with varying methodology, had worked there, especially with the type of actress classified as 'starlet'. He had accepted what his big cars, his name, his well-established and enormous money—old Protestant money, for some reason more potent than any other kind—could bring in the way of these women, and men too when he wanted them to do things for him. Just knowing he was Walter Danforth Prince bought certain people lock, stock and soul. He had enjoyed it, for a while. Young men take what they can get any way they can get it. Young rick men take for a short while, and then settle down.

But Bucky hadn't settled down and hadn't wanted to settle down. Bucky had been restless. His dream was not one of Real

Society affairs and raising more Princes in the Big Money mold and forgetting the world of untasted experience, unknown adventure. He wanted to build his fortune, yes, but that was just *one* of the things he wanted. The others he couldn't specify; being a master sailor, perhaps ... but that was only part of it, a single symptom and not the whole sickness. To live, to move outside the safe, square world of the super rich. To do ... *something*. And still, to have money.

He had been transferred to the home office in Philadelphia, where his parents and even his playboy brother Tad, who had married and gone right on playing, had been certain he would soon find his lifetime heiress.

They were wrong. After L.A. and Philadelphia and New York (at which time the company began to falter and he was recalled to home base), he still kept looking, kept experimenting with life. And his father, in the brief time left to him, became aware that his son differed from the Real Society norm, and was saddened. Bucky also began to see how he differed from the generally smug, basically square men of money. Most rich men bought their wives, those very women supposedly beyond purchase because of their own wealth. But they had to marry money, didn't they? They had to raise their children in Real Society, didn't they? Anything else was unthinkable!

And so Bucky Prince had never met a woman, inside or out of Real Society, whom he had wanted to marry ... because any woman he could buy he didn't want, and to some extent he felt *all* women could be bought.

And wasn't that another reason for his love of sailing, sailing *alone*? No one could prejudice the sea with money, nor the winds, nor the currents. No one could buy good weather.

But the rich spoiled even this with hired men to do their sailing, with crowded yachts and cruisers, with stinking engines; extensions of the purchasing power of money, attempts to make the sea their whore. And to the degree they succeeded, that was the degree to which they reduced the meaning of being sailors. To the degree they succeeded, that was the measure of their failure to find the essence of going down to the sea in ships.

In this, at least, he felt the non rich were superior ... even if not by choice.

The days Bucky Prince best remembered were those days alone with *Spray I* and a good wind.

The women he best remembered were the ones who had made him expend personality in relating to them.

He had Olaf bring him a fresh drink, lit a fresh cigarètte and told himself it was all nonsense, all mind-play, all beside the point ... that point being, he had to get *back* into Real Society, not attack it! That point being, he had to *have* money before deciding what it was he didn't like about having it!

He watched Ceecee Mortonson down the bar with her foot on the rail and her black hair swinging, as she laughed along with her blond Clyde. He had another drink and felt he was getting drunk and knew he couldn't get drunk even though others around the bar were; he had to stay cool and clear and watch them because they were his prey. He put down the glass. He smoked and waited for his head to clear and made himself listen to the talk of those who owned the world.

'... bothering the President about his visits to, and I quote, an all white, all Christian enclave of entrenched wealth. That's yellow journalism for you! And he only comes to see his old friend Charley Vener ...'

'... keep up my membership in The Links and The Knickerbocker even if I never leave Prouts Neck again.'

'... about to bid on the Idol's Eye necklace, but then my agent found one with a smaller center piece, sixty three point eight carats as compared to the Idol's seventy point twenty and a much finer stone ...'

'... ought to get Cecil Beaton or Carleton Varney to turn Number Twelve into a decent club.'

Charles and Karen Vener came up then, the dominant members of the Vener brewing clan, his neighbors in Number Two. They said just what he expected they would say, and in unison: 'Hi, neighbor!' Karen was, as all Vener wives, German born and quite a bit younger than her husband. Such a pleasant couple with a five-year-old son named for a friend who lived in the White House; such easy-going people, really, if one forgot their massive donations to the John Birch Society and several virulent 'patriotic' organizations.

They talked. Was he married, Karen asked forthrightly, and on learning he wasn't, said, 'You must come for dinner soon.' Bucky said, 'Certainly,' and Charles laughed. 'Better be careful, Bucky. She's got a sister.'

Ceecee stayed at her end of the bar and Bucky kept meeting other residents and getting more invitations; and accepting them. He would see for himself just how many Picassos and French Impressionist masterpieces the Veners kept on the island. And whether Lambert and Patricia Whiteson had brought much of their extensive jade figurine collection from Boston. And during the course of what would appear a very general conversation, someone would be bound to come up with the answer to whether Allie Mortonson actually did keep a million dollars in cash always close to his person. And he'd have had to be totally blind not to see all the fine jewelry on all the fine women, and this only a very casual Monday night gathering.

Yes, he was back among the Beautiful People again.

Vincent Drang was also present, a broad, dark man, very sedate in dress and very carefully in the background. (Rumor had it he'd been *far* in the background when he'd used a purchasing agent to buy his Bay Island home for him, and by the time the club committee learned who the real buyer was, it was too late to do anything without a scandal. They had voted more against scandal than for Vincent Drang.) Not so sedate was the woman standing with him, a striking ash blonde in her early thirties. Charles Vener offered the information; 'Beth Larkin, Drang's sister-in-law.' He beckoned Drang, murmuring, 'I know Karen will hate me for this...' In a moment, the introductions were made and Bucky found himself alone with Beth Larkin as the others wandered away.

'Is your sister here?' he asked, by way of openers.

'No, a touch of virus. I've heard the name Prince before. Sailing or polo, I'm not sure which.'

'Both, as far as the family goes. Just sailing for me, and not much of it, I'm afraid. Not any more.'

'Well, there *àre* other pastimes,' she said blandly.

He waited. She was medium-sized, richly endowed fore and aft, with a perfect baby face. Her dress was mini, on top as well as bottom. She was a very sexy woman and knew it. 'Golf, tennis, croquet...'

'Business,' he said.

'That's too bad,' she said, and moved up on a newly vacated stool and smiled at him. He smiled back and looking past her, saw that Ceecee Mortonson was smiling at her Clyde, and past

him. Their eyes met. Ceecee kept smiling and talking. He felt
something—that goddam chemistry—and asked Beth Larkin if
she cared for a bite of supper.

They went to a table. They ate and talked. Every so often he
saw Ceecee. There was rock music now and she danced with
her Clyde. She danced the way she walked, with shocking sensuality, whipping her long arms, her long, beautiful body fren-
etically, tirelessly. People watched her. Bucky watched her and
Beth noticed he was watching her.

'That's quite a girl,' she said, after turning in her seat.

'Who?'

She smiled.

He shrugged. 'Hard not to look.'

'Yes, like a dirty movie.'

'The rain's stopped,' he said. 'Why don't we walk?'

They walked in the chill, wet gardens. He heard the music;
the wild sensuous music. He kissed Beth Larkin. She was a
very warm armful. She said, 'Why don't you take me out on
your boat tomorrow?' He said, 'Yes.' They went back inside,
she said bye-bye and returned to her brother-in-law. Vincent
Drang, né Drangostine, retained at least a little of his Mafia
antecedents. He smiled at Prince, but it was a suspicious,
Italian-brother smile. Beth Larkin smiled at Prince. No suspicion there. Just considerable interest.

Ceecee Mortonson was still dancing. She'd worn out her
Clyde and had another young partner. This one worked hard
to keep up with her, but he wasn't succeeding. Allie Mortonson came over and put his arm around Bucky's shoulders. A
heady aroma of booze and cigars preceding his words, he said,
'What the devil did you do to my daughter Saturday night?'

Bucky looked at him.

Allie laughed. 'Whatever it was, I thank you, Bucky. I thank
you with all my heart. She's been ... well, if not a different
girl, at least a far happier one. Out all day Sunday with young
Blake, nephew of Chin Miller. Didn't get in until long after I'd
gone to bed. That's Blake dancing with her now. And today, in
Miami with Lad and Nabby Waters' youngest. Tall blond boy
who danced with her before. And she's making dates and accepting invitations as if trying to corner the market.'

Bucky nodded, chuckled and murmured, 'Marvelous.' And
went home. Where Sandy was in the entry hall, almost as if
she'd been waiting there. She wasn't wearing her maid's uni-

form. She was wearing a leather outfit, high boots and an uncertain smile. He ended the uncertainty. He took her hand and led her up the stairs. If she wanted it that badly, then Vino was obviously failing, as the French put it, to honor madame's signature. Or Sandy needed more honoring than any one man could provide, or they were breaking up.

Whatever it was, the old Prince appetite was sharp tonight and rationalization had set in. He knew it was a mistake but Bucky Prince always survived mistakes of this kind.

She had big white thighs. He stood behind her, facing the dresser mirror, raising the leather miniskirt and kissing her neck. Her reflection smiled when he stopped. 'Surprise, baby.' She wore no pants. He turned her around and watched his hand clutching her abundant flesh, more flesh than he could manage with both hands. Then he let go and she took off her jacket, blouse and bra. She stopped. He saluted her breasts with his lips. She said, voice a thick whisper, 'I'll leave the rest on, huh?' He said, 'Certainly,' and took her to bed. She lay down and stretched out and ran her hands up and down the insides of those big thighs, watching as he undressed. When he came at her, she put her booted legs up over his shoulders and said, 'Bang me! Bang me, Bucky!' It was exactly what he had in mind; no more, no less.

Back at the house, Yang served them coffee in the living room and Ceecee was high enough to ask him where his friend Yin was. He smiled slightly, but his eyes reproached her. She said, 'I resisted almost a year, didn't I? How many of your friends held out *that* long?' He murmured, 'Of my friends, Miss Mortonson, *all*.'

'Servants,' Ceecee said. 'Whatever happened to the good old servile kind?'

Father shook his head slightly; square old Dad who feared losing a good houseboy. But this time she saw the young Oriental grin as he turned away.

'I'm glad you snapped out of it,' Father said.

'Oh, yes, the depression runs its course and then the manic takes over.'

His cup stopped short of his lips.

She shook her head, laughing. 'Another funny, Father. I'm having a good time now.'

He smiled and drank his coffee. 'It *was* a damned good

party, wasn't it.' He took out his cigar case. She took out her cigarette case. He said, 'You're smoking entirely too much.'

'Pot calling kettle black.'

'Cigars? I don't inhale. All the cancer reports...'

'I'll quit one of these days, Father. When I'm safely married.'

He lit his cigar, muttering, 'Plenty of time yet before you have to think of *that*.'

He had said similar things recently. Now that she thought of it, he had said similar things for as long as she could remember. She smoked, looking at him. He examined his cigar ash.

'Don't you want me to marry?' she asked.

He looked up. 'Marry? Of course, when you're ready. But you're obviously not even close to that state of grace.'

She was going to say something about mind readers, but he quickly changed the subject, discussing their 'little Monday bash' and how they'd started at the Waters' with just six people and gone onto five of the island's eleven houses and ended up at the club with 'twenty-six people, as close as I was able to count'.

She nodded, and felt her high slipping away. He couldn't know that she and Jock Waters had been on pot all afternoon and had smoked a final stick just before joining the party at his parents' home. But that was hours ago and she would have welcomed another stick to keep it going. Because since Saturday and Bucky Prince, too many evil spirits had returned to haunt her. And now Father was doing *something*—or was it that he was failing to do something?—that was strengthening their grip on her.

She rose. 'Good night.'

'Good night, dear.'

'Breakfast on the patio at ten, ten thirty?'

'I won't be here. I'm going into Miami and see if I can't bribe someone to get me two gardeners. Goddam difficult to find help this season.'

'I thought those two the agency sent...'

'No, they didn't work out.'

She hesitated, wanting to ask was it because they were Negroes. They had never had Negro servants, as long as she could remember. And while he never said anything bad about blacks, that wasn't really a point in his favor because he didn't mention them at all, not even to comment on news stories, just didn't seem to know they existed on this planet. And in *this* day and age, that had to mean something!

She went up to his chair and bent to kiss him. He presented his cheek, as always.

'I want a real kiss,' she said.

'What?' He stared up at her.

She bent to him again, aiming at his lips.

'What's the matter ...?' he began.

She moved slowly, deliberately, and he laughed with what she felt was considerable embarrassment. She kissed his lips. Dry lips. Remote lips. Lips sealed away from the heart for this kiss. Lips that turned immediately to receive the cigar, and the cigar was taken with far greater warmth than his daughter's lips.

An old evil spirit slipped into her heart. A Daddy never loved me evil spirit. A cliché evil spirit found in every girls' school, in every nation, in every time of man's history she supposed. A spirit not worthy of Straight A Ceecee Mortonson.

Her insides hurt as she went to her room. First Bucky Prince's face as seen from the bathroom doorway. And now this dumb old evil spirit. She tried to bring up all the triumphs, all the men who had wanted her, all those who'd had her and continued to want her. But tonight it did no good.

To bed, to bed! And screw all evil spirits and evil thoughts. And screw Bucky Prince and his shallow, cunt-hunting soul.

Before she slept she heard the memory words, 'Love you, love you, Bucky, yes, a little, for now.'

She *didn't* love him; had simply gone ape for a handsome face and rich voice and educated cock. Nothing, really. Just ... a *feeling*, a lech that had caught her by surprise.

No one loved on first sight. It was a Grandma-Grandpa myth. An impossibility! Definitely!

Bertram Alvah Mortonson, good old Allie to his social Society peers, sat long with his cigar, but he didn't enjoy it. There were signs that she was finally beginning to notice. Her unasked questions about the two Negro gardeners he'd failed to hire. The slip—his—about marriage, but then again he'd been drinking too much tonight. And finally the kiss.

Goddam it! Why *couldn't* he kiss his own daughter?

He dropped the cigar stub in the ashtray and stood up. Ay, *there* was the rub. *His own daughter.*

In his room, he picked up the silver framed photograph of Greta. Not a particularly good-looking woman. Good family, yes. Fine breeding. High intelligence. But they hadn't gotten along very well after the first few years. Many reasons; prime among them his having married without being in love. Realized that too late. But they might have made a success of it if they'd been able to have children. They hadn't. It was never pinned down, medically, who was to blame, if 'blame' was the correct word. He had always assumed it was Greta. Perhaps he'd even said as much.

Then one day she'd told him she was pregnant. He had been delighted. And she? She had been strangely remote. Happy, yes, but strangely apart from him.

He had never thought to suspect Ceecee wasn't his. He had engaged in sex with Greta two and three times a week all during their marriage, and there was no reason to doubt Ceecee was his. A dark, lean child, not at all like fair Greta and not at all like any Mortonson, but still, why suspect anything? The child would *grow* into a LeMain, a Mortonson.

Long before he understood she never would, Ceecee was taken from him. Not physically. She remained with him, at least at those times when she wasn't at one of the fine boarding schools he chose for her. And then Oldfields School at Glencoe, and then Skidmore (though she had wanted Berkeley and he had thought, *Call of the blood?* and laughed at himself). And now an end to education, after she refused to go for her Master's as he had suggested, and more than suggested. An end of schools and the putting away in schools of this girl and what she represented.

Greta's heart had failed seventeen years ago. A coronary for so young a woman. Well, not unheard of, but a curse and a cause for the beginning of love. Yes, he began to care for her; for the woman whose courage amazed him. Another coronary was possible, more than that, expected, but she fought to live without bringing the shadow of death to her child, then three, and to her husband. She still went out and played golf, sharpening her game with the pro who, because of his style and education, because of his ability as a teacher, was the only Negro professional the Whiteoak Club had ever had. (The last too, as long as Allie Mortonson would live!)

The second attack left her alive, but barely. She had hours, perhaps a day or two. Once she gathered this from the faces and voices of her doctors and her husband, she waited until she and Allie were alone. And told him.

He had begun to love too late. She had hated far too long. He had said things, left things unsaid, and the pride and strength of character of this woman who was more like her father Corliss LeMain than either of Corliss's sons (and Corliss came from whaler stock, smuggler stock, refined into railroads and banking but always tough), this woman had proved *he* was the sterile one, and proved it with Eddie Cromson, the Negro golf pro.

'But not just because he was there,' she whispered from her bed, smiling slightly into his unbelieving face. 'Not just because he told me he loved me. But because he was the man I would have married if I'd had the chance to know him and be with him. Because *I* love *him*. How much of his love is for the wealth and position, the white world of power I represent, I don't know. A good deal of it, I suspect, almost inevitably. But there was nothing he could give me, besides himself. I love him and I will until the moment I die, today or tomorrow.'

He began to turn away.

'He's Ceecee's father,' she said.

She died two hours later. He was at her side, and her death was a fighting and crying and choking, no final words which he feared might be overheard by doctors or nurses. Her death was a forgetting of love and hate and a clutching at breath. He lost his fear, held her hand and tried to *will* her that breath. But when she was gone and a day had passed, he found he was relieved. His four-year-old daughter came to him for her kisses, her fondling. He had none to give.

He'd had none to give from that day on. Oh, a minimal touching of hand to hand, lips to cheek; and housekeepers had given her whatever they'd had to give. Allie Mortonson had told himself the child didn't know, couldn't distinguish between what had been before that day of death and afterward. And, in a conscious sense, he knew he was right. And, in an unconscious, subconscious, deep inside the child sense he knew he was wrong. But those were vagaries and easy to dismiss. And besides, it was not a matter of choice. Ceecee didn't exactly repel him, but there was something that made it impossible for him to love her beyond that minimal touching, that

85

minimal kissing.

Schools were the blessing. Schools in which to shut away the living symbol of his failure and of his betrayal. Yet every so often, Ceecee would *not* stay in school, would return home and insist on living there; would refuse to go to any place that did not allow her to return home each day to her father.

So Allie Mortonson stayed away for long periods too. Allie Mortonson worked a little harder, played a little harder and never brought another woman into his home as wife. His women were kept in other homes and with them, he tried to erase Greta's assertion that Ceecee was a black man's daughter. (Well, not *black*, since Eddie Cromson was a finely shaded man, a tan and beautiful man, and even that amount of color had failed to show in Ceecee.) Allie Mortonson had tried to impregnate every woman he slept with and never once succeeded. So while he told himself there was still doubt—was even doubt Greta had mated with Cromson; she might have told that story in a last attempt to hurt him as he had hurt her—at the same time, he grew more and more certain Ceecee wasn't his.

He watched for signs of her nigrescence. There weren't any, and there were, according to how hard he looked on any particular day. A certain coarseness of hair. A certain deepness of tan when she sunned. A certain fullness of lip.

It was in her lips, her mouth, that he most often found the spoor of Eddie Cromson.

And yet she was his child, in the sense that she had grown up calling him Father. She was his child in the sense that he would leave her whatever he owned. She was his child in the sense that he cared more for her than for any child on earth.

She was his child, but in an adopted sense. And Allie's pride made this distinction terribly important in another sense—the human, loving sense.

Now she was beginning to know. Or had known and was beginning to show she knew. He hoped he was wrong. He didn't want her to be hurt.

But God, how he feared black babies!

Then the *world* would know!

Unless, of course, she married a black man. He had thought of this often. But Ceecee had never indicated she cared for that kind of ground-breaking, that kind of crusade or rebellion. And when she had gone into a period of gloom, a grayness of

86

heart and spirit, he had hurt for her and feared for her. He had wanted men for her.

Damned dichotomy! Ugly ambivalence! He needed to know (to alleviate his own guilt, his own part in her sadness) that she was gay, popular and successful with men, men who could give her what he had not been able to give. At the same time, he feared like he feared eternal hell itself her choosing one of those men, her marrying and giving forth children.

He had never spoken to anyone about this. He had never allowed himself to think about this—except in momentary flashes of insight—until this night.

A crossroads for Allie Mortonson.

He put down the picture, rang for Anders and had a diathermy treatment for his bad hip. A crossroads, but Allie never hesitated, never deviated from his established path and pattern. The treatment finished, he washed up.

He wanted for her. He feared for himself.

He wondered what Bucky Prince had thought of her. She was young for Bucky, certainly, but that date had marked a sharp turning in her attitude.

Another brief insight: *Had she been hurt?*

Anger flared, a father's anger, and died. Allie Mortonson went to bed, shrugging mentally and resigning himself to what he was and what he would probably remain all his life.

Poor Ceecee ...

TUESDAY, JANUARY 28

Beaufort made his nine to ten a.m. rounds, starting with the bridge and after three inland and three coastline checkpoints, ended up in Walter Prince's driveway. All his men were alert, wide-awake, on their toes. They goddam better well be. He had rid himself of two goldbrickers his first year on the island. One had tried to give him some backtalk, saying, 'Nothing ever happens here anyway, so why're you running around playing tin soldier?' After, Beaufort had sunk his fist wrist-deep into the bastard's belly and dragged him to his feet, and then explained that nothing ever happened until it *did* happen; like that fool kid with his sawed-off shotgun and his pillowcase full of loot from the Vener home.

Getting out of his car, he smiled—a slight widening of the wide lips in the big, pitted face—thinking he owed that kid something, this great job to be exact.

He rang the bell and asked the butler for Mr. Prince.

'If you'll wait a minute, please.'

Beaufort waited closer to five minutes but he wasn't at all impatient. He stood in the marble floored anteroom and hummed tunelessly, enjoying the feel of the house, as he enjoyed any house on this island. He'd talked to Granny Blayle last week; Granny had worked with him on the Miami force, and was now out in Palm Beach. They'd compared notes and Beaufort had felt Palm Beach was slipping, no matter how much big money was there, what with the kooks and jet-setters and phonies. Too much mixing. Servants screwing debutantes. Waitresses dating rich boys. Plenty of robbery, though they kept the stories down. Even a rape earlier in the season. Not a *safe* enough setup for a good family.

Beaufort wouldn't have traded with ole J. Edgar himself! He was going to *die* in this job!

The butler returned and Beaufort followed him out to a back patio. Prince was sitting at a table, eating. 'Good morning, Beaufort. Beautiful, isn't it, after yesterday's rain? Sit down and have some breakfast.'

Beaufort flushed a little at the greeting and took a chair, placing his thin zipper case on the flagstone floor. 'Thank you, Mr. Prince. Coffee would be good right now.' He looked at the dock and the boat. 'Looks like you put some new sail on her.'

'You're observant,' Prince said, pouring from a tall, silver pot into a cup the butler had brought.

Beaufort caught himself flushing and quickly raised his cup. The coffee was really something. 'You've got yourself a cook.'

'Yes, one of the best.'

'Which brings me to the point of my visit,' Beaufort said, picking up his zipper case.

A maid came out with a tray of rolls and buns. Beaufort said, 'No, thanks,' then took a second look at her. Cute piece. Lots of meat and lots of movement. She smiled at him. He cleared his throat, touched his collar, returned his eyes to Prince. He wondered if he could ask her out. She was new enough here not to have made many contacts.

Not that he was hurting for it. He still had Gloria and her

88

girls and it was always free for old Beaufort who had been on
Gloria's payroll when he worked for the force. But a steady
diet of whores left a man wanting.

'What *is* the point of your visit?' Prince was asking.

'Sorry, thinking...' He opened the case and began to explain about Consolidated Investigations. 'Security checks,
they're automatic and periodic, paid for by the Owners' Association. I send in the names of your employees; Consolidated
runs the checks. In two weeks, sometimes a little longer, they
send me a file for my records.' He smiled. 'Run a check on you
too, Mr. Prince.'

Prince barely answered his smile. '*That's* flattering.'

'They tell me it was established by the original twelve...'

'And by now it's taken on the strength of religious ritual.'
Prince was no longer bothering to smile. Beaufort had run into
this before. They hated to be bothered and they worried about
losing their servants. Servants quit real fast nowadays, for any
little thing, because they could get jobs just about anywhere—
say in Palm Beach, where the shortage, according to Granny,
was terrific.

But rules were rules, though he could show he understood. 'I
know it's an inconvenience, Mr. Prince...'

Prince nodded, glancing at the maid who was arranging the
serving cart. His voice dropped. 'They're new help. I found
them in Miami, in a hurry, and I was fortunate ... as you
mentioned about the cook. They'll resent...' He stopped and
lit a cigarette.

Beaufort felt lousy. He fingered the cards in his hand, until
Prince's eyes brought him around.

'These cards ... if they'll fill them out with names and
Social Security and the other things; get a small passport type
picture ... Well, I'll leave them with you. Afterwards, have
them come down to the office. I'll fingerprint them, check
licenses and other identification...' Prince's stony look stopped him.

'I wish someone had told me about this beforehand,' Prince
said. 'I wish you had come around when they first arrived.
Now that I've grown accustomed to them...' The maid left,
wheeling the cart, and Prince stood up.

Beaufort said, 'No point doing it when they first arrive, Mr.
Prince. I like to wait at least a month, even longer when I can.
The shakedown period for servants, new ones, I mean, is about

that long, wouldn't you say?'

Prince looked puzzled. 'If I'm going to dismiss a servant, I generally do it within a two month period, yes.'

'That's what I mean. A waste of time and money to investigate people who might not be here when the reports come in.'

'Then ... why are you here *now*? It's not a month...'

'Just to deliver the cards, Mr. Prince. They can bring them to me, say, the first week in March.' He paused. 'By then the season'll almost be over. Even if one of them gets snippy...'

Prince said, 'I'm staying on for a while,' but he seemed to be thinking of something else. He sat down and said, 'Well, if it can't be helped ...' He sighed. 'How involved we become with servants. The law of supply and demand really squeezes us here.'

Beaufort nodded, relieved that the worst was past. Mr. Brandy had thrown a real fit when he'd found out his Cuban housekeeper was going to be fingerprinted. But then again, Brandy wasn't *old* family and he'd also been sick.

'They bring you the cards the first week in March,' Prince asked, pouring fresh coffee for both of them, 'and a month later you get the results?'

'Two weeks to a month.' He took cream and sugar, stirring his coffee.

Prince pushed cigarettes across the table. Beaufort lit up and inhaled deeply. He looked around, at the dock boat and bay. Yes, one hell of a beautiful day, sitting here and having coffee and smokes with a man like Mr. Prince. One hell of a beautiful job.

The moment the door closed behind the security officer, Vino came into the study where Bucky was at the desk, making notations on a sheet of paper. Right behind Vino came the others, and they all began to speak at once. Bucky said, 'Now just a moment. Whatever Sandy told you, it's not as bad as it first appeared. You'll bring him the cards on March eighth; perhaps even hold off until the Monday of the second week, the tenth. The reports on your fingerprints will take another month...'

'He said two weeks, mostly,' Sandy muttered, proving she'd been listening from inside.

'All right; two weeks. That still brings us far past the fifteenth, and that's the only date we have to worry about. On the sixteenth you'll be gone, no matter what he gets on you.'

'There's nothing to get on *me*,' Sandy said. 'I'm clean.'

'But the rest of us,' Fanny said. 'That *cochon*!'

'He could ask for the cards sooner,' Vino said. 'He could get a hunch and push for a fast report. And you should've mentioned that something like this might come up. We should've been prepared.'

'The odds are heavily in our favor,' Bucky murmured, feeling the justice of Vino's complaint.

'Odds are okay when gambling for bread,' Vino said grimly, 'but not when it's your freedom.'

'Or your life,' Fanny added. 'What if he gets the hunch, like Vino said, and has us watched?'

'It's my freedom too,' Bucky said quietly. 'My life too. You're allowing yourselves to be carried away by *if's*.'

'We can do it sooner,' Rollins offered.

Vino nodded vigorously. 'The sooner the better. I say the first party.'

Bucky glanced at his sheet of paper. 'That's next Saturday, February first. Bramms can't possibly have the LC ...'

'Then to hell with the LC!' Vino interrupted. 'We can do without it!'

Bucky looked at him. 'I'd rather drop it completely than commit suicide.'

'I'm with Bu ...' Sandy began. 'I'm with Mr. Prince.'

'I *know* you are,' Vino snapped.

Bucky waited. The two looked at each other. Sandy said, 'No strings on anyone, right?'

Vino looked away. He didn't answer but he was pale. Bucky said, 'That's another thing. We can't have any trouble about women. If I ...' He paused, hating having to say this in front of them all, but knowing it had to be said. 'If I stepped on anyone's toes, tell me.'

'You *didn't*,' Sandy said.

'All right,' Vino said, and he looked at Bucky. 'You didn't. But she gets the hell out of my room.'

'She can come in with me,' Fanny said. 'I have a folding cot in the closet.'

'Then that's settled,' Bucky said, still watching Vino.

'Yeah, settled,' Vino said bitterly.

Rollins cleared his throat. He began to speak, stopped, began again. Sandy cut him short. 'Let's stop talking about me like I belong to everyone in the group!'

'Well you do!' Vino said. 'Everyone but Fanny, the way I see it!'

'The way you see it isn't so! I belong to *me*! What I do or don't do ...'

'You belong in a whorehouse! Why I never thought ...'

Bucky stood up. 'If this is what we've become, it's off. I'll return as much of your investments as I can.'

First Ceecee Mortonson and now Sandy. Unnecessary complications, both of them, in an already complicated affair ... but, like liquor, a Prince weakness. And he should have anticipated at least the *possibility* of a security check, even though the island had seemed so tightly controlled an enclave—at least in his childhood memories of it—that extra checks hadn't appeared likely. And no one else had brought it up. And now pressure was building on pressure and tearing apart his hastily assembled group, a group that would have had trouble at the best of times, and this was fast becoming the worst of times.

He felt sick, deep-down sick, and yet he was already beginning to plan on a new set of 'servants'. Where he would find the extra money, he didn't know, but there was no turning back for Bucky Prince.

Rollins's voice was uncertain, apologetic. 'I was only gonna ask when the second party is.'

Vino didn't look quite as pale, quite as angry now. 'The second party might be it.' He cleared his throat, grinned (albeit unconvincingly), included Sandy and Bucky in a quick glance around. 'I'm over my mad. Business is business, especially when it's as *big* as this. No one wants to call it off, right?'

The others murmured their agreement.

Bucky sat down, knees weak ... with relief. He didn't want to call it off either.

But neither did he want to rush it. 'The second gala is a definite possibility. That's on February fifteenth, and Bramms might be ready by then, if he knows he has to be. Then there's the third gala on March first ...' He paused, fingering his sheet of notations. 'But all the galas except the last lack a very important ingredient.'

No one asked questions.

'That ingredient is ... the largest possible take. I'm reasonably sure Mrs. Greshen will wear her Light of Stars diamond at the final gala. She always did, when she attended. And she's definitely going to attend this year, because I'm going to escort her. That's almost three million dollars right there, according to the agent of a very affluent Levantine who, I hear, wants to hang it around the neck of an ancient Greek statue in his private vault room.'

Vino made a sound somewhere between a whistle and a groan.

'And the other residents ... any single gala is attended by upwards of half of them and their guests, averaging about six per family. But the final gala brings them *all* out, with guests flying in from every part of the world. And brings them out in all their jeweled glory. I doubt whether we'd get even *half* the jewelry at any other gala.'

Deepening silence.

'Finally, it's the only *costume* party of the season. A *masked* ball. The other galas...' He shook his head. 'We'd have to change the plan and change it radically. Make it a blatant and dangerous stickup.'

'You *have* the plan?' Fanny asked.

'Just about.'

'Then shouldn't you tell us?'

'Not until I can say I have it complete and absolute. In a week, maybe two. That's why it's dangerous to try and step up the schedule. Every time I walk out of this house, I'm revising, finding weaknesses, plugging up holes in the dike. It's complex —it has to be, to succeed. But you already know that, from the basics we agreed upon.'

'So we're back to that final party,' Vino muttered.

'Unless you feel the risk is too great. In that case, I'd prefer to call it off.'

'And try later with another group, right?'

Bucky hesitated only an instant before nodding.

'It figures. I'd do the same.' He looked at Fanny. 'I'll play Russian Roulette for the payoff that last party will bring. How about you?'

Bucky intervened with, 'It's not *that* big a gamble.'

Fanny said, 'Yes, all right, but we must be ... better with each other.'

Vino nodded. Rollins said, offhandedly, 'Anything you people say, okay.'

Sandy said, 'I *never* wanted any change.'

Bucky looked at his sheet of paper. 'I'd like to do some thinking . . .'

After they left, he covered two more sheets with his heavy scrawl, checked over the first sheet, then crumpled all three and burned them in the ashtray. He sat and smoked and figured angles; new angles. One thought—vagrant as yet—concerned Beaufort and the way he looked at Sandy. If he ever made a move in her direction . . .

It might prove useful. Not that Bucky envied her such an assignment.

Beaufort as lover.

He winced a little.

Another thought, not quite as vagrant, was Beaufort's check on *him*. There had been no card for Walter Prince, no talk of fingerprints or photographs. A *name* check, obviously. But how deep would it go? Beyond family history? Beyond the rumors of *reduction* of wealth to a searching out of total disaster?

That could mean trouble, *after* March fifteenth. That could build suspicion . . .

But then again, it was almost impossible to pin down exactly what a once-rich man owned.

He barely heard the tapping and Sandy entered. She closed the door softly behind her and began to smile. He said, 'Honey, it was very nice. *But . . . no . . . more.*'

Her smile faltered, then regained strength. 'All right. At least until you feel different.'

'I won't, Sandy. I can't. And believe me, there's nothing in it for you.'

She nodded, as if to say, 'Sure, sure,' blew him a kiss and went out, shaking her abundant rear at him. He lit a cigarette and began working on the post-robbery pattern. After a while, he rang for service. Vino came. 'Gin and tonic, please.' Vino went out, cold and correct.

He had three drinks, about par for any boozer's morning, and then it was time to dress for his sailing date with Beth Larkin. Beth arrived on the dot of noon. She wore a white skirt and blue blouse and was altogether a neat little sailor girl. But once out in the bay, the sailor suit came off to reveal a most interesting bikini. And the quart thermos in her straw bag was full of extra-dry martinis.

94

They sailed, drank and ate a few small sandwiches, then returned to his home ... and his bed. It was fast, it was fun and it meant nothing; like all his one-night stands, his one-week or one-month stands; like all the women in his life.

And that included Ceecee Mortonson, chemistry or not!

Vino came into the Pelican, caught Bramms's eye in the back of the bar mirror and gestured for the squat man to come out-side. In the darkness of the parking lot, they stood together.

'Where's Prince?' Bramms asked.

'In the Caddy. C'mon.'

'What's wrong with being comfortable over a drink?'

'Comfortable? What if someone—one of the servants, or security men, or anyone else who works on the island—what if they came in and saw him drinking in a place like the Pelican? You think millionaires come to joints like *this*, with people like *us*?'

Bramms grunted and they went on to a shadowy corner of the lot. There, Vino got behind the wheel of the Cadillac, motioning Bramms in front beside him. Prince said, 'Mr. Bramms, I'm Walter Prince,' and put his hand over from the back seat. After they shook, Prince added, 'I know you've already talked to Vino, but I'd like to hear for myself. I understand a bit more about such things than our landlubber friend.'

Vino chuckled, glancing at Bramms. Bramms smiled a little.

'And I might be able to avoid problems by learning your strong points. Though I must say, from what Vino tells me, you're comprised of little *but* strong points. And that's as it should be, since you're doing considerably more than the rest of us.'

Bramms murmured, 'I wouldn't say that,' and Vino breathed a sigh of relief. Bramms was flattered.

Vino drove and the other two talked and it went well, none of Bramms's nuttiness showing. Vino didn't want Prince scared off because, nut or not, Bramms could definitely do the job. That was the important thing. That was what he had spotted from the beginning, when Sandy had brought Bramms to the Seashell Motel in downtown Miami Beach where they'd been living before the house on Bay Island became available. Bramms thought he was going to have a drink with a pretty girl and, maybe, make it with her ... but he'd sure sparked to the idea of the robbery when Vino had begun hinting about it, kidding about a 'crazy idea'. Bramms had jumped right to the point, saying, 'Listen, if that's why the girl picked me up, if that's what you're talking about, if it's a robbery with a big payoff, I want *in*!' He'd leaned forward in his chair, his face tight and his eyes digging into Vino's, and he hadn't bothered looking at Sandy from then on. And Vino had thought, even at that early stage, 'This guy's a nut,' but in a short time he'd also thought, 'This guy's a *find*!' Bramms went right on to admit—no, *brag*—about how he'd stolen a speedboat right in front of Sandy.

Sandy had been sunning on the beach and seen the boat break down offshore. The couple on board had worked on the engine a while, then given up and swum ashore, leaving the boat anchored where it had stalled. When they'd disappeared through a street exit, a short guy sitting down the beach a ways had swum out to the boat, started it without too much trouble and hauled up the anchor. That's when Sandy had decided he was copping it, and stood up, waved and got him to come in and pick her up. The way she showed in her bikini, it was no trick at all! After a little ride, they anchored the boat back where it had been and went to the motel ... where he got Vino along with his drink.

A real break, Vino had thought at the time. Even better than spotting Fanny, who had been parked out along the shoulder of the General Causeway, casing Bay Island with binoculars when Vino and Sandy drove by one day. Vino thought she looked familiar but he hadn't pushed it, since he was working down a list of hotel employees who'd looked good to a jewel-heist mob, one of whom had been Vino's cellmate during a short stretch in Danemora. There were always a few willing hands among the beach boys and cabana boys, and among the kitchen help too, but the trick was to find those with staying power, those who wouldn't chicken-out at the first squeeze. When the rented Ford was back on the causeway shoulder two days later, Vino had stopped nearby and strolled over. And recognized Fanny Lescou. A quick chat and she was in. (But she never *had* explained how she'd hoped to rob the island by herself, a smart, cautious professional like Fanny.)

Since Vino had come to Miami with Sandy and Rollins, that left only one opening—the man to handle the LC—and within a week Sandy brought him Bramms. Only later, after they'd talked a few times, did Vino understand just *how* nutty Bramms was! But by then, Bramms was filled in on the rough details of his job. Besides, there was no way of making a man like Bramms *resign*. He was in and he would stay in, unless someone killed him.

Bramms and Prince were talking LCVP's and swimming and coastal charts and other things and they kept right on after Prince said to return to the Pelican. They talked up to the minute Bramms got out and shook hands through the back window. Then the squat man really made Vino happy.

'I'm glad we could meet, Mr. Prince. I'm not worried about anything, now that I see who's running things.'

Prince was quiet until they hit Surfside. 'A sensitive type,' he murmured. 'Something *tight* about him.'

'Yeah,' Vino replied cautiously. 'But he knows his stuff.'

Prince didn't answer right away. 'Well, he'll do. I'm sure of it.'

Vino nodded, and smiled a little. At least *this* had gone right. A few minutes later his smiled died as he glanced in the rear-view and saw Prince's face—a helluva good-looking man, no getting away from it—and thought of how Sandy went for him.

All right, she was cock happy. No surprises there; he'd known it all along. He'd known she took other men when she could get them, and she could always get them. He'd also known that if he complained too much, she might cut out. But never before had she pushed it in his face, and she had always cared more for him than for anyone else.

Things had changed since she'd met Prince.

Sure, Prince would never take her seriously; anyone could see that ... anyone except Sandy. And now that they'd had it out in front of the others, Prince wouldn't touch her with a ten-foot pole.

But she ... She wanted Prince too goddam much!

Could a hot-pants like Sandy fall in *love*?

He knew the answer to that. Even old freewheeling Vino had finally fallen. And just his luck to pick on a dirty little whore!

But he couldn't think of her that way, not for long. Even as he raged against her, he was thinking that it would all blow over soon; that they would get together soon. Six, seven weeks, and she would never see Prince again. After that, it would all work out.

By the time they'd reached the island bridge, his pleasure at the way the evening had gone had returned and so had his little smile.

BOOK II

SATURDAY, FEBRUARY 15

There was a knock at the door and Sandy said, 'Bucky?'

He was getting dressed for dinner and said, 'Just a minute.' When he had his trousers on, he said, 'All right.' She came in, closed the door and leaned against it. He got into the white dinner jacket as she stood there, trying to catch his eye. She was a little sullen, as she'd been the last few times they'd spoken, beginning to understand, he supposed, that her fantasies concerning him weren't going to come true.

'Vino's all excited,' she said.

'Oh?' He turned to the mirror. 'Byuferd call you again?'

'He did, but it's not that.'

'What have you decided to do about Byuferd?'

'I'd like to tell him to shove his date, far up!'

'You know my opinion but I'm not pushing it.'

'Vino doesn't think it's a good idea for any of us to get too close to that guy.'

'I think you might learn something.'

'Like what?'

He was examining his face, noticing that despite the tan those dark circles under his eyes were deepening, almost to Chicago proportions. He hadn't been sleeping well lately. Not at all. Dreams. Idiotic dreams. About sailing. About the robbery. About Tad and Father. About himself becoming Tad and becoming dead. And a few about Ceecee Mortonson.

Not that he had any trouble with Ceecee *awake*. He'd met her at the first gala two weeks ago, they'd spoken and spent some time together at a table—he, Beth, Ceecee and young Jock Waters. All very pleasant. All very cool...

'I asked what you think I can learn from that pig!'

Sandy's voice was a near shout and he turned to see her flushed and angry. 'Easy,' he murmured.

'You never listen when I talk!'

99

'Sorry.' He spoke quietly, trying to placate her. 'You can learn many things from Byuferd ... especially his arrangements for the final gala. For example, if he's planning to assign anyone besides the usual door guard. And if he's thinking of our security checks. Any and all information concerning island security.' He smiled. 'And even if it doesn't end up doing any good, dinner and a few drinks with him can't hurt.'

'Yeah, can't hurt *you*. You don't have to go out with that pig. What if he makes a pass?'

He maintained his smile. 'Your virtue won't be in danger.'

Again the red anger hit her face. 'You don't give a damn who gets me, do you?'

He didn't try to answer that. He turned back to the mirror, adjusting his bow tie. 'Exactly what is it that's bothering Vino?'

'Something on the radio,' she said, voice heavy. 'Something about the President. He wants you to come down. He's listening to it right now.'

He went to the door. She didn't step aside. He put his hands on her shoulders to move her. She tried to come up against him. He sighed, shaking his head.

'Bucky, honey ...'

He pushed her back, firmly.

'I ... I've got it bad,' she whispered.

He stopped with his hand on the knob. 'You don't mean that.'

'I do.' Her mouth quivered. 'I wish I didn't but I do. It was so damned good with you.'

'Make up with Vino.'

'We did already. But even if I move back in with him, it won't change things. I just keep remembering ...'

'I'm sorry.' He went down to the kitchen. Vino was turning off the radio. Fanny and Rollins stood with him at the counter. They looked at Bucky as he came in. 'The President,' Vino said. 'The goddam President.'

'What about him?'

'It was on the news. We were eating and listening to the radio and they said President Lacton's coming to Miami to stay with friends, on Bay Island.'

'All right. He's done it before. There'll be tight security while he's here, but once he leaves ...'

'He's coming for three days. March thirteenth to fifteenth!'

Bucky went to the table and sank into a chair. 'Charley Vener,' he said, 'Lacton's friend and supporter.'

Rollins came over and picked up a half-eaten sandwich. 'The way *I* heard it, they weren't sure he was going to come, or if he did, whether he would stay the three full days. You know how it is with the *President.*'

Bucky looked up at him. Rollins took a bite of sandwich; then his eyes slid to the doorway. 'Maybe Sandy can date him and keep him and his guards in her bedroom.'

'You're turning into a real funny character,' Sandy said. 'I liked you better when you couldn't talk about anything but Jews.'

Rollins grinned. Fanny said, 'He's right. How many times does a President have to give up pleasure for some sort of crisis? He *plans* to spend three days with his friends. He *plans* to attend the party.'

'And how long do you think the President would stay at a party anyway?' Rollins asked.

'And even if he stays...' Sandy began impetuously.

Fanny shook her head. 'We could not steal a toothpick with all those Secret Service men, police ... no, it's unthinkable.'

Bucky was still looking at Rollins. The boy chewed calmly and said, 'No use worrying about it, that's for sure.'

'Bright,' Vino muttered. 'Very bright. What the hell *are* we supposed to worry about if not that?'

'About when we get the complete plan from Mr. Prince. About Bramms getting the LC into the bay. About when we meet for the split, once the loot is sold. Things like that. Things we can handle. Not things out of reach like the President of the United States coming here, or Byuferd finding out we got records before we do the job.'

Vino stared at him. Fanny nodded. '*Oui*, he makes sense. We should continue as before, until we *cannot* continue.'

'So say we *don't* worry,' Vino said drily. 'Say we continue as before, and the President shows up at the party. What then?'

'The worst,' Rollins said, finishing his sandwich, 'is that we quit.'

Bucky thought that Buddy-Boy might yet turn out to be a prize bargain, the most valuable man in the group. 'I'll try to get further information tonight. Vener will know more than the newsmen. After all, the President will be *his* guest.'

'Right next door,' Vino said, barking out laughter and

shaking his head. 'I mean, Jesus Christ, did you ever *hear* of such a thing? It looked so good a few weeks ago; then everything, and I mean *everything*, started happening!'

Bucky stood up.

'When do we get the plan?' Rollins asked, 'I think it's time, Mr. Prince.'

'Yes, it is.' He paused. 'The end of the week at the latest. But there will still be certain options, a few decisions we'll have to make the night of the gala. We can't go to more than two or three homes after leaving the club. We won't know *whose* homes until the very last minute, when we see who left what jewelry in the safe. And then we have to decide on paintings, perhaps Mortonson's cash, if it's true he keeps a million...'

'You should be pumping Mortonson's daughter,' Vino interrupted bluntly, 'instead of that *mafioso's* sister-in-law.'

'Oh, he *pumps* 'em all,' Sandy muttered.

Bucky looked at them both, and decided against any sort of call-down. He smiled slightly. 'As long as we're discussing man–woman—I think Sandy should accept Byuferd's invitation. It makes more sense than ever now. He's bound to know something about the President's security. At least he will, in a few days. The Secret Service sets these things up far in advance and in minute detail.' He spoke to her. 'Why not make it for next Saturday? By then he should have plenty to talk about.'

'Vino don't want me to,' she muttered. 'Besides, I get a sick feeling...'

'I changed my mind,' Vino said.

She looked at him, nodding sourly. 'Maybe I'll change *my* mind about what we were talking...'

'This is no time for making trouble!' Fanny snapped. 'There has been too much foolishness about you and ... and your men!'

'You know what *she* needs,' Sandy said, smiling maliciously.

Fanny rushed to the door. Sandy stiffened but held her ground. Fanny slid by her, whispering, *'Putain!'*

'What's that mean?' Sandy asked.

'From the sound of it,' Rollins said, 'I wouldn't want to know.'

'That goddam frog bitch!'

'She's been kinda tense lately,' Rollins said.

'Yellow,' Sandy said. 'The closer we get the more...'

'Not Fanny Lescou,' Vino said. 'Not anything that has to do

with a job. She's a pro. She and her husband pulled off something in Montreal you wouldn't believe. They robbed this big
place, then settled down in it for two days, calling real estate
agents. They got themselves a ten-grand down payment! I
mean, without knowing when the family was coming back,
they *sold* the house!'

'I didn't know she had a husband,' Sandy said.

'Back in Toronto, and maybe that's it. I wanted him in on
the job, but she said he was sick. Maybe he's worse.'

'She got any kids?' Rollins asked.

Sandy laughed. 'That cold-hearted witch? *Kids?*' She
laughed again.

'I don't think so,' Vino said. 'She never talked about kids.'

'She could have,' Rollins insisted quietly.

'And how would *you* know?' Sandy mocked. 'You're not
much more than a kid yourself.'

'Maybe that's why,' Rollins replied, lighting up a cigarette.
'She's sort of ... nice to me, making me eat and all that. I kind
of get the feeling she has someone around my age.'

'Whether she's tense or not,' Bucky said, 'she's right. Too
much unnecessary trouble.' Sandy began to answer angrily.
Bucky caught her eyes, looked straight into them. 'Let's not
lose sight of our goal, Sandy. We'll have the rest of our lives to
play games with men, with women, with anything we want.
But first we have to get by March fifteenth.'

Held by his eyes, she nodded. He went out of the kitchen,
and heard Vino say, 'Call him now.'

He left the house, glad to escape the bickering, the tension,
the general unpleasantness. It was a clear, perfect evening, the
air slightly cool, delicately sweet. He wondered what it was
like out on the bay, out in the Atlantic.

*Sailing alone, free of tension, of unpleasantness, of am-
bition* ...

Now he was *awake* and dreaming that nonsense!

Rollins had brought around the Mercedes. He drove quickly,
forcing his mind to tonight's party, the second gala, and how
he was going to learn things, encouraging things.

Even if Lacton did come to the final gala, all was not auto-
matically lost. If they changed the timing, made it much
later ...

He parked far off to the side of the club house, sitting in the
deeper darkness of the banyan tree, thinking that despite his

youth Rollins was emerging as a cool and clear-headed man ...
but that in one matter, he was quite wrong.

They *didn't* quit, no matter what!

Ceecee had hoped Bucky wouldn't show up at this gala, but in
he came with Beth Larkin, the two looking as chummy as
rumor had them. She told herself it *didn't* hurt and for the
hundredth time asked herself how she could be so foolish as to
carry on this way for a man whom she'd dated just once, slept
with just once. Sleeping with a man was no ultra-special thing
for Ceecee Mortonson, as it wasn't for most of her class and
generation.

Perhaps it *might* have been ultra-special if Father hadn't
worried about kidnappings when she was eleven years old and
hired that 'reliable ex policeman' Chris Adams and at the
tender age of twelve ...

She turned to Jock Waters, who had become her steady because he was basically a good kid and didn't press too hard
when she resisted going to bed with him. (For some reason, she
was resisting that with everyone.) And besides, he had a good
supply of pot. She put her hand on his arm as he watched the
people dancing to what he classified as 'waltzes' (all the non
rock dances) and said, 'Hey, Mr. Pusher, you got another of
those 'licious cigarettes?'

'*Here?* What if someone identifies the smell?'

'Let's risk it. I'm too young to drink,' and she downed her
second gimlet.

'Well,' he muttered, 'all right.' He took out his thin gold case
and she took one of the very normal-looking cigarettes except
that it had no brand name, but even that wasn't particularly
unusual here where so many of the people had tobacconists
back home make up blends to suit their tastes. They lit up and
he blew smoke down at his feet and the band went into another
'waltz'. Bucky Prince and Beth Larkin began dancing. Ceecee
sat watching them from the table near the bandstand, watching
and inhaling deeply and feeling the troubles of the world re-
cede and the goo*ood* feeling take over.

'Hey baby,' she said. 'Hey Jock boy. I've been a bitch, haven't
I?'

'You have?' he murmured, still so damned nervous that the
pot wasn't taking hold as it should have.

'No loving for poor Jock.'

104

He leaned closer. 'I'm glad you brought that up. I was about to change deodorants.'

'You should change girls, Jock boy.'

'There aren't that many around this flippin' island.'

She squeezed his hand, liking his cool.

'Can we leave early?' he asked. 'I'd like to show you my collection of dirty pictures.'

She smiled.

'I really have them,' he said. 'They're my father's. And are they *funny*!'

'If I laugh, won't that defeat their purpose?'

'Who the hell uses dirty pictures for seduction except the Momma-Poppa generation?'

She was watching the dancers, only a handful in their twenties, most past thirty, and forty, and fifty. She was watching Bucky Prince and Beth Larkin because she was facing their way and why make an effort *not* to look? She smoked the pot, inhaling as deeply as she could, getting her high as far up as she could. 'That's a profundity,' she said, seeing them pressing together and insisting she didn't give a damn. 'A truth of our times. Everyone over thirty is hung up on sex—black lace panties, garter belts and high heels, dirty words, dirty books and dirty pictures.' (But it hadn't been that way with Bucky Prince, not at all...) She dragged on the stick and went on developing her thesis. 'We, on the other hand, throw our genitals in each other's faces and it's healthy, cools the whole thing down, makes it part of just living.'

'Let's go throw our genitals...'

'But if you look around, if you see what these others are like, it makes you want to laugh.' She watched Bucky Prince and Beth Larkin and wanted to cry.

'Ceecee, let's cut out right now.'

She looked at him. Nice big fair almost-white-haired boy. She said, 'I'd rather stay here and laugh.'

'I don't think you meant a word you said.'

'Of course I did. I said we're open about sex and it cools the whole thing down, didn't I?'

'You also said...'

But he was debating with Straight A Ceecee Mortonson who had always been able to twist a truth to suit herself. 'And I'm all cooled down, Jock boy. I'm healthy and sex is just part of living and I'm not hung up on it, are you?'

The question came so swiftly, accompanied by such a penetrating stare, that he had to give her the answer she wanted.
'Me? Hung up? Hell no! It just...' He shrugged.

She patted his hand, poor kid, and wondered what she was
doing with him when she wanted that old man, that salacious,
cunt-hunting, thirty-four-year-old Bucky Prince.

It was the pot. She was shaking Bucky Prince from her mind
a little more each day. He'd be out of mind completely, if it
wasn't for that one little cloud on the horizon; the fact that she
was more than a week overdue for her period.

But nothing as corny as a *pregnancy* could happen to
Straight A Ceecee Mortonson. Not after one lone sex experi-
encé this month! It was laughable! She laughed.

Jock Waters stood up. 'You'll forgive me but I've had it.
You can laugh at someone else from now on. And *away* he
went.

She stared after him. He strode across the dance floor, past
the bar ... going, going, gone. She shook her head, dragged on
her stick, singed her fingers. She took a frantic last drag and
put it out in the ashtray, then remembered and dropped it to
the floor and ground it into shreds under her shoe. Well, no
more pot, unless she could find another source of supply.

She was nice and high now, but behind the high was a dark
area of fear. She had never, no *never* missed a period. She was
as regular as the big old clock that had stood in the entryway
back home for as long as she could remember.

She felt tears pushing at her eyes, and quickly looked
around for Father, for anyone to talk to and be with. She saw
Bucky Prince going by the bar toward the rest rooms, and
didn't think, walked between the dancers and caught up with
him as he paused to speak to Olaf, the bartender, whose hail-
fellow-well-met bluff and hearty personality she disliked and
mistrusted because it reminded her of Chris Adams and his
hearty red face and his hearty red...

She said, '*Hello* there, Mr. Prince. Isn't it lovely weather
we're having? And hasn't the racing been *great* at Hialeah?
And what do you think of the President coming to our little
island? And ... oh yes, I believe I'm knocked up.'

He had been smiling and his smile froze and he said, 'You're
drunk,' and took her arm and walked her away from Olaf and
his hearty red face.

'No, just winging a little on pot. You're hurting my arm.'

He smiled at people and said things and then they were outside and walking through the parking lot.

'Did I stop you from going wee-wee?' she asked. 'If I did, you'll be uncomfortable.'

They were at a car and he opened the door and none too gently shoved her in. By the time he entered from the other side, she realized she was crying. She wiped at her eyes and told herself, 'Stop, stop, *stop*!'

'Now what's all this?'

She wiped away a last tear and smiled. 'When I put someone on, I do a job.'

He kept looking at her.

She opened the door. 'A joke, Mr. Prince, or don't you recognize...'

He pulled her back inside and, leaning across her, slammed the door. She said, 'Well, if you insist on playing heavy,' and turned the rear view mirror and began checking her mascara in the dim light.

'I asked, what's all this?'

'And I told you. All this, sir, is a joke, a gag, a put-on. If I open the door again, will you allow me to get back to the party?'

He didn't answer. She turned from the mirror and smiled at him. No more tears got in the way. 'A *bad* joke, but I'm a little high.'

'I don't think it's a joke.'

She had other bright things to say but realized that if she wanted to get away from him before she made even *more* of a fool of herself, she had better give him something he could believe; at least part of the truth. 'I missed my period. Rather, it's late. Of course, I've skipped it completely several times before, so no sweat. How are you and Miss Larkin getting along? I have to admit she suits you. A handsome couple, as my father has said. But does she have enough loot to match the Prince portfolio? I recall you said money was your bag, your true love, and from what I hear, Miss Larkin—or does she call herself *Mrs.* since there are two marriages...'

'Ceecee,' he said, face and voice grim, 'I've done you one lousy turn, haven't I? I thought you were a woman and would look after yourself and you're a little girl and didn't. Now we're in trouble. What do you want me to do?'

She put back her head and laughed. Jock had run from her

laughter and now she would give Bucky Prince the same treatment. She kept laughing, shaking her head and pointing at him and saying, '*What do you want me to do!* Oh Sir Lancelot of the Lake, are you ever delightful!'

He didn't run. He waited, and when she had no more laughter to give, he said, 'We'll count on the very worst happening. If it's just a skip, fine. If not, we'll know what to do. There are several ways to go. The obvious is an abortion.'

She tried another sharp laugh. It didn't stop him.

'Or you can have the baby and keep it secret from everyone, including your father, if that's important.'

'Give me a cigarette.'

He lighted two and gave her one. They smoked. He said, 'Then there's marriage but that might be compounding the mistake since ... well, I don't think this is any basis for a marriage, do you?'

'That's the understatement of the century! You've got fourteen years on me! We've known each other a grand total of half a dozen hours, tops! And during those half a dozen hours, we fought more than we talked! Oh, you're quite right, Mr. Prince. Fifteen minutes fucking is *not* a basis for marriage!' And she laughed and dragged furiously on her cigarette and wanted to get away from here, wanted to leave this insanity behind!

'Then abortion or a secluded ...'

'There's not going to *be* any pregnancy. I just told you, I've skipped before.'

'Fine. We'll hope you're right. But if you aren't ...'

'If I'm growing *your* baby, I'll cut it out so fast, so damned fast ... !'

He didn't say anything. But when she glanced at him, she could almost *hear* him thinking, 'Methinks the lady doth protest too much.'

'Sorry,' she said, lowering her voice. 'Gin and pot are a rough combination. I guess I'm more than a little drunk.' She took a deep drag of smoke. 'Yes, an abortion, if it comes down to that, which I doubt.'

'Will you want your father to know?'

'You needn't worry. I'll want no one to know.'

He was quiet. She looked at him from the corners of her eyes. Something seemed to have gone out of him; he sat slumped in the seat. She cleared her throat, said, 'I don't know *what* got into me, acting as if you'd seduced me. *Ruined* me is the way the Victorians would put it, isn't it?'

He smiled a little. 'Maybe they were right. *I'm* not running any risks.'

'Neither am I, Bucky.' It was the first time she'd addressed him without malice, without rancor. He looked at her. She smiled for him. He put out his hand and touched her face. She jerked back, and he quickly turned away, reaching for the door, convinced now she wanted no part of him.

She said, 'Can we finish our cigarettes?'

'Of course.'

She still had Chris Adams on her mind; or, more accurately, had herself and her feelings for men on her mind. As Dr. Drexler had put it during her abortive nine months' analysis two years ago: 'There *has* to be a connection,' the *way* in which she was drawn to sex, far from the cool-healthy-just-part-of-living line she'd fed Jock Waters.

'I *did* think of protecting myself, Bucky.'

'Then why didn't you do it?' It was a soft question, not accusatory or angry.

'I don't know. I could feel you ... getting ready. I said to myself, "Say something. Tell him you're no longer on the pill." I knew if I did, you would either pull out in time, or put on a rubber.'

He nodded.

'I ... I was carried away.'

'Lost control?'

'I guess so.' But it wasn't true. She had *wanted* his discharge. And go and explain *that*, Straight A Ceecee Mortonson! She said, 'Do you know what the greatest hangup a wealthy parent has about his child? The *bête noir* of Real Society?'

'I know several. Marriage outside the proper class ...'

'When the child is still quite young.'

'You mean kidnapping?'

She nodded. 'Did you ever have a private guard?'

He said no, but the butler had been required to have a pistol permit and for a while after a heavily publicized kidnapping, had escorted him and his brother on various trips and errands.

'When I was eleven,' she said, 'there was a rash of kidnappings. Father had me spend a year at home. I had a guard, a retired police officer. At least he said he was retired. He was young for that, I think, about forty. He might have been *forced* to retire, in the way they cover so many ugly little things in government agencies and big companies.'

He looked puzzled, and she knew he was wondering what this story had to do with him.

'I'm telling you this because I'm high, and because I'm trying to explain, somehow, why I did what I did that night with you and why I am the way I am with men in general. And I'm not sure this *will* explain it. Do you want me to stop? Will Miss Larkin be wondering where you are?'

'She'll be wondering but I don't want you to stop.'

'There's not much to tell anyway. We became rather close. At least *he* was close to *me*. I might be coloring the picture *after* the fact, but I seem to remember not really liking him, not being comfortable with him, even though he was a rather good looking man. I'd been friendly with other servants, so it wasn't that he was someone who worked for us. It's just ...' She shook her head. 'He got into the habit of coming to my room a few times each week to say good night. Not all the time, but now that I think of it, when my father was out or Bertha, our housekeeper, wasn't nearby. Not that it would have aroused suspicion. He was my guard and checking on me in my room was being properly vigilant. He would sit on a chair beside my bed and talk a few minutes and then lean over and kiss my mouth; a goodnight kiss, he said. Sometimes I turned away and he would chuckle ... he had a red face like Olaf and the same type of laugh, deep and hearty and oh so innocent.' She laughed nervously. 'I know I'm doing Olaf a disservice, but Chris Adams *was* very much like him. One evening, it was about a month after my twelfth birthday—I was beginning to develop then, too, tall and with breasts and I would catch him *looking* at me if we were alone—well, this time I didn't turn away from his goodnight kiss. He kept his lips on mine longer than usual, and then he said something like, "Ceecee, I have something. Give me your hand, Ceecee. Something wonderful, Ceecee."'

'Oh Lord,' Prince said, and he seemed genuinely pained.

She made the laughing sound again. 'You guessed it. He had his fly open. I don't think I understood what it was I was holding at first. My arm was at a funny angle, so I asked him to wait while I got more comfortable. I sat up and he stood up, still holding my hand. I saw it then, and I *did* understand. At

110

least I knew it was something forbidden, but ... I didn't cry out.'

'Afraid to?'

'I don't think so. He didn't threaten me or anything like that. He was caressing my head, and then my arms and shoulders, but he didn't try to touch any forbidden part of *my* body. So I let him move my hand over his penis and after a while he made a sound and twisted away. I saw his handkerchief, and later of course I knew he'd had an orgasm. He walked out and I lay down and tried to sleep. I remember my heart pounding and my mouth being dry. I remember being sickened, or excited, or both.'

'What did he do the next day?'

'I never saw him again. He left that night; packed all his things and left when no one was awake and that was it. My father asked me if anything had happened and I told him. But I don't know what, if anything, he did about it. And since the kidnapping scare was over for the while, he sent me back to school.'

'You think that changed your attitude toward sex?'

'An analyst once said that if it didn't change it, it certainly helped *form* it. I still remember what seemed like a swollen, throbbing pole, red and incredibly large. It wasn't that large, couldn't be, but I was a child and anything coming out of a person's belly, as I thought of it, that way would seem enormous to me. And I guess I'm still looking for that enormous throbbing pole and it doesn't exist...' She suddenly laughed, sorry she'd gone this far. 'No reflection on you, Bucky.'

He gave her the mandatory smile but waited for her to go on.

'It's all ... foolishness. He didn't hurt me. Didn't really *do* anything.'

'He made a memory,' Prince said, and again his hand reached out, only this time he drew it back before it touched her, drew it back without her having to do anything.

And she *wouldn't* have done anything! She wanted his touch, wanted it so badly she opened the door and said, 'End of spicy story. Meaningless spicy story.'

'*Not* meaningless. He gave you a memory of sex out of context to your age and your position in life. He set up either an appetite, or an anti-appetite, neither natural and therefore neither good.'

111

'You're almost as glib as Dr. Drexler, my old analyst. If only you knew what you were talking about.'

They laughed a little together, and he said, 'I minored in abnormal psychology.'

'Abnormal psychology. Now *there's* a basis for marriage!'

She got out. He joined her as she started back to the club, and said, 'But I didn't take enough courses to understand how that particular experience would stop you from protecting yourself during the sex act.'

'Vell, mein dear friend,' she said in what she hoped would come through as an Austrian-Freudian dialect, 'he denied me his ejaculation, you see, so I was driven to find a substitute, and dere you ver, Mr. Bucky Princh, you and your ejaculation.'

'I don't think so,' he said, smiling slightly.

She didn't either. But talking about Chris Adams had brought back details of her sessions with Dr. Drexler and something he had said about her description of Adams and her description of her father. She had rejected the idea with laughter (and hidden disgust for Drexler), and shortly afterward discontinued treatment. But now the memory words came at her, and she had no laughter. She grew very quiet, and Prince said something about calling her regularly. 'We'll keep in touch ...' She said, 'Yes,' and walked quickly ahead of him into the music and talk and laughter.

It was rock music now. The younger people were having their time. She saw the Millers' nephew, Blake, another nice kid, and swung herself toward him. He was with a little blonde trick, but he said, 'Hey,' and moved his smile all over her, up and down, head to toe. She looked first at the dance floor and then at Blake and he said, 'Excuse me, Merry, but this is a *challenge*!' And away they went to snap crackle pop with the rock group.

She tried hard not to think any further about Chris Adams and whom he looked like, or whom she had thought he looked like when she was a child. And while she danced she didn't. But then they stopped and she went to the bar for a coke and there was Father. He turned and smiled and she knew that she should have stayed with Drexler; knew that the big fair man who wanted to kiss her lips and the big fair man who put her hand on his prick and the big fair man she carried in her mind and her erotic fantasies were *this* big fair man. Silently she said, 'God, *no*!' and aloud she said, 'I'm going home now,' and went quickly out and didn't think to take Father's car but ran down the dark road to Bay Drive and across the drive to where the lights of their house shone; ran, ran shaking her head because it was such an *ugly* thing to carry in your mind, such an *ugly* way to get hung up by that Daddy-doesn't-love-me evil spirit.

She ran out of breath and walked and couldn't stop thinking of Chris Adams always wanting to kiss her lips and her father never wanting to kiss her lips and a certain type of big fair man who had always been able to make it with her.

Bucky Prince was tall, yes, but not big, not the way Chris and Father were.

Bucky Prince was *dark*, not fair.

Dr. Drexler would have approved of Bucky Prince. Whatever her reasons for wanting Bucky, it was certainly removed from the ugliness.

But what the hell good was it realizing she could love this man without taint or ugliness if he cared little or nothing for her? And remembering his face from the bathroom door, she was assured he cared nothing. And remembering tonight, when he had offered her everything but marriage ...

Marriage? She wanted marriage?

She laughed aloud.

Marriage? She had *eons* to go before marriage!

But then again, a knocked-up broad had all sorts of biological-social needs for marriage, and she was a knocked-up broad.

Not certain yet. Could be her first menstrual irregularity.

Why *hadn't* she stopped him? There had been tremendous excitement, yes, but still she had known she was close to her fertile period, should have feared, could have said something, had *not* been rendered speechless or gone totally out of control.

Never before had she done such a thing, and from seventeen to a few weeks shy of twenty-one, she had experienced some two dozen boys and men, including a series of big, fair teachers ranging from instructors to full professors, none of whom felt they were being used for good grades since Straight A Ceecee Mortonson hadn't needed help. So why ...?

Because she had wanted him ... and still wanted him, though she couldn't give specific reasons for her wanting. His looks? He was a beautiful, beautiful man to Ceecee; beautiful even in his worn-at-the-edges look. And that strange reticence, that vague air of being apart from things; and then too, a girl always wanted what she couldn't get. Wanted him as husband and father of her children and all the other insane Mamma-Poppa goodies she didn't believe in; no, dammit, *didn't* want and didn't even understand because she wasn't anywhere near ready for that!

But an abortion? If it came to killing his seed?

She had reached the house. Yang let her in and she asked him to serve her a pot of tea and milk in her room. Tea had always settled her. By the time it arrived, the concept of abortion was an impossible one.

She drank and leafed through a magazine. She was calm now; remarkably calm. She was approaching a decision, had actually made it without admitting it, and it was going to change her entire life in ways she couldn't yet foresee.

If she was pregnant, she would have Bucky Prince's child.

Beyond that she couldn't say.

Beyond that she didn't care.

She put on her bedside radio. It was tuned to a Miami rock and roll station. She listened a while, and somehow didn't enjoy it. She searched the dial, rejecting talk shows and pop-tune shows ... and stopped at string-heavy, melodramatic music. She listened while reading her magazine, and later an announcer said, 'This has been an hour of Rachmaninoff.'

Bucky would approve.

Bucky would never know. She would stay far away from him. They were finished, her first real love and she, finished after fifteen minutes and the creation of a child.

She tasted that for tragedy, comedy, tears, laughter. She yawned.

There would be problems, but money wasn't one of them ... even if Father went Victorian and played cut-you-off-without-a-cent. She would come into complete possession of Mother's forty million in stock and real estate on March thirtieth, her twenty-first birthday.

She put out the lights but left the radio on. Chris Adams and Father were still part of her ... but less than before this long, long night. She closed her eyes, sighing, feeling bone tired ... and somehow more complete than she could ever remember feeling.

With Prince at the party, Vino and Sandy having a reunion celebration in Miami Beach and Rollins watching television on the color set in the study, Fanny had a chance to make her call. She put a washcloth over the mouthpiece and dialed one-three. The phone rang five times, there was an unusual series of clicks, and a man said, 'Bridge. Mr. Byuferd's not around at the moment. Anything I can do?'

Just as well. She had to find out how to proceed in the event he didn't answer his phone. She spoke in as deep a voice as she could.

'It's personal. How do I get him?'

'Personal you say? If you leave a number...'

'Can I get him *now*?'

'Well, not for personal things, not as a rule. You can always get him on security matters. He leaves a number. I'm not supposed to give it unless it's security.'

'And he *always* answers? *Always* gets to the island?'

The guard said, 'Inside of fifteen minutes, Mister. And that's no joke. He's never more than fifteen minutes away from his job. Now if you want to make it a security matter...' He chuckled.

Fanny said, 'No, no, I'll call again,' and as the guard tried to ask for 'his' name, she hung up.

Voilà. It was begun. Now the trick was to accomplish her *pure* goal, while yet coming away with the money she'd been promised, the money she needed to make Armand's final days free of want, full of comfort. There was danger in this dual goal, yes, but she was certain it could be carried off successfully. Much depended upon what Prince told them tomorrow or the day after. Much depended upon where she would be in relation to Bramms, Beaufort and Prince the night of the robbery. Much depended upon how she could release the furies in those violent men; release and direct it.

And if direction failed, then she herself could strike in the darkness and confusion of that final night.

Only one thing frightened her, and that was the possibility that the President's visit would cause the entire operation to be called off. Then what would she do? For money, perhaps a quick hotel robbery, if she could contact a bell captain, or some other minor functionary with access to keys. But what about her *second* goal, the destruction of her enemy?

Simply shooting him would leave Armand alone during the

115

time he would *most* need her. She could *not* do that. And Armand would not want her to do that; would suffer too much for her if she did that, compounding his agony.

No, it had to be done through indirection; and the March fifteenth robbery had suddenly appeared as the perfect solution while she was living in Miami and casing the island, trying to think of a way. She'd been parked on the shoulder of the Grand Causeway, examining the little white bridge through binoculars, still not settled on a course of action, when the man walked over and she recognized Charles DeVino, who had served time with Armand six years ago after she and her husband had worked the New York side of the border. Immediately after she'd agreed to join Vino, she had gone to church and given ten dollars to the collection for the poor and thanked *le bon Dieu* for such a miracle.

Now it was threatened.

But as Rollins had said, there was no sense in worrying about what they could not control.

She would try, however, to control it the only way she could think of. God had helped her once; why not again?

She got up, faced the chair, sank to her knees and placed her elbows on the wicker seat. She clasped her hands and bowed her head. 'Help me, Holy Mother, in the name of a mother's love for her dead son, which you above all others understand.'

Beth Larkin had been annoyed at his disappearing with Cee-cee. She had seen them leave the club together and since he was in no mood to try false explanations she assumed hanky-panky. Bucky shrugged at her lifted eyebrows, ignored her sudden frown and nodded silently when she said perhaps it was time they called it quits. She was surprised and then insulted. He was sorry for that but his appetite was appeased ... at least with her. He was finally beginning to settle down to the job, and the job alone.

Later, on finally making it to the men's room, he met Vincent Drang. They exchanged hellos, and Drang said, 'Beth's gone home.'

'Oh?'

'I, ah ... don't think it would be advisable for you to contact her again.'

Bucky turned to the washbasin. 'That's exactly what Beth and I decided, Vince. No outside help was needed.'

116

Drang left then, and Bucky went home and to bed. He was awakened by someone touching his face. 'Bucky ... wake up, honey. I couldn't get away before this.'

He jerked erect. It was Sandy, and she was pulling off a nightgown. He lay down again, saying nothing. He had said it all before and she hadn't listened.

Stripped, she got under the covers and pressed up against him. She began to kiss him, murmuring about her inability to stop wanting him and how he would get to want her too, wait and see. And she was correct, in an immediate sense. There was no resisting the delicate maneuver of grabbing a penis and massaging it. He sighed deeply. She murmured, 'Ready now, sweetie?' He didn't answer. She kept massaging. He turned his head away from her, biting his lip. She said, 'Anything wrong?'—certain from the evidence in her hand that nothing could be. He didn't answer.

The instant he began to spasm, she jerked her hand away.

He finished it himself as she lay beside him, stiff, unmoving. Then he said, 'Sorry,' and went to the bathroom.

She was gone when he came out.

Well, at least one problem was solved—women. He had run out of them.

SUNDAY, FEBRUARY 16

Sundays were especially bad days for Curt Bramms, always had been, as far back into childhood as he could remember, when everyone in the small South Carolina town of his birth would go to church; everyone but the Abramsons and three other families who lived in the downtown area near their businesses, Abramson's Dry-Goods being about the poorest. 'Little Jew businesses' that earned the owners a living and considerable contempt from the Gentile citizens of Vennson. Why this should be, when Gentiles also had shops and *weren't* mocked, was not a question Lou asked himself; he was one who accepted the majority, WASP opinion blindly, with initial pain and later with a fierce partisanship.

Lou had wanted to go to church. That way, he felt, he would have been safe from the bestiality beginning in Germany

117

and finding sympathetic verbal counterpart in much of the Southern United States as well as in certain select Eastern areas, such as the German belt of Pennsylvania and the Bund enclave of Yorkville, Manhattan. Going to church would also have been a refutation of his father, being his father, and his mother, being his mother, matters of growing importance to him as he entered a period of increasingly psychotic behavior.

But he hadn't been able to go to church, not as long as he was a child, and not as long as he lived in the town where he was born and bred a Jew. But in pharmacy school, he had thought to begin the process and started showing up at Sunday chapel. Not that he gave a damn about their Jesus Christ; another Jew and insane to boot, according to his reasoning. It was the *uniform*, the *badge* of Christianity that he desired. And even that was denied him.

Three times he attended chapel. The Wednesday following that third time, he was in his dormitory room with a group of five assiduously cultivated friends when a package was brought up by the custodian, marked Special Delivery. He was puzzled, but not worried. He had instructed his mother in the strongest terms never to send him food, that way making certain he would never receive anything that could be classified as Jewish. Besides, this hadn't been sent from Vennson but from right here in Columbia, where the University of South Carolina was located. Yet he hadn't bought anything, hadn't ordered anything...

He could hesitate no longer because his new friends were accusing him of holding out some toothsome delicacy. He opened the package and at first didn't understand. A few of the boys had laughed. One had begun, 'Hey, I thought you said...' and then cut himself short as another shook his head. All had fallen silent and the silence had thickened with embarrassment, because the exposing of a man who has hidden his race, his religion, is a shabby and embarrassing thing. The embarrassment was compounded, was blended with pity and contempt, since that man had talked *hatred* of his race and religion.

Curt Bramms (he had already changed his name) had been too stricken to come up with the proper words; though it is doubtful whether any words could have weakened the evidence of his flaming face. Out of the package had tumbled two Hebrew newspapers and a shiny black skull cap.

There had been more. He had tried to laugh and show he didn't care by tossing them openly on the bed. A kosher salami. A jar of *gefulte* fish. A tasseled prayer shawl.

He had wanted to leave school that night. Instead, he had changed his quarters and given up trying to make any friends whatsoever. And he had watched the faces of Jewish students, wondering which one—or ones—had attacked him this way; for it could only be another Jew who would know, and hate him for trying to 'pass'.

He still longed to go to church. And almost thirty years later, the traumatic shock of that college shaming had still not allowed him to go to church.

This Sunday, however, the stresses were so enormous that he dressed, left the motel and drove to a modern brick building in Golden Beach. This Sunday the growing tension of what was to happen March fifteenth, and the daily tensions of being Curt Bramms, combined to reach such a peak that the uniform, the badge of Christianity (or proof of non-Jewishness) was absolutely necessary.

He didn't even note the denomination, just that it wasn't Roman Catholic. He parked in the lot, saw people at the doors, walked in with them and waited ten minutes while the church grew two-thirds full. Then the minister appeared. Then the service began.

He was in the second from the last row, almost alone. He kept his head down, the words of the sermon and prayers swirling toward him and around him, but not entering into him. He sat where no Jew should sit and this was good. He heard, 'our Lord Jesus Christ', forbidden to him (as a Jew), and that too was good. The collection plate was passed and he gave a dollar and with payment made looked up and around, beginning to feel part of this provenly non-Jewish group, and that was *very* good.

But then it was over and people began to leave. Then they went out to their lives and there he couldn't follow. Then he too was forced to leave and get back into his car and drive away. And it was still Sunday and he was still apart from them and still alone.

Aloneness was Jewish; apartness was Jewish; had always been Jewish for Curt Bramms. And it was still Sunday and weeks away from the great triumph that would save him from all the Sundays to come, that would end the aloneness and the

119

apartness because he would have money to organize a group and he would be the center, the *Fuhrer* ...

He was shaking when he entered the Pelican Bar. He had two drinks before he was able to look at the bartender, start a conversation and lead it around to the point where he could say, 'Just got back from church.'

The bartender nodded.

'Don't you go to church on Sunday?'

'Used to. The wife goes. Back home, we were closed on Sundays. Now ...' He shrugged.

'You should,' Bramms said piously.

'Guess so.' The man went away to serve a young couple. They laughed a lot together. Bramms was certain the couple was Jewish. Too many Jews in the Miami Beach area.

The bartender answered Bramms's signal for a third drink. He was still smiling. Bramms said, 'You get lots of those people in here, don't you?'

'What?'

'You know.' But he was suddenly cautious because you never knew where their tools, their agents could be found.

'Oh, yeah. Tell you the truth, I thought *you* were Jewish, till you said about church.' He chuckled.

Bramms made himself smile. '*Me?* Hell, I'm no Hebe.'

The bartender said, 'They spend real well. Wish I had more.' He began to leave; then added, 'Do me a favor. Don't go saying Hebe and things like that in here. I don't want trouble.'

'Trouble?' Bramms laughed. 'You ever know any that could fight worth a damn?'

The bartender nodded slowly. 'I think so. And take that million and a half in Israel, you figure they're Irish or something?' He walked away.

Bramms drank a great deal. He lost count of how much he drank. And later he was in the men's room when that young guy who was with the girl came in and used the urinal. Bramms stood at the single sink and looked at him. Tall. Slim. Couldn't be much muscle under that sporty jacket. The man finished and waited behind him. Bramms decided to wash his hands again, and then to comb his hair, and then to examine his face.

'You mind if I wash ...'

'You're goddam right I mind, Izzy!'

The man stared at him. The man smiled and said, 'Little

120

man, you're bombed.'

Bramms slapped him. Bramms began to call him everything he could think of. Bramms felt the fist in his mouth and the pain as he slammed into the sink. He was surprised. But he struck back. The trouble was he'd been hit by surprise, sneak attack, Pearl Harbor, and he couldn't get going. The man hit him twice more and he found himself on the floor, his lips swelling, his nose bleeding. He struggled to his feet. He was alone. He flung himself out the door, and the couple was gone. He began to run toward the entrance. The bartender was somehow in his path. He said, 'That goddam ...'

The bartender said, 'Shut up. He told me. He's a good customer, he, his wife and their friends. I told him he'd never have to put up with anything like that again.'

'*He?* Just look what ...'

'I warned you, didn't I? I know your kind.' He held Bramms's arm and walked him to the door and outside. He looked around, then let Bramms go. 'Don't come back.'

'If I weren't full of your rotten booze ...'

The bartender was a big man and he put his hand under his apron and waited. Bramms was suddenly sober. Blackjack. Well, he had something in his car that would take care of that!

He went to the Chevvy in a stumbling run. He opened the passenger door and the glove compartment and then remembered he'd put the gun in his dresser, under the shirts. He'd been worried about carrying it since he had no license, and with March fifteenth coming up, he could afford to take no chances.

But now the rage was building, the self-hate too, and when the self-hate came, there was no way out except through a triumph. Making that bartender crawl was the only triumph he could think of.

He drove back to the motel. He went up to the room and got the gun. He held it, a solid Colt ·357 with four-inch barrel and target sights; a Trooper that fired ·38 bullets as well as the more powerful, magnum-style ·357's. And it was loaded with magnums. And one slug would kill a bear, not to say a bartender.

Holding it, he began to quiet. He had loved guns since adolescence. Guns were American.

Guns also made the smallest, most frightened man the

121

physical superior of anything alive.

He sat down on the bed, broke open the cylinder and snapped it closed, thinking of March fifteenth and how he couldn't afford to go to the Pelican and get into trouble. Perhaps if he hid in the parking lot until the place closed...

He played with the gun. After a while he put it away, dressed in his riding outfit, slapped his crop on his thigh and went to the phone and dialed Annie's number. He'd had her ten days ago and it had gone as well as the time before. If only she would answer...

She did. He asked her to come over. She said he would have to pay for the cab as well as for her, unless he would pick her up. He said, 'Goddam it, stop trying to Jew me!' She said, 'You talk like a Panther, baby.' He didn't want that either! They had no right to confuse things with black anti-Semitism! It ... it bothered the hell out of him! Negroes and Jews were allies, the blacks being the tools of Jewish imperialism.

'The hell with that! Get down here!'

'You sound beautiful, Curt.'

He didn't like her using his first name. 'Are you coming?'

'Okay,' she said. 'About two hours.'

'Two hours!'

'I want a bath and something to eat. 'Bye.'

He was shouting at her to come *this very moment* when she hung up.

He went to the bed and lay down. He told himself he would close his eyes, sleep and it would seem like no time at all. But he didn't.

Perhaps that was why he failed, he was tired, that and her asking questions about his swollen lips and bruised nose. Perhaps that was why he couldn't even fake it. To salvage some part of his manhood, he threw her out without paying, telling her she was so filthy a normal man couldn't *stand* her. She didn't take it. She stood outside his door, shouting that he was sick and crazy and that if she didn't get her money she would tell everyone in this building...

He got his gun and, no longer thinking, just reacting, ripped off his bathrobe and went to the door, naked. He listened to her shrill clamor another moment, then opened the door. She took one look, made a choking sound and ran. Only then, did he realize he had jammed the revolver into his groin; a lethal penis, pointing out at her.

He closed the door and looked at the gun ... and for one clear moment understood that there was only one way to solve Curt Bramms's problems permanently.

Bobby was still up and still insisting on playing Monopoly with Miss Egret and his father. He had stopped asking his mother because he'd learned, even at five years of age, that she was just not tuned in to that particular game. Karen laughed as he threatened to run away, and said, 'You will have to run away in your pajamas. To bed, now, *raus!*' Miss Egret looked grateful and Karen felt it necessary to add, quietly, 'Since his sickness, we have been perhaps too easy. But now that he is well, your authority will return.'

Charles had been on the phone most of the evening, talking to people in Washington. He was still on the phone, sitting in a corner of the comfortable, lodgelike living room, with exposed oak beams and heavy teak furniture, a wonderful room if not very 'dress-up', as Karen thought of it. She heard his heavy laughter, and he said, '... costs me a good five thousand a day when he's here, so let's not go into the *pleasures*. And the Secret Service all over the place ...' He paused. 'To *live* here, permanently? Well ... the residents would be honored but time enough for that when he leaves the White House, and he certainly expects a second term.' Another pause. 'The last time, it disrupted TV reception ... yes, I know it's necessary to have a communications set-up. Over my garage ... haven't touched the room since then. But haven't they found a way ... ? I'm sure the island heliport can handle it. *That* many? Well ...'

Karen left the room, mouth turned sour when she was alone. She disliked having the routine of her existence disturbed under any circumstances, but—and this was something she could tell no one, especially Charles—she *hated* what happened when Bob Lacton visited, here or at home. Having to worry about his savage temper was only part of it ...

She tried to stop the thoughts, telling herself his face wasn't really *lumpy*, wasn't really repellent to her. It was probably that she was so happy with Charles, she would hate *any* man who pawed her.

And how did you reject the President of the United States so that he did not feel rejected, did not grow too angry? Charles had a deep ambition; he wasn't satisfied, as she was, with business and home and society. He wanted to get into government. He had ideas. He especially wanted to get into a position where he could fight what he called 'the insidious socialist clique that prevents industry from utilizing all that wasted land, much more land than the country needs for parks and wildlife refuges, and especially more than it needs for wilderness areas. Conservationists, they call themselves, but their public stands on oil and logging prove they're leftists and it's time they were fought.' He wanted a position in the Department of the Interior. His views weren't too well known, so it was possible he might get it ... *if* Bob Lacton offered it to him.

The President hadn't, as yet. But when he visited last time, he spoke to Karen one evening—the glib yet nonspecific kind of talk at which he was so skilled, never really saying anything but *sounding* as if he were—and she got the idea, vague though it was, that *she* was preventing Charles from getting his appointment.

That too she hated! Being used! She, Karen Vener!

Again she tried to stop the trend of thought. Soon he would be here, and without Maggie this time; which would make it worse, she supposed.

If only Charley wouldn't show him those electric dolls he'd bought in Hong Kong. Those fantastic little dolls she enjoyed when she and Charley watched them alone, doing their naughty little tricks in so lifelike a manner she was always moved to shocked laughter. But Lacton had watched the dolls with them the last time, and even with Maggie in the room his eyes had jerked to Karen, to her breasts, her generous Prussian hips and rear, and she had known he would be trying again, trying in that indirect and talky and hand-brushing way of his.

She sat at the vanity mirror, combing out her reddish hair, not willing to call Linda and allow her unhappiness, her inner turmoil, to show. How she wished Lacton had been defeated in the election! So close ... and if the Democrat had won, there would have been no Secret Service moving in, disrupting her life, the life of all Bay Island, for three miserable days.

The phone rang twice. She continued combing her hair. The buzzer sounded and she lifted the French-style handset.

'Mr. Walter Prince, madam,' Everett said.

'Yes, please put him on.'

'Karen,' the deep well-modulated voice said, 'sorry I missed your call.'

'Oh, just a little invitation, Bucky. Just a spur-of-the-moment thing, a dinner party for a few of us.' She laughed and added, 'Before all sorts of people descend and make life impossible.'

'Ah, the President and entourage.'

'Yes, but let's not talk of that.'

'It must be exciting. I can't promise not to talk of it. When do you want me?'

'Just remember that this is Florida, no engraved invitations and no formal dress ... and it's Tuesday.' Again she laughed. She had decided to call people only this afternoon. She had decided in a sort of desperation to enjoy people, the right *kind* of people, and forget Bob Lacton. 'What must you think of me!'

'Enough to say I'll be delighted.'

'That's a good friend! I'll be sure to bother you with many more such invitations all during the season.'

'I'll hold you to the promise.'

They talked a little more then said good-bye, and she was pleased. No one had declined her invitation, despite the short notice.

She had finally lost the ugly thoughts. She decided she would, indeed, have these 'surprise' dinners often.

When Charles came up, he was exhilarated. His complaints were always jovial, his pleasure always obvious at having what he called 'the single most important man on earth' as his friend and guest. (Though he felt the man weak in curbing radical elements; felt the government badly needed someone like himself to influence the President in a healthy conservative direction.)

'How's my *hausfrau* tonight?' he asked, voice booming as it did in moments of pleasure. He came up behind her as she stood near the dresser, just changed into a delicate pink night-gown. He took her around from the back, hands stroking her stomach and then her breasts, his manhood rising, pressing into her buttocks.

'Charles,' she murmured, as if surprised. But pleasure often did this to him.

'*Achtung!*' he snapped, and pointed at the bed.

She laughed, shaking her head, and turned to the bathroom.

125

He caught her, swept her up, held her as if she were a child. At age forty, he was twelve years her senior, but a healthy, vigorous man. One hand, low on her thigh, moved, and her giggle was followed by a long sigh.

He carried her to the bed. He removed her nightgown, then stripped quickly. Looking at his virile member, she wanted to take it and kiss it, but she remembered vividly how he had reacted the first, the only, time she'd ever tried it. He had lost desire. He had been repelled, almost panicked she would have said.

He sat down beside her. She touched his member. Even this he rarely permitted; at least not more than a touch. She stroked him. He began to climb on her. She said, 'Charles, wait ... play with me.'

His fingers went into her. She said, 'No ... Charles ... other things.'

He went to her breasts. Her crotch and her breasts, and nothing else, ever. And she wanted something else, something more. She read, she heard, and before marriage she had experienced briefly some of those other things. She stroked him, and held tight when he tried to draw away. He grunted in surprise. And before he could say anything, she bent and took him in her mouth.

She felt his entire body grow rigid; then he left her, so violently there was no stopping him. She sat up and he was turning away, shaking; yes, his entire body shaking. 'You've been drinking,' he said, voice also shaking.

'No ... I just ... just to love you ... for fun, Charles!'

'Fun? Degeneracy between man and wife is *fun*?'

He walked to the closet and got his robe and she saw he was no longer erect, he was small and shriveled.

'But ... even the dolls, Charles! The dolls do it, and you laugh and joke with Bob Lacton, so why...?'

'Dirty little Chinese dolls? Dirty movies ... they do it there too. *That's* what you want to emulate? What's the matter with you, Karen!'

She didn't feel the shame he obviously expected her to feel. She felt that the correct question was, 'What is the matter with *you*, Charles?' She didn't ask it, but her eyes did, her face did. When he started for the bathroom, she said, 'Don't leave like this, please. When did it happen to you?'

He went onto the bathroom. The door closed and the water

ran. He didn't come out for almost half an hour, but when he did she was still waiting ... and so was her question. 'When did it happen, Charley?'

She didn't expect he would answer without a fight. She expected him to say, 'When did *what* happen?' and then laugh at her hints. She expected to return to the subject next week, and perhaps again the week after, and in a gentle way to bring it all out.

But he suddenly fell apart.

One minute he was taking his pajamas from the drawer ... and the next minute he was sinking into a chair, head down, talking, his voice so choked she suspected tears—*tears*, from her Charles!—the words pouring out of him as if they had been dammed up so long that now, given the chance to be heard, they were running wild.

'A boy at Choate, the school I went to before Deerfield, I didn't tell you about Choate because this boy, a goddam Englishman, I swear Hitler was right about the English, *verdamte* degenerate shopkeepers, this goddam boy, I never thought because he was good at sports, much better than most of us even though he was only in the country two years from England and still he played baseball and football like a professional, a tall, fair boy...' He drew a breath as if he were drowning, the air rasping through his throat. 'He said they played a game in good public schools, you know, the English public schools are the private schools ... a game called, hell, he didn't worry about what we thought, just said it, Cocks All Around, said it was mentioned in realistic English literature, he meant pornography, as far back as the eighteen hundreds. We sat in a circle one night in his room, he and his roommate and another boy. The roommate was a sissy type and I should have understood why they got along so well when they weren't at all alike ... the roommate, Christ...'

Again the rasping inhalation; and now Karen was frightened, was sorry she had started this. Perhaps it was better not to know?

'We sat in a circle, four of us, holding each other's ... yes, God, and *why* I did it I don't understand except that there we were with only a candle burning and you know how kids are about a dare and how teen-age boys are, how quick, how excited ... so we were all stiff and it was the roommate holding mine and he didn't just hold it like the rest of them, at least I

127

think the others just held it, he was like a woman with it, stroking, and God I didn't know what to do, but *he* did, the lousy faggot! *He* did!'

Now she could *see* he was crying, the tears running down his big face, and she whispered, 'Just a childish ...'

'No, *not* childish, because ... I stayed when the other boy who didn't belong in the room said he had to study. He didn't have an orgasm. He didn't want to. But ... I did. I wanted ... and when he left, the one holding me began to do ... what you wanted to do, and the other, the goddam Englishman, he forced me ... no, he didn't have to *force* me, no, I wanted to ... I did it to him and the roommate did it to me.'

The sob seemed torn from the very bottom of his stomach. 'I stayed there half the night! I couldn't get enough! And every chance we had the next week. And when I finally realized what was happening to me, I got sick and went home and I wouldn't go back, and that's when I transferred to Deerfield and never, I swear, *never,* touched another male, or let anyone even put his arm around my shoulders so that I got the reputation of being a cold fish, but I knew I had to stay away, I knew because ... I couldn't help it ...'

She held out her arms.

He came to her, without hesitation. They hugged. They kissed. He wasn't ... No, she had panicked, just as he had; exaggerated, just as he had. Her beautiful life was still beautiful. Nothing had changed, really, except that she understood him a little better.

Except that she had opened a door on something frightening.

She kissed him wildly, stroked his body (but stayed away from his penis), drew him down to her breasts.

Breasts and vagina were all right because the English boy and his roommate hadn't had breasts and vaginas.

She kissed him, afraid even to use her tongue, and finally felt the stiffness return. Anxious to prove that her beautiful life was still intact, she took him and rammed him into her.

Yes, that was all right, because they hadn't been able to do that.

He made love to her just as he always did, with short, rhythmic strokes, lips to her cheek, eyes closed ...

Eyes always closed. What went on behind those eyes in the brain that held memories not connected with breasts and vaginas and Karen Hoffenter?

128

He was of good German stock! He ran his breweries with strength and skill, had diversified and was a success by even the highest standards! He was as much a man as any she had known! *More! More!*

He raised himself a little, opening his eyes to look at her, to question her. She was late. She smiled and murmured, 'In a minute.'

He went back to her cheek. He went on with his unvarying rhythmic strokes. Nothing was happening to her, so she played at orgasm, crying out and tossing her head from side to side as when it was real, doing it for him, not to risk adding to his night of anguish.

He squeezed her and shortly after, she felt the spasm and the wetness.

Later, as he slept beside her, she stared into the darkness and thought it all out and told herself there was nothing to fear. She would experience satisfaction with Charley again. The shock of the evening would soon wear off and it would be good for her again. As for him, he had relieved his mind; she had drawn out the poison lurking there; he was normal and had proved it decisively.

Or had he? Wasn't it possible to desire something and settle for something else, something less?

Tears came. She cried into the pillow, it helped and her eyes closed. Half asleep, she went back to her previous line of thought; the visit. And though she wasn't aware of it, her memories of Lacton, of his words and glances and surreptitious, tenuous touches weren't tinged with *quite* as much dislike as before.

A strangely unattractive man, not her type at all . . . but still, as Charley had said, the single most important man on earth. And after knowing Maggie Lacton, with her thin face and thin lips and thin, angular body, one could understand and, yes, almost sympathize with his need, his hunger.

The single most important man on earth . . . and one thing she knew, he desired Karen Vener.

Fanny looked out the window near the sink, hearing the deep voice humming one of those foolish rock 'n roll songs. And simple as the tune was, he couldn't carry it. She smiled. It sounded good to her anyway; hearing the boy happy at his work. He *liked* gardening: it wasn't just a pose for the robbery.

He was doing something to a bush beside the window. She said, 'Hey, *mon cher*, what sort of plant is that?'

Rollins looked up, surprised. 'Fanny? I thought it was your day off?'

'I traded with Vino.' She hadn't wanted to go into Miami or Miami Beach. What could she do there? She knew no one and wanted to know no one.

'Next time trade with *me*.'

She would. 'Ah, you want to chase the girls?'

He shrugged. He didn't seem at all embarrassed. Different from her little one in that . . .

She stopped those thoughts. Too deep; too raw. Forever too deep and too raw.

'I was thinking of swimming, lying on the beach. Look at this morning! Not even ten yet, and it's up over seventy-five.'

'Of course, swimming.'

He grinned and returned to work. He tore up the ground near the roots of the plant and poured blue liquid from a pail.

'What are you doing?' she asked, to keep talking to him, to lose the deep, raw feeling of loss.

'Feeding acid to an evergreen. Bush like this—mugho pine— can leach off the concrete foundation and sicken . . .' He went on and she didn't understand and didn't care about understanding. She was content listening to him.

After a while he stood up, wiping sweat from his forehead. His tan shirt was damp across the shoulders and under the armpits. So were his pants at the waistband and behind the knees.

'You want something cold, Rollins? I have a pitcher of lemonade . . . fresh lemons and pieces of orange.'

130

'Man!' he said, and disappeared.

He came inside and sat at the table and drank four glasses, fast. He was a big boy and had a big thirst. She made a sandwich with much ham and Swiss cheese and put some cold white beans on the side and he ate it almost without noticing. When he lit a cigarette, she muttered, 'Smoking is for blind ones. Dangerous, very dangerous. All the information about cancer...'

He nodded and stood up. 'Well, back to work.'

And she suddenly said something she hadn't planned on saying, something she had thought several times but had no business saying.

'You shouldn't be in this kind of a thing, Rollins. No, not a nice boy like you. What would your mother think? You spoke so *strongly* of her, that Jewish mother of yours. What would she say?'

He was turning away and stopped, looking over his shoulder at her, eyes full of surprise. Then he laughed.

She felt her face growing hot and moved quickly to clear the table and bring the plate and glass to the sink. 'That *was* foolish,' she muttered.

'No, Fanny.' He was right behind her, timidly touching her arm. 'I didn't mean ... I wasn't laughing at *you*, honest.'

He was upset, truly upset. Her embarrassment left as quickly as it had come and she was touched by his concern for her.

'I laughed because...' He made a helpless gesture. He went back to the table and sat down and smoked his cigarette. She washed the few dishes by hand rather than put them in the dishwasher. She dried them, and he said, 'It's ... okay watching you do that, y'know?'

She didn't know.

'I mean, I used to sit in the kitchen back home—oh, Christ, nothing like this!' They both laughed. 'But I used to watch Mom and it was okay, then.'

She got herself a glass and filled it with lemonade and sat down opposite him. He was still smoking and still looked as if he was trying to explain his laughter.

She waited. He said, 'I *wasn't* laughing at you.' She pressured him with, 'And even if you were, it's not important.' He fiddled with the ashtray and wet his lips and began to speak. And what she heard hurt her, because no matter how he tried to make it sound, it had hurt him and deeply, had turned his

131

whole life around. What she heard made the tears well up in her eyes, though she hid them and smiled and murmured things like, 'Ah, sensitive sons,' and, 'Not *all* in your mind but much.' And wished he had been born to *her*; and quickly caught that wish and drove it away.

His brother had been older than he and much better in school, much more successful in the things a mother values. His brother had been the mother's favorite but not so much that it twisted Buddy-Boy's life. Then came Vietnam and the brother had been killed in one of the first American sweeps towards the DMZ. And a fifteen-year-old boy had come home from school to find his home a crypt, a tomb, a temple dedicated to a dead son turned god.

Buddy-Boy had been alone with his mother, the father having died some years before. Buddy-Boy had done all the things the doctor had told him to do for her—the medicine and the meals, and afterward the cheerful talk and the little trips. A year later the mother began to move back toward sanity, though she was still subject to frequent descents into blackness and despair. (And how Fanny understood this, though *she* had gone right on with life. But still, the darkness and despair had been *inside* her, and she knew just what he was saying.)

In the early days of her insanity of grief, the mother had moaned such things as, 'He was so good, so beautiful, and he's dead and you're alive. Why?' Buddy-Boy believed she was right; he believed his brother *had* been more worthy of life and love; he had loved the brother himself and missed him and wished himself dead in his place.

But he changed in this. In the second year of his travail, he hardened without knowing he hardened. He began to block out the brother's name, the brother's memory. He was *supposed* to do this, for the mother, for her sanity ... but he did it for himself too. And in him grew a small anger that became a large anger.

He never showed it ... not once in the two years that he served his mother in all the ways he could, in ways that went beyond trips and cheerful talk, in ways that included sitting, simply sitting beside her, holding her hand as they watched television shows. For two years—the years from fifteen to seventeen—for those two irreplaceable, precious years he belonged to his mother, and she grew whole and began to see

132

him and began to love him as she had never loved anyone, understanding finally what he had given her, understanding and responding.

The day she was able to take a job to help their desperate finances, that was the day she told him he was the finest son a woman could desire. The day she told him this, the small anger that had become a large anger reared up and even as he smiled and kissed her and walked with her to the bus, the anger was working. He went on toward school. He went on and past the school. He had saved four dollars and he went downtown and found a movie and found a girl, a girl to help him spend three of his four dollars; a girl to teach him that he could get girls easily enough and that he didn't always need three dollars.

He went back to school after a week of truancy, and after the return of pain to his mother's eyes. He stole a car. He got away with it, but instead of dumping the flashy Oldsmobile hardtop, he kept it for three weeks and of course he was caught.

He received a suspended sentence when the mother stood up in court and talked of her Buddy-Boy and his two years of servitude. He died a little as she did.

He stole another car. He shoplifted. He held up two pawn shops, the second with a gun from the first. He had many girls, including one who became pregnant. Her father turned in a gift he'd given her and it was on a make sheet and Buddy-Boy Rollins went to jail—not youth house or reform school but jail, for armed robbery. Five months before the end of his three-year sentence, his mother died of a massive coronary.

Buddy-Boy Rollins's cellmate told him to look up several people on the outside. One was Charles DeVino ...

'And where did all this happen?' Fanny asked, when he fell silent, to ask something, and also because he had never mentioned a town, a city, a place where he'd lived.

He shook his head. 'All forgotten,' he muttered. 'Wiped out.'

She then realized he hadn't given names for his mother, his brother, his cellmate. There was only Buddy-Boy Rollins and a world of shadows.

It was one way to reduce the past.

He went out and she began preparing a salad. Prince wasn't dining at home today; not lunch and not dinner. She would go upstairs soon and see how Sandy was doing with the cleaning.

133

She would keep busy.

It was necessary to keep busy if one was not to think too much.

She heard him singing again a while later. She stopped chopping onion to listen. What would happen to him? How much chance did he have in his innocence—yes, innocence, despite his courage and strength and three years in jail—of getting away after it was all over?

Very little chance, she felt.

Very little chance once the money was in his hands and he was out in the world.

The vultures would find him. And soon he would be robbing again. And soon he would be back in that old life of jails and cellmates...

But one had one's own life, one's own problems.

She set her mouth in its accustomed hard line and chopped determinedly, vigorously, and any watering of the eyes was from the onion and not foolish sentiment. No more mixing in his life. No more thinking of him as *le pauvre* and *mon cher* and just a boy. Rollins was a thief, as were they all. He would face his fate alone, as would they all.

Dick Brandy came out into the sunshine and waved Claude away. The chauffeur looked as if he couldn't believe it. Dick didn't really believe it himself but he set off down the road, walking steadily if not briskly, and he breathed the air tinged with aroma of salt water and he looked at the palm trees, the grass, a car that went by with a male face turning to stare at him (because people didn't *walk* from place to place here), and everything looked brighter and greener and finer than he could ever remember.

He was at the side road to the club. Amazing! Walking was a great new discovery! Walking was the one activity, sport, pleasure—whatever it was, and it was all three and more to him—he had truly missed. They could keep their golf and tennis and polo and everything else, including the swimming and boating his doctor had told him he could try next week, 'with caution, of course'. They could keep everything, if only they left him his walking, 'they' being the gods, fate, whoever or whatever might have a hand in determining Dick Brandy's future.

'Oh you beautiful things you,' he said to his legs as they

134

carried him nicely, though with just a *touch* of weariness up to the double front doors of the Bay Island Country Club. 'You get your rest now.'

As soon as he entered the club, someone waved at him. He went across the room, *quite* tired now. It was Vincent Drang, and while Dick had nothing but foul memories of the racket boys—especially from his beginnings in show biz when he'd played the smaller clubs—he wanted company. Besides, Vince was so far removed from the rackets now it no longer counted.

He seated himself and they exchanged a few words and the waitress came. At the same time, Walter Prince entered and walked to a table about as far from theirs as he could get. Dick caught his eye after he sat down. They exchanged smiles and nods. Vince, Dick noticed, concentrated on his old fashioned.

'You know him, Dick?'

'Not really. I played a Philadelphia Hunt Club affair some time ago . . .'

And suddenly he remembered. His body had grown stronger, and so had his mind. 'I'll be damned,' he said, looking over at Prince again. 'He recouped rather quickly . . . or could it have all been a lie?'

'You've left me at the post,' Vince said, using race talk; always race or horse talk, never anything that might remind you of hoods or Cosa Nostra.

Dick hesitated; but he didn't see any harm in discussing it, especially with Drang who, like himself, could never become part of Real Society even though he lived cheek by jowl with it. Besides, Prince was here, wasn't he? He wouldn't be here if he hadn't recouped his fortune, or if the loss of fortune wasn't a vicious lie in the first place.

He went into it in some detail, testing his memory and finding it as good as it had ever been. . . .

It was three years ago, almost to the month. The dance was in full swing, a buffet dinner having been cleared away from the sides of the large ballroom an hour before. The Brandy Man, as he had been known, had played and sung his old-time favorites, the current hits, and gone on into Latin numbers. It was a mature group of celebrants, in the main, though a rock quartet was waiting to go on behind the curtain of the half-circle stage. Dick Brandy was also waiting for them to go on. Lately his energy had been low, his staying power less than satisfactory. He felt rather as if he were coming down with the flu ... and had felt that way for weeks.

At the band switch, he left his musicians to their own devices (the Brandy Band knew how to mix, respectfully, with its society audiences) and hurried to the bar for a double Scotch. It was while taking his first long swallow that the trouble erupted.

'... as near to a swindle as it *could* be and not a police matter,' a slender, balding man was saying. 'Prince *was* a swindler, in point of fact, and his dying doesn't change ...'

Someone brushed Dick aside, spilling part of his drink; a tall, dark man, his face worn beyond its years. The balding man stopped speaking abruptly; then put down his glass and said, 'I'm glad you heard, Tad. Now you're going to hear it all.'

'Shut up, Chick,' the dark man said. His body swayed. He looked half-potted.

Chick's companion—the man he'd been talking to originally —was big, heavyset, built like a body-contact athlete. He murmured, 'Uh, Chick, you think this is the place ...?'

Chick ignored him. 'I put close to half a million into your father's new mines, and it's highly doubtful those mines ever existed. And whether they did or not, I've now been informed that you and Bucky aren't going to make good ...'

'Shut *up*!' Tad Prince said, voice shaking.

At this point, another man, equally tall and dark but not nearly as worn as Tad Prince, nor as angry, arrived on the scene. He put his hand on Tad's arm. Tad shook it loose. 'I won't tell you to shut up again, Chick!'

Chick glanced at his companion. 'That's typical Prince reaction to statement of fact.'

Tad began to swing. Dick was caught in a sudden press of four moving bodies, but had the presence of mind to duck. Tad's fist missed his nose, but by considerably less than it missed its target. Chick's body-contact friend lived up to his appearance. He threw two punches, very quickly and very hard, into Tad's middle. The tall man buckled and began to retch.

That should have ended it. Bucky led his brother down the side of the hall toward the rest rooms, nodding a little at the sympathetic glances and smiles of those who assumed Tad, as usual, had drunk too much. New people were pushing up for drinks and the rock band was fracturing everyone's eardrums

136

and no one seemed particularly interested in what had happened, so quickly, at the far end of the bar.

Dick ordered a second double and saw that Bucky Prince was back. Prince spoke quietly, smiling a little, but there was a look in his eyes . . .

Dick moved slightly away.

'It's true,' Bucky said to Chick, 'that you invested money in Prince Mining. But it's also also true that no one guarantees an investment—not in U.S. Steel and not in I.B.M. and certainly not in high yield mining futures. The name of the game is risk, as you very well know. You also know just where the Securities and Exchange Commission is located. *That's* the place to do your talking, not here.'

'There's such a thing as operating within the framework of the law, and *still* being crooked. In this case . . .'

Bucky Prince lowered his voice, his eyes flicking between Chick and his muscular friend. 'You're an unmitigated crybaby sonovabitch, Chick. If you'll step outside with me a moment, I'll give you proper reason to cry.'

The muscular friend said, 'You know Chick has heart trouble.'

'I *don't* know. And neither did Tad. But . . . in that case, I'll accept an apology.'

Chick laughed.

The muscular friend said, 'Want a drink, Chick?'

Bucky looked at him. 'Come to think of it, it was *you* who threw the punches.'

The man spread his hands.

Bucky kept looking. 'I don't know you, do I?'

The man said nothing.

'Just who are you? What are you doing here?'

The man smiled and shrugged. Bucky stared a moment longer, then turned to Chick. 'A hired hand,' he said. 'A bully boy; a bodyguard.' For the first time, he seemed truly shocked and angry. 'I heard you'd made enemies, but to bring a guard to a party . . .'

The man called Chick flushed. He said, 'The question is, just who are *you*? And what are *you* doing here? You certainly don't belong with us. Your damned father was a thief and so are you and your brother. You're declaring bankruptcy without even trying . . .'

'No bankruptcy,' Prince interrupted, and he was quite pale

now. Dick, who didn't want any more fists whistling past his nose, moved away again, but not so far that he couldn't hear what was said. No one paid him the slightest attention. 'No bankruptcy, because no debts. Investments in speculative stock aren't loans and don't require repayment if the speculation fails. We've made you money on our speculations and now we've lost you money. Other people have also made and lost with us. No one else is crying. Our basic operation will continue, in reduced form, until we recoup...'

'You're wiped out! You haven't a dime to...'

'Chick,' the muscular man murmured.

Chick was breathing hard. He glared and abruptly stalked off.

Prince finally glanced around to see if he'd been overheard. Dick concentrated on his drink. Prince said, 'I guess he *does* need you, even here, with that temperament of his.' The bodyguard said, 'Shove it.'

Dick was turning to place his empty glass on the bar. He heard a grunting sound and a woman's cry of surprise. He turned back to see the muscular man slumping back against the bar, hands over his stomach. Prince was in the process of hitting him again, in the face this time. The man slumped lower, bending his head, but didn't fall. Voice choked, he said, 'If you wait...'

Prince waited. Several people were staring now. The bodyguard said, 'If Chick ever gives me the word...' Prince walked away.

'And that was it,' Dick said, glancing across the room at Bucky Prince, older looking now and by more than three years; more as his brother had been.

Vincent Drang was concentrating on the plate of sea trout and wild rice that had just been served him. Dick turned his attention to his own plate. The boiled beef with horseradish sauce was marvelous. Even his palate seemed stronger, more receptive!

It wasn't until the coffee that Vince spoke. 'What was that Chick fellow's full name?'

Dick shrugged. 'Never heard it mentioned. Why?'

'Good to know a man like that,' Vince said, pouring cream. 'In order to avoid him, that is.'

Dick chuckled. A few minutes later he excused himself. As he walked out, he saw that Vince was watching Bucky over the rim of his cup. He wondered, briefly, whether he'd been wise to tell that story.

But Vince wouldn't repeat it. He was a cautious man, very cautious and very careful of his standing here on the island. Prince could make it uncomfortable for him if he wanted to. Anyone could. Vince was *tolerated*, at best. And Prince, whether simply a millionaire now instead of a centimillionaire, was Real Society.

Vincent Drang waited until Prince left the club; then he too left. He drove to his home and went directly into his study and locked the door. He made three long-distance telephone calls. He had friends in Philadelphia, though he rarely contacted them. Now he wanted information.

His calls completed, he smoked a long Havana cigar and thought how *sweet* it would be if he could find out something to use against Prince. Not that he expected he would. Too many ways for wealth to remain hidden, no matter what went on in Philadelphia. Of all people, Vincent Drang well understood Swiss banks, hidden accounts, secret safety deposit boxes.

But say, just say, that Prince *was* broke.

Say he was spending his last few thousand here on the island.

What would be the *point* of it?

A business deal involving one of the residents? Building confidence in a mark? Heiress hunting?

Vince smoked and considered possibilities, including the one that Prince had indeed recouped at business. He sincerely hoped that wasn't so. Beth hadn't said much but Vince suspected that Prince had used her, and used her badly. That was reason enough to do Mr. Walter Danforth Prince a bad turn, should the opportunity arise. And then there was another reason, a reason that had already caused some friction between his wife and himself. He had a growing interest, a festering lech, for his luscious sister-in-law. He had a long-range hope, a slow fuse plan, to get her in his bed and to keep her there as occasional solace for the aridity of this square, legal life. So Bucky Prince was far from his favorite person; Bucky Prince who had sampled, and discarded, what Vince so avidly coveted.

Vince would keep his eyes and ears open. Nothing much

139

else to do on Bay Island anyway. Nothing much else to do since he'd retired from 'business'. Nothing but remember who he'd been, how much power he'd had, how no one had dared deal with him, and with *his*, the way Prince had.

If there was a way of cutting that WASP bastard's throat, he would find it.

The dinner held two surprises for Ceecee Mortonson. One was Walter Prince, placed straightforwardly beside her by Karen Vener. That it was also a surprise to Walter Prince she could only surmise, since he had considerable control of his emotional reactions, or so she felt at that stage of the evening.

They didn't talk much, she and Walter Prince. They talked to people on their *other* sides. The talk centred around President Lacton, referred to here at the Veners' as 'Bob' and not without a certain backhanded pride that masqueraded as critical humor.

She drank quite a bit of white wine and felt that it increased her sense of cool detachment and her ability to observe with scalpel-sharp vision ... and so she understood that she was getting gassed and stopped the wine bit because getting gassed with Walter Bucky Prince so close might be dangerous, especially with her father on the other side and down-table two seats. Oh, yes, *dangerous*, because she'd had the frog test yesterday and phoned for the results today and confirmed what she'd known anyway; she was indeed going to add to the population explosion.

She turned to Prince. He was starting on his strawberry mousse. She said, loud and clear, 'And how does an eligible bachelor feel about Bay Island after a month's residence?'

He smiled. 'Satisfied.'

'You're not bored with the limitations? There is, for example, only a handful of single women.'

Others were listening to them now and she told herself it was harmless.

'A handful is about my quota.'

Karen Vener thought that funny. Ceecee waited out her laughter.

'And tell me, what sort of bachelor pad can a man maintain on Bay Island, Mr. Prince? I mean, I can visualize it in Manhattan—Park Avenue or Central Park South. Or Philadelphia ...'

140

At that moment, her father said, 'I've been wondering about your home myself, Bucky. How's it turning out?'

And off they went into square-feet-of-living space, docks and servants and she had to put away her stiletto, and after a while, was grateful to old Allie for interrupting, because while she'd been right to stop sipping that nice white wine, she hadn't stopped quite soon enough.

They went into the rustic living room and sat around and she talked with Flap Cornwall and asked where Toots had bought that simply *devastating* gown and Flap, the dirty old man, put his hand on her thigh and murmured, 'I'd trade Toots *and* her gown for one kiss, you man killer you!' She smiled into his flushed face, thinking he had drunk a lot more than she, and not just white wine, and let him move his hand around over the thin lace of her nightgown-turned-evening-gown. When Toots wasn't looking and Bucky was, she gave Flap his kiss and his hand tightened on her thigh. She said, 'Now where do I pick up Toots and the gown?'

'Walk in the garden with me and we'll discuss it.'

Sunuvagun, he meant it. She leaned back, thinking time and Toots would cool him off but she didn't have to wait that long. Once again, it was dear old Dad to the rescue, strolling over amiably but oh-so-firmly. Flap's hand flew away, and a moment later, under Daddy's cold eye, so did Flap himself.

She looked up at him. 'Now, now,' she murmured, 'you know footsie is perfectly acceptable among us grown ups.'

He smiled. Maybe she was being a little too scalpel-sharp in her observations, but the smile wasn't real and his eyes were ... strange. She became uncomfortable.

He turned away. She sat alone, smoking, letting the wine take her and soothe her. Walter Prince sat down on the couch with her; not close, no—a respectable distance away.

'That's a very beautiful gown,' he said, looking her over.

'Sent me by an aunt in London.'

'I can't quite remember seeing anything like it.'

'Thank goodness.'

'It seems—the material that is—quite old. Is it?'

'Yes. Lace with silk overlay. It was a nightgown. No way of being certain, but one of Queen Victoria's ladies in waiting supposedly owned it. My aunt suggested I give it to a good designer and see what happened. The nightgown cost about fifty dollars in a flea market. The *couturière* charged a mere twelve hundred.'

'It was worth it,' he said, and went away to talk to Karen Vener.

She tasted his voice. She wished she could hear him say it again, the same way, so she could feel...

She lost the fleeting feeling.

The second of the evening's two surprises came when her father reached down and helped her up. 'Bucky's invited us over to his place for a quick look-around. I haven't been in Number One since I quarreled over Eisenhower's leftist tendencies with Chip Barnestadt, the previous owner.'

Bucky was standing close by, and from his smile and from what he said Ceecee felt sure the 'invitation' had been forced out of him by her father and her father's curiosity.

'You'll have to excuse what, as you put it before, Ceecee, is just a bachelor pad. I haven't prepared for guests...'

'No formalities, Bucky,' Allie boomed, and hustled them through their goodnights and out to the cars, theirs *avec chauffeur* as befitted the Mortonsons on a two-mile drive to a local dinner party, Bucky's deadly little buglike racer.

He pulled away so fast, Gerald, the chauffeur, couldn't contain himself and whistled softly under his breath.

'It can *move*,' Allie said.

She nodded, and wondered why he was in such a hurry. And guessed at a house that might not be prepared for guests and a staff that wasn't yet broken in or under proper control.

He met them at the door, along with his butler, who seemed just to have thrown on his jacket. Or was it more of the gassed-up scalpel-sharp vision that, now that the gas was evaporating, she no longer trusted?

They went through the house, Prince talking rather more than usual; rather more, she felt, than necessary even when giving the grand tour spiel. Nervousness would explain it. But nervousness wasn't part of the Prince style. And what was there to be nervous about? It was a house, rather small and moderately furnished. The servants ... well, there she had some intimation of problems, though everyone seemed alert and respectful, despite the hour and the unexpectedness of the visit. The maid was quite a trick.

Could Mr. Prince be playing at upstairs bedroom with the downstairs maid? It was far from unheard of, and the girl *was*, to put it mildly, nubile. And it would explain Bucky's nervous-

142

ness, if indeed he was nervous, which she wasn't at all certain of.

She decided never again to stray from the virtuous pot to the insidious little white wine. There ought to be a law.

And yet, coming down from the bedrooms, preceding the master of the house and listening to him chatter away to her father, she again felt there was something ... perhaps *wrong* was not the word. Something *different* about Prince here in this house. Or in the house itself.

The chauffeur—if she had the servants straight and the young, good-looking one with all the muscle was the chauffeur —threw light switches and this-way-pleased them and they went out to the patio and then the dock to look at Prince's boat in the moonlight. 'A nice home,' her father said; which, knowing him as she did, meant, 'Nothing much.'

'Comfortable enough,' Prince said, looking at her and finally, seeming to be himself, 'for a bachelor pad.'

She smiled, suddenly tired and ready to go home and sleep and let whatever was going to happen happen. Last razor-sharp vision of the evening, very last one: Something *was* going to happen. Not just in her belly. Something else; something to do with her feeling of strangeness here.

She laughed a little, at herself, not really believing, and Prince said 'Private joke?'

Father was already walking back to the house. They were alone for a moment, the very first moment during this night of perceptions and doubts and alcohol. She said, 'I don't think it's private. I think it includes you.'

He waited for her to explain. She waved her hand. 'Did you perchance notice how much of the grape I consumed at dinner?'

'Yes. More than a bottle of nineteen sixty four Bâtard Montrechet, a wine not to be guzzled.'

'And I guzzled. So I laugh and make obscure statements.'

'Make a clear one. Say you'll sail with me tomorrow. I need a crew.'

She shook her head. 'Tomorrow I play tennis. I've reserved a court for nine. You can be my opponent, if you wish, because Jock Waters has deserted me and I plan to grab whomever I can. You can be he who gets grabbed.'

He seemed less than delighted, but nodded. She would have told him not to bother if Father hadn't called, 'Fallen off the

143

dock, you two?'

And that was something else; the change she felt in dear old Dad.

Oh my, Injun no can drink firewater and neither can drug-generation heiress.

They went out to the car. Prince stood at the door, smiling and waving, master of the manor seeing his guests off, and she still felt something was wrong.

Wrong, wrong with Prince and Father and this night.

Wrong, wrong, and she was insane!

Later, almost asleep, she murmured, 'Yes, not clean enough,' and tried to awaken fully, couldn't and forgot her flash insight.

Her insight into a basic wrongness about Prince's home that might have explained some of the things she had felt that evening.

Her insight built on an unconscious comparison between his home and every other home on the island, every other home *anywhere* inhabited by the very rich: Those perfectly neat, smug, shining-clean homes maintained by men and women whose jobs included cleaning, cleaning, three and four times a day, because what else did they have to do, what else did they get paid for? Clean, clean, super clean for the super-rich.

Number One Bay Drive hadn't been smug enough and hadn't been clean enough; not for Bay Island and not for Walter Danforth Prince.

Wrong, wrong, and she slept and forgot it, for the while.

WEDNESDAY, FEBRUARY 19

Bucky Prince's right arm felt heavier each time he swung the racket. His chest ached, clear back to his laboring lungs. He hadn't played lawn tennis in more than three years, and his life in those years hadn't been in any way a preparation for the courts. But he persisted, because he couldn't allow Ceecee Mortonson to defeat him. He was determined to triumph and was convinced he would by concentrated will power wedded to the remains of his old skill.

She defeated him anyway, in straight sets, with several

humiliating tumbles attending his back-court sprints and lunges, and by such lopsided scores that he refused to be aware of them, despite the attendant's stentorian bellowing of numbers and that ridiculous term, 'love'. Then, as he stood panting and stretching his sweat drenched face in a grin, she came around the net, looking even younger than she was, in a snug cotton blouse and pleated white skirt so short it showed her tight white pants with each stride, her hair tied into twin black braids with bits of ribbon. On the court to their left he saw a man, reasonably young but no boy, a guest of Charles and Karen Vener's, openly admiring her as he readied himself for a serve. His blatant, smiling stare annoyed Walt. He stepped forward as she reached him, blocking the man's view. 'Well played,' he gasped. 'Of course, it's been a while ...'

'And encroaching age.'

He chuckled. 'Give me a week or two and then see.'

'Sorry. No rematches. I risk no victory to chance of turnabout.'

'That's not very sportsmanlike, is it?' (But he was relieved, because it would take more than a few weeks to eradicate nearly three years of drinking, night owling and lack of exercise.)

Her eyebrows climbed. 'Is sportsmanship important to a *laissez faire* businessman?'

'It is when he can't recoup any other way.'

She smiled. 'And that's what they taught you at Harvard Business.'

'Actually before that, at Andover. Harvard's too open to the masses ...'

Charles Vener interrupted, calling from the other court. 'Bucky, Ceecee, I'd like you to meet a friend.'

The friend was the blatantly staring young man, who was still staring.

'Bud Franklin, advance man for President Lacton's security forces, arrived a few hours ago.'

'So young,' Ceecee said, meeting his smiling stare, 'for so important a job.'

Franklin flushed a little, a broad, muscular Rollins-type with smoother face and lighter hair. 'It's a young man's business, Miss Mortonson.'

'Ceecee,' she said.

'Well, Ceecee ...' He hesitated, as if summoning up his

145

courage, then spoke quickly. 'I'd like to tell you about my work, say at lunch?'

She nodded. 'One o'clock, at the club.'

Franklin's smile was positively blinding. 'Nice to have met *you*, sir!' And he trotted back to the court where Karen Vener waited for his serve.

'Bright fellow,' Charles Vener said. 'Good future. And here's something that might surprise you, Bucky. He's a member of *the* Franklins, up your way in Bryn Athyn. That's the reason Bob Lacton uses him as advance man here and at other social establishments.'

Ceecee was watching Franklin. Bucky said, 'Plays well, doesn't he?'

Vener had turned to watch the government agent's serve. He seemed preoccupied and a little under the weather, as he had last night, despite much loud talk and laughter. Bucky repeated his statement.

Vener said, 'Oh, yes,' and unaccountably flushed under his tan. 'Made it to Forest Hills several years ago.' He put his arm around Ceecee's waist, grinning. 'You ought to try him, honey. Old Bucky here wasn't much competition for you, not that *we* could see.' He let her go, punched Bucky's shoulder and laughed uproariously.

Ceecee smiled. 'I'll do that. Now I have to buy my victim a cold beer.'

'Just as long as it's not a Vener Brewery product,' Bucky muttered as they walked to the club.

'Worried about the mother of your child?'

He kept his expression bland, though inside he winced. She was a goddam savage! 'That too, of course. But do you realize he's bringing screaming Bob Lacton down on our heads?'

'Then it's true about the President's lack of ... control?'

'The wildest tantrums this side of the nursery, when he's, and I use the word advisedly, relaxing.'

'Still, he *is* the President, and he *will* liven our last week. After which, the island can relapse into somnolence for another nine months.'

'I expect to be part of that somnolence.'

They were entering the club; she glanced at him in surprise; he realized he'd made a mistake. He made nothing *but* mistakes with this girl!

A waitress showed them to a table and took their order.

Bucky said, 'I overworked this year, so I'm extending my stay past the mid-March deadline. Do you realize that in places like Palm Beach, the season now continues well into April?'

Their beer and boiled shrimp came. She used her fingers to dip and eat. Except for that one distasteful mother-of-your-child crack, she hadn't really broached the subject; a subject that must have been very much on her mind, as it had been on his since Saturday night.

'Have you done anything yet?' he asked.

She looked up, licking cocktail sauce from her fingers. Such long, slender, childlike fingers, he thought; then he reached for cigarettes.

'Done anything?' she murmured.

'The rabbit or frog test for pregnancy. Or do you expect to *guess* for a month or two?' He'd revealed his tension; her face changed in relation to it, as did her attitude.

She drank beer. She looked around the near empty room. She ate another shrimp. 'What I do or don't do is *my* business.'

'I think it's also *my* business, unless you've had second thoughts about who the father actually is.'

'Yes,' she said.

He froze with his lighter ablaze.

'Blaming you was some sort of vestigal self protective reaction. I mean, picking on the older man, the man more likely to pay the bills. Once I realized how foolish that was, I decided to tell you the truth. You're one of three prospects, and since I can afford to pay for my own abortion...'

'Do you have a doctor?'

'When the time comes, I'll fly to New York. It's quite easy there, and I'll be back in two weeks, with time out for visiting friends.' She picked up another shrimp. 'Or I could combine it with a vacation and go to Denmark. Have you ever been to Scandinavia?'

'I lived in Oslo for three months. We had an office on the Torggt.' It was gone, along with the Prince fortune. He was going to bring it back, if Bob Lacton didn't stop him. And his task was a little easier now that Ceecee was off his conscience. Yet he heard himself say, 'I don't believe you.'

She shrugged. 'Nothing I can do about that.' She pushed back her chair.

'You haven't finished your beer.'

'Don't want to ruin my appetite. James Bond awaits.' She

147

smiled a little. 'Do you realize that I'm free to do what I want with whom I want, now that there's no longer any fear of pregnancy? Even with a diaphragm or the pill, a girl worries; an instinctive worry. Only when she's pregnant...'

'Can we sail later in the week?'

'Why? You don't have to keep in touch, now that I've told you the truth.'

'Can we sail?'

'Oh, I think I understand. You've decided to declare yourself in on the goodies since there's no longer danger of involvement.'

He finally lit his cigarette. 'Are the other two candidates for Daddy getting goodies?'

'*Yes*,' she said, and somehow he was pleased to see the faint tinge of red moving into her cheeks. 'But they didn't panic the way you did.'

He felt heat moving into his own face, and masked it with a smile.

She stood up. He said, '*Can* we sail?'

She didn't look at him, and when she spoke her voice was thin. 'I don't know. It depends upon what I feel like doing at the time. If I want to screw the Secret Service, no. If I want to blow Jock Waters, no. If I want a decadent father image to ferry me around the bay, perhaps.'

'That's reasonable,' he murmured, his foot itching to kick her nicely rounded ass.

She walked off without further word or look. He finished his beer, ate every last shrimp, had another beer. What he really wanted was a martini, but it was only eleven o'clock and wouldn't have looked right. And *wasn't* right, dammit! Still too much drinking...

He thought of Tad, and was afraid. The Princes had always believed in breeding. His father had been fond of phrasing and rephrasing, 'What's bred in the bone...' And what was bred in Tad's bones was bred into Bucky's; and that was deterioration and death.

And yet, it had taken years for it to show in Tad. He had been a Prince in terms of sports and solid scholastic achievement before the excessive drinking and sexual athleticism. At twenty-two, with eighteen-year-old Bucky rooting in the stands, Tad had gone all the way to the finals at Forest Hills—and then lost in straight sets in some of the worst tennis ever seen in championship play. That too was typical of Tad—to do superbly well and then to throw it all away. Later, because of a threatened paternity suit (avoided by a generous settlement), the family learned Tad had been seeing a Long Island belle all during the tournament, and had been out with her the entire night before his final game.

Such escapades failed to reduce young Bucky's hero worship. Tad was his big brother. It was from Tad that he received his early sex education and assurances that women were placed on earth primarily for use by male Princes. It was from Tad rather than from an instructor that he learned to play tennis and later, polo.

But not to sail.

He thought of that. Sailing had come from Grandfather Cleve, and from Father ... and finally and most importantly, from self knowledge; from growth of personal technique and instinct. Sailing was now his own.

But boys don't have such personal skills, such self knowledge. Boys are products of their families, schools and friends; and most important among these was Tad. His influence was basic and strong, and it lasted until Bucky's twenty-first birthday. It might have lasted even longer, as twenty-five-year-old Thadeus Prince was a very attractive and manly figure, if it hadn't been for the girl who called herself April Wynd; Wynd, as in find.

Tad was working in the firm's Los Angeles office at the time. With Father in South America setting up what would eventually become their most disastrous speculation, Bucky decided to spend August 23 and his twenty-first birthday with big brother. Tad expressed delight and said there would be 'considerable fireworks to celebrate your majority'. These became evident as soon as Bucky stepped off the jet. A new aluminum-and-glass chartered bus was waiting, marked 'Bucky's Baby'. It held ten men and eleven women, the men a mixture of upper echelon employees of Prince Mining, Tad's friends ... and three studio executives who provided most of the women. The odd woman, a sleek and talky brunette who knew exactly what she wanted and how to get it, bore the label 'starlet'. As Bucky soon discovered, she could easily have borne an older—*the* very oldest—label of female professionalism. She was, as Tad put it, Bucky's 'to have and to hold till jet do you part'. And as soon as drinks were served and the bus started on a five day tour of California pleasure spots—some of them definitely *not* on any map or chamber of commerce brochure—she worked her hand inside Bucky's fly. He looked at her. She kissed his ear and murmured, 'You like, baby?' He grunted, but he *didn't* like. Certainly, his penis reacted as expected. Certainly, he would screw his 'birthday gift'. But he felt reduced in pride by big brother.

At twenty-one, Bucky Prince was an accomplished woman-izer in his own right; no outside help needed, thank you. Fixing him up like some visiting fireman was a bad scene.

As soon as he could manage it, he excused himself, slid by the surprised brunette and went up front where Tad and three others were playing stud poker for high stakes. There was no room for a fifth hand at the lap top board table set up between two seats and so he ordered a bourbon from the red-jacketed barman and stood swaying in the aisle beside a blonde girl who leaned over Tad's seat. A while later, after Tad had taken a big pot, she looked up at him, smiled broadly and said, her voice even younger than she was—and he guessed at no more than nineteen—'The old Prince magic, right?' He found her smile infectious, and said, 'Right!' She wanted another drink and he signalled the barman. The rocking of the bus became rather much and they took an empty double seat. He gave her a cigarette; she gave him her name. 'I'm April Wynd ... and no, of course it's not my real name. But don't ask my real name because I won't tell you.'

He asked instead, what she did. She smoked and sipped her drink and looked across the aisle at Tad. 'Grub, I guess.'

'What?'

'You know ... live off the land. Or the man.' Then, quickly, she added 'But I was working in a theater—the ticket booth—when I met Tad. He wanted me to be available more than on my days off and ...' She shrugged. 'I liked him. I did it.'

'You want to be an actress?'

'I can't act. I can dance but not good enough for movies.' Again her eyes went to Tad, but no smile this time. 'I'm strictly housewife material.'

Her hair was long, straight, silky. Her smile, when it came again, revealed small, slightly spaced-out front teeth. Her figure was on the plump side, but much to Bucky's liking. Her voice, along with her smile, warmed him; a soft, little-girl voice that would have driven a Women's Lib advocate to fury

150

and turned on almost any man. It turned on Bucky Prince. And this, as became evident, wasn't lost on big brother, despite his seeming concentration on poker.

Their first stop was at a Los Angeles rock joint. There Bucky danced with several of the women, and saw Tad speaking to the sleek brunette. The brunette smiled and nodded. The next stop was at a very unusual Chinese restaurant near Santa Monica Canyon; it was also a private club. Available were various forms of entertainment, including the erotic. They watched a performance by two men and two women which covered just about every possibility, then retired to separate dining rooms. Bucky found himself alone in a cubicle with delicate silk screen decorations, a low table and a rush mat made to conform to American modes of comfort by a foam-rubber underlay. The first course, soup and appetizers, was served, and a moment later April Wynd entered. He rose. She stood there, as if unable to decide what to do.

'Whatever happened,' he said, pulling out a low stool for her, 'I'm glad we're dining together.'

'Dining together,' she said, her smile all wrong. And he began to suspect why.

She sat down. The meal had twelve courses. She ate a great deal and he told himself that his suspicions were foolish, because a woman wouldn't be able to eat that way when ... well, he was wrong.

But he wasn't. She was a different girl, a grim, preoccupied girl; a girl who was eating out of a sense of frustration and unhappiness. He finally said, 'Did Tad tell you you *had* to come in here?'

'No one tells me I *have* to do anything!' This was said with real anger. 'I'm not angling for parts in movies. I do what I want to do.'

'Then you're here because you want to be?'

She didn't answer.

He rose.

'Please don't go. It'll spoil everything.'

'Then you *are* here because you have to be.'

'No ... I mean, I can leave any time I want to. I'm not going to get anything much if I stay, and so I won't lose anything much if I leave. I ...' She was fumbling for words. 'I'm not very good at explaining things. Can't we just eat?'

He said, 'No, April.' He was feeling very low now. And not

just because of April Wynd. Because of admired brother
Thadeus Prince, who had lost points today and was going to
lose many more. He went to the door. She said, 'Give me a
minute.'

It took considerably longer than a minute. It took three of
the exotic rum drinks served in coconut shells, and some
cautious prodding, and then it came out.

'Well, Tad said you liked me and it was your birthday and
you'd be going back home in a week and so what was the harm
since . . . I wasn't born yesterday, you know, and it's not as if I
don't like you . . .'

Tad had asked her to spend the next few days with Bucky.
She was in love with Tad and knew she would never have him,
except briefly, and that was what she meant by not going to get
much if she stayed and not losing much if she left. 'But
still . . .' her words were slurring now . . . 'I guess even a few
more weeks . . . I guess I want them.'

He rose again. She said, 'But if you walk out, I won't even
get that.'

He hesitated. She looked at him. There were no tears in her
eyes. There wasn't much expression in her face. She merely
looked at him, a girl who expected little . . . and he couldn't
take that little away from her.

She had taken more than a little away from him. Tad was
no longer important in his life.

They drank. He asked how long she was expected to stay
with him. She said, 'We're sleeping here. We go on to Sequoia
in the morning. And then Frisco. Your big birthday party. I'm
your present.' She rubbed her eyes and yawned.

He finished his fifth drink.

She looked at the rattan mat. He said, 'Go ahead. I'm not
tired.'

'That's silly. As long as I'm here, what difference . . .?'

'A great deal of difference, to me.'

She smiled then, the gay and innocent smile, the ebullient
smile. 'Like those old dumb movies on television. Clark Gable
and Claudette Colbert and *It Happened One Night*. You ever
see it?'

He said yes. She moved close to him, touched his face,
kissed his lips. He said there was no need for that; he'd tell
Tad anything she wanted him to. She said, 'Shit, what's the big

152

deal? So tonight it can't be Tad Prince. So come on, Bucky Prince.'

On the rattan mat it was good, this in spite of everything else he was feeling—resentment, pity and shame. It was good more than once, and toward morning she said, 'You look like him and you're as good as him with a woman. I wish I'd met you first.'

He held her close and said, 'It wouldn't have made any difference, in the long run.'

'I know that.'

He wanted to leave the bus that day but he didn't. Tad was giving him his big time, his birthday present, and he couldn't deny the gift. And he couldn't deny April her few extra weeks with Tad. He went on; and April stayed with him and watched Tad and the sleek brunette having their own big time. And Bucky took her each night. And at the end, he shook hands with his brother and stepped aboard the jet and flew back to Philadelphia.

At Christmas, when Tad came home, Bucky asked about April.

'Who?'

'April Wynd. My birthday present.'

'Oh, yes. I got her a job with a studio. Receptionist. She'll make some casting director happy.'

Bucky Prince had a drink with Tad and Father, and left to attend a party; Bucky Prince, the man, not the kid brother.

And now Tad and Father were dead and what was bred in the bone . . .

He signed the bill and left the dining room to find another game of tennis. He played Charley Vener and won, probably because Charley was off his game, but also because he could feel some of his old skill, and some of his old style, returning.

He called Ceecee as soon as he reached home. 'Sorry we had to quarrel . . .'

'Was that a quarrel? Please don't answer. I really have to leave now.'

'I just wanted to make sure that you know I . . . care what happens, Ceecee, and let's forget that there are other men involved.'

'If it serves your male ego, fine.'

He took a deep breath and said, 'It does. Friday or Saturday for boating, all right?'

She said nothing.

'I won't try for goodies, if that's what's bothering you.'

And that, judging by a brittle spate of laughter, seemed another mistake. But involvement with Ceecee now, *re*involvement that is, was insane! There was a possibility he wouldn't even be *alive* by March sixteenth.

A moment later, he was assured she wanted no involvement ... as he'd been assured Saturday night when she had avoided the slightest physical contact with him.

'Under those circumstances and those circumstances only, all right. Make it Saturday, early. I have a date which starts about five thirty.'

'Workingman's hours,' he said, to try to end this lightly.

'Oh, he'll be working all right.'

He said good-bye first.

He had Fanny pack him a lunch and sailed the *Spray II* all the way to Vizcaya, passing under five causeways and checking landmarks carefully before entering them on his charts. It wouldn't be easy making the trip at night. If the police thought to drive to one of the causeways, especially the Venetian where the complex of islands reduced areas of passage for his purposes, they might be able to bring the *Spray* under fire.

He passed Vizcaya about two hundred feet offshore, returning the waves of a group of tourists strolling around the back terrace. No one was on the stone barge breakwater and landing, because the museum provided no bridge or boat from the house. No one was ever on the breakwater. It was perfect!

He was tired, but couldn't rest on the way back because the bay had turned choppy and on the last third of his voyage there were heavy gusts of wind and splatterings of rain. He had to take down the genoa, no easy job in a rough sea, and go on the jib alone. Then the skies opened up and he was inundated by a tropical downpour that had chill elements of an eastern spring storm. Drenched, he wanted to go below for his foul-weather gear, but didn't dare leave the wheel on self-steer now. The changing air currents worried him.

It was almost six before the island appeared as a gray shadow in the lashing rain and failing light, and he was so glad to see it, he laughed aloud and wondered what men like Chichester, who had sailed vast distances alone, had felt during storms. A

154

storm in mid Atlantic, for example. A storm going around the Cape.

He was ashamed then of his exhaustion, and refused to excuse it with the awkward tennis he'd played this morning. He was ashamed of what he had become, remembering the man who had sailed five straight days with a practically useless crew of one lovely debutante ('practically' because there *were* those moments below decks) and attended a party the night he'd docked at Newport Harbor Yacht Club. And sailed onto Southampton two days later to play winning tennis at one of the Meadow Club's innumerable Invitation Tournaments. And made it back to Philadelphia to work a frantic three weeks during one of the many crises that had begun afflicting the Prince interests after Father's *gaffe* with that insurance investment. And then driven to Bryn Athyn to tour the Saturday parties, from afternoon until five A.M., making his mark wherever he went among admiring women and, occasionally, irritated men.

He wondered what it would have been like meeting Ceecee Mortonson ten years ago, Ceecee as she was now and he as he had been then. And tying up at the dock, knew that the earlier Bucky Prince was dead and gone.

He ached for the man he once had been. But was it simply aching for a more youthful man, a richer man, a man happier in his time and his place? Or did he really *admire* the man he had been, Bucky Prince, 'sailor, playboy and delightful bastard' as some girl or other had dubbed him?

He had Sandy prepare a hot tub and bring up a rum toddy. When she left him, withdrawn and silent as she'd been since Saturday, he drank and scrubbed away the weariness and bone chill and came out ravenous for one of Fanny's fine dishes.

She had prepared a saddle of lamb with a sauce she called *vivant*, something more Lescou than *haute cuisine,* but excellent, and he ate two large portions and limited himself to a single glass of wine feeling content and sleepy.

He was rising from the table when Vino, who had served him, came in and said, 'We've got to settle something.'

He sat down again. 'Of course.'

'We've been talking, Sandy and Fanny and Rollins and me. And I drove into Miami Beach this morning and talked to Bramms. We all feel it's better to try the third gala. Bramms says he can rush the boat fitters and get the LC on time. He's going to South Carolina this week for the rockets and stuff. We're all agreed. Better a smaller take than no take at all.'

'Why didn't you talk to *me*?' Bucky asked mildly. 'Why line up support as if dealing with an enemy?'

'You've been keeping things to *your*self, haven't you? We don't even know the plan...'

'Call the others in, please.'

'We still feel...'

'Call them in,' he said, and reached for the bottle.

He filled, drained and refilled the glass, his good intentions once again disappearing under stress. And it was stress, not thieves falling out, that was causing trouble in his group. The stress of Beaufort and the President's visit.

He added one more area of stress a moment after they all had entered. Sandy came to the table, pulled out the chair beside his and plumped herself down as if daring him to say anything.

He spoke to Vino. 'Not worried about bad habits any more, Vino?'

Vino said, 'It works both ways. What about your bad habits with *us*?'

Sandy lit a cigarette. Bucky wanted to go ahead, to ignore the girl sitting there. After all, what did it mean? They would be parting in a few weeks, and after that, he would meet only Vino, and him only twice for the payoffs.

And still he didn't speak. He had to be in charge. If he wasn't there was no telling what would happen, what sudden changes they might initiate on their own the night of the robbery. It was the same in business; there could be only one chairman of the board.

The silence stretched out. He sipped wine and lit a cigarette.

Rollins finally said, 'Sandy.'

She looked at him, mock wide-eyed, a burlesque innocent act.

'Get up.'

'Who are *you*...?'

'He's right,' Fanny said. 'Stand with us. It is the way we started and the way we will finish. It has nothing to do with what I always say. Not this. It has to do with keeping things ... orderly.'

Sandy shrugged. 'I don't agree and I get a full vote in this operation. Vino don't agree either, do you, baby?'

Vino said, 'Listen, Prince, let's get on with it.'

Bucky looked at him and said nothing. Vino's face reddened. Rollins moved swiftly; he came to the table, took Sandy's arm and, as she squealed in outrage, yanked her out of the chair and back across the room with him. Vino said, 'Let her go!'

Rollins said, mildly, 'Sure,' and he did.

'Don't you ... don't ever touch her again!'

'Not unless she asks,' Rollins said. 'And you know how she likes to ask.'

Vino stepped up to him and threw a quick punch; but not quick enough. It landed on Rollins's upraised forearm. Rollins said, 'You're right, Vino. I shouldn't have said that.' But he didn't back away; and suddenly he wasn't just a big kid but the biggest man in the room. His thick arms, his wide shoulders, his strong stance, all clearly foretold what would happen if the slighter, smaller man persisted in throwing punches.

Vino glared a moment longer, then nodded and cleared his throat. 'Okay. If you're sorry, okay.'

Rollins looked at Sandy. 'Sorry,' he said, his voice level, unemotional.

Sandy glared at Vino and began to leave the room.

'You'll have to hear this,' Bucky said, 'if you're going to be part of it.'

She kept going. Vino said, 'C'mon, honey.'

'*Honey,*' she said. 'First making me date that pig Byuferd, and now this.' But she stopped near the door.

Bucky said, 'In twenty-four days, we reach the final gala. That's exactly how long we have to tolerate each other. Not a day longer.'

'Only we're not waiting *that* long,' Vino said. 'We're going for the third gala on March first.'

Bucky looked at Rollins. 'You certain that's what you want?'

'Only if the last one's impossible, like Vino says.'

'And it is! The President ...'

'And you, Fanny?'

'What Rollins said.'

'And you, Sandy?'

'I just want to get it over with!' She was near tears.

Bucky was back to Vino. The man was tight lipped and his forehead glistened with an oily film. 'I thought we decided this

157

once before, Vino?'

'That was with Byuferd. The President is too big a risk. Too much security. I read once he has about fifteen agents when he travels. And if he's near a coastline, like here, a Coast Guard boat too. If we wait, we'll lose our chance at *any* gala!'

'What you say about the President's security may be true. I don't know the exact number of his men and the various kinds of protection, but it's bound to be considerable. *While he's here.*' He paused to let that sink in. 'The moment he's *not* here, neither are the Secret Service or anything else. They leave with the President. And from what I learned last night, it's far from certain that he'll stay for the gala. As it stands now, he's going to arrive on the thirteenth and leave on the fifteenth. *When* on the fifteenth, no one knows. It's my opinion that he'll leave during the afternoon.'

'His friends said that?' Rollins asked.

'It was the general trend of the conversation.' Before anyone could dig into his ambiguity, he added, 'And even if he *does* attend, he's known as an in-and-outer, early to arrive and quick to depart. A few hours is his limit, generally.'

'Generally, yeah,' Vino said, 'but what if *this* time he stays until the end?'

'He won't. He'll leave no later than ten, ten thirty, and fly right back to Washington.'

'Your crystal ball tell you that?' Vino said, not bothering to hide what now seemed a full-fledged mistrust.

'No, my experience with Presidents. I've attended parties with them before. There's a certain blueprint for their appearances and disappearances. They can't stay around all night, drinking with the boys and flirting with the girls, now can they? They can't get soused. They can't dance too often with a pretty woman. All they can do is put in an appearance and leave. Only at the Inaugural Ball ...'

'All right. So we don't know anything about Presidents' balling habits. So you do.' There was a degree of contempt in his voice, working class contempt of the upper class.

'That's the point of it all, isn't it, Vino? What I know about Presidents and millionaires and this island! If not for that, you wouldn't need me, would you? You and everyone else who wanted a few million would be rifling this treasure house at will.'

When no answer was forthcoming, he began speaking

158

slowly, deliberately.

'This is the way it will go on Saturday, March fifteenth. We'll make changes to suit the President's schedule but I expect all changes will be for the better.

'Rollins will take a cab into Miami Beach at eight A.M. and meet Bramms at a prearranged spot, say the corner of Collins and Lincoln. They'll drive in Bramms's car to that town near Delray...' He paused.

'Berrywood,' Vino offered, and glanced at Rollins, who looked unhappy. Vino said, 'Could we get someone else to drive Bramms?'

'Not without considerable trouble. Besides,' looking at Rollins, 'you'll only be together the hour or so of the trip to Berrywood.'

Rollins shrugged. 'I didn't say anything.' He still looked unhappy.

'Vino,' Bucky continued, 'will have his afternoon's work cut out for him. You're to get the Thorazine and the guns ... and I hope everything is proceeding smoothly?'

'If you mean the whole picture...' Vino muttered.

'I mean the Thorazine and the guns,' Bucky said, voice cold.

They locked eyes. Fanny said, 'Vino, please, let us at least hear him out.'

Vino looked away. 'The order's in. No problem about the knockout drug; it's more or less legal. The guns will be ready on time. It's costing us three hundred each for five stolen pieces.' He returned his eyes to Bucky. 'You don't carry one, right? Eight hundred for Bramms's submachine gun, which I'll get two days earlier. All with ammo. My contact can't say *what* guns we'll get, only that they'll be good and no one'll be able to trace them to us.'

'Fine. They're only to be used as threats anyway, with the exception of Bramms's little off-shore display. Now, after delivering Bramms to the Berrywood shipyard, Rollins will return to Miami and drive onto the General Causeway. A hundred feet past the road to Bay Island, you'll develop engine trouble, pull over to the side and leave the car on the shoulder. You'll walk back to the entrance road, then to the bridge, then to the house. If the guard asks any questions, you were given a ride to the road and are simply walking home.' He glanced at Vino. 'Do you see why it's impractical to send someone else in Rollins's place? You'll be getting the drug and guns. And having Sandy or Fanny walk all that distance...'

Vino and Rollins both nodded.

'One thing, Buddy-boy. You must remember to lock Bramms's car so no one can enter it or move it. Not that the highway patrol will bother it unless it's obviously been abandoned. But we can't take chances. It has to be there when he swims back from the island. He has another key ... But that's getting ahead of myself.

'What I'll describe now will be subject to change, in case there *is* a Coast Guard cutter off shore and Secret Service agents on shore. But the change will simply be one of *time* ... we'll just postpone everything and Bramms won't show himself with his LC near the island until it's safe to do so. It complicates matters, I know, but I'll have an alternative plan for Bramms and his diversionary tactic.

'Bramms will take possession of the LC and pilot it down the coast from Delray to Miami Beach, and through the Bakers Haulover Cut which leads to Biscayne Bay. He'll proceed slowly, so as to reach the bay about an hour before sundown. Then he'll maneuver around off Bay Island, until the security men on the bridge and along the shore are sure to have noticed him. But he won't get too close, so they won't have any reason to bother him. Nor will they know—and this won't occur to them until later—whether more men are hidden aboard, since there'll be a tarpaulin covering most of the LC's interior.

'By the way, he'll have heavy armaments—actually fireworks changed by a dealer in South Carolina into approximations of anti-personnel rockets. They won't be able to do too much damage, but the security men won't know that. He'll have brought them aboard in Berrywood, along with his submachine gun, in two or three large suitcases.

'At sundown, he'll be off the south shore, between here and the causeway, and he'll begin coming in closer, on a line with this house. He won't use any running lights, and the guards are certain to be bothered by that. But not until he gets the signal that the robbery is to commence, will he make his move.'

'And if the President...?' Fanny began.

'The signal will be given when I phone Vino that the time is right. That means when the President has left. And I'll give him half an hour or more to get off the island.'

'If he *gets* off the island,' Vino muttered.

160

'We're back to that never-ending series of suppositions,' Bucky said; and went on: 'By this time, Fanny, Sandy, Rollins and I will be at the party. I'll go first, in the Porsche. Rollins will drive Sandy and Fanny in the Caddy. Vino will keep the Mercedes and will be waiting at the house for my call. By the way, you're all to go to Miami and buy costumes. I suggest the following. Ski togs with winter face mask. Knight's armor—cloth made to look like mail, for example—and a light metal helmet. A clown's outfit with pull-over make up mask. A glamorized burglar's outfit, with tights, striped shirt and nylon stocking mask.'

Fanny chuckled. 'That would be going as ourselves.'

'Well, you get the idea. Bramms won't need a costume. He'll be wearing a skin diver's wet suit and will slip a Navy face mask on under his view mask when Vino picks him up.'

'How do I know where to find him?' Vino asked.

'Let me go step by step. You'll all have invitations to the gala. Each resident is getting ten tickets for family and guests. That means there will be more than a hundred people present, not counting the club staff. We can lose ourselves very nicely in that crowd. As I said, Fanny, Sandy, Rollins and I will be at the party and Vino will be waiting at the house. At eleven thirty or thereabouts—certainly well before the one A.M. unmasking...'

'Don't they unmask at midnight?' Sandy asked. 'That's the way it always is in the movies.'

'This party starts at eight, technically, but it won't get going until about ten, and it'll hit its stride between eleven and twelve. So they have the unmasking at one, sometimes even later, in order to milk the mystery element properly. If Lacton puts in an appearance, he should stay an hour, two at the most. It depends on *when* he arrives, of course. By past performance, that should be about nine. Any later...' He shrugged. 'We would have to play it by ear.'

'My God,' Fanny murmured, 'what a tune that will be! A funeral march if he comes at *ten*, or *eleven*!'

'Not likely, and even so, we'd probably be able to make it. But again, there's no point talking about unpredictables.'

This time he didn't push ahead but waited, feeling he had to see what resistance remained and where it was located.

No one spoke. All looked anxious to hear the rest; even Sandy, whose sullen, angry look had been replaced by a childishly intent, tell-me-a-story expression, right down to the parted lips.

He'd felt it all along—the robbery itself was the solution to all his problems. Let the action commence and what had seemed insurmountable would dissolve into nothing! After the fifteenth, Vino, Sandy, the others, all would be gone and he would have *real* servants and a *real* life. Beth, Ceecee, most of the other residents would also be gone, the season ending with the costume gala, and he would have time to take his trips, dispose of the loot and begin rebuilding the Prince fortune.

He leaned forward. 'Now it gets a little more complicated. I'll phone Vino from the club and tell him to signal Bramms. The signal will be a shot from my flare gun. When Bramms sees it, he'll throw on his spotlight. This will catch the attention of the bridge guard, as well as the other guards on the south shore, and they'll hail him and give him orders, probably to come in under their guns for inspection. They'll also call for the security speedboat, which is usually at the marina after dark. Bramms will be moving toward shore, and he'll cut his light. This will bring them all on the run, from Beaufort on down. Bramms will pull back from shore, but they won't know it. He'll shout, give orders, turn on a tape recording of men's voices, and the guards will think they're being invaded by a gang of seaborne thieves. When they open up with their guns and their speedboat approaches, Bramms will pull a special scuttling plug and go over the side ... but not before he puts a dozen or more holes into the security boat, at and under the water line. The speedboat will have to go into shore, if it makes it. The LC should sink in five to ten minutes, certainly before anyone can get another boat out there and find it. By then, Bramms will have swum to shore, to the wooded area between houses Two and Three. There Vino will be waiting.

'You'll pull the Mercedes off the road, Vino, in among the trees. You and Bramms have to find each other as best you can, without aid of lights or raised voices. The guards will be farther east, near here in fact, but they won't stay in one place long. They'll begin by covering the entire island coast, but about the time we're ready to use the coast, they should be going inland.

'Vino will have a bath towel and extra gun in the Mercedes. Bramms will dry and arm himself and, still wearing his skin diving outfit, go with Vino to the club. There won't be any

162

problem with the guard at the door. You'll have two of the invitations assigned to me, as will Fanny and Sandy. Later, I'll say you obviously took them from my desk ...'

'You sure there'll only be that *one* guard at the door?' Vino asked.

'There's never been more than one guard at a gala. There's no reason for more than one guard. In fact, there's no real reason for him, except as a ticket-taker, this being the tightly closed community it is.'

'But if the President ...'

'Let's not go back to that. Let's go ahead. When I finish, you'll give me your decision.'

Rollins said, 'We're all in the club now and the President's long gone and the security guards are running around the shore, looking for invaders.'

'Yes. That's when we—I mean you four and Bramms—pull your weapons, bring in the door guard, tear out the phones, line the men up on one side of the room and the women near the bar. You'll choose several men, I'll be among them, to strip the women of their jewelry.'

'Bet you're the best,' Vino said, smiling for the first time. He seemed to be gradually accepting the plan.

Bucky nodded. 'But see to it that the others are also good at it. Don't get too near anyone, keeping clear of trouble that way, but make certain no woman is left with any piece of jewelry. And *don't* bother with the men.'

'You mean we don't go for their wallets?' Vino asked, incredulously. 'Most of them must carry a grand or two, and wear good rings and jeweled watches.'

'Yes, there might be as much as a hundred thousand among them. But we haven't time for such small pickings. We'll get the jewelry, choose three hostages—again, myself among them —and leave. Sandy and Bramms will take the hostages to the Caddy, and drive back here.'

'What if we run into a security guard?' Sandy asked.

'There's small chance of that, since they should be concentrating on the coast, probably the other side by that time. But if we do, we might have to take him prisoner and keep him with the hostages.'

'Or plug him,' Vino said.

'No. Gunfire could bring the whole security force down on our heads.'

'Not if it's from a silenced gun. I asked for silencers. My contact promised all he could get.'

Bucky shook his head. 'No point in killing. Remember that I'll be one of the hostages. I'll be able to identify myself and say something, whatever best suits the situation. Perhaps that we're going to my place to continue the party, or taking our guests on a drive around the island. Something, anything, and if the guard is still suspicious, then I'll help you take him prisoner.'

'That would blow your cover,' Rollins said quietly. 'You can't do that, Mr. Prince. Without you, there's no payoff.'

'I'm not saying we'll go around massacring people,' Vino said, 'but there just might have to be some shooting. You've got everything down pretty pat, but you're dodging one thing. This is a heist, not a society game. I've never killed anyone yet, but I've put bullets into two.'

'I once had to sap a woman,' Rollins said. 'She was screaming. Then I prayed she wouldn't die.'

'And did she?' Fanny asked.

'I don't think so. I left town...'

'Remember when I hit that watchman, Vino?' It was Sandy, face alight with remembered excitement. 'We went to a warehouse, a nothing job, but this watchman showed up sooner than he was supposed to. So Vino put up his hands and I came out behind the old pig and *bam*! I hit him with a flashlight as big as my arm. Then *I* did some praying!'

Vino grinned. 'He was up and chasing us in about a minute and a half, but I'd taken his gun.'

Fanny said, 'My Armand once shot a fool who came upon us at a bad moment. The fool lived, but barely. If we had been caught for *that* night's work, it would have meant twenty years each.' She muttered a quick Hail Mary.

Bucky nodded, trying not to show his feelings. Vino was right. He *did* refuse to consider violence. And their open exchange of bloody reminiscences shocked him. He'd known they were professional thieves, but somehow...

'If anyone gets killed,' Vino said, 'you've got to remember it isn't because we want it. You've got to be ready to go on and finish the job. Just like you're describing every little part of the plan so we should know how it's going to be, so we can be prepared for it, I'm telling you that there might be a stiff or two before the night's over, and *you've* got to be prepared for it.'

Again Bucky nodded, but he refused to admit anyone might be killed. Hurt, perhaps, to the extent of a bruise or two, but not killed. If he admitted *that* possibility to himself, he wouldn't be able to go through with the robbery.

'Sandy, you and Bramms get the hostages onto my boat and below decks. Take them down to the cabin and tie, gag and blindfold them. Say things to indicate that the third hostage is being forced to accompany the rest of the gang ... and that's just where I'll be, with Vino, Rollins and Fanny. Then while Bramms gets ready to leave, you'll inject them with a massive dose of tranquilizer. They'll be unconscious in ten of fifteen minutes, and stay unconscious six or seven hours. That'll keep them until after sunrise.'

'Inject,' Sandy muttered. 'Gee, I've never ...'

'I'll instruct you,' Bucky said. 'Bramms will swim back to the causeway, climb the slope to his car and drive away. It's very important that he accomplish this, because he'll be carrying all the jewelry from the club.'

Vino's expression changed, grew worried. 'That's quite a swim, maybe with guards on the bridge watching and another boat around.'

'No one will see him, because he'll be using scuba equipment—self contained, underwater, breathing apparatus. He'll come to the island from the barge as a skin diver, using a snorkel. But for the trip back, longer and more dangerous, he'll use a tank of air and a mouthpiece connection that will be waiting on the *Spray*. He'll be deep underwater and quite safe from detection. He *did* say he was an experienced skin and scuba diver.'

'Yeah,' Vino muttered. 'But that's still quite a swim.'

'Not for even a moderately skilled diver.'

'How will he carry the jewelry?' Fanny asked.

'A collection bag attached to his belt instead of the lead weights which he'd otherwise need. But those are details that I'll discuss with Bramms. Minor details.' He paused to gather his thoughts. 'While Sandy guards the hostages, I'll be with the others, entering two or three homes. Just *what* homes will depend on what I learn between now and March fifteenth.'

Rollins said, 'Won't people—I mean servants—in those houses recognize you, or at least be able to describe your costume so you'll be identified as one of the group?'

'Yes, and that almost stopped me from going along. But I felt it was counterbalanced by *need*. I can get the doors to open for us, quickly and without violence. Once inside, Vino can keep a gun on me, threaten me with death if I don't cooperate, and so on. Afterward, we'll return here with another collection of jewelry and other valuables. This constitutes the second, smaller haul, and since Bramms will already have left the island, we'll have to bury it, wrapped in plastic, in a spot where freshly turned earth won't be noticed.'

Rollins said, 'Near the rosebushes. You could bury an elephant near that double row of bushes and no one would know.'

'Then that's where it goes, to await my European vacation.'

'All this time I'm watching those hostages?' Sandy asked. 'What if someone comes along?'

'You'll be below decks. No one is likely to bother you.'

'And if they do,' Vino said, 'you'll have your gun. You can always give another injection to a snooper.'

She sighed and nodded.

Fanny said, 'I have a confession, and a favor to ask. I ... am not as young as I would like to be. The robbery at the club will be difficult, yes, but I am not worried about that. Later, however, going to two or three houses...' She shook her head. 'I do not think I want to test my strength *that* far.' She turned to Sandy. 'But if I could change jobs with you; if I could watch the hostages...' She spread her hands, a helpless and apologetic gesture. 'One thing—I am expert at giving injections. My father was a diabetic.'

Sandy glanced at Bucky. Bucky said, 'It makes no difference to the plan. I thought Fanny would be more experienced at house burglary, but then again she can put that experience to use in case anyone comes to the dock.'

'They would not leave to cause trouble,' Fanny said. 'That I can assure you.'

'It's okay with me,' Sandy said. She wet her lips. 'Boy, knocking over a club and then two, three houses! What a night's work!'

'And what a payoff!' Vino said, his reservations seemingly forgotten. 'How much, Prince? How much do you guess at now that you've been here a month?'

'Ten, twelve, fifteen million, give or take three or four million.'

'*Mon Dieu!*'

'In English,' Rollins said, grinning, 'that's Jesus H. Christ.'

'Don't blaspheme,' Fanny murmured, shaking her head at him. 'We will need God, all of us, that night.'

Rollins nodded, still grinning. 'I'll say a prayer, Fanny, honest.' He turned to Bucky. 'We'll need a couple of *thousand* prayers for the getaway, won't we, Mr. Prince?'

Bucky smiled a little. 'Not quite that many. After we bury the second collection of valuables, we all get on the *Spray* with the two hostages and sail to Vizcaya. It will be deserted, except for a watchman ... and that's where we have to do a little more research. I want Vino or Rollins to get lost there one day at closing time and see just how long it takes before the watchman finds you. I'll land you on the mainland near the back entrance to the mansion, and you'll make your way out through the front, where we'll have a rented car waiting.'

Vino said, 'What happens to those hostages after we leave? And what about *you*?'

'I'll maneuver the boat away from the mainland to a little docking area on a stone breakwater, tie up, inject myself with the Thorazine, and after getting rid of the hostages' gags and blindfolds, lie down next to them for a good night's sleep.'

He was suddenly very tired, and discouraged. A momentary depression, he was sure, but it was a strange turnabout— now that it was all set, the others were enthusiastic and he was full of doubt. 'When I speak to Bramms next week, I'll tell him where he's to leave the jewelry. Something simple, like a rental storage locker, should do. He'll send me the key and I'll collect the jewelry when I feel it's safe.' He poured another glass of wine and tossed it down.

Sandy said, 'We have to trust you an awful lot, don't we?'

'Not really. You could destroy me at any time. Actually, I have to trust *you* much more than you have to trust me. Because you disappear, go underground, while I stay out in the open, vulnerable to all sorts of pressures.' He watched her. Her eyes fell.

Vino said, 'I knew that from point one. That's why I never worried about our money.'

Rollins said, 'We shouldn't even talk about such things. It makes trouble.'

Fanny said, 'We are comrades in arms.'

Bucky nodded, wanting another drink ... and stronger than wine. 'Yes, comrades in arms. Or else comrades in disaster.'

'And Bramms?' Rollins murmured. 'I have to say this, Mr. Prince. He's not like the rest of us. We have our faults, sure ... but he's something else again.'

Bucky said, 'He seemed all right to me,' and looked at Vino. Vino spoke with his old assurance. 'I vouch for Bramms. He's a nut, yeah, but who else would do the job he's doing? And he's got pride by the ton. He'll want to do better than all of us.'

'And afterward?' Bucky asked.

'Afterward he'll play it straight, or he won't play at all. I hired him and I'll take care of him.'

'Then that's it. Unless there are questions.'

'About the hostages,' Rollins said. 'Shouldn't we try and pick two in advance? I mean, people with important family?'

'Everyone here has important family,' Vino said.

'I think we should take women,' Rollins said. 'First, they're easier to handle. I mean, purely on the muscle. Second, it's a thing with Americans, isn't it, Mr. Prince, that they're more worried about a wife or daughter than a husband or son? There's at least an *edge* there, right? Women and children first, that kind of thing?'

'I'll give it some thought,' Bucky said, because he couldn't right now. Couldn't think at all any more.

He stood up. They looked at him and at each other. Then Vino said, 'All right, March fifteenth. For the big haul. And to hell with worrying about it!'

When they were gone, Bucky went to the study, thinking to read, to listen to Bach, to relax and say to hell with worrying too. But there was a decanter of brandy and two glasses on a tray and he didn't have to ring for anyone and reveal just how badly he needed a drink, just how worried he was. He had a large one and a larger one. They didn't help and he sat at the desk and was as weary in mind as he had been in body after the trip to Vizcaya.

He got up and went out onto the terrace. It was still chill and damp, but patches of sky had cleared and the stars were beginning to show. Stars to steer by. Stars to make one's way across open sea by. The old-time sailor had used the sky, the stars ...

But sailors, ships, business, women—all the good things of

168

life—seemed far away from Bucky Prince tonight; very far away.

He took the decanter upstairs with him, walking softly so that no one would hear. And for the first time since Chicago, he drank himself to sleep.

Fanny went to her room. The others were in the kitchen, having drinks and talking about the plan. It was a good plan, they felt. She agreed. It was a perfect plan, for *her*, since she had managed to find her perfect place in it.

She felt like calling Toronto, but didn't. Someone might interrupt. Someone might overhear. So instead of telling Armand about her good fortune, she told God.

On her knees, she whispered, 'Thank You for helping me. I will be at the boat, alone except for the *fou*, and there will be time to dispense justice. But You must help me a little more, in my telephone call, in my bringing them together. After that, I will light candles for a month. After that, I will thank You every day of my life.' She began to get up then said, 'I know there are things you will not do, Holy Mother, but if you could see to it that Armand does not suffer too much...'

SATURDAY, FEBRUARY 22

The Greshen colors were deep blue and pale gold. The footmen, only two now, still wore them. They sat in front, beside the chauffeur, jackets gold and breeches satiny-blue, two young men who, she knew, were far from happy with this area of their duties. They sat stiffly, their necks red.

Willa Dorcas Greshen sat behind them, on the other side of the glass panel in back of the Rolls-Royce, not one of those new, undistinguished automobiles made for anyone with twenty or thirty thousand dollars, but a 1936 custom limousine, as luxurious a vehicle as had ever been manufactured. It had been made to Trent's own specifications, the only change from the original being air conditioning, which had been installed after the war. So she was certainly comfortable ... but she was far from at ease. She didn't enjoy going off the island.

Still, she had to shop for the final gala. She had to get a costume; a new Marie Antoinette gown and high white wig and soft white mask. And accessories. Her old gown displeased her, seemed not only to be yellowing but was much too large. (Had she really lost *that* much weight?)

She was on her way to Palm Beach, her first off-island excursion in more than a year. She had heard that there was a fine costumer among the boutiques on the Via Mizener, and had assured herself she would enjoy the experience and afterward might visit the Bath and Tennis Club. She hadn't been to the Club since ... since when? That time Dr. Kayle (and he was dead now, dead, as all her contemporaries were) had talked to Willis and Lambert Miller about making her go out and 'partake of life' and at that time (why couldn't she remember whether it was two years or three or five?) she had still listened to friends, still *had* friends, and allowed herself to be convinced. They had driven her to Palm Beach and the Club, where she and Trent had once spent pleasant days on outings from Bay Island. She had lunched there ...

She began to remember, *really* remember that day, and was stricken. She had lunched at a table under an umbrella while people, not all young but all younger than she was, played and swam and laughed and drank, and stared at her as if she were already beyond noticing or caring; and she had known it was a mistake ever to leave her island home ...

She became aware of a car to her right, holding its speed equal to the Rolls-Royce's, a gaudy red station wagon full of children, all looking, pointing and laughing. Her suit of pale blue linen and wide sunshade hat suddenly were suspect; they and the Rolls itself. But it was the footmen who were the main cause of amusement; now their necks were almost purple.

Deliberately, she stared at the driver of the station wagon, and eventually he glanced her way. Her look told him what she thought of his manners. Her look caused him to increase speed and pull away. One of the children in back waved; a very little boy with a chocolate smeared face, far too young to mock what was strange since all the world was strange at his age. A smile flickered at the corners of Willa Greshen's thin lips; her hand twitched, beginning to rise. But the station wagon was gone, the child was gone and she closed her eyes and rested, conserving her strength for the time when she would leave the car and go into the costumer's.

The section of Via Mizener where the shop was located was closed to automobiles and Carl, the chauffeur, said she would have to walk several streets. She sat quite still as the footmen, faces frozen but flushed, their livery brilliant in the glare of sunshine, stepped out, one to open the door and the other to help her to the pavement. People stopped and watched, smiled and murmured, even here in what had been the stronghold of the nation's best families. Even here . . . and what must the rest of this nation be like now that footmen were laughed at and Willa Dorcas Greshen was a curiosity, a museum piece, in Palm Beach?

'That won't be necessary,' she said, wincing at the blast of heated air from the open door. 'We'll go back.'

They were inexperienced, these footmen. She'd had to hire half a dozen in the last few years, since none stayed long. These two had only a few months of service. They exchanged a glance.

They drove home. Long before Bay Island, she had need of a bathroom. But it was impossible to think of stopping at any of those restaurants or service stations and using a public toilet, with people staring . . .

She felt frightened. She had never been frightened before, of anything—distressed, yes; despairing, yes; but never frightened —and now she was frightened of everything, of the *world*. She sat trembling, biting her lip with the shameful need to empty her bladder, waiting for the island to appear.

It finally did. She finally entered sanctuary.

Later, she had Mildred telephone the costumer's and, after much conversation, a home fitting was arranged, which was what she should have done in the first place. Then she sent for Bellet and instructed him to discharge the footmen. When the butler asked if he should hire replacements, she said, 'No,' sitting at her window and looking out at the garden. 'One doesn't seem to need footmen any more.'

She had iced tea and slowly, slowly the fear drained away and her inner trembling lessened. She told herself she had been very foolish. But even so, it was difficult to think of the final gala now. There would be so many guests, strangers, and they too might see her as a curiosity, a museum piece.

And still, she wanted to accompany that handsome Prince boy. She wanted to wear her Light of Stars and know people were admiring her again . . .

171

Life!

She was standing, hands clenched.

She wanted some portion of life! She wanted something other than this sitting, this waiting!

She was breathing heavily, a pulse hammering in her throat. Not wise to react so violently. Dangerous, in fact.

She sat down, sipped tea and looked out the window at the garden. She quieted, and after a while nodded and dozed.

Bucky busied himself on the *Spray*, belaying lines and checking the deck where Rollins had sanded and varnished. Soon, it would be necessary to haul...

But his thoughts weren't really on the boat, and he jumped to the dock. Shading his eyes, he looked toward the woods between houses One and Two where, briefly, Bay Drive showed. Ceecee was late for their sailing date. He had called the Mortonson house and a servant had informed him that 'Miss Mortonson left; dressed for yachting, I believe.' That was almost an hour ago, and still no Ceecee.

He went aboard again and down to the cabin—compact, utilitarian, sleeping four, with fiberglass icebox, stainless steel, two-burner alcohol stove, sink, and everything else he would need if he ever decided to sail off for two or three or ten days, he and a companion.

He realized where *those* thoughts were heading and went up on deck to check the auxiliary engine. Rollins had run it for several hours during the week to charge up the battery, which in turn powered the running lights. Not that Walt planned any night sailing, at least not before March fifteenth, and then he would use no lights. But everything had to be kept shipshape.

He went aft and examined the wheel, a rare feature on a sloop this size. It had added considerably to the cost of the twenty-nine footer, but for sailing alone it was almost a necessity, certainly an enormous advantage...

Where the devil was she!

He was examining the mast when he heard an engine, its sound growing rapidly as he turned to the bay. A speedboat was coming from the east, prow high, skipping over the swells, just now passing under the island bridge. A male in white ducks, bare above the waist, was at the wheel. A female lounged in the wide padded seat behind him, also wearing white...

No, the white was in a pile beside her. As the craft came closer, he saw the flash of orangey-red—a bikini.

He shaded his eyes. The boat cut in toward him. The girl—it was Ceecee Mortonson—raised her arm and waved. Mechanically, he waved back. The boat, a small cabin cruiser, came closer, its prow dropping as its speed dropped, its raucous sound also dropping so that the male's shouted message could be heard.

'Ceecee says ... forgot date ... sorry ...'

The speedboat was quite close now, not more than ten yards off, and he could see her smile, her languid mocking smile, and the boy's smile—not the Secret Service man as he'd first thought but that boy she'd danced with, pale blond and broad shouldered—Jock Waters, smiling as he and Ceecee shared the joke of standing him up.

He dropped his arm and turned his back. He heard her laughter, her voice, just before the engine accelerated, its roar an ugliness, its smell an abomination, her laughter a razor slicing at his suddenly raw nerves.

'... yo, ho, *blow* the man down ...'

He remembered, against his will, what she had said to him in the club after their game of tennis, her answer to his invitation to sail today:

'If I want to screw the Secret Service, no. If I want to blow Jock Waters, no ...'

The engine's roar faded into a petulant buzzing and then nothing at all. He told himself, *Good riddance!* Now he was through with her; his responsibility discharged.

He decided more tennis was just what he needed, violent exercise. And after dinner, a tour of the Miami Beach clubs. A little free-wheeling ...

But he still seemed to hear that high, mocking voice: '... yo, ho, *blow* the man down.'

The obscene little bitch!

'*You* called *me*,' Jock pointed out as she looked at him askance. They were moored off the dock of his parents' home. It was dark. They sat on the boat's couchlike seat, smoking. He had just, for the first time in their long day of cruising, swimming, eating, drinking and smoking pot, made a strong pass. His hand was pressing her pubic bulge; not pushing between her legs but merely pressing from the outside. Her bikini was

173

still wet from their last swim and she said, 'I know, Jock, but I want to change, I'm cold, my suit's wet.'

'Go ahead and change.' He dragged deeply on his stick. He'd told her he had roughly five hundred, all rolled beautifully, like the custom blends his parents smoked. 'Change right here. I'll close my eyes. Well, one anyway.' He didn't take his hand away. He pressed gently and a response, a slight warmth, made her move a little and smile a little. At that, he pressed harder and his other arm drew her close and his lips pressed her cheek and nose and finally her lips.

'All right,' she said. 'I'll change ... if you'll give me a hundred sticks.'

His fingers began to move, and soon she wouldn't be able to make bargains. She put her hand on the bulge in his trousers. He said, 'Ceecee, baby...' sighing and arching his pelvis upward.

'A hundred sticks.' She opened him up and took out a real wonder of a penis. This was a *big* boy! She said so, and he was pleased enough to remove his hand from her and look down at himself, grinning and sighing. 'You think so? Really big?'

She took the opportunity to cross her legs, at the same time stroking him. It was nice. She enjoyed feeling the heated, gristly flesh. Huge, like her old hangup ...

He was suddenly trying to free himself, gasping, 'No, please ... Ceecee...'

He wasn't circumcised, which made things easier. She continued hooding and unhooding his thick glans, following as he tried to shift away. Then he was sinking back, his expression a mixture of shame and ecstasy. She bent to his panting mouth and gave him a deep kiss, feeling the bellows rush of breath. 'I know,' she murmured. 'You wanted it all day. Don't fight, Jock. Let go. Let *go*.' She stroked harder, faster.

He had an impressive orgasm. Afterward, she rose and said, 'When do I get my hundred sticks?'

'You'd kill yourself with a hundred,' he muttered, using a handkerchief on his white ducks.

She glanced down the dock toward the house. Still no lights. Everyone out and the servants at the boob tube. She removed her bikini top and said, 'Hey, man, you want to do business?'

He looked up and grew still.

'You will, you know, in about ten or fifteen minutes, big strong boy like you.' She smiled, feeling a little bitchy and a

174

litfle randy and, most of all, wanting those sticks. It was going to be a long, hard time before March sixteenth and leaving this island and trying to forget. It would take some doing, but she had done fine today, for starters. Bucky should be beginning to hate her. She would find a clincher soon, and then she could be *certain* he would never try to see her again . . . and could begin to hate him in return.

She took off her bottoms and sat down beside him, stretching her long legs out in the moonlight and smiling and murmuring, 'It's a kick, feeling the air all over. Try it.'

He nodded, and soon they were sitting side by side, not touching, naked, and looking at each other. They smoked. He finished his stick and put his arm around her, cupping a breast, and bent to find the nipple with his mouth. She allowed him a moment, then stood up.

'Is it a deal?'

He was grinning that foolish high grin and touching himself. 'C'mon, Ceecee, you don't want to be a whore for a little shit, do you?'

They laughed giddily together, but she nodded. 'A hundred sticks, Jock, or good night.'

He hesitated. She understood. A hundred sticks was *something*. Not just money but what money couldn't always buy. She suddenly bent and planted a big, open-mouthed kiss on the head of his penis. He said, 'Christ, yes, let's go!'

She sat down beside him, melting against him, smiling with desire, murmuring, 'Word of honor, Jock? A hundred?' Her hand closed over the dream penis, her lips came up to his. 'Say it.'

'Hundred sticks, word of honor.'

And away they went, really rocking the boat.

It should have been great. It was, for him. At nineteen, he had plenty of spunk. He went three times to her one, and her one came close to his third and wasn't what she would classify as anything to remember.

He took her home in his Jag convertible. She sat slumped back, eyes closed, holding the cedar-wood box with the hundred marijuana cigarettes.

Well, so much for the big prick hangup and the dream of super sex with super man. She'd heard girls say the size didn't matter, but she hadn't believed them. She did now. Jock had been educational. Jock had done her a good turn. He'd have to

175

live a long time and do a lot of practicing and, she felt, he still would never be the lover Walter Prince was.

She patted Jock's fly and he jumped a little, the car swerving. She said, 'If anyone deserves the vote, Jock, you do.'

He found that very funny.

He also wanted to make a date for tomorrow, or Monday, or any day she was free. She said she would let him know. Tomorrow was the Secret Service again. She wondered if she would give him more than the kiss she'd given him after their lunch and evening of movies—three of them—in Miami Beach. He was nice, bright and cleancut and she had nothing against the fuzz and she had nothing against Jock and nothing against any well hung young male on God's earth.

She sighed, walking to the front door.

Nothing against them and nothing for them. Nothing, period, was what it added up to.

It would change. Once off this island, and once settled in her plans to have the baby and once free of Bucky Prince, it would change. *But no details, Ceecee. Just ride with the tide and have your kicks and soon it will be better.*

She had another stick before bedtime, and it was better already.

Beaufort surprised her. Sandy hadn't known what to expect, but it certainly wasn't the respectful, talkative man who held doors for her on getting in and out of his car and going into the restaurant at the city of Miami end of the causeway, a well-lighted, family-style place and not one of the bar-room eateries she associated with his kind of guy. He had her completely off balance, talking about sports, movies and Bay Island, beckoning the waitress every time she wanted something.

She began to relax, forgetting her fears. She'd worked herself up into such a sweat, she'd been sick to her stomach all afternoon. Now she wanted to laugh at herself, and at the others too. He still *looked* like the toughest thing since King Kong, but wait'll she told them back at the house what a simple square he *really* was!

He asked her why she was smiling. She cut into the prime rib, finding her appetite for the first time since last night. 'Private joke, Byuferd. Girl's joke.'

He said, 'Ummm,' as if he understood, and then his eyes went past her. The manager came over and said, 'Evening,

Byuferd, miss. Everything all right?'

Beaufort said, 'Fine, Bill. No calls for me?'

The manager shook his head. 'If there was, you know we'd tell you immediately.' He chuckled. 'I guess we'd better. Wouldn't want to lose a good customer.'

When he left, Beaufort muttered, 'He'd lose more than that,' and cut into his T-bone.

Sandy ate, thinking of what she'd just heard. 'You get business calls while out on dates, Byuferd?'

'Just stay in touch with the island. In case anything happens, they have to know where to reach me. We can get back to the bridge in under ten minutes, breaking a few laws.'

'What if you're farther away?'

He shook his head.

'I don't understand,' she said.

'I'm never farther away. Fifteen minutes, tops. I've got this restaurant and I've got a few hotels at the Miami Beach end, where I go for drinks and music. No place else.'

'Ever?'

'Ever.'

She began to think of getting information. 'Seems like a waste of free time, since nothing happens on that island, from what I hear.'

'Nothing happens because I won't let it.' His eyes had risen, pale brown eyes, strangely flat. They were looking right into hers, she smiled uncomfortably and concentrated on her prime rib. 'Where you from, Sandy?'

'New York.' She had her little story all ready. 'Got tired of the winters and decided I could be a maid in Florida as well as anywhere else.'

'Sure. You always been a maid?'

'I used to be a high school student.' She laughed.

He smiled, but his eyes were still digging at her. She began to tighten up again; then told herself not to be dumb. She would talk to him and he would tell her what she wanted to know. After all, that was why she was here.

'That visit ... I mean the President ... that's going to mean a lot of extra work for you, isn't it, Byuferd?'

'No. The government boys handle that. We'll just go on with our usual security. Oh, we might concentrate a bit on Number Two, but not so you'll notice. The President isn't as important as the residents, as far as Bay Island security is concerned.' He smiled a little at the end, and she smiled too and cut another piece of rib.

'Where are all those government men going to stay? I mean, there aren't any motels ...'

'The Veners have rooms over their garage. And there's a guest house that can hold five or six. And the Yacht Club has accommodations for visiting crews.'

She stopped eating. 'So *many* men?'

He shrugged. 'Last time he came there were seventeen, all told.'

Her insides grew cold. 'Wow,' she said, and made a smile. 'Seventeen. I never thought ...'

'Waste of the taxpayers' money, if you ask me. Bay Island isn't like other places. A few bodyguards would be enough. But who can tell Republicans how to run a country, huh?'

She smiled. 'I'm a Democrat too.'

'I'd've bet on it, but I'm not.'

Her eyes blinked.

'Conservative. We're growing, y'know. Wallace isn't finished, not by a long shot. Wait'll next election.' He smiled, a hard smile, and pushed his plate away. 'Not that *he's* tough enough to straighten things out. But he's a beginning. The right man'll come along. People want law and order ... the real thing.'

She nodded. 'Those riots ... terrible.'

He looked around for the waitress, asking Sandy what she wanted for dessert. And to think she'd been worried about having him rape her! She'd probably have to kiss *him* good-night, just to—as Vino put it—keep the lines of information open. It wouldn't be *too* bad, having dinner and a few drinks with him once or twice more before the job. Not that she enjoyed looking at him. That pitted face; those strange flat eyes; and his hands, not so much big as ... thick, cruel looking.

Still, looks could be all wrong. Never judge a book by its cover, as Mom used to say. Beaufort was just another cop ... and not nearly as rough as one or two she'd known. Like the one who'd caught her and Pete on the dirt road near the old sand pit. Said he was going to take her home himself, make sure no more hanky-panky, and Pete had been glad to get out of it and drove off. So in the police car, with the radio growling, that goddam pig (real father type with belly and heavy face and half his hair gone when he took off his cap) told her

178

just what she had to do or she'd end up in juvenile court. 'Suck, little girl, suck.' And when she'd hesitated he'd cracked her face a good one. She hadn't been able to get the taste of that bastard out of her mouth for a month! Support your local police, Pop always said, and half of them working the lovers lanes and giving it to the kids, not like men but like animals, and the other half with their 'car checks' and how come it was mostly young women they checked?

'That's not a happy look,' Beaufort was saying.

She said, 'Well, not all thoughts are happy thoughts.'

'Tonight they are.'

She smiled. 'Okay, tonight they are.'

They went back across the causeway, past the Bay Island turnoff, to the Miami Beach side and the Grenoble Hotel, one of the older ones but with a real nice club and three different bands; regular, Latin and rock. Here too Beaufort talked to the man up front, the captain, and the man nodded and said, 'You'll be informed immediately, Mr. Byuferd.'

'Had to make sure,' Beaufort murmured as they followed a waiter through crowded tables in the dim, circular room. 'Don't come to this place much. Too expensive for ordinary dates.'

She glanced back at him then, smiling, and caught his eyes going over her. All of a sudden, he didn't look so gentlemanly.

When they were at their table, he surprised her again, asking if she wanted to dance. She just couldn't see Beaufort dancing. Not that he really *danced*; say like Vino who could have gone professional, he was so sweet on his feet. Beaufort just sort of rocked back and forth. But he held her close and she didn't like it—the feel of his big body, and a certain smell...

Not that he wasn't clean. A smell of tobacco, because he smoked. But then again, so did she. Another smell; his very flesh, it seemed. A slightly sour smell. Maybe his clothes?

No, it was only her mind.

But it wasn't her mind that made her feel what happened after a few minutes on the floor. He was coming up aces. She detached herself and smiled a little (but God the feeling of fear, of disgust was back!) and said, 'I'd like my drink now, Byuferd, if you don't mind.'

'Sure.' He held her arm on the way back to the table. She had a second drink, and by then the floor show began and she didn't have to dance with him any more. (Thank God!) It

179

wasn't a bad show. A good dirty comic, a magician and some singers and dancers.

Beaufort didn't laugh, didn't do much of anything, just watched with those flat, brown eyes. He checked his watch when the Emcee said, 'And so, good night, ladies and gentlemen, and don't forget, keep Miami Beach green, bring money!' The lights came up and people started leaving. 'Almost one,' he said.

'I guess you have to get back,' she said, hoping.

He nodded. 'Don't like to stay away too long. But if you want another drink...?'

'No, I'm fine.' She laughed. 'Wouldn't want to get loaded on you.'

He said, 'That would suit me fine,' and snapped his fingers for the waiter, who was at a nearby table and gave him an annoyed look. Beaufort said, 'Waiter, bring the check.'

The waiter was going to put him off, she could see it, but Beaufort kept looking at him and after a minute the waiter said something to the people at the other table and came to theirs and made up the check. When he put it down, he murmured, 'In a hurry, sir?'

Beaufort laid out money. 'Always.' His voice was like lead.

He drove over the Bay Island bridge, but not to Number One. He drove instead to his cottage. 'Uh-oh,' she said, hiding her tension with humor. 'Here come the etchings. But I really got to get back, Byuferd. Breakfast's early tomorrow because Mr. Prince...'

'This won't take long.'

She said, 'What won't?' before thinking, and then laughed and said, 'I mean, it's not right for me to go into your place. I mean, the first date and all.' It sounded stupid.

'It's not my home I want to show you. It's my office, my jail.' He got out of the car and walked around the front and opened the door for her, just as polite as could be. What the hell was she so worried about?

'You going to lock me up?' she asked, making it little girl cute. He took a good long look at her legs, which he hadn't done when she'd gotten in and out of the car before. She knew how much she showed in her minis, but she didn't own anything that was less than four inches above the knee. He said, 'Maybe. You and all the rest of Prince's crew, if you're not nice to me.'

She laughed, but he was leading her to the stone cottage and he didn't laugh with her and she couldn't see his face and wasn't sure if he was even smiling.

For a moment, panic swept over her. He knew something! He was going to spring it on her, force her to put out for him, then pull the rug from under the robbery! He had her, like that pig at the sand pits ...

But when they came into the cottage, a light was burning and she could see his face and he was smiling a little and she called herself all kinds of fool. But Christ, she just couldn't keep her balance with this man!

He showed her his office and the special phone with small switchboard of buttons which could get him any number on the island just by pressing. 'Anything happens, I'm into it right away.' He showed her the single, large cell with the double-tiered bunks. 'I can put six, seven in here, in a pinch.' She smiled for him, but the place gave her the crawlies.

Still, it was all right. He turned away from the little hallway with the door at the end, saying, 'My living quarters.' No grins and stuff about showing her the workshop or anything like that, which had led her into plenty of bedrooms in her time ... though she'd *wanted* to be led into them. Not this time though. No, thinking of that brutal pitted face pressed to hers, that body with its strange sour smell—maybe like *death*; but how could that be?—thinking of him pressing down on her ...

'I really got to go now, Byuferd. It's been a swell evening. Thank you.'

He nodded, but he was standing near his desk, looking down at some papers, and he didn't move. The fear that he knew something, had learned something about the others, leaped back into mind, and she swallowed drily and was afraid to say anything more.

Still looking down, he said, 'I got a very good job here, Sandy. Nice place to live too. If I wanted to marry ...'

Her relief was so ... *explosive*, she almost laughed. The jerk! The square stupid, jerk!

She said, 'We'll talk again, Byuferd. But now I'm late ...' She had turned as she spoke, and was stepping toward the door.

And he did it. He proved himself to be what she'd feared. He did it and right after saying what he'd said!

She almost screamed when she felt his hands, one grasping

181

her shoulder, stopping her dead, the other feeling her ass, but not just an ordinary pat or squeeze or feel. He went right into her, his thumb goosing and the rest reaching between her legs and it was so goddam fast, so goddam unexpected.

She couldn't scream. He was the fuzz on this island. She said, 'Byuferd!'

He turned her around and his hands were everywhere, but he was cool as ever. 'You're gorgeous,' he said, only his voice was different; a little higher. 'Gorgeous.' The word sounded so weird coming from him, she would have laughed if he hadn't been at her breasts and under her dress and all so cool, like he was touching her hand! He said, 'Now don't tell me you don't know what it's all about because I *know* you do, I been around and I know a girl and I know a woman and you're a woman, all woman.' She was pulled into him, and her hands pressing at his chest meant nothing because he was strong, about the strongest man she'd ever known. He had her up against him and was kissing her and while it was bad at least he'd had to let go of the rest of her. But he had her up against him and he was hard and she felt she was going to puke.

When he came up for air, she said, keeping her voice as level as she could, 'Yes, I'm a woman, Byuferd, but ... but I'm not a tramp. You're going to let me go now. If you don't ...' Tears pushed at her eyes, but letting him see how weak and helpless she felt could be dangerous. He might just take her then. She'd have no more chance of stopping him than she would of stopping a train with her bare hands; and while it had never been important to stop anyone before, it was now. But if he didn't stop, who could she complain to? The police?

'If you don't,' she concluded, 'I'll never see you again.'

He didn't let go for what seemed like a long, long time. Then suddenly she was free and he was stepping back. He said, 'I'm sorry.' He didn't look sorry. 'I'll take you home now.' Again she turned to the door, hoping he wouldn't see her trembling. 'On one condition,' he said.

She froze.

'Next Saturday night again.'

'I'll let you know.'

His hand came down on her shoulder.

'All right,' she said, quickly, to forestall that other hand, the hand with the dirty tricks.

He drove her to Number One and parked and cut his lights

and engine. *Not again!* She reached for the door handle. He stopped her with that hand on her shoulder; that heavy heavy hand. 'Good night, Sandy. I really had a good time. I really ... respect ... you know, honey.' He bent to her. She closed her eyes against that brutal, pock-marked face and gave him his kiss. His head rose, but his hand remained heavy, holding her like she'd once seen Pop hold a rabbit he'd wounded and was about to kill; helpless, trembling...

Oh God, help me out of here!

He kissed her again, but lightly, briefly; then got out and went around the car to open the door for her. 'See you next Saturday,' he said. 'I'll have something for you, a present.'

She managed the smile and got the hell out of there.

In the hallway, she leaned against the door and laughter came; near-hysterical laughter. When Vino and Fanny came she couldn't say anything, just shook her head and kept laughing. They stared at her, and Rollins showed up and said, 'What's so funny?' and she bent double, laughing so hard it really hurt. Because ... because ... (and she couldn't speak a word, couldn't explain it to them since they hadn't been there and hadn't seen and hadn't felt the multiplicity of feelings she'd felt) ... because if he treated someone he *liked*, someone he *respected*, someone he'd hinted he was *serious* about, the way he'd treated her, how the hell did he treat the girls he just wanted to lay?

Laugh? She thought she'd drop with laughing!

Afterward, she cried. Then she was able to tell them what had happened; at least the outlines. They didn't understand. Not even Vino, who looked surprised that she was so sensitive about 'a little feel'.

'A little feel from a ... a yellow eyed dog!'

But they still didn't understand. They felt she'd made a bogyman in her mind.

Prince would have understood. She was sure of it.

She said she'd accepted his invitation for next Saturday but wouldn't go.

Fanny gave her coffee and they sat around and after a while she felt better. Vino asked questions. She told him about the President's Secret Service guards and how Beaufort was always in touch. No, he hadn't mentioned their cards and security checks.

'You'll learn more, next week,' Vino said, and the others

183

nodded and Fanny said, 'Prince, he will be satisfied with this.'

Satisfied! Satisfied with putting her into a snake pit!

But after another cup of coffee it didn't seem as ... as *ugly* as it first had. She couldn't remember how many men had felt her up—lots after less time than Beaufort had taken—so maybe it *was* a bogy-man ...

She drank so much coffee she couldn't fall asleep. Not that Vino was about to *let* her sleep. Since they'd made up, he was at her more than ever. And she wanted it *less* than ever ... from him.

Still, tonight it was good. Having him hold her close was good. Feeling his nice lean body was good. But then he was asleep and she was alone again and afraid again.

SUNDAY, FEBRUARY 23–MONDAY, FEBRUARY 24

During his first month of White House occupancy, still secretly confused and disturbed by living in a mansion of sixty-eight rooms with another eighty-two in the wings, including private solarium, swimming pool, movie theater and medical offices, still in shock from his first official reception at which five thousand guests had been served hors d'œuvres and drinks and looked at him as he had always wanted to be looked at and yet had not been prepared to be looked at, still waiting to be freed from a fear of his high office, Bob Lacton had come down alone and unannounced from his second floor living quarters, wandered into a hallway near the vast kitchen complex and overheard a fragment of conversation. It was only a few words exchanged between two unimportant people—a secretarial hold-over from the previous administration and a member of the kitchen staff—but it had led to his first loss of temper as President.

The secretary had been saying, '... in the place where Lincoln and F.D.R. and Kennedy lived, imagine! How could it have happened?'

Bob Lacton had assumed the worst. In a fury, he had slapped the secretary (female) and punched the elderly Negro cook (male). Both had been so stunned, so dismayed, that it was relatively easy for Gordon McKentry, Lacton's long-time

184

friend and now press secretary, to smooth over the awkward situation, explaining that 'world affairs' had reached such a tense stage that the President was almost beside himself.

Lacton had given them a personal apology (he was good at apologies, having had to issue quite a few in his time, though several had failed in his pre-White House days, resulting in some bad publicity). He was especially sincere in his talk with the Negro cook, since *that* could cost him dearly, in the next election as well as in current prestige, and who knew what some crazy militant might try to do to him *personally*! Bob Lacton worried a good deal about assassination, though he felt that, unlike Kennedy, Truman, F.D.R. and Lincoln, he was a *healer* of the nation's rifts and not a creator of such rifts. Second to his personal safety, Lacton worried most about the next election. It was force of habit, since he had lost so many. Even now, after three years as President, there were times he could hardly believe it; especially on first waking up in the morning.

Mornings, opening his eyes, seeing Maggie, tasting the ever-present worry—always some worry that lingered from the previous day; always, since childhood—he was at first unable to remember who and where he was. She, certainly, hadn't changed, except to grow older. Their relationship certainly hadn't changed, except to grow even colder. He hadn't touched her in three weeks, and soon the pressure to do so would have them both edgy. Not that either wanted to, but at least once a month they mated, to keep things 'normal'.

This morning he stared foggily at her, and mind returned, and he wondered what it would have been like if Lois West had accepted his proposal and he hadn't bounced over to Maggie a month later. Lois with her plumpish body, so unlike this hard, angular woman...

Maggie stirred and came awake. He said, 'Good morning, Madam President.' She liked that. She gave him her thin smile. He took a deep breath, and reached out for her. She seemed about to reject him, but when he murmured, 'It's been so long,' she got the message and they went at it.

He thought of Karen Vener. He had been thinking of her all week. So much like Lois in her generous flesh, her rounded curves. He thought of Charley's Chinese dolls and of himself and Karen watching them, alone.

Afterward, Maggie talked of the boys, one at Yale and the

other married and living in California. He listened carefully, because he rarely asked about them and their communication was, except for public consumption, solely with their mother. He had had some minor guilt about them, especially Abner, the older. Ab had lived through some rough periods...

But no time to think of that now. It was eight thirty and they had to prepare for church. Later, he would have a free hour or two until lunch; then a series of ambassadorial-level meetings on the perennial problem of Soviet pressure, once again reaching a peak in the Mediterranean. He would rely heavily on Jason Goodwell, his Secretary of State, as he relied heavily on all his cabinet. He had yet to face a truly serious moment of decision and believed this was due not to good fortune but to his own foreign policy. Those who said he had avoided all meaningful moves in both foreign and domestic fields were correct, he was fond of telling newsmen. He avoided *conflict*.

He showered, thinking how he had been offered the chairmanship of a huge advertising agency after that first presidential defeat. He would have known how to run it; would have been far more than a figurehead. And the money, the stock, the women...

He smiled a little, a thin and bitter smile. One thing he'd had as a political loser, women. Not many, but every so often there had been an opportunity and he had taken it. Now he was President of the United States and, no matter what they said about various of his predecessors, there was no opportunity whatsoever for that sort of thing. Not the way the news media had grown. No, unthinkable...

And yet he thought of it.

And he realized that Bay Island, and Karen Vener, were his only chance; would be his only chance until he was no longer President, and since his chances as incumbent were excellent, it would be another five years. And by then, he might not give a damn.

He called down for two breakfast trays, as was their Sunday habit; then dressed, leading Maggie into a discussion of her March thirteenth trip to Ab and his family in Los Angeles. He enjoyed hearing her talk about her plans, because they created a background of reality against which to place his dreams. He couldn't call his thoughts of Karen Vener 'plans', knowing as he did that she was far from willing, yet.

186

Yet. But he was prepared to offer something in return for her favors. She knew what Charley wanted. He would make her understand that it was within her power to give it to him.

Maggie began to dress. He went to the oval study where his breakfast tray waited, along with three folders relating to the Soviet naval situation. Every President since World War II had faced similar folders. Nothing irremediable had happened before; nothing irremediable would happen now.

He remembered to mutter, 'Please, God,' under his breath, determined to serve two terms without making a mistake. Oh, they were all waiting for him to make a mistake, he knew it, but he'd fool them. He'd go down in history as a President of peace in an era of war; a President of cool deliberation . . .

But he didn't want to think of that now. Fear attended thoughts of that. Knowledge of self created the fear.

He had coffee and toast, then lifted his phone and placed a call to Bay Island. He glanced at the door to his left, which led to his bedroom . . . which was now his *and* Maggie's, since he had insisted that they share a room, a bed, and so give the electorate a close, *normal* American family. It was worth votes. He had instructed Garson to get the message across via the press. Few Americans were aware of the two bedroom setup for the President and his Lady, or for that matter in the homes of all who could afford it. A damned good idea, in terms of him and Maggie, anywhere else but here.

His luck was good; Karen came on the line. He kept his eyes on that bedroom door, and said he was calling to ask about his namesake. Karen said her son was fine. He asked about Charley.

'Just wonderful. Out at the polo field, getting ready for a match.'

'One game I never mastered,' Lacton said.

'I doubt you ever will, Bob. It's a dangerous sport . . .'

'I've never avoided . . .' he began, annoyed, though the truth was he had never really mastered *any* sport.

'No, my dear,' she interrupted. 'I mean that the nation's interests . . .'

'Ah.' He was surprised. The tone of her voice—the *personal* tone and approach—was something new. Whatever Bod Lacton wasn't, he was a consummate artist in judging people's reactions to *him*, and even on the phone he was able to make a judgment, an evaluation, instinctive but registering on his consciousness and changing his approach instantly.

'Are you alone?' he asked, eyes still on the door leading to his bedroom.

'Why ... yes.'

'I've missed you.'

'Mr. *President*!' she said, in mock reproach.

He no longer doubted. His heart hammered as it hadn't since the returns from New York had indicated he might lose that second election. And even though it was victory he sensed now, the fear was there too. He had lived his life with fear, was brother to fear, and while he could never defeat fear he knew well how to function within its sweaty strictures.

'I can't wait to see you,' he said.

'Charley talks of nothing *but* your visit.'

'You,' he wanted to say. 'What do *you* talk of? How do *you* feel about my visit?' What he said was, 'Can anyone listen in on this conversation?'

'There are at least six extensions that I can remember.'

'Then it will have to wait.'

When she said, 'What will?' her voice kittenish, he gripped the phone hard, as if it were her fine breasts he was gripping, her luscious backside.

'I'm going to have to get you a scrambler phone,' he muttered.

She laughed softly.

He felt it was time to say good-bye. He could change his daydreams to actual plans now; figure out how—if Charley didn't do it himself—he could get the man away from the house for several hours each of the three days of his visit. By the time he attended that gala, he wanted to be able to look at Karen with a sense of absolute possession.

Yet her laughter lasted and the sound of it was an invitation to continue and it had been so long since he'd actually *enjoyed* anything that he said, 'Do you still have those incredible little dolls?'

'I'm afraid so, though we've been considering getting rid of them.'

'Don't, Karen. At least not until we see them again, one more time.'

'I think Charley's tired of them.'

She was giving him opening after opening!

'Then just the two of us.'

She laughed. 'Would I be safe?'

'No.'

'You must be working very hard, Mr. President, because you sound ready for relaxation.'

'I've been ready for years,' he said, and he said it flat, a statement of fact. 'The question is, Karen, when did *you* become ready?' And then before she could answer, 'Afraid I have to go now. Good-bye.'

He was reading the second folder when Maggie came into the study. They went downstairs, picking up their Secret Service men, and went out to the car. The usual Sunday morning crowd was pressed up against the fence. He tried to estimate how many people were gathered, remembering Reston's claim that he drew the smallest crowds since Herbert Hoover. Cloudy and cold, but there still seemed to be a few hundred. Well, perhaps a hundred. Truman hadn't drawn more than that, had he?

He allowed his mind to drift during the sermon. Another overseas tour in early spring. He liked traveling ... as the President of the United States. Then preparations for the next election could begin, and this he liked best of all, because this was his forte, his one true enthusiasm. Outside of Karen Vener, that is.

A line of pickets was waiting when they returned to the White House; Negroes, some in African dress. Shouts were hurled at him. He heard an epithet. Maggie murmured, 'Too much!' though her face remained calm. His own anger came alive. But with pickets, with masses of people, with the electorate, he had good control. Never catch him *that* way!

He waved, grinning through bulletproof glass into their stern or angry faces. Then they were gone and he was on his way into the home of Presidents, thinking they would have five more years to stew before they got another soft touch, another liberal Democrat to throw money into the bottomless pit of their poverty and inability. But on Wednesday, he would address a coalition of Negro ... had to remember to call them *black* ... a coalition of black organizations, and he would soothe and palliate and give them what another pinko ... *very* taboo word ... what a *Washington Post* columnist had called 'his special brand of pillow talk'. But the *majority* liked it. And the Bay Islanders *loved* it, all except the blind, the far right fools who didn't understand that it was suicide for the establishment to act openly like an establishment these days.

Bay Island, he thought as he left the luncheon table and went toward the cabinet room. Karen Vener and a chance to be himself ...

To be himself.

Could he remember that far back? Even in high school, he had followed the lead of the majority, basing his opinions on the conglomerate, middle class mean.

To be himself.

Assistant Secretary of Defense Raber was beginning his analysis of recent Soviet naval provocations. President Bob Lacton leaned forward, eyes narrowed and seemingly attentive. But it was Bay Island he thought of.

SATURDAY, MARCH 1

She wasn't sure whether she'd planned it or whether it just happened by itself. Anyway, she felt sick in the restaurant and had to go to the rest room and there she thought of how it would be a way out and suddenly she was throwing up. Afterward, she felt faint and the colored woman rubbed her neck and said she'd better sit at the vanity a while. Sandy asked her to get word to Mr. Beaufort at a booth in back, and the woman went out. Sandy felt better right away. Now he would have to take her home and no stopping at his place and if she acted *real* sick he might not try anything in the car.

She knew Vino would be mad. But if she insisted it was something she ate or drank, how could he say it wasn't?

From the minute Beaufort had picked her up and given her the orchid corsage, she'd been shaking inside, her stomach churning, feeling sicker and sicker. God, his face, his eyes, the man he *was*, just made her feel that way and she couldn't help it and she knew it was *impossible* to go through with this evening! What made it worse was that yesterday Prince had decided they, the servants, weren't to bring Beaufort their cards as promised. He wanted the extra few days that putting it off until Monday would give them on that security check. And sure enough, what did Beaufort say when they began to eat but, 'Hope you like your meal, Sandy, 'cause I don't serve

190

such fancy stuff in my cell and I'm going to have to put you in there ... you and all your friends.'

She'd known he was kidding, but even so the shrimp had turned bitter in her mouth and her, 'What do you mean, Byuferd?' sounded more like a death rattle than the sweet, innocent question she'd meant it to be. He'd explained about expecting her and the other servants today, at the latest. 'Now I'll have to put a rush on those reports so I can find out just what desperate characters I'm dealing with, especially a cute little con artist...' She'd laughed, not only to stop him but to stop her own panic from showing. She'd gone on eating, and turned the conversation to other things, and all the time she'd been thinking she had to end this evening. A moment later, she'd felt nausea.

When she finally came out of the ladies' room, Beaufort was waiting. He said, 'I told the manager the shrimp ought to be examined...'

'Maybe it wasn't that,' she said, voice weak, and leaned on his arm. 'But I just got to get home and into bed.'

He said, 'Sure. I'd planned on that anyway.'

She smiled faintly.

In the car, she leaned back and closed her eyes. He talked a little, but she didn't answer, just moaned once in a while. And being this close to him, the sickness began tickling her throat again.

When they stopped at Number One, he leaned over her. 'Feeling a little better now, honey?'

'No ... not really.' She reached for the door. 'I'm sorry I spoiled your evening.'

He took her around the shoulders and pressed a long kiss to her cheek and then turned her head, his fingers gripping her chin and allowing no resistance, and kissed her mouth and tongued her and she could feel the sickness rising and couldn't move because he handled her like a ... a *thing*! When he lifted his head, she belched loud and clear. Served him right!

But he only laughed. 'We'll make it next Saturday.'

'Oh, not next Saturday, Byuferd. I ... I got friends visiting from home.' Before he could ask for another night, she said, 'I'll be taken up with them until, let's see ...' She wrinkled her brow in thought. 'Well, until after the fifteenth, anyway.'

He said nothing. She shot a quick glance at him. His face was heavy, lowering. She added, 'Of course, after then, I'd be happy ...'

'Can't find even one free night?' he muttered, eyes lying on her like fists.

'Well, not as it stands, but if there's any change in plans ... you know how friends from home are.'

'I don't know,' he said. 'I never allow anyone to get in the way of what I want to do.'

'I guess we're not all so strong in our ways as you.' She gave him what she hoped was an admiring smile. He continued to stare at her. She swallowed, and said something before she had thought it through, and then was sorry. 'Anyway, I'll see you Monday, for the fingerprinting and all.'

He nodded. 'And I'll be sure to lean on Consolidated for quick reports.'

Her laugh came out better than she expected. 'You hoping to get something on me, Byuferd? You *that* mad at me for being sick?'

He shrugged and got out and came around to open her door. She gave him her hand. Now she hoped he would kiss her again, hoped he would forget his anger.

Beaufort didn't kiss her, so she did what she had to do. She came up against him, closed her eyes and put her lips to his. When she felt him stiffening against her belly, when his arms tightened around her so that she could barely breathe, she murmured, 'Until after the fifteenth, Byuferd.' She slowly removed his arms and he allowed it. She gave him as steamy a look as she could manage, went to the house and turned. 'Think of me until then, will you?'

Unsmilingly, he said, 'I will.' She quickly rejected the thought that there was considerable menace in his voice. There *couldn't* be, now that she had practically promised him he would get what he wanted. And so he didn't have any reason to 'lean on' the investigators for their security reports. And so she didn't have to worry the others by telling them about this.

When she stepped inside, she heard voices from the kitchen and moved silently through the foyer and to the servants' quarters. Vino didn't come to the room until about an hour later, and he stopped dead in the doorway, staring at her. She said, 'Got in a few minutes ago and just had to lie down. Whew! That sonofabitch! Lucky for me he had some sort of work to do at ten thirty. And he's tied up for a couple of weeks, which lets me off the hook. Anyway, there's nothing more he can tell us.'

Vino said, 'Yeah?' and began to ask questions.

She kicked back the covers, saying it sure was hot tonight, and let him get a good look at what the shortie nightgown didn't cover, which was just about everything.

He forgot his questions.

He went to the third gala and sat at the bar and drank. He knew he'd been drinking far too much the past week, almost as much as he had in Chicago, but that didn't mean anything. Purely temporary. It would change in two weeks. His entire life would change in two weeks. No sense worrying about a little alcohol when he would soon have his new start...

'Run through that handful of single women already, Bucky?'

It was Karen Vener, and she looked flushed and excited and quite lovely in a *zaftig* Bavarian manner. Her gown was lavender and black, several layers of gossamer thin material that molded hips and breasts as if wet and sticking to her. His eyes must have been bolder, and drunker, than he realized because she flushed more deeply and murmured, 'Now what can you find so interesting in an old married woman?'

Signals from Karen Vener? Whatever could be happening to that happy millionaire couple with the child named after a friend in the White House?

He rose from the bar stool, saying. 'The phrase, "old married woman", would appear to be two-thirds correct. "Married" and "woman". But that "old" changes it to something that doesn't apply in the slightest to anyone who looks like you do.'

She laughed. 'Quite a speech.'

He agreed. He was getting stiff on martinis and making stiff little speeches. 'Join me?'

'Then you *are* alone.'

'Yes.' He was alone and wanted to remain alone, despite the obligatory invitation. He had come to see and be seen and have a few drinks and then go home. And among those he had seen and been seen by was Ceecee Mortonson who had passed within touching distance, laughing into the face of her escort, Jock Waters, and while her eyes had flicked to him she hadn't acknowledged his presence and he had told himself it was fortunate she hadn't because he'd have cut her dead. And watching them as they had moved to the dance floor, and watching them as they had danced, he had recognized an intimacy that hadn't been there before, a physical intimacy that he felt was embarrassingly obvious, and he'd thought that if he were her father he'd have slapped her face!

'... at our table,' Karen was saying.

He smiled. 'Forgive me. The noise and all.'

'I asked if you'd care to join the group at our table?'

He finished his martini—fifth, sixth?—and tried to think of a graceful way out. Before he succeeded, she had taken his hand and he was drawn along after her, through the crowd and the noise and the dancers, and there was Ceecee again and her dancing was an obscene fertility rite and he wanted to stop her and tell her, 'Too much!' And behind his anger—was it *anger*?—lay a question: *Why?* Why was her dancing and walking and laughing too much now? Why was Ceecee in totality so different now from what she had been before, even though before there had been wildness and abandon too? Why was she doing this; what was driving her to this excess of excess?

There was an answer, felt if not articulated in his mind, only he could not accept that either, because there was the fifteenth of March to consider; always and always the fifteenth of March.

They were past Ceecee, threading through the extra tables set up for these galas, and then they stopped at a large, round table. Faces turned up to him and he breathed deeply to clear his mind and eyes. The air wasn't pure enough to do much good and yet he had to be sober, had to be *right*, because he was the hunter and this was his prey.

He was introduced to a young looking man and a not so young looking woman who were, surprisingly, Mr. and Mrs. Someone; surprisingly until, a few minutes later, Karen murmured to him that *she* was Real Society and *he* wasn't. Marriage for money. It was a way ... just as March fifteenth was a way.

Allie Mortonson was part of the group. He had a woman with him and the woman was from Pennsylvania and talked about Bryn Athyn. Bucky made appropriate remarks and accepted the drink served him and nursed it. The woman was big, blonde and handsome, and very impressed with her escort's daughter. She said, 'Cecily is *quite* a girl. To be honest, Allie, I just don't see much of you in her.'

The others laughed and Charley Vener said, 'Is that a compliment or what, Lolo?'

Lolo also laughed. 'Merely an observation. They're both wonderful, in their ways, their very different ways.'

Allie Mortonson began talking about the performance of conglomerates on the New York Exchange. Karen, who seemed totally engrossed in the conversation, touched Bucky's hand under the table. Just as he had to stay reasonably sober and articulate when dealing with his prey, he also had to play their little games. He took the hand and squeezed it as Allie was saying, 'Now, more than at any other time in our history, keeping meaningful sums of money out of the market or real estate is wasteful and economically dangerous.' Karen's knee slid along Bucky's thigh, and she said, 'Then how do you explain that famous million of yours, Allie? The one that follows you from home to home, and even on short vacations? The one that's supposedly in your bedroom safe here on the island?'

Bucky was watching Charley, who was drinking steadily and grinning steadily, but there was a touch of something about the eyes and voice; something that Bucky felt he had seen in his own eyes when shaving, when dressing, when looking at himself in mirrors. *Pressure.*

Allie said, 'I was talking about *meaningful* sums of money, *considerable* sums of money, not a lousy million.'

The laughter was loud now; though tinged with some resentment and envy, Bucky felt. Allie outranked everyone at this table and he hadn't bothered to take the curse off his remark with smile or shrug or anything else. In fact, he wasn't even looking at them; he was watching the dancers, was watching Ceecee, Bucky guessed. And Bucky watched her himself, for a moment, and then stopped watching because she was still in excess of her usual excess.

He saw Beth Larkin with a new man. He saw Vincent Drang, and Drang looked away from him. He kept his eyes moving, moving ... everywhere but to Ceecee Mortonson.

He was grateful to Karen for providing him with that vital piece of information about Allie's million and its location, and began playing her under the-table game a little more actively, caressing her thigh. She turned to him and smiled and said, 'This gentleman here is a problem. I want him at all my dinner parties, for his looks and charm...'

He murmured his little disclaimer.

'But he's unattached, imagine, and so I need unattached females...'

He made a jocular reference to being quite satisfied sharing his hostess with his host, and Charley said, 'Hear hear,' and drained his glass. Karen said, 'My it's getting so *stuffy*,' and Bucky offered to escort her on a breath-of-fresh-air stroll.

Outside, they walked through the bright-sky evening past the tennis courts and she glanced behind them twice as if worrying, or hoping, that they were being followed. In the shadows of a line of stately pines separating courts from golf course, she turned to him and he took her by the forearms and kissed her, gently, thinking that if she wanted him he would oblige. She dropped her head. He waited, puzzled. After a while, she looked at him and came to him and kissed him fiercely, her body straining against his until he responded. And then, when his hands were beginning to move over her, she withdrew, whispering, 'You don't ... not enough, Bucky.' He said, 'I think it's the other way around, Karen.' She said, 'Maybe, but if the man is very strong in his wanting ... Are you in love with someone?' He said, 'No,' quickly. She said, 'I ... I'm sorry,' and laughed. 'I don't really expect you to be in love with me after half an hour's flirting.' They started back toward the club, and he said, 'Is there anything I can do? Advice, aid, succor, anything at all? Do you want to talk?'

'No, I just ... too much to drink.' She smiled at him. 'And you *are* the most attractive man on this island.'

'With a line like that, you'll never lack lovers. Once you decide you really want them, that is.'

She laughed and it was close to being legitimate. 'That makes two of us, Bucky.' Then, quietly, 'Please, let's forget about this, can we?'

'In the way you mean, of course. But in another way, I'll always remember you chose me.' He took her hand, feeling that there was need and confusion here, also feeling a resurgence of his own need, his own confusion. If she had wanted him *this* moment, if she had come up against him as she had a few minutes ago, he'd have swept her away. Because there was reason now, motivation now.

She must have sensed something of what he felt. Her hand warmed in his and she smiled at him and when she spoke her

196

voice was soft. But what she said was completely without meaning for him. 'Ah, Bucky, if only you were President.'

He laughed. She did too, leaning up against him. His arm went around her shoulders and they stumbled along, laughing wildly. And then the voice exploded out at them, bringing them to a startled halt.

'Damn, damn, *damn*! Is there anyplace on this fúckin' island free of them? Anyplace at all?'

It was Ceecee, sitting on a car fender with Jock Waters, both holding lighted cigarettes. The boy was as startled as Bucky was, and muttered, 'Cool it, Ceecee. You've been going too strong tonight.'

But she didn't cool it. 'Is there anyplace on *earth* where we don't have to see them playing their stupid little dirty little square little games, the marrieds and the unmarrieds and the wives with the...'

Jock put his hand over her mouth.

Bucky said, 'I'm glad you did that. I'd have slapped...'

Jock cried out, jerking his hand away. Ceecee threw herself off the car and ran, hard and fast as a boy, toward the club. Jock shook his hand, bent over in pain. 'Christ! I think she took a piece out of it!'

'What's *wrong* with her?' Karen asked.

The boy was standing now. 'Drunk. Really drunk, I'm afraid.' He looked at his hand, raised his other hand to drag on his cigarette, then quickly dropped the cigarette and ground it under his shoe. Bucky caught a sweetness, a strange difference in the smoke, and guessed what Ceecee had been 'going too strong' on tonight.

Karen examined Jock's hand. 'The skin is broken,' she said. 'Olaf has a first-aid kit...'

They walked to the club together. By the time they reached the doors, Jock was making light of the whole thing. Bucky left them and went back to Allie, Lolo and the guest couple. Charley was gone. Allie was watching the dance floor again, his expression strained. Ceecee was swinging away in a rock and roll dance with another youngster, only the music wasn't rock and roll. The boy was embarrassed, but not willing to stop. Ceecee seemed about to perform coitus right then and there.

As Bucky watched, heart thudding, other dancers stopped to form a widening circle around Ceecee and the boy. And then the music faltered, blurred and became rock. Ceecee swung up close to the boy, her cigarette hanging from her lips, her pelvis snapping frantically. The boy, who was quite good in his way, backed off a bit, but used his arms and legs wildly. Ceecee pursued him. The crowd began to clap the beat; at least the men did, egging Ceecee on.

Allie stood up. He spoke to Lolo, and Bucky caught, '...chauffeur back for you.'

She said, 'That's all right. Mr. Prince will see to me until then, won't you, dear?'

Bucky said, 'With pleasure,' but his heart continued to thud and he watched as Allie went onto the dance floor and pushed through the circle and put his hand on Ceecee's shoulder. She stopped dancing. He smiled and spoke close to her ear. She didn't reply, didn't move, merely stood there. The circle of people dissolved; the music stopped briefly, then resumed in fox-trot tempo. Bucky lost sight of Allie and Ceecee. Lolo was speaking to him, saying that Ceecee had 'a little too much spirit, or is that *spirits*?' He smiled, nodded at something the guest couple was saying, saw Allie and Ceecee passing the bar on their way out. Allie had her firmly by the arm.

Lolo was rising. He rose with her and followed her onto the dance floor. He didn't want to stay any longer. He wanted to drink where he couldn't be seen. He wanted the days to pass; to pass without his having to experience anything more with anyone on this island.

He wanted the fifteenth of March, dammit! He wanted it over and done with! He felt he was being ripped open, being torn into small, bloody pieces!

'You dance beautifully,' he said to Lolo.

'Anyone would, Bucky, with you leading.'

Finally, she had enough, and he was able to say good night. At the bar, Charley Vener was talking with a group of three men. They exchanged good nights; Vener's eyes jumped away from his.

At the end of the bar, Karen sat with Jock Waters. She'd put three band-aids on his hand and Bucky said the boy looked like a disabled war veteran and they all laughed.

Then he went home. Everyone seemed to be asleep and he took a decanter from the set of six in the dining room and didn't bother looking at what it was and sat in a hot tub and drank Scotch, as it turned out. He didn't finish the decanter.

He merely had a few drinks—six or seven. And was spared thought. Which was the name of his game now, wasn't it? Which made him smile, albeit sloppily, and stumble into bed.

He had an instant of fear, remembering Tad.

But Tad hadn't had a March fifteenth to look forward to, to solve everything for him.

'Kill or cure,' he mumbled. 'Kill or cure.' Over and over. His prayer . . .

SUNDAY, MARCH 2

It was graying up now; dawn was an hour or less away. The *Hatteras* drifted at anchor about a mile south of the island, dead center of the bay, its running lights defining its forty-one-foot length in red, green and white dots. Allie Mortonson smoked a cigar, sitting back in the swivel chair, in the hurricane-deck cockpit, looking out into nothing; no land, no other boats, no sound except that of water slapping the fiberglass hull.

Limbo. Peace. And yet he was waiting for something.

He turned his head to the right and one of two padded benches framing the cockpit. Ceecee lay there, curled under a blanket, asleep. The air was crisp, cool, but not cool enough, he felt, for her trembling chill of two hours ago. Chill from within. Chill that had reached out to him too. And so he was waiting for something, waiting for her to awaken and break limbo, shatter peace.

When he had taken her from the country club, she'd come along as if in a trance. He'd expected a fight, after that insane exhibition on the dance floor, but she'd climbed into the back of the car with him and looked at Gerald as he'd started the engine and said, 'Do the others use their chauffeurs for a mile or two?' He'd begun to answer that he didn't care *what* the others did, he used his servants as he saw fit, and she'd interrupted quietly:

'I won't go home.'

Before he could grow angry, her head had fallen and her voice had broken as she'd whispered, 'Please don't make me go home. Take me someplace. Please, I'm afraid to go home, to

199

stop, to go to bed. Please ...' Her hand had come to his; cold, cold, hand; trembling hand. 'Please, Daddy, take me someplace.' And she hadn't called him Daddy in years and he had nodded.

They had gone to the Yacht Club, empty because of the gala, and ordered seafood platters and English ale. He had eaten and she had looked at her plate and sipped the ale, smoked and grown dull and sleepy. He'd suggested they go home now. Her head had come up, her eyes widening and clearing, filling with something like panic. 'No, you promised to take me someplace ...'

He'd had Yang bring the *Hatteras* to the Yacht Club dock and return home with Gerald. He and Ceecee had gone out into the bay. They had cruised along the Miami coast, looking at the lights. He had tried to speak to her, to ask what was wrong, but she'd shaken her head. Later, on the way back, she'd said, 'The engine is so noisy.' He had moved further out into the bay, as close to dead center as he could judge by shorelights and instruments, and anchored. Again he had asked what was wrong. She had begun trembling, said she was cold, said she was *freezing*. He'd gone below for a blanket, and when he returned to the cockpit she was lying down, huddled into herself, teeth chattering. Her dress was a frothy little thing ... but still, it was over sixty degrees and she had never been delicate that way. He'd covered her, and without further ado she'd fallen into heavy slumber.

That was two hours ago. He took a last puff of his cigar, threw it overboard and stretched.

He heard her moan, and turned to her again. She sat up slowly, rubbing her eyes, a little girl awakening. And she was so very beautiful, this daughter who was also a stranger, and his heart moved as it hadn't in too many years. He smiled and said, 'Good morning.'

'Morning.' She looked around. 'Oh, the boat.'

He chuckled.

She felt on the seat until she found her cigarette case. He said, 'Don't smoke any more of that.'

She looked at him.

'I broke one open. I know they're not supposed to be more dangerous than whiskey, but you've had so many.'

She put the case down; then took it up again. 'I'm sorry. I need it.'

200

'Why? What's wrong?'

She lit one, inhaled deeply, turned on the seat to stare into the grayness. 'When will the sun come up?'

He checked his watch. 'Half an hour; a little more. What is it that's bothering you? A boy?'

'Or a girl.'

He told himself he didn't know what she meant but the blood rushed to his head and he made a choking sound. She turned to look at him. He said, 'Don't joke about such a thing, ever!'

'How quickly you understood,' she murmured. 'I wasn't going to tell you. At least I don't think I was...'

'Be quiet!' And it was as if he had been living with the immediate knowledge for days now. 'It's not true!'

'Wishes won't wash dishes, as Grandma liked to say.' She turned back to the gray limbo of Biscayne Bay. 'Besides, it doesn't concern you. I'm on my own in this. I'm going to have the child, but I'm not asking for anything. As of the thirtieth, I'll be free, white, twenty-one and worth forty million.'

The laugh was torn from his throat. 'Free, white and twenty-one!'

Again she looked at him. 'Do you want to spank me or something?'

'Free, *white* and twenty-one!' *He* was trembling now. 'Dear Jesus!'

Her face questioned him.

'Who is the father?' he asked harshly.

She shook her head and drew on her marijuana cigarette; so calm, so damned calm in the face of this terrible disaster! Without planning it, he lunged from his seat, tore the cigarette from her hand and slapped her across the face. She rocked sideways, staring at him, then spoke evenly.

'I don't know who the father is. There are three, perhaps four candidates. I can give you a *list* of names, but not one. And I can lengthen the list, if you'd like to know all the men...'

'No,' he muttered, turning away. 'No... it's not true. You wouldn't joke if you understood. You can't have a child. It'll be black. Everyone will know. What will we do with a black child?'

And then he realized he'd said it, it was out, and he stumbled to his chair and sank back down.

'Black?'

He told her. It was actually a relief. He told her everything, waiting for the shock to reach her face; that and the horror of what she had done. He concluded with, 'That's why I always kept a million in cash available. In case anyone found out. Blackmailer or not, I'd be able to silence him. I'd have done more, if money wasn't enough. I'd have protected you, our name...'

She laughed; once, briefly.

Shock. Hysteria.

She laughed again, shaking her head and staring at him.

Disbelief. He didn't blame her.

She laughed and laughed, bending over.

'Please, Ceecee, control yourself.'

She nodded. 'I'll try.' And still she laughed. 'But it's hard. I mean, such a *joke*!'

'Joke?' It must be part of her hysteria. Bitter joke, she meant. Terrible joke.

'Joke on *you*, Father. Joke on all the people like you. Big joke on society. Get it?'

He knew hysteria didn't deserve rational response, but he shook his head.

'It's so damned *unimportant,* this revelation of yours. It's such a *nothing*, this enormous black secret of yours. *That's* the joke.'

He said, 'We have to talk sensibly,' and waited for her to say she realized now she couldn't bear a child, had to have an abortion. He looked at her face; her face still filled with laughter. And then he saw the laughter fade as her eyes met his. And then he saw her mouth twisting, her eyes blazing.

'You *idiot*! So *that's* why you couldn't touch me!'

Hatred. And he could understand it just as he understood her hysteria. Hatred of him for having been the unwitting cause of her disaster—for his inability to conceive, his incapacity to love her mother until it was too late and so pushing her into the black man's arms. He could take it. He understood her pain and so he could take it.

'I'm sorry, Ceecee.'

'You goddam idiot!' She was standing, staring down at him. 'To ruin everything for us because of such ... such *incidentals*!'

His mouth sagged open.

202

'And black babies!' She laughed again. 'Didn't you ever discuss this with a doctor, or at least with a friend who had some knowledge of genetics?'

'Discuss? How could I discuss *this* with anyone?'

'Didn't you try to find out ... try to *read* ... don't you know the simplest facts about the matter that's dominated your existence, that's twisted your feeling for me and our life together?'

'What was there to find out? Everyone knows...'

'Everyone knows? Old wives' tales! Myths from the past! But multi-millionaire Allie Mortonson?' Her tone and expression were not to be tolerated. She wasn't hysterical, had never been hysterical. She had been shocked, yes ... but at *him*. And now she was full of contempt ... and pity. Shame began to mount, even before he knew exactly what there was to be ashamed of. And so he said, 'Watch your tongue! Just because I never had the advantages of higher education...'

'My God!'

'I had to *work*, to build the family fortune at a time when the economy was shaky. I didn't have the time, or inclination, to sit around a university...'

'I can't have a black baby,' she interrupted quietly. 'I can't have a child darker than either me or the father, darker than the darkest of the parents.'

'But ... throwbacks to the grandparent, or great-grandparent...?'

'Any college biology text could have saved you that worry. Mendel has been revised, Father. Or do you prefer that I call you Allie?'

He couldn't believe it. Everyone had heard stories ... people hiding black babies ... it was part of American history and tradition. 'Exceptions to the rule,' he said. 'There are always exceptions...'

'Shall I give you the entire three-credit course? Shall I quote Curt Stern and other established geneticists? It is *impossible* for any of the offspring of a white and black mating—like Ceecee Mortonson—if mated to a white spouse, to produce a child as dark as the original dark grandparent. Stern says there are no known exceptions to this generalization, hearsay and folk tales notwithstanding. I remember my own biology professor saying, "Ignore those rumors you hear from time to time about a white-skinned couple supposedly producing a

203

black-skinned child because one of the parents has what we call hidden Negro blood." If I'd known then he was talking about me...' She turned away and went down the ladder to the deck.

He still couldn't accept it. How could so many people believe in something so wrong? He wasn't an ignorant man. He read occasionally; not biology or genetic texts, but still...

He got up. They had to talk. They had to decide on a course of action. If the child was white...

He was at the ladder, looking down. She was pulling her dress up over her head.

'What are you doing?'

'I want to swim.' She stood in silky blue panties and brassière, kicking off her shoes.

'There's a suit and bathing cap...'

She stepped onto the stern.

'Don't go too...'

She dived cleanly, cutting into the water with hardly a sound, and came to the surface some five or six feet from the *Hatteras*, stroking hard and fast. It was lighter now, the gray changing to a milky white, but there was considerable mist and she disappeared even as he called. 'Don't lose sight of the boat!'

He ran down the ladder, his previous fear, rage and shame forgotten as a new emotion seized hold of him. *Terror!*

He reached the deck and peered out over the stern. Nothing! He listened, trying to hold his breath and quiet his thundering heart and pulse. 'Ceecee!' he shouted.

How could he have been so stupid, so insensitive to *her* feelings! She had been hit with something that, despite her attempts to make light of it, must have torn *deep* into her! She was just a child, an emotional one at that, and she was swimming away from the boat, away from him, away ... from life?

'Ceecee!'

He thought he heard something from the bow, and ran around there and heard nothing but the breath whistling harshly in his throat. He said, 'God, please!' and regretted, regretted ... all the years that he had failed to love her; all the wasted years.

Another sound, from the port side. He ran, stumbling over a carelessly placed cushion, and cursed and screamed, 'Ceecee!

204

Please answer! *Please!*' He was gasping now, sobbing drily, certain she would never return; and his mind showed her as she had been a few minutes ago, tanned and beautiful, her limbs and breast ...

No, that wasn't the way he should remember her.

Remember her! She couldn't do this! 'Ceecee!' He was tearing at his clothes as he ran back to the stern. He had his shirt and undershirt off and bent, pulling at his shoes. He straightened, shouting her name, ripping down his trousers. She mustn't die! As he kicked away clothing and jumped onto the stern in stockings and underpants, she appeared out of the mist. She was swimming easily, coming from the port side in toward the bow.

He stepped down to the deck, backing away until he bumped the cabin housing. She came up the stern ladder, hair streaming. She climbed onto the deck and shook her head, flinging water in all directions, some of it sprinkling his face. He lifted a hand to his cheek, numb with relief. She looked at him and said, 'Can I have a towel?' She was panting, her chest heaving. He said, 'Of course,' but didn't move. The wet panties clung to her, defining her pubic area clearly, so very clearly that he could see the dark mass of hair and even the line of division ...

He turned abruptly to the cabin, went down and grabbed a towel from the pile Yang had placed on the lower port bunk, went back up again. She was facing away from him, and before she turned for the towel he saw the ripeness of her buttocks, the incredible beauty and curve of them, protruding from the wet nylon and delineated by the fabric. His breath caught low in his throat and he felt he was choking.

She took the towel and began drying herself. He wanted to turn away—or told himself to turn away and wanted to look at her, this beautiful girl, his daughter who had loved many men ...

Not *his* daughter. A woman who had lived with him since her childhood, but a stranger, biologically. No common blood flowed in their veins. And she was carrying a child and wasn't even sure of the father and didn't men copulate with blood relatives like nieces and cousins. And she was less than that and he only wanted to look at her and touch her and give her the love now bursting free after so many years ...

She was bending to her legs. Her breasts hung round and full

205

within the water soaked brassière. She straightened, putting the towel around behind her, trying to dry her back.

'Here, let me do that.' He didn't recognize his voice, it was so hoarse, and she gave him a startled glance. He smiled then, made himself smile then, and came to her and took the towel and the pulse in his temples mounted as she turned her back, turned her eyes away and her mind away and he was left with only the beauty of her, only the body of her. The pulse hammered, hammered, and he began rubbing her gently—her neck, her back, lower, where the ripeness began.

'You frightened me,' he said, still in that deeply hoarse voice. 'I thought you'd drowned.'

'I was able to see the running lights,' she said. 'I swam around the boat and I was always ...'

His head bent as if under an unendurable weight. His lips pressed the nape of her neck. 'I thought I'd lost you. Only then did I realize how much you meant to me.'

She had grown very still. He lifted his head and somehow the towel had fallen and he held her damp, cool arms. 'I didn't want to live then, Ceecee. I thought how right you were about my ruining everything for us. I thought of the waste, the waste, and I wanted to die.'

She was turning. There was a look on her face, a little girl look of longing and delight, of need and wonder. He raised one hand and stroked her cheek.

'My little Ceecee,' he whispered. He bent and his lips touched her lips. 'My own lovely girl.'

She had waited for this and waited for this, and now it was here. She had missed it all her life, missed being touched by her father, missed the cuddling and the kissing that would have told her how valuable she was, how loved she was. She had ached for it through childhood and adolescence and as recently as a month ago. Now it was here. Now his lips pressed her lips and his hands stroked her arms and his voice called her his little Ceecee, his own lovely girl.

She leaned into him, head going to his chest, eyes closing. It was here and she was being healed by it, being made complete by it.

His hands left her arms. His hands fondled her sides, her back. His hands were at her waist, and one moved down over her hip.

'Let me love you,' he was saying, his voice hoarse and shak-

206

ing, and suddenly she didn't recognize it, didn't recognize *him*; she couldn't see her father with her head on his chest, couldn't *feel* her father.

She tried to look up then. One hand pressed her head back to his chest. 'Forgive me the lost years, Ceecee. Let me make up for it, my beautiful girl.'

'Yes,' she said. 'I will . . .'

'Let me, Ceecee,' the strange voice, the somehow terrible voice whispered. 'Let me love you.'

This time he allowed her to draw back and look at him. She saw his face poised over her, flushed and trickling sweat, almost filling the universe. She wondered at the pain of it, the incredible pain of it . . .

And then wondered no more. And then was filled with understanding. And then in the single instant it took to feel what was rising and pressing into her belly, was robbed of the healing, the completeness, the joy.

She said, *'No!'* tore away and turned to the bay and stood poised to jump. Inside she said, over and over, 'God, God, God, God . . .'

She heard him move away. She heard him climb the ladder. She heard the engines start.

She grabbed her clothing and ran down to the cabin and sat on the bunk as the *Hatteras* began to move.

He would never admit it and she would never mention it and it would never come to words between them. But they were strangers now. She would go to the final gala with him and return home to Boston with him. And then, on March thirtieth, she would come into her maturity and into her inheritance. And leave him forever.

She pulled on her dress and lay down and tried to think. And thought of Bucky Prince.

Always back to Bucky. All the hang ups solved now but that one.

If she told him what Father had told her; if he reacted the way she expected he would, the way most Americans *had* to by virtue of their unconscious racism (and she too had felt a touch of horror, and only the fact that she was who she was and looked as she did and had forty million dollars had made it unimportant); if Walter Prince showed even a *little* of what he was bound to feel, then she could finally despair of him, and free herself of him forever.

207

'Hey Bucky-baby, the mother of your child is a jigaboo!'

That's how she would tell him. That was the clincher she'd been looking for; the key to happiness.

'Oh happy, happy day,' she murmured.

The call from Beaufort came at eight thirty, after she and Fanny had cleaned up the dinner tables, both Prince's in the dining room and their own in the kitchen. Prince had gone right out, and was he ever bombed! Vino was a little worried about it; Prince had been lushing pretty heavy lately. But Rollins hit the nail right on the head when he said, 'He'll be sober for the job and that's all that counts.'

Beaufort said, 'Sandy? Sorry to bother you. Your card wasn't filled out properly. Could you come down to the office for a few minutes?'

'Oh ... I thought you already sent them away.'

'No rush, is there?'

She laughed quickly. 'You're asking me?'

He chuckled heavily.

Vino, standing behind her, whispered, 'What does he want?' She shook her head, and spoke into the phone. 'You mean right now, Byuferd?'

'That's what I mean. Not still sick, are you?'

'No ... at least not like I was. Just a touch ...'

'All right then. I'll expect you.' Before she could say anything more, he'd hung up.

Vino asked questions, and she explained, and Vino muttered, 'I don't like it. What mistake could you have made?'

She shrugged and asked him to drive her down. He hesitated, and then shook his head. 'It'll look funny, someone waiting for you. He thinks you're his girl. You can take the Mercedes and drive yourself.'

She didn't like it. She *wanted* someone waiting for her. Not that she was really worried, as she'd been on their dates, but it would've made her feel better to have Vino outside.

She didn't bother changing, just slipped a light cardigan sweater on over her uniform and got the car from the garage. She was at the stone cottage in under five minutes and Beaufort was waiting for her behind his desk.

'Hi,' she said, smiling brightly. 'Hope it won't take long. I've still got some cleaning to do.'

He stood up. 'It won't take long.' He walked ahead of her to the foyer leading past the cell to his quarters. 'This way.'

She said, 'But that's ...'

He was out of sight. She followed slowly, wondering, but still not worrying. And not worrying was a mistake. He was in the foyer, and grabbed her hand and pulled her quickly along as she said, 'What's going on? Byuferd! C'mon now. Where's my card?'

He opened a door, yanked hard and she went flying inside. He closed the door. 'Your card's on its way to Consolidated Investigations,' he said. 'Take off your sweater, your under-things, but leave on the maid's outfit.'

She looked around. It was a bedroom. She looked at him and tried to smile. 'Stop kidding, Byuferd. They're waiting for me back at the house. Mr. Prince ...'

'Mr. Prince left the island half an hour ago. You going to do as I say, or am I going to have to hurt you a little?'

He came toward her. She backed up, shaking her head. 'You're crazy,' she whispered. 'You can't just ... you can't expect ...'

His hand shot out, but not at her face. With stiff fingers, he jabbed her in the belly. She folded over, gagging.

'I did that easy,' he said. 'The next time it'll be harder. You ever get jabbed hard in the belly? And the kidneys ... that's a very pleasant feeling, getting hooked in the kidneys. Want to check it out?'

She shook her head. She was in agony, but stronger than the physical pain was the overwhelming fear of this man. Still bent over, she began to struggle out of her sweater.

'That's the girl.' His terrible, terrible face, like pitted stone, shifted in a smile, which made it only *more* terrible because it was a ... a *dirty* smile. She got the sweater off and began to cry.

'The underthings,' he said, his smile disappearing. '*Fast!* I haven't got all night!'

She moved her hands toward the hem of her skirt and stopped and sobbed, 'Why're you doing this? Why're you hurting me, and ... and making trouble for yourself? Let me go now and we'll forget all ...'

He stepped toward her and she cried out and twisted away. Another mistake, turning her back on him. She found out about that 'very pleasant feeling' of being hit in the kidneys. She fell on the bed, writhing in pain, the screams choked off by her tightened throat. And besides, he was pressing her face into the bedding so that she thought she would smother.

After a while, the pain let up and so did he. And she realized he had his hand under her skirt and inside her pants, feeling her ass. But he was looking at her in that same icy, brutal way.

'Why?' she gasped, and quickly added, 'I'll do it, but why?'

A finger made her gasp. He smiled that dirty smile. 'You must think me as stupid as the men you're used to. You couldn't stand being with me. I gave it two dates. I was going to give it three, maybe four, but that cop-out with getting sick and having friends coming to visit ... that clinched it.' He leaned over her, eyes gleaming dog yellow. 'I spent good money on you. I said straight things to you. No one takes Byuferd. If you were a man, I'd beat the shit out of you. But you're not a man.' His dirty smile returned. His hand resumed its explorations. She grunted, jumped, said, 'Please,' but without hope. He said, 'Thank God you're not a man.'

'This is wrong, Byuferd. I'll do it, but ... *forcing* a woman is a sin.'

He laughed. It was the first time she had ever heard him laugh, really laugh, and he laughed quite a while, shaking his head. 'You dirty cunt,' he finally said, 'what do you take me for? I've dealt with your kind all my life. I could put my hand in up to the elbow, that's how much you care about *sin*. Get those underthings off. I want to be served by my maid. Get them off and get down here.' He pointed at his feet.

She knew now she was in the hands of a pig, a real pig like the one at the sand pit back home when she was a kid.

Trying to pull down her panties without revealing too much, she said, 'You know what this means, Byuferd? Rape is a serious ...'

He stepped toward her, fist raised, and she wailed and cowered and said, 'No, I won't tell! I won't, Byuferd, honest to God I won't!'

'You're goddam right you won't. If you do, I'll say you were absolutely compliant and my word's a lot better'n yours. And I'll make your life a hell. I'll check back to the day you crawled out of your bitch-mother. I'll check every day from then to now. And I've got friends in every police department from here to Vancouver. You'll come to me on your knees, *begging* me to lay off ...'

'Byuferd,' she wept. 'Byuferd, I'll be good! Honest, just

don't hurt me! Just ... be nice to me.'

He snapped his fingers. 'Move!' She quickly pulled the panties down over her shoes and fumbled at her blouse. Her fingers shook so badly she couldn't get the buttons open. She was afraid he would think she was stalling and hit her and said, 'Wait, I can't ... just a minute...' She got the blouse open and stopped, her mind not functioning. 'I ... I have to take it off to take off the brassière.'

'What the hell do I care *how* you do it. Just do it!' She nodded and began to remove the blouse, and now that she didn't expect it his hand lashed out and sent her sprawling, ears ringing from the blow. Her skirt was up and numbly she began to tug it down. 'Leave it up,' he said. She did. She sat on the floor and took off her blouse and removed her brassière. He said, 'Nice tits. Shake them.' She looked at him. 'I said shake them!' She moved her shoulders. She was crying and she knew he didn't like that but she couldn't help it. He said, 'C'mon!' She shook her shoulders and her breasts bounced and he nodded. 'All right, put the top back on and get over here.'

By the time she had her blouse on he had opened his fly and removed his penis. It drooped out the opening and he said, 'Suck it up nice and hard now, Miss Blake.'

She came across the room as if to her execution and went down on her knees and fought back the sobs. 'Now you answer me, Miss Blake.' His hand was heavy on her head. 'Answer me like you'd answer Mr. Prince if he asked you to do this.'

'Yes ... sir,' she wept.

'Yes sir what? Say it!'

'Yes sir I'll suck it up good and hard.'

'Now do it!'

She did it. She gagged at the feel and taste and smell of him, and kept telling herself it was all in her mind and she'd done it before and enjoyed it. And still she gagged, remembering that cop back home, and this was worse, much worse. Yet she hoped he would finish this way, bad as it was; just didn't want to go to that bed. God, she couldn't face going to that bed and having him ...

'All right,' he gasped, pulling away from her. She looked up. He was pointing at the bed. 'On your ass, hurry!'

Shivering, she went to the bed and lay down on her back. 'Spread!'

She parted her legs.

'Wide!'

She closed her eyes and opened her legs as far as she could. First, she felt his hands. For a long time she felt his hands, and then his weight was on her. She was sick and she was crying, but she was grateful for one thing: He hadn't undressed. She didn't care how he was built; she couldn't have stood his naked body.

'Damn you!' he said, and her head rocked with the force of his slap.

'I'm sorry,' she sobbed. 'I ... I can't help it!'

'You'd better help it.' He was raising himself, his fist drawing back over her naked belly.

'Wait! Please, I'll ...' But how did you make the juice of love flow when you were sick to your stomach?

She spat on her hand and put it between her legs. She did it again and again, and he began to laugh. 'Play with yourself,' he said.

'Yes sir.'

She spat and played and, for the first time in years, she really prayed. Prayed for this to be over.

He got back on her. He got in, though it still wasn't right, and she clenched her jaws and fought back moans of pain. He pounded away, grunting each time he slammed down on her body, and then he began to spew obscenities. He mauled her breasts through the blouse and pounded and spoke filth and she thought desperately of what it was like with Vino, with Rollins, with any human being ... and finally she had to think of what it was like with Prince.

'Shake your ... shake your big ass!' he panted, and slapped at her thighs and bottom until she had to cry out. He made it then and for the first time tonight kissed her. He took her face in one big hand, palm cupping her chin and fingers digging into her cheeks, and he put his own mouth over her mouth and sucked at her.

That she didn't throw up was a miracle. A moment later he got off her and said, 'All right, get the hell out.'

She couldn't believe it! She had thought she would *die* here!

She jumped off the bed and headed right for the door. 'Take your stinking underwear,' he said, and yawned.

She was afraid to approach him, and he was standing near her brassière. Yet she had to obey. She came over, bent down, and he kicked her behind. Not too hard, but she fell over. He laughed. 'You're the lousiest piece of tail I *ever* had. But you suck all right.'

She scrambled to her panties and sweater, then ran to the door. He said, 'Hey!'

She stopped.

'I gave you a compliment. What do you say?'

'Thank you.'

'Thank you *what*!' He took a step toward her.

'Thank you *sir*! I'm sorry, *sir*! Good night, *sir*!'

He laughed. He put a hand inside his fly and scratched himself. 'Maybe I oughta make you lick me clean.'

She stood there, wanting to scream and able only to wait. If he told her to do it, she would have to do it. She could call for no one, tell no one, not even the others at the house. They would know she had fouled up with Beaufort. They would blame her if anything happened with those reports. If only she had gone through with last night's date, all this might not have happened!

He said, 'But you're probably out of spit,' and laughed some more.

She made herself smile.

He waved her out.

She was hurrying down the foyer when she heard, 'Hold it!'

'Hail Mary...' she began, trying to remember the rest and not able to and feeling that if it went on much longer she would crack and shriek and he would do what he'd said and not only would March fifteenth be finished but he would hound her...

He was in the bedroom doorway. He pointed at her. 'Just you be good now, hear? I don't want any problems with you.'

'Yes sir.'

He closed the door.

She ran past the cell and through the office and outside, clutching her sweater and underthings. She got inside the car and lay down on the seat and pushed her face into the upholstery, screaming deep in her throat. Then the thought that he might look out the window and see she was still there and come out made her jerk erect and drive away with a spinning of wheels.

She stopped again, in a dark spot at the side of Bay Drive. She checked the dashboard clock, and it had only been a half-hour. *A half-hour!*

She wept.

After getting into his bathrobe and sitting down at his desk with a cold beer, Beaufort began to feel something besides satisfaction. Something that eluded him.

He'd carried it through just as he'd planned, so what else *was* there to feel but satisfaction? He'd had his piece and paid the little bitch back for trying to make a fool of him. He'd figured her just right, judged her fear . . .

Her fear.

Why had he judged her fear to be so great that she would take whatever he dished out? She wasn't a whore like those he used to roust for soliciting and take to his room for a few hours of fun. Or a shoplifter, or a kid caught in a car with a boy. She wasn't anyone who had to fear the law or publicity and was blocked from recourse to the courts . . . and yet he had sensed his power over her from the beginning.

He had also sensed her dislike of him from the beginning . . .

So why had she accepted his invitations? Why had she tried to make a fool of him? For a free meal, a few drinks and a hotel show? Not likely . . . but why else? Why hadn't she turned him down that first time? And that second time?

She was afraid of him and he had counted on it tonight but he didn't know *why*.

He lit a cigarette and sipped his beer and stared at nothing. He turned to an adjacent filing cabinet, removed a folder marked, 'Bay One', and went through the typewritten sheets, routine abstracts of the scanty information on Walter Prince's servants. He thought back to Sandy and their first date, trying to remember everything. And that second date, before she'd played sick.

He read the abstracts again and placed a mental picture of a person alongside each name. Charles DeVino. Fanny Lescou. Broderick Rollins. And, of course, Sandra Blake.

He leaned back and closed his eyes, letting his mind, his experienced cop's mind, roam free. He played What-If. Then he swung his chair around to the typewriter, inserted a sheet with the Bay Island Security letterhead, and addressed it to Bob McGuire at Consolidated Investigations. It was a brief note. It stated that something had come up that required a rush response on the following names. He hesitated; then shrugged, smiling at himself and his what-if game, and added the name, Walter Danforth Prince.

214

Book III

SATURDAY, MARCH 15

It was eight a.m. when Bucky boarded the *Spray*. Rollins had just left by cab to meet Bramms in Miami Beach. The sky was a heavy, leaden blue, an oppressive color despite the absence of any but the highest, whitest of clouds above the faint haze. There was practically no wind to speak of on shore, and it was already warm, giving promise of real heat later in the day.

As the *Spray* nosed slowly, sluggishly away from the dock, Bucky could see the sleek Coast Guard cutter in Coast Guard gray anchored some two hundred feet off the Vener dock. Three men lounged around the forward deck, and another sat sunning himself near a post-mounted, ostentatiously exposed machine gun. From what he'd been able to gather by observing the cutter since Thursday afternoon, Bucky guessed it carried a crew of at least eight, possibly ten, all of whom wore sidearms, even when stripped to the waist for sunbathing.

They were watching him now, he knew, even though he kept busy with wheel and sheets. They watched every craft in the area, turning away those that didn't match specifications given by the yacht club; the few, that is, that managed to elude Beaufort's security speedboat which had been circling the island constantly, night and day, since Bob Lacton's arrival. There would be no chance whatsoever for Bramms to bring the LC into these waters as matters now stood. And no chance of changing the plan to exclude Bramms and try the robbery any other way, because of the mass of security agents; seventeen, as Bucky had learned from the Veners, and as Beaufort had told Sandy. These included three helicopter pilots and two communications experts, but since all were armed, only an army of madmen would buck such odds!

Bucky was passing between the cutter and the Vener dock, and turned to wave at the Coast Guard craft. The men fore waved back; the man at the machine gun saluted casually.

Very polite, all of them, along with all the agents ashore. Very aware of the island's VIP status. But very, very alert, nonetheless.

He was past the cutter now, moving toward the island's west end, picking up a little more wind and headway, but just a little. If Lacton left early in the evening and the robbery did take place, lack of wind might pose a problem...

He came past what Bay Islanders called Mortonson's Finger, a thinly wooded strip of land probing eighty or so feet out into the bay, acting as a breakwater and giving Allie's dock a degree of protection during storms. And there was Ceecee standing on the dock, using binoculars on him.

She waved. He ignored it. He had no time to waste, no thought to spare on her now.

'Bucky,' she shouted. 'Bucky...'

She had phoned him twice in the past week. He hadn't returned the calls. He had his plans, his fear and his whiskey. It was all he could handle.

But he found himself looking at her. She was wearing her tennis outfit. She was a little girl in white and he couldn't ignore her. He waved, hoping that would suffice.

Her voice reached him through the still air. 'Come in...'

He shouted, 'Sorry, previous engagement,' swinging south for the General Causeway and open bay water. He saw her bend and take off her shoes. He told himself to concentrate on sailing, but kept watching. She came up from her crouch in a run, and went off the dock in a shallow racing dive.

He could probably outrun her, if the breeze held and he wasn't becalmed. But knowing her, he thought she would probably swim until she sank of exhaustion, and his lifesaving abilities were no longer what they should be. He came about, emptying his sail, and lay dead in the water. She swam beautifully, he had to give her that. He watched as she came closer and took a towel from the drawer under the stern seat. She didn't need instructions or a rope ladder, to board the low-lying *Spray*. She grasped the fender, made of canvas and filled with ground cork, and caught her breath. Then, reaching up for his hand, she came aboard in one smooth motion.

He worked with wheel and sheets, and got the sloop moving again. When he had time to look, she was drying her hair. 'I've got a robe in the cabin,' he said.

'That's all right. The sun's warm. I'll dry quickly.'

He sat at the wheel. He felt a thousand years removed from the man who had made love to her. He didn't understand why she was here. He didn't want her here.

'I'm surprised you can sail on such a calm day.'

'In sailor's terminology,' he said, voice cool and precise, 'calm means wind of less than one mile per hour. This isn't calm.'

She sat down on the deck close to the wheel, hugging her knees, looking up at him. He kept his eyes out on the bay for a while, then had to turn to her. 'Is that so?' she murmured. 'And will you correct me in that professorial manner no matter *what* I say?'

'Not if you say, "I'm surprised you can sail in such light air." Light air is wind of one to three miles per hour. We're doing a little better than that now, as you might be able to judge, if you watch our wake. We're catching a slight breeze, four to seven . . .'

'And what, Professor, would you say if I told you I'm a Negro?'

He was trying not to look at her legs, her long and lovely legs, and her face, her lean and piquant face. He was trying to forget her very presence, because the minutes were ticking away and soon would become hours and his chance at the good life was slipping by.

But she never said the expected; always threw him off pace. 'A black?'

She nodded.

'I'd say black is beautiful.'

'I mean it. Allie told me my real father was Negro, light-skinned but identifiably Negro. That's why I phoned you. I wanted you to know.'

'Why?'

She waved an arm impatiently. 'I'm telling you something vital and you're . . .'

'Vital to you, perhaps. But why should it be of interest to me?'

'You're angry because of that broken sailing date. And my exhibition at the last gala. You're letting little things get in the way of a big thing.'

'Again, a big thing to you, but why should it be *anything* to me?'

She stared at him and despite the cold coil of fear and tension that had been dominating his insides for three days, he was pleased at the red beginning to tinge her cheeks.

'You're one of the candidates for daddy, remember?'

'Oh, *I* remember. And *that* was of some importance to me. But you made it plain it meant nothing to you.'

She leaped up, face twisting. 'Can't you understand what I'm saying! Do you think I'd joke about something like this!'

'I didn't think you were joking.' And he *hadn't*. It just didn't mean anything to him. Didn't change anything for him, and didn't change anything for *them*.

'Then ... what if it's *your* child? Aren't you concerned? Do you think a Negro child can have a decent life in this country?'

He laughed. He couldn't help it. 'You seem to be doing all right. Or you could, if you were a little less intent on playing Emancipated Woman. And a child born of you and me, or you and that Waters boy, or you and any other Bay Island male, could hardly be classified as "a black child".'

'Yes he would!'

She was really angry now and he didn't understand it. But then again, he had never understood her. She had always confused and puzzled him. Upset him too, only this time he couldn't see anything to be upset about, beyond her presence here.

'One remote ancestor and a man or woman is classified as black!' she said.

'By whom? People you care anything about? And why bother to tell anyone, if it frightens you that much? Which brings us back to my original question—why bother to tell *me*?'

'Because ... you might be the father and ... don't you know what they say about throwbacks and ... would you ever admit to the paternity of a black ...'

'Come on now,' he interrupted, irritated, beginning to doubt everything she'd told him. Because she was certainly better educated than *that;* or even if she wasn't, she would have looked into the subject as soon as she'd found out about her real father. 'You know that's nonsense!'

She moved her lips. She clenched her fists. She turned abruptly away, stepping toward the side.

He felt she was going to dive overboard and try to swim back to the island, a dangerously long swim now. The breeze had grown to Moderate; he spun the wheel hard to starboard. The *Spray* heeled and Ceecee fell to her hands and knees. 'Raise the jib,' he said.

She didn't move.

'*Jump!*'

She looked back at him, startled. 'I don't know how.'

As he turned the boat into the wind, he pointed at the jib halyard and told her to pull on it. She got up and followed his repeated instructions until the sail was at the top of the stay. He helped her secure the halyard to the cleat, and turned the wheel so that he was now heading on a port tack.

'Pull in the leeward jib sheet until the jib stops luffing.' He pointed, nodded and smiled as her eyes flew upward at the pistol shots of sound resulting from the main spilling its wind and flapping in the breeze. 'That's luffing,' he added, and set his course for Bay Island.

When she sat down beside him again, she was panting. He said she had the makings of a good sailor. She said he had the makings of an *excellent* Captain Bligh. 'Seriously,' he said, 'you have the right instincts.'

She looked down at her left hand, where she'd suffered a slight rope burn. 'But you won't sail with anyone. Chichester and all that.'

'I'm no Chichester,' he muttered. 'Just never found anyone I *wanted* to sail with before.' Immediately he was sorry he'd said that ... and then told himself he was *not* disappointed when she didn't pick it up.

'I meant what I said, Bucky. About being part black.'

'Does it make you unhappy?'

She raised her head, catching his eyes, trying to hold them. He looked quickly away.

'Did you see ... black characteristics?' she asked.

'What?'

'When you looked away from me?'

'I don't know what the hell you're talking about!'

'My mouth ... and I'm dark ... and perhaps other things ... my genetic inheritance.'

'And the Prince family had a Southern branch and plantations and I'm dark and my lower lip is full and who the hell actually knows what he is when ...'

'All right,' she said. 'Don't shout.'

With all that was on his mind she had to bother him with

219

this goddam foolishness! Why couldn't she leave him alone!

A little later, approaching the Mortonson dock, he was sorry. He didn't know why; perhaps because he wasn't able to concentrate on something that was hurting her. She had asked for his help, he guessed—though the *way* she'd done it had been more challenge than request.

She was looking up at the mainsail.

'You're not *really* worried about a dark child, are you?'

She shook her head, still staring at the sail.

'And you know who you are and that hasn't changed with some words about Negro blood, has it?'

She shook her head again, and then, looking at him, 'But you never even asked how it came about.' She suddenly seemed surprised. 'You haven't asked the right questions. After all, you'd think ...' She shrugged and rose, touching her white tennis skirt. 'All dry. But I've missed my game with James Bond.'

'I didn't think he'd have the time.'

'He always has time for me. He has hopes, Mr. Bond does.'

'Yes?'

'With good reason.'

'Yes.'

She stepped up on the cabin housing and held to the mast. 'I've been reading books on black history. I know a little more than I knew before. I'm a little more compassionate than I was before. And I'll read more and learn more. And maybe ...'

When she didn't go on, he finished for her. 'And maybe it's a good thing. Maybe it's going to enrich your life, if you allow it to.'

He'd thought she would like that, would finally smile, but what she did was jump to the deck, say, 'We're close enough, thanks,' and dived overboard.

On the way back home, he tried to understand what her point had been in telling him all this. The obvious answer was that she was distraught over learning she had Negro blood and wanted a sympathetic ear. At the same time, he could *not* believe it would really bother her. He felt that way because he didn't believe it would bother *him*. If a person's life would be drastically and negatively changed, his livelihood threatened, his family destroyed, *then* there was reason to be distraught. But none of that applied to Ceecee. Her father had known all along. Her baby wouldn't suffer ...

It probably all came back to that very real and literally grow-ing problem; the fact that she was going to have a baby. And she might have told him because she actually knew *he* was the father.

He waved at the Coast Guard cutter. He concentrated on lowering sail and using the auxiliary to dock. She had said he was only one of three prospects for daddy and he believed her. There was no reason for him not to believe her.

Walking toward the house, he was again caught up in the grip of tension. Vino, Sandy and Fanny were waiting. What could he say to them?

Ceecee went directly to her room, showered and got into a bathrobe. A helicopter chuck-chucked overhead, as they'd been doing since Thursday, and she said quietly, 'Oh damn,' and lay down and closed her eyes thinking of how she'd made a fool of herself and how he never, no *never*, did what she wanted him to ... that mothering ...

The phone rang; her buzzer sounded; it was Bud Franklin, her James Bond. 'I'm sorry, Bud, I wasn't feeling well.'

'Gee, I was worried, Ceecee. No one could find you.'

'Went for a long walk, by myself.'

'Will I see you at the costume party tonight?'

'Yes. Is it definite then you'll be there? I mean, the Presi-dent ...'

'As of last night, the word is go for the gala.' He chuckled, and she gave him a little laugh in return, and he was happy.

'See you then,' he said.

Yes, see you then. Her last night on this fucking island. And nothing settled because Bucky Prince never acted the way she expected him to act and today he hadn't even seemed to understand what she was saying.

He hadn't believed her. That was it. Or he was great at covering up.

Or he was the man she wanted, the man who didn't give a good goddam about such a thing.

She was still standing at the phone, and almost called him.

But then she remembered his face from the bathroom that one night of love. And his words in the car at the country club that night she'd told him she was pregnant. And Beth Larkin and Karen Vener and maybe his fat-assed little maid and any-one else he could get. And she remembered her feeling, her

221

knowledge, that he was remote from her, that even when he was with her some vital part of him wasn't. And with all the needles she'd been slipping him lately, he no longer even *liked* her, as evidenced by his ignoring her phone calls and ignoring her at the dock ...

Why the hell was she wasting time and tears—yes, *tears,* standing there and crying like a fool!—over him when she had written him off; written him off at least a dozen times!

She went back to the bed and lay down. Well, she would write him off one more time. Tomorrow, she wouldn't even know him any more.

She rolled over on her face; and the thought came that she would know him all her life, through his child.

It hurt and it felt good.

She told herself she was a madwoman and got up to examine her costume for the gala.

Bramms drove his Chevvy and Buddy-Boy kept his eyes out the window on the scenery. It was only an hour to the boat-yard in Berrywood. Only an hour, and all he had to do was give Bramms a breakdown on the latest information and keep his cool and then he would drive back to the causeway and walk back to the house. Nothing to it.

And yet, as soon as he'd entered the car beside the squat man, he'd felt himself tensing, tightening, wanting to lash out at that flat, ugly face! He felt certain Bramms would do something to hurt them all, do something to ruin the robbery.

'You mean that Coast Guard boat's still there and all the Secret Service men too? Then what the hell am I doing with that goddam LC!'

The shout made Buddy-Boy's mouth twist but he kept his eyes to the window. 'You know the answer to that. We all do what we're supposed to do until ...'

'Until that idiot Prince calls it all off! But meanwhile I'm supposed to explain to the cops why I'm cruising around in a landing craft with a submachine gun and rockets and ...'

'Until the President leaves,' Buddy-Boy went on, keeping his voice level. 'You know the alternative plan. You spoke to Prince and Vino Wednesday. You cruise a mile or two east of the island, using your binoculars ...'

'Don't get snotty with me, sonny boy!'

Rollins's big hands began to clench but he became aware of it

222

and opened them. 'That's Buddy-Boy,' he intoned.

'What? *What!*'

Buddy-Boy sighed, and looked at Bramms. 'I said, that's Buddy-Boy.'

Bramms glanced away from the road to glare at him and began to shout, and Buddy-Boy said, 'Listen, if you've got to get your head beaten in, if you've just *got* to, stop the car and I'll do it for you and then we can get on with the job.'

Bramms swerved off the highway, slamming on his brakes. Buddy-Boy was out of the car as soon as it stopped. He was sorry in a way, because he had promised Prince and Vino it would all go smooth but he was glad too, because he had wanted to lay into Curt Bramms since the day they'd met.

Bramms was standing with his back to the highway, in his hand was a big revolver, Buddy-Boy froze. They looked at each other. Bramms's face was white and crazy. Buddy-Boy didn't say anything. He knew, suddenly, that Bramms was nut enough to kill him. But he didn't back off and he didn't plead; just waited.

Finally, Bramms spoke, voice thin and shaky. 'After the job, I'll come looking for you after the job.'

'Good enough,' Buddy-Boy said carefully. He wanted to add that Bramms wouldn't have to come looking.

The rest of the trip passed in complete silence. At Berrywood, he helped Bramms carry the four big suitcases aboard the freshly painted deep blue barge, then walked away as Bramms handed the envelope of cash to the man at the canal dock. If it wasn't for the robbery, he would have prayed for the barge to be blasted out of the water by that Coast Guard cutter!

He calmed down somewhat on the trip back to the General Causeway. By the time he abandoned the Chevvy on the shoulder and began walking toward the Bay Island entrance road, he had convinced himself that nothing very much had happened.

And yet, deep down in his mind where he'd put it away, the thought, the *conviction*, that Bramms had to be destroyed lay in wait.

Manny Kahn drove his little red and blue mail wagon over the bridge ... and seeing Beaufort's Dodge just entering Bay Drive, tapped his horn lightly and waved. Then he made a motion for Beaufort to stop.

Beaufort looked, barely nodded and kept going. *Well screw him!* Manny thought. Beaufort was the least friendly guy in all Miami!

But still, he had a Special Delivery for him ... and so he really leaned on his horn and turned after the security chief. Beaufort slammed on his brakes, backed up with a screech of tires and shouted out his window: 'Where the hell you think you are anyway!'

Manny began to answer but Beaufort just kept shouting.

'Don't you go honking horns around here! I've got the President of the United States to take care of, so whatever the hell you got to say can wait!'

He rocketed off.

Manny turned and drove to the stone cottage. He brought Beaufort's five pieces of mail inside—*The American Rifleman* magazine, three junks and the Special from Consolidated Investigations—and placed them on the desk. Then he took the Special from the top of the little pile and humming quietly, slid it underneath, so it was completely hidden. Whatever the hell the Special had to say could wait too.

He had the engine running at about two thirds maximum. The LCVP moved along at under four knots, some three hundred feet off shore. The sky was hazy blue; the water as calm as he could have hoped for; other boats had been few in the two hours since he'd left the Berrywood Canal. He had stretched the tarpaulin over the front half of the craft and working under it for brief periods, with frequent withdrawals to check the wheel, his course and any curious boats. He had placed the firework rockets in their low stand, unpacked the machine gun, wet suit, binoculars, tape-recorder-player and amplifier-speaker and tried out the stern-mounted spotlight.

And then, surprisingly, there was nothing more to do. All that anticipation, and now he had hours and hours to kill, just sitting at the wheel and listening to the engine chugging and feeling the LC bounce even in this mild sea. He looked up at the sky again, wondering if the weather forecasters could be mistaken about the storm bypassing Miami. That brassy, hazy blue ... it smelled like bad weather to him.

What if the forecast had changed? What if right now they were broadcasting small-craft warnings for this evening, or even this afternoon? This floating dump truck wouldn't be safe in a strong breeze, and a moderate gale would send it to the bottom.

He began to get up, and then sank back, moaning, 'Shit!' He'd forgotten his transistor radio, which he'd wanted simply as an aid in killing time. Now he had no way of finding out about changes in the forecast ... unless he hailed another craft and asked.

But he couldn't do that. He'd glared at the two speed boats that had come close to inspect him and had turned his back on a girl who had called from the first, 'What do you call your boat?'

But that was before he'd finished stretching the tarpaulin. Now he looked like a cargo barge, or hoped he did.

It was ten thirty and the weekend boaters were more in evidence. A Rhodes 19 class sailboat was coming towards him from shore, a large power cruiser from behind. The cruiser swerved and went roaring out to sea. The one man in the small sailboat put a hand to his eyes and peered at the LCVP; then maneuvered to come in closer on the starboard. Bramms almost welcomed the approach, because he was beginning to think of that bastard Rollins and how cocky he'd been; as if Bramms would have allowed him to land even a single punch! Just wait until the job was over!

'Ahoy, LC! Haven't seen one of those since Anzio!' It was the man in the Rhodes 19. Bramms nodded and looked away. 'Using her for cargo?' the man called, now only some twenty feet away. Bramms wanted to answer, to engage the man in conversation, and then to ask if there'd been any change in the marine forecast. But he hesitated, and by the time he turned to the Rhodes 19, ready to take a chance and enter into conversation, the little sailboat was tacking toward shore.

Bramms opened the neck of his blue cotton work shirt as the sun climbed higher and grew hotter. (His inner turmoil climbed too, creating heat of its own.) The rest of his outfit was levis and tennis shoes, to give a workman-sailor appearance, instead of the usual whites or swim outfit of the pleasure boatsman. Except for handkerchief and self sealing plastic identification holder with driver's license, twenty dollar bill, two photographs and the LC's ownership papers, he carried nothing in his pockets. He would have lost anything else when he changed into wetsuit and scuttled the LC.

225

He reached to the deck for his charts, but he really didn't have to check them. It was all simple pilotage, simple landmark identification. Right now he was approaching Pompano Beach, a third of the way to Miami. If he made as good time the rest of the way, he would reach Miami about three to three thirty and Bay Island at four thirty to five. Too early, even at this snail's pace. Too early because of the change in plans due to that lousy Coast Guard boat! And yet, he couldn't cut back his speed very much more than he already had. As Prince had said, there was always the possibility that the President would leave before the party and then the original plan would go back into effect. To cover that possibility, Bramms had to be somewhere near the island at about five thirty or six o'clock.

But as things stood, he would have to stay several miles away and watch the Coast Guard cutter through binoculars, hoping not to arouse suspicion; then, after nightfall, move in closer, still managing to remain unseen by the Coast Guard, and watch for the flare that would signal the beginning of the feint. And *then* he would have to do everything so damned fast—spotlight, tape-recorder, rockets, machine gun and scuttling—all so damned fast that there was practically no chance at all that it could go as planned. The best to be hoped for was that he would manage to get ashore after making some minor disturbance, because he wouldn't have time for the off-shore cruising that would create suspicion...

He opened another button on his shirt, feeling he was choking. He didn't mind taking chances, *wanted* to take chances but he also wanted some chance of success, and the way it shaped up now success was remote.

'Christ,' he muttered, using his handkerchief on balding head, face and neck.

He wanted a cigarette ... and had forgotten them too. They were in the glove compartment of his car and his car was back in Miami now, parked off the causeway. Hours and hours before he could have a cigarette! A full day before he could have a cigarette!

He was sweating, clenching and unclenching his fists, in a frenzy of self hatred and despair.

He got up, went to the tarpaulin, then back to the wheel. It was a little choppier, and the flat bottomed craft began bouncing in a more pronounced manner. He sat down again, one hand on the wheel. With the other hand, he took the clear

226

plastic identification case from his back pocket and pulled the little flap that opened the self sealing edge. He removed the two wallet-sized photographs and put the case away. He looked at the pictures of two women, one dead and one, so far as he knew, alive. One blonde and angular and rather plain looking, the other dark and curved and pretty. One the late Ivy Bramms, the other the chastened Barbara Amaley; reminders of his two ritual bloodlettings, ultimate proofs of his manhood, his strength, his ability to triumph over society, over the world that continually threatened to destroy him.

He held the pictures tightly, hand sweating. They represented his one sure means of salvation; a means that would be repeated tonight. He forced his mind back to the past, the triumph of the past...

Ivy had threatened to leave him. Actually, he'd wanted nothing more than that; he despised and feared her. Despised her for her inability to arouse him, and feared her for her growing knowledge of what he really was. And then, after the last failure in bed, she had said something he could *not* forgive: 'You're not a man, Curt. You're impotent.' He had struck her and screamed, 'Only with you!' which hadn't been quite the truth but which hadn't been quite a lie either; not at *that* time. Only recently...

She decided to leave him. She had hired a lawyer, a Jew named Richard Beiler, and the Jew had asked him to come in and discuss terms of the separation. But they were still living together in the roomy apartment over the drugstore in the town of Agrew, South Carolina, about two hundred miles from where his mother still lived. And he'd understood that allowing her to leave would be allowing her to carry away a memory of him as a non man.

There was no way out but to destroy her. No other way. And so he begged her not to leave him, said he would seek medical help, said he loved her and couldn't live without her. She found the last hard to accept, after some of the scenes they'd had, some of the things he'd said to her. But it had confused her just enough so that she had hesitated, told her lawyer to wait, decided to think it over. And he had immediately begun planning her death.

Poison was out. He was a druggist. Anything to do with the tools of his trade was out.

In fact, anything at *all* should have been out, since people

227

knew she was thinking of leaving him, neighbors had heard him ranting...

But he had to kill her. Had to take his chances. Anticipated being suspected and therefore had to find a way in which the chances of his being convicted, if tried, would be minimal.

An accident. Something that would stand up as an accident—a *possible* accident—no matter how much suspicion was cast on him.

He rode horseback. She occasionally accompanied him. He had his own horse at a stable outside of town. She rented horses, generally gentle ones. She would fall from her horse and die of the injuries.

They rode one Sunday morning, and his tension was always a little higher on Sunday mornings because even while married to a WASP he hadn't been able to go to church. Ivy was agnostic and mocked church.

It was early winter. They rode along a downward sloping and mildly turning bridle path. There was one sharp right turn and then a wooded section. If a horse were to bolt off the path between the trees, the rider was bound to get knocked off by low branches.

Bramms said, 'Ivy.'

He had allowed her to get slightly ahead of him, and she turned. Her angular features were ugly, not just plain, to him now. It was because of her, he told himself, that he was failing at sex. Once rid of her, once with someone softer, prettier, more feminine, all would be well.

He raised his riding crop. Her face began to change. Before it could complete the transference from a questioning glance to one of horror, he had brought the gelding forward, blocking her mount's side movement, and slashed down with the crop. The mare bolted as he'd thought she would, off the path and through the trees.

He followed as quickly as he could, hanging low alongside the gelding's neck to escape the branches. The mare was already out of sight, its hoofbeats fading rapidly. But Ivy was lying under a tree not more than a hundred feet from the path. He stopped and looked down at her, beginning to feel release, joy and triumph. She lay on her back, arms outflung, one leg twisted beneath her, head also twisted and face bloody ... but even as he leaned off the gelding to determine if she breathed, her eyes opened and she groaned. She didn't see him at first,

228

and then her eyes moved and she saw his horse and tried to sit up. Struggling, she opened her mouth and looked at him. 'Please,' he heard. 'Oh please . . .'

He said, 'Hyeah!' and kicked the gelding sharply. It neighed and danced sideways as Ivy screamed. He kicked it again, and it went right over her. Her scream was cut short this time.

He reined up and turned and saw she was lying still. He came up close and noticing the deep dent in the side of her head and the whitish muck mixing with trickling red. He sucked in breath, trembling with delight.

After making certain she was dead, he got back on his horse and maneuvered it around so as to thoroughly confuse the tracks. Then he rode toward the stable, rehearsing his story.

It was too bad the fall hadn't killed her, for he would have to admit he had run over her. While trying to catch her run-away horse, of course. While trying to save her life. And then she had fallen and he hadn't been able to stop his gelding and the tragedy had happened.

Her Jew lawyer talked to the D.A. and the D.A. talked to Bramms. For three weeks, almost every day, that damned D.A. talked to him. But he admitted to only the evidence they had—his running over her with the gelding—and an expert was unwilling to say more than that the tracks were 'suspicious' and his only bad moment came when a twenty-five thousand dollars life insurance policy turned up in her father's safe deposit box, with *him* as the beneficiary. He hadn't known a thing about it!

It almost put him on trial for his life; but almost doesn't count and the coroner's jury finally labeled the death acci-dental. Curt Bramms had sold his drugstore a few weeks later and what with Ivy's insurance, the savings they'd put aside for twelve years and the good price he'd gotten for the store, he was worth over a hundred thousand dollars. A hundred and eighteen thousand, to be exact. He was free and he was well off! Certainly well enough to live better than he had ever had before.

He found a store for sale in a town on the North Carolina border, not too far from the Atlantic. He also found a house, isolated on a sixteen acre site; a beautiful four room house that had been part of an old estate and included a barn with stable for his horse. He furnished it in wood and leather and bought a whole new wardrobe. He piloted a Cessna and sky-dived with a weekend club, boated and skin-dived out of Myrtle Beach. He skied, skated and tobogganed on flying trips to Vermont. He did everything that his mythological Jew could not do and thought often of how he had killed, beginning to want a woman. He found her in a fine tavern-restaurant he frequented for dinner. They spoke at the bar. Her name was Barbara Amaley, a musical comedy dancer who had come home after three years of failure and near-alcoholism. She was twenty-eight and beautiful in a dark, sultry, overripe manner, and was looking for someone, anyone to foot the bills. Curt Bramms seemed the answer to her not-so-maidenly prayers. After one successful evening, she moved in with him.

For five months Curt Bramms lived the life he'd dreamed of. True, there were occasional failures in bed, but if he paced himself at twice a week, he could just about eliminate them. And true, he didn't like Barbara's frequent trips to Bennton 'to see my mother and uncle', trips from which she returned too exhilarated to suit him. But his business went well and his life went well ... for five months.

Then the tensions began to mount. Barbara wasn't the same. She didn't treat him with quite the ... the *respect* he needed. Her visits to Bennton became more frequent. His failures became more frequent. (Or had it been the other way around, the more frequent failures preceding the more frequent visits?) And so one day, he left his assistant in charge of the store and drove to Bennton and located Barbara's red Ford convertible on a sleepy sidestreet, not too difficult a task in the town of three thousand. He parked around the corner and went into a bar and looked through the local phone book and could find no listing for Ameley. Of course, that could have been a stage name, though it wasn't smooth or professional enough, it seemed to him. Or perhaps her mother had married again, and her uncle was on the mother's side ...

He had a few drinks and went around the corner, the red Ford was still there. It stayed there for almost six hours, and then Barbara came out of a frame house with a wide porch, with her was a boy, a kid no more than eighteen, if that.

Could he be her *son*?

It was growing dark but the porch had a light and the way the boy put his arm around her waist as they walked to the street and the way he leaned into the window of the car and the way they kissed told Curt Bramms it was *not* a mother and

230

son relationship.

But a goddam *kid*!

He got home before she did. They had dinner at the tavern. They went to a movie and she laughed heartily at the Jerry Lewis comedy and he sat there with the humiliation and rage building as he glanced sideways at her and could see certain things now—her nose, her entire face—that made him begin to understand.

She was a Jew!

With that, he no longer cared anything about her.

They went home and went to bed, and he went at her in a fury ... and failed. She sighed and turned over, her smooth backside a taunt and a reproach, a mockery of what he was.

After she fell asleep, he arose. Quietly, he got his riding outfit and crop from the closet and dressed in the darkness. Then he put on the ceiling light. She still slept, nude atop the covers in the humid summer night. He came close, drew back his arm, and cut her across the rear. She cried out, convulsed, fell off the bed as she tried to run while half asleep. He came around and stood over her. She looked up at him, looked at the riding crop, touched her rear. He said, 'Who is that boy in Bennton?'

'Did you ...?' She blinked, came fully awake, began to get to her feet and shout at the same time. 'You have no right ...!'

He put his hand on her head, shoved her back down, cut her across the breasts. She screeched, clutching at herself, then rocked in pain.

'Who is the boy?'

She wept. She shook her head.

He raised the crop. She said, quickly, 'A cousin.'

'Your mother and uncle don't live in Bennton. He isn't a cousin.' His crop was still raised over her. There was a livid welt across her full breasts. It excited him. He wanted to beat her until she was covered with such welts. But a thought was beginning to shape in his mind, and he merely waited.

She wept again. He lowered the crop. He turned away, head bowed as if in grief. He heard her scrambling to her feet. He said, his back to her, 'I understand. You ... you're not satisfied with me.'

When he faced her, she was sitting on the edge of the bed, the sheet wrapped around her. The tears had stopped.

'You want to leave me,' he said, his voice as tremulous as he

231

could make it. 'You want that boy.'

She watched him carefully.

'Don't leave me,' he said, and put the riding crop on the dresser. 'Please. I'll never hurt you again. Stay . . .'

'After what you did?' she interrupted, beginning to regain courage. 'I'd never be able to sleep peacefully again! I'm packing . . . first thing in the morning!'

He wasn't worried in the slightest. She had no money. She liked this house and she liked his paying the bills and she wouldn't be likely to give that up for a boy; *certainly* wouldn't if he gave her a way to have boy and comforts both.

'I swear to you, Barbara, I . . . I won't set any conditions. You can be free. You can . . . you can even have your friends visit you here. It's your home.'

She laughed sharply but stared at him.

'Just as long,' he said, voice sinking in shameful subjugation, 'as you don't have anyone when I'm home.' His voice sank further, to a whisper. 'Just as long as you don't let me find out about it, or let anyone else find out about it.'

'I wouldn't,' she muttered. And then, 'Do you mean it?' And before he could answer, 'Because I'll leave right now if you don't swear that you mean every word. I can have friends in when you're not around and you won't interfere?'

He nodded humbly. 'Just don't go running off to Bennton any more.'

She lowered the sheet, examining her breasts. 'Look what you did to me,' she said. 'And why? It's not my fault you can't . . . you know.'

'I know,' he said; and he wanted to slash her to ribbons! But he couldn't. He could only strike at her through that boy.

She put on a robe and they went to the living room to drink. He kissed her and stroked her head, and all the time, he held his savagery under tight control. Soon . . . soon . . .

He kept pouring bourbon. She grew drunk and more confident of her hold over him. 'Y'know, I'd never . . . no, I wouldn't have, I mean it . . . never have bothered with Peter if you'd been able to do the job.' She drank and laughed and then touching her breasts, stopped laughing. Her face turned to him and it was vicious now, vengeful now. 'Picked him up at a movie. He's an usher. Went to Bennton to get a man, any man, and he's more man at eighteen than you ever was, ever will be. He gives me more loving in one night than you do in a

232

month. S'help me. One night . . .'

He left her then, but as he left he said, 'I'm sorry.' And he was—that he wasn't able to slit open her belly and drag out her intestines with his bare hands!

It took a while, and that while was pure hell for Curt Bramms. He had his idea, but it wasn't a plan, couldn't be a plan, because he didn't know just how it would come about. The boy had to enter his home at night. He had to be able to kill the boy as a prowler and make sure that Barbara never said anything to dispute it.

He began taking twice monthly 'business trips' to Charleston on the first and third Mondays of the month. He always left home at ten p.m. on Sunday, drove straight through, called Barbara after checking into his hotel at about two a.m., visited various wholesalers the next day for cosmetic, novelty and drug items, returning home shortly after six p.m. He established absolute rigidity of habit in this. He did it for three solid months, and during those months, he never once tried to spy on her, never once asked questions (even when she grew careless and he saw the cigarette butts without filters and without lipstick; even when she fell asleep one Monday afternoon and left two sets of plates on the kitchen table with the remains of two steak dinners). He was no longer capable of making love to her; no longer even attempted to. But the stupid bitch thought that just having her with him was so important that he would tolerate everything!

In his store, with his employees and customers, it was understood that he and Barbara were as good as married; common-law, as it were, and that they soon would make it legal. There had been some talk about them, but now, after eight months, it was an accepted thing.

Finishing his usual late dinner on the first Sunday in November, he packed his bag and kissed Barbara on the cheek. 'See you tomorrow at six.' She nodded, patted his shoulder and went back to applying nail polish to her toes. He drove away, went fifty miles and stopped at a service station. While the elderly attendant was pumping gas, he said, 'Good Lord, I forgot my wallet!' The man cut the pump off instantly. 'That's two-seventy already, mister.' Bramms searched his pockets and came up with a quarter. The man sighed. Bramms said, 'That's all right, I'm Curt Bramms of Bramms Pharmacy in Langley.' He showed the man a card. 'Maybe so,' the man said, 'but I don't know you from Adam and I'm not the boss and it'll come outa *my* pocket if . . .' Bramms settled matters by leaving his gold wristwatch and card . . . and headed back to Langley. In the glove compartment of his car was a ·45 caliber automatic and license to carry it.

It was a few minutes to twelve when he quietly let himself into the house. They were in the bedroom, talking. He heard Barbara laugh. He smiled, the sweat beginning to trickle down his sides, and took the ·45 automatic from his pocket and removed the safety. He went across the dark living room and into the foyer and then to the bedroom door.

The boy said, 'What's that?'

Barbara said, 'What's what?'

'I heard . . .'

Bramms stepped into the room, left hand finding the wall switch. The ceiling light went on. Barbara and the boy were just where he expected they would be, in bed. The boy was nude and Barbara wore her black nightgown. The boy had her breasts out and, even as he stared in shock, his hand caressed one. Barbara made a soft, choking sound.

'Get up,' Bramms said to the boy, trying not to see his aroused genitals. 'Get up! Get up!'

The boy got up. He was tall and lean and his face was the face of a child. But his erection, now disappearing, was that of a man, the man responsible for Curt Bramms's betrayal and humiliation.

'You a Jew, boy?'

The boy shook his head. 'Listen, I was told . . .'

'Get dressed.'

'You said I could . . .' Barbara began. Bramms moved swiftly, eyes on the boy who was stepping to the chair which held his clothing. He reached the bed, switched the gun to his left hand, took out his handkerchief and wrapped it around his right. As she said, 'You promised!' he swung and caught her a glancing blow on the ear. She shouted, 'Pete!' and cowered. Bramms punched again, straight down, catching her full in the mouth. The feel of teeth breaking under his knuckles was beautiful, simply beautiful!

She cried out in pain. He returned the gun to his right hand and said, 'You just watch and be quiet. Or I'll kill you.'

Sobbing, hand over her mouth, she scrunched back against the headboard and away from him. He considered hitting her

234

again, to make certain that signs of her 'assault' would be sufficient. But he could always take care of that afterward.

Strangely, she began to look good to him, cowering that way; and the boy fumbling desperately to get into his clothes, unmanned and glancing at him fearfully every few seconds ... all that began to arouse him. But that too could wait for afterward.

The boy was dressed. Bramms told him to tie his shoelaces. The boy did. Bramms looked him over, said, 'What's your name, your full name?'

'Pete Smith. But listen, Barb told me it was all right with you if ...'

Curt Bramms shot him once, carefully, dead center of the chest. The roar of the ·45 blended with Barbara's shriek. The boy's mouth was open as he fell straight back, head hitting the chair. If he made any sound, Bramms didn't hear it, and he was sorry for that. He lay with his head between the legs of the overturned chair, his tan shirt splotched in the middle, a red stain spreading rapidly under him.

Bramms came close, looked down, waved his gun to quiet the now hysterical Barbara. She wouldn't stop screaming and he wanted to concentrate on this man he'd just killed. He turned briefly to point the gun at her. She was jammed up against the headboard, eyes bulging, and grew silent. He said, 'If you want to live ...'

She nodded violently.

'Then do as I say.'

He looked down at the boy, and he was happy. He looked at his work and when he turned to Barbara, he felt his manhood rising. He put the gun down on the dresser and went to the bed and told her what to do. She stretched out as instructed. He didn't waste time in preliminaries or niceties. He relieved himself and arranged his clothing. And told her exactly what she was to say, how she was to act, if she didn't want to be displayed before the town, the state, the entire nation, as the dirty whore she was.

Her eyes stayed on him. Wide on him. He slapped her face to make sure she wasn't in shock. She said, 'Yes, Curt, I will,' lisping because two of her front teeth were broken in half.

'Fine. I'm going to call Chief Redmond now.'

'All right, Curt.'

'You can put on a bathrobe.'

She got off the bed, started around it and then stopped, hand rising to her bruised mouth, staring at the boy and shaking and whimpering.

'Your robe,' he ordered. Oh God, if only he could feel this way *all* the time! So full of power, purpose and manhood! He picked up the gun. He held it out as she walked around the boy's body. He said, 'This if you try anything.' He opened the top drawer and took out the envelope he'd prepared and showed her the money. 'This if you do it right.'

Chief Redmond came. The local doctor who doubled as coroner came. Then all sorts of people came. Barbara wept and was perfect. Yes, she'd known the boy briefly, spoken to him in the movie house at Bennton. Yes, he knew where she lived. She'd thought him a pleasant boy and they'd chatted a few times and she'd mentioned Curt and how he went to Charleston twice a month ... perhaps to explain why she was in the movie alone, she wasn't sure, she couldn't remember. And then tonight he'd come here and beaten her—'look at my mouth'—and tried to rape her. But thank God Curt had returned and they'd fought ...

It wasn't as simple as it had been with Ivy. Not nearly as simple. He was indicted. He feared for his life, his freedom, and hired the best lawyer available. People had seen Barbara and the boy, a drifter who called himself Pete Smith and who was never identified as anyone else, in Bennton together, and not just in the movie. The prosecution made much of the fact that Curt had returned home this one time alone of all the times he had gone to Charleston, this night of the rape. The D.A. tried to refer to Ivy's death too, but was stopped by threat of mis-trial.

It lasted five days, and every minute of those days Bramms worried about Barbara. But her mother and uncle did exist—living in Columbia, not Bennton—and came to the trial and how could she display herself for what she was in front of *them*?

He paid in sweat for those five days and he paid in money. He had Roger Atwiller, the well-known criminal attorney, and Atwiller insisted on fifty thousand dollars in advance. Curt Bramms had signed over his store and house to Atwiller, and after the trial, the attorney sold quickly and without regard for top value. He got his fee and Bramms was left with about forty-five thousand, all told.

Barbara returned to the house with him the day he was acquitted. She asked for the envelope of money. He laughed. He looked at her and laughed. She moved away from him. At the door, she tried to strike back by saying it had cost him his business, his home, just about everything he valued. He answered, 'It was worth it. If I could do it to you for the money I've got left, that would be worth it too. If I could raise fifty thousand every few years and spend it this way ...'

She fled. He had a week to vacate the house but began packing immediately. The phone rang and the doorbell rang and he knew it was reporters.

He packed and waited and when the phone was silent and the last car had driven off, he waited some more. At four a.m., he left for Florida. He had settled in Hollywood Beach and lived frugally and looked for some way out ... and instead of his finding it, the way had found him via Sandy and Vino.

And now, the LC bouncing heavily as the wind increased, with a speedboat cutting across his bow and two girls waving and laughing, with Bay Island and government agents and millions of dollars waiting, he stared at the photographs and thought only of the two triumphs they represented, the two ritual slayings that had brought him the only *real* pleasure he'd ever known. And then he thought of tonight. And tonight could bring—*would* bring—the third! Maybe the fourth!

Karen knew she was playing the bitch. For two days, since his Thursday noon arrival, she had used her eyes and, occasionally, her body to keep Bob Lacton at fever pitch. At the same time, she had used Charley to keep the President from doing anything about it. They had boated together, swum together, played golf and eaten three meals a day together, and all the time she had smiled at him, allowed him to brush her hand, her hip; and last night when he'd touched her leg under the table she had moved it closer to him and allowed him to caress her bare thigh. But always there was Charley, talking sports, economics and politics. Always Charley, protecting her from what she wasn't sure she desired but *was* sure she feared.

But Charley was different since that night of revelation and confession; Charley was no longer her ardent lover. And at eleven this morning, Charley had left for the polo field behind the golf course for the big match between a Palm Beach club and the team made up of Bay Island residents and their guests.

She and Lacton were supposed to have watched the match, but the President said, I have to stay close to the phone; something I can't discuss,' and Charley, always the perfect host, suggested she keep him company. 'There's that traditional luncheon tendered the victors and I won't be able to get away until three or four. Can't leave the world's Number One guest alone *that* long!'

They still hadn't been alone; not with Lon Creesey, the President's personal bodyguard, and four other Secret Service agents in the house. And Press Secretary Garson McKentry and the servants. Far from alone, and so she hadn't felt things would come to a head.

She was wrong. Lacton asked her to take him to the game room, which was also the projection room, telling Creesey he and Mrs. Vener were going to view some highly 'secret' film of both their families at an outing—'Don't want anyone laughing at the President, now do we'—locked the door and lowered the shades. When he turned to her, she understood the moment had arrived. And she knew she still wasn't ready for it.

'I suppose you want to see those dolls,' she said, laughing, hoping to put off the moment of truth.

He hesitated, then smiled and nodded. The erotic little things had appealed to him from the moment Charley had first displayed them.

She went to the big cabinet under the dartboard, and shook the key out of the narrow green vase. She unlocked the double doors, aware all the time of his eyes on her, and glanced down as she squatted, seeing her bare legs exposed to upper thigh by the short tan skirt. Quickly, she took the transformer out, much like the one that controlled Bobby's electric trains at home, except that this was a remote control radio sending unit and would activate receiving units in each doll within a radius, as Charley had proven, of eight feet. She straightened and he was walking up to her. 'If you'll get the dolls,' she murmured, eyes flicking to and away from his face. (No, *not* lumpy!)

He said, 'Of course,' and she was pleased, reassured, to hear the tremor in his voice. He was nervous and uncertain too. Maybe it *wouldn't* happen today. Maybe he would watch the dolls and kiss and paw her a little, and then talk of their having a rendezvous later, when she and Charley visited Washington. Maybe it would be put off for weeks, for months, until they were both fully adjusted to the idea.

238

She set the control unit up at the side of the billiard table, and he brought over the large teakwood box and put it down. She handed him the electrical cord and he went to the wall and plugged it into the outlet. She hesitated before opening the box, because that would bring sexuality into the room, bring them face to face with what they merely had played at for two days. But she had suggested the dolls herself. And he was asking if she wanted his help.

'No, I've watched Charley do it many times.' She raised the lid. As always, she had a moment of revulsion, seeing those four incredibly likelife figures, plastic skin tinted softly pink; one brunette couple and one blond couple, the males a foot high, the females an inch shorter. The hair was lifelike too because it was *real*, was human hair ... and not only on their heads. The pubic hair was also authentic. Totally realistic in all ways, with the possible exception of the genitals. Not that there weren't men and women built that large, but because of their function, these dolls were hung and slitted to the extreme of human possibility. And, of course, the penises were always erect.

There they lay, faces up and perfectly molded in cheeks, chins and dimples, two beautiful little women and two beautiful little men. They were Occidental, since Charley had ordered them and he was an Occidental. The men's eyes were glistening blue with curving lashes; the girls' pale brown with longer lashes and thinner brows and an under-scoring of mascara. The boys' mouths were pink and curved in lecherous smiles; the girls' red and twisted in two variations of the agony of passion ... which was, Charley said, the manufacturer's sole error, because it was as Oriental as Japanese erotica and not at all a Western concept. Still, it was exciting, far more exciting than a simple smile. The boys' arms, legs, bellies and chests were muscular and defined in straining tendons and delicately delineated veins; the penises, especially, were done to perfection in an angry reddish hue and tiny tracing of blood vessels. The girls had full breasts hiding, Charley had informed her, tiny electromagnets to make certain the boys' hands always found their marks. Electromagnets were also hidden beneath the fleshlike plastic of bulging female buttocks and within the vaginal slits.

There they lay, four victims of a warlock's art, cursed with toy size and insatiable lust.

'Anything wrong?' Lacton asked, standing close beside her. 'Forget how to make them work?' His voice was thick and slightly hoarse. She felt him brush her hip, and quickly reached into the coffin ...

She laughed, shaking her head as she placed the first, a boy, in the center of the table. Warlock ... coffin ... The gruesome German fairy tales of her childhood always returned to haunt her when she saw these incredible toys. 'They're a little frightening, aren't they ... Bob?'

She had said his name, and it was the most intimate thing to have passed between them, ever. His name, here alone with the screwing dolls. His name, an opening of the door.

He must have felt it too. He took out one of the females and placed it alongside the male. 'I guess so, but when they start to move...' His left hand seized her right. She laughed, said, 'To work, to work,' and freed herself to take a doll in each hand. 'Put the box on the floor, please.'

He did. All four dolls lay face up on the green felt. She turned the dial to *on*. A click sounded, and then a faint humming. She said, 'Oh, I have to separate them or both males might go for one female.'

'Charley did that ...'

'I'm not as adept as he is.' She placed one couple a foot from the other.

He was brushing her side with his. 'Not as adept? It's my impression ...'

She laughed, laughed and shook her head, turning the dial to *One*. The dolls moved, went into their first act. The males rolled over, the dark one a little quicker than the blond, moving their arms and legs, jointed at wrists and elbows, hips, knees and ankles; moving their heads toward the females. (More magnets? Or were they like science-fiction androids, created in laboratories with near-human capabilities? Charley insisted it was only a sophisticated use of magnets, but seeing them smile, move and crawl smoothly toward the girls, who now turned *their* heads toward the males and used all *their* joints to raise arms and spread legs and move pelvises, created the doubt, the fear that these things were truly alive while the current was on!)

She almost turned them off. But she heard Lacton catch his breath as the males mounted and their little hands moved over breasts and buttocks and the pink, smiling mouths pressed

240

down to the red, passion wrenched mouths ... and she shivered as the voices began. She knew it was only a recording—a tiny tape somewhere in the transformer—but still, those voices, those sweet girl voices and deep male voices, the final touch of realism ...

'Ah, darling, come to me, come to me.'

'I'm here, my dearest. Your breasts are so sweet, your bottom so ripe.'

Lacton laughed quickly, nervously.

'Kiss me, my strong lover.'

'Oh, my beautiful girl, how I long to enter into you.'

Lacton said, 'Whoever wrote those lines was a little behind the times.' His arm went around her waist. 'And they sound Chinese, don't they?'

'Yes,' she said. 'But ... it's still the nicest thing about them.'

The dolls went on talking, kissing, caressing each other.

'I *long* for you!' the boy voice said passionately.

'You must be patient.'

'Oh. I can't wait!'

'Neither can I, my lover! Kiss my breasts! Fondle my behind!'

'The latest models,' she said, feeling Lacton's hand slipping up toward her breast, 'speak in more modern fashion. Charley says they use all the dirty words.'

'Oh, oh, I'm not able to wait ... I'm not able to wait!'

There was a slight pause, and then the girl's voice repeated her first line, 'Ah, darling, come to me, come to me.'

'End of act one,' Karen said, and turned the dial to *Two*.

When she straightened, Lacton's hand cupped her breast. She tried to laugh. Nothing came out. He caressed her and she watched the dolls begin to copulate.

The penises moved down, hesitated, found their mark, moved partly inside.

'Now I am entering you, my true love,' the male voice said, trembling.

'Oh, deeper, deeper!' the female said.

The male bodies moved at hips and knees. The penises disappeared; the dolls lay belly to belly. And then the rise and fall began and the tape played ecstatic groans and cries.

'Oh, darling!'

'Ah, dearest!'

'Ahhh, my love!'

241

'More, more!'

The little people screwed and she watched them and wished she were one of the women because those little men were beautiful and this man beside her was not. Yet he was arousing her now, his body turned into her, his rigidity pressing her hip, his hand squeezing and massaging her breast, fingers rolling her nipple. She looked at the beautiful little men, who were approaching their orgasm, and Lacton's lips pressed her cheek and he murmured her name. She kept her eyes on the dolls, listened to their voices alone.

'Oh, oh, my true love!' the girl voice cried. 'I faint, I die, I ... I spend!'

The boy voice groaned long and true to life. 'My life spurts into you!'

She watched them, eyes blurring, seeing real lovers writhing in ecstasy. She had occasionally noticed little mechanical imperfections, slight jolting movements, cessations, pauses that proved these were dolls, even if they cost eleven thousand dollars and were the best in the world. But now she invested them with life.

They came to a halt, flattening out as if in exhaustion. Lacton murmured, 'Karen, I've waited years for this.'

She preferred the tiny tape voices. As he tried to turn her to face him, she said, 'Wait ... the next act,' and set the dial at *Three*. The males began to reverse themselves over the females; to place themselves in position for oral lovemaking. (And she suddenly wondered if that last setting on the control, *Four*, which was non-operational *was* operational for other customers who wanted to see homosexual love. Charley, of course, wouldn't. Even this third setting disturbed him.)

Lacton said, 'Karen!' and turned her strongly. She closed her eyes as he kissed her, as his stiffness came up against her. 'I'll give Charley that post,' he muttered thickly. 'You'll live in Washington ...'

She still preferred the dolls.

'Oh, my sweetest, put your mouth to my seat of love. Be not ashamed, my darling boy.'

'I will do *everything*, my heart's desire. I will sip from your bowl of honey. But will you take me within your heavenly lips?'

'Yes, though it will stretch my poor mouth and nearly choke me!'

Lacton was backing her toward the black leather couch, his hands under her dress, panting heavily and drowning out the doll voices. She moved her head aside to hear better, feeling his hands slide inside her pants.

'Now, my darling, I will prove my love!'

'And I, oh bull of a man!'

The sucking, gurgling sounds followed, and she felt her legs hit the couch and sat down. The cries of orgasm came, but she could no longer see the dolls. She could only see President Robert Lacton standing over her, and then he was sitting beside her. The moans of ecstasy died. There was no one to turn the dolls back to the first setting. They lay relaxed and still, she knew, their three cycles ended, their lovemaking ended. And hers was just beginning.

He kissed her, his hands everywhere; and then he placed her hand on his fly. She kept her eyes on his face. His mouth gaped and he was groaning.

His penis was in her hand. It was thick ... and lumpy.

She laughed. His eyes, half closed, opened. 'What?' he muttered.

She shook her head. Lumpy Lacton, his political enemies had called him during that first presidential election. Lumpy Lacton who came off so badly on television.

The laughter wouldn't stop. She shook her head, but it wouldn't stop. He was staring at her and she said, 'No, wait ...' and tried not to look at his face and tried not to look at his penis. But where else was there to look at a man when he was making love to you? His nose?

She simply *roared* laughter, sinking weakly into the couch. His nose was the lumpiest part of all!

The blows ended her laughter. He was shrieking obscenities that the dolls would never dream of and swinging both fists at her as if she were a male opponent in a prize fight. He hit her in the neck and in the breast and she fell all the way back against the arm of the couch.

She screamed and he leaped back, raising his hand palm outward to stop her, the white rage still there but fear conquering it. She stopped. She said, 'You'd better go now.' His fear dipped and rage struggled to dominate again. She said, 'Shall I scream you into national disgrace?'

He closed his fly and whirled toward the door, which at that moment was opened from outside. Everett, the butler, had

243

used his master key. Everett who was gentle, fragile and sixty-two years old. Lacton rushed toward him, and as the butler tried to step aside, Lacton punched him viciously in the stomach. 'Filthy bitch!' the single most important man on earth screamed.

She ran to the butler, who had sunk gracefully and soundlessly to his knees. She bent to him, and heard Lacton shouting, 'Get everyone! We're leaving! Damn it, move! I said we're *leaving*!'

Everett murmured, 'The President bumped into me, madam.'

'Yes,' she said. 'He was upset.'

The graying, crewcut man of forty came to the door and looked in. Karen said to Lon Creesey, the President's bodyguard, 'A little accident. The President hurt his hand playing billiards. You know how a man will rage when he hits his thumb with a hammer? Like that. As he ran out, in pain, he bumped into Everett.'

The butler struggled to his feet, very pale but managing a smile. 'Please give my apologies to the President,' he said.

Creesey looked at him, and at Karen, and murmured, 'I'll do that.' He went away. Karen kept her arm around Everett's waist and led him to the couch. Only then did she remember the dolls. She hurried to the table and put them back in their box. Everett was sitting quietly, hands to his stomach. She said, 'Are you all right?'

He nodded, breathing heavily.

'I think I'd better call a doctor.'

'Perhaps ... a little later.'

'If you're sure you can wait?'

'Yes, it's not that bad. I just want to make certain I'm not ...' He smiled. 'Old men worry.'

She sat down beside him, taking one of his hands. He said, 'Are *you* all right?'

She said, 'Yes, perfectly,' but her left breast ached.

Everett withdrew his hand and rose. 'Thank you, madam.'

'Thank *you*, Everett.'

He went out and she put away the dolls and poured a Scotch from the bottle on the sideboard. She returned to the couch and sipped, touching her breast, hoping it wouldn't bruise badly enough for Charley to notice.

Poor Charley. He would never get the position he wanted.

Poor Charley. He would never get *anything* he wanted.

She finished her drink and blinked away tears.

Poor Karen, would *she* get anything she wanted?

There was always divorce.

But she didn't want to consider that, yet. There was hope. There was always hope.

She listened as footsteps ran all over the house and doors opened and closed. Voices called orders. Cars began driving up.

Miss Egret knocked and came in with Bobby. 'The child insists on seeing you,' she said. 'I told him you're very busy with the President...'

Karen held out her arms, not the right thing to do when the governess was standing there, trying to make a point with her charge. But Karen couldn't help it; she needed her baby. He ran to her. She kissed him, and held him murmuring, 'It's all right, Miss Egret. The President is leaving. We'll spend a little time together now, thank you.' Miss Egret left and Karen took Bobby on her lap and they talked and she ignored the slamming of doors and the roaring of cars. Sometime later, she heard the awful racket of helicopters, several of them. Then it grew quiet, both inside and outside the house.

She wrestled with Bobby and bit his neck a little and he said, 'The President came to visit *us*, didn't he, Mommy?'

She nodded.

'And everyone *loves* the President.'

'Of course.'

'Because he takes care of our country.'

'Yes.' She said a quick prayer for the country.

It was Rollins who first noticed it. With Vino in Miami picking up the guns, drugs and a few last-minute accessories for their costumes, and Prince at that polo match, he had no one to discuss it with except Sandy or Fanny. He entered the house and went to the kitchen, expecting Fanny, but found Sandy instead. She was at the table, lacing a cup of coffee with brandy.

He said, 'Hey.'

She started and the brandy spilled. 'Don't sneak up on me like that!'

He came to the table. She'd been playing cat on a hot tin roof all week, and so had Vino. He expected it from her, but Vino surprised and worried him. 'Take it easy,' he said.

She went to the sink, got a sponge and returned to wipe up the liquor. 'Sure, take it easy!'

He was sitting now and she was standing close beside him, leaning over the table. Looking at her he put his hand on her can. She slapped it away. 'Is *that* all you got on your mind!'

He laughed. 'Now there's a switch.'

She glared at him. He met it with his smile, and again gave her can a feel. She jerked away. He chuckled, but he wanted it, needed it. He hadn't been to Miami in two weeks and hadn't managed to make it but once since that night with Sandy. And maybe this was *his* way of reacting to tension?

'I was on the dock,' he said, when she returned to her seat and her spiked coffee. 'I've been working on the boat, you know, checking things...'

'How can you go on as if everything is all right?' She looked at him, looked hard. 'Are you stupid or something, Buddy-Boy? Do you know what's happening?'

He leaned forward, mimicking her intense expression. But he liked looking at her from close up; liked the smell of her skin and hair; liked everything about her today. He grasped her wrist. 'Yeah, Sandy, girl, do *you*?' She didn't try to pull away, so he stroked the wrist with his fingers, thinking of that big ass, and began to turn on strong.

'You men,' she muttered. 'Too much.'

He didn't get that. The Sandy he knew would never say 'too much'.

'Yeah, so I was outside working and all those helicopters were batting around, maybe even more than usual, and then suddenly I heard it. Or *didn't* hear it. It was quiet. Listen, the whole island is quiet, like it was before Thursday.'

She began to answer; then stopped and turned her eyes to the window and listened. 'It *is* quiet.'

He slid his fingers up from her wrist to her hand. She tugged a little, but he held on. He tickled her palm. 'Watch it,' she said.

He smiled. 'Here's something that should make you happy; maybe even calm Vino.'

'We got a right to worry! Vino's a pro! He doesn't close his eyes to trouble!'

'That Coast Guard boat's gone.'

Her lips parted and she slowly put down the cup. 'What do you mean, gone?'

'What *can* I mean?' He laughed at her funny, little girl expression. 'Not there. Split the scene. How else do you want me to say it?'

'Maybe ... maybe it just ... moved to another spot?'

'Maybe. But why? It's supposed to guard the Vener dock, right? It's been guarding it for two days, right? So why move?'

She ran out of the kitchen.

He found her at the end of the dock, near the boat, looking around. 'I wish Vino was here,' she said. 'Or Prince. They'd know if it means anything.'

He glanced back at the house. 'Where's Fanny?'

'Lying down. She got a headache.'

He took her by the arms and pressed up behind her. 'Honey, everyone's gone.'

She turned. 'What's that supposed to mean?'

He grinned.

She slowly shook her head. 'I got to admit it, Buddy-Boy, you're something else again. Don't you worry even a little about what's going to happen tonight? I mean, even if the boat's gone and those helicopters...'

He drew her close and tried to kiss her, but she turned her mouth aside. 'What the hell do you think you're doing!'

He was suddenly tired of all the bullshit. 'I'm trying to throw a fuck into you, that's what. I'm so turned on I can't think of anything else. If you want me to worry about the job, I'll do it ... after you get me off the hook.' And he really grabbed her and kissed her and put it right between her legs and socked it to her.

When he finally let go, she was breathing hard and her face was pink. 'What ... if Prince or Vino...?'

He took her hand. He led her around the house to the garage and showed her the little room upstairs. It didn't look as if it had been used in a long time and was dirty and dusty, but he stripped the sheet off the bed and the mattress wasn't bad. Then he sat down and waited. She came to him. 'You know why?' she murmured. 'Not because you need it. Not because of anything *I* want, though I'm starting to.'

She was close now, and he put an arm around her waist and a hand under her dress, stroking that great ass and sighed, not caring what she was saying but letting her finish because he didn't want her getting mad.

'Because Vino's scared and Prince is scared and we're all

247

scared. But not you. No one can think of anything except the job, and you can't think of anything but...' She laughed.

'But *you*,' he muttered, and dragged her pants down and lifted her dress and kissed her there and tongued her there and could have eaten her alive! When he felt her begin to writhe, he stopped and got her on her hands and knees and went to work.

Two fast tricks, for both of them, and then he was stretched out, relaxed and happy, holding her and kissing her lightly. 'You're a great old girl.'

'Old yet,' she murmured. 'Everyone's old compared to you.'

They heard a car drive up to the house, and that noisy engine could only be Prince's Porsche. They went down, and when they found him in the study he was looking out at the bay. He turned, smiling. Rollins couldn't remember his smiling, really smiling, in weeks. He'd been looking bad—shot around the eyes and worn from boozing—but now, suddenly, it was as if his face had been wiped clean. He laughed and pointed to the window. 'It's gone!'

'I noticed,' Rollins said, as Fanny entered the room. 'Does it mean anything?'

'The President has left the island! I heard it at the polo match and wanted to come right home, but decided I'd better not. Lacton simply up and left. It must have been a sudden decision, because Charley Vener didn't bother hiding his surprise. Said it was probably due to a hush-hush call that kept Lacton at the house.'

'Then everything can go as planned?' Fanny asked.

'Yes, everything, especially Bramms and the LC. It's not quite three o'clock and the President and all his staff are gone!'

'You sure *all* those agents are gone?' Rollins asked.

'That's what I heard. Lacton said to pack up and leave, and they left. The whole thing didn't take an hour.'

They looked at each other, Sandy laughed, and Fanny said, 'God is with us!'

Rollins said, 'We'll make it now, won't we, Mr. Prince?'

Prince nodded. 'I don't see what's to stop us. With just a *little* luck...'

When Vino came in, they had to explain from the beginning. It was like New Year's Eve, twice.

He'd begun his passage through Baker's Haulover Cut at four

fifteen, glancing at the park and beach, seeing people turned to him. Not many cargo barges came this way. This was pleasure-craft area.

He'd left the Atlantic and, as soon as he'd entered the bay, the water quieted and the LC's skipping was reduced; which was fine with Bramms because, though an experienced sailor, the heavy motion had been getting to him, making him feel ill.

Now it was almost five, he was passing the Harbor Islands and heading under the Broad Causeway. Another fifteen, twenty minutes and he would reach Bay Island ... or rather make a detour on the Miami mainland side of the island to avoid being hailed by that Coast Guard cutter. He had driven along the General Causeway yesterday, seen the cutter and cursed and cursed. And as he thought of it now, he cursed and cursed. The speedboat that cut across his bow and the teen-aged boy who shouted and waved got nothing more than a malevolent glare and a muttered, 'Fuck off.'

The sky had turned grayish, though not with clouds; a thickening of the haze that had persisted all day. Visibility still wasn't bad, but neither was it unlimited. Bramms turned the wheel, beginning his detour, and only then, took the binoculars from the case around his neck and trained them on the spot where the cutter was.

Where the cutter *should* have been ... because it wasn't there now.

His heart began to pound. The heavy, bitter feeling began to lift and he warned himself to look carefully and not do anything foolish.

He looked carefully. If there was a boat off that south shore, it was a submarine!

He changed course with one hand, keeping the glasses to his eyes with the other. He began following the original plan, the original course, but remained alert to switch back to the alternative if the cutter hove into view.

He came closer, closer, until he had to decide whether to pass under the Bay Island Bridge (the first step in Prince's original plan to create a diversion), or to turn and go north, then west around the island so as to avoid the house where the President was staying.

He saw nothing. He kept going. He came under the wide center span and the city cop on the causeway sidestepped to the railing and looked down at him. Bramms kept his face away, but raised a hand in greeting. He didn't see if it was answered. And he didn't look back once he'd passed under the bridge and was approaching the area of houses and docks. He kept his distance, of course, hewing closer to the causeway than the island. It wasn't time to worry the guards, yet.

He passed Prince's dock and boat, no one was there. But that too was part of the plan. No chances would be taken that a bridge guard would see them communicate.

There was a cabin cruiser tied up at the Veners', but no guards, no people and no activity of any sort. Either the President had left, or he'd moved to another part of the island and his security had moved with him.

Bramms went on. He came around the western end, still no Coast Guard and still no security. Now he began to catch a brisk southwesterly wind, sweeping in from the open reaches of Biscayne Bay. Now the LC rolled and bounced as if back in the Atlantic, but the movements lessened when he came around the north shore, heading east, standing in closer to shore. Still no Coast Guard. Still no security.

He had almost reached the eastern end, with its water tower and Yacht Club marina, when he decided that Lacton had left the island. He'd been sweeping the shore with his binoculars and there just wasn't any sign of Presidential-type security.

He turned the LC, now he didn't miss his cigarettes, transistor radio or anything else.

It was six when he came back around to the south shore. The sun was fading, the twilight growing, night pressing close behind. He cut the engine to slow and crawled toward the island bridge. This time both guards—cop and island security— came to the railing to watch him. They were only curious; perhaps just a little more than curious. Curt Bramms smiled tightly. Soon, they would begin to worry.

Willa Dorcas Greshen didn't begin dressing until eight. She hadn't even been sure she *would* dress, but then Walter Prince phoned and said he would call for her at nine and joy had infused her. She'd been afraid he would forget, or change his mind, or do something that would make going impossible ... because she couldn't face all those people alone.

Mildred helped her into the new Marie Antoinette costume and high-piled white wig. She tried on the white satin mask.

250

Then she went alone to the small parlor, using a thin cane of lacquered Malacca, and got the Light of Stars from the safe. Mildred met her outside the door and helped her down the stairs. She sat in the hallway, and the maid said, 'How lovely you look, Mrs. Greshen! Like a queen!'

Willa smiled faintly.

'And the diamond! It's ... it's unbelievable!'

Willa looked down at the huge stone. 'Haven't you seen it before?'

'No, Mrs. Greshen. You haven't worn it since I'm here.'

So many people hadn't seen it; new people on the island. Well, they would tonight. They might not look twice at *her*, but they'd look at the Light of Stars.

Yet when Walter Prince arrived, lean and handsome in a ballet dancer's black tights, puff-sleeved, lacy shirt and velvet vest, he said nothing about the stone, bending over her hand to murmur, 'How *could* they have guillotined you?' She laughed and he helped her out to his car, one of those little foreign things which she looked at with suspicion and dismay, but which held her very nicely once he'd guided her inside. He drove rather fast and, to her surprise, she found she was enjoying it. He glanced at her and asked, 'Once around Bay Drive?'

'Yes, that would be nice.'

He insisted on hooking up her seat belt, an over-the-shoulder affair, and drove even faster. She caught her breath and laughed quite loudly and said, 'Cleve...' and remembered to murmur pardon and change that to 'Walter ... you're not at Le Mans.' He slowed and she said, 'No, please, I was only joking.' He drove fast again and she caught her breath again and it was so good to feel alive, alive and excited!

'I'm going to be happy tonight,' she thought.

When he looked at her, she realized she'd spoken the thought, and so she smiled and added, 'I know I am, because of you.'

He turned quickly away, and for a moment she felt he'd looked sad.

But why should he be sad when it was the night of the final gala and he was trying to make her happy—sweet, kind boy!—and she had told him she *was* happy?

There was no reason for sadness. Not tonight. A night she was certain she would always remember.

251

Beaufort came into his cottage at ten twenty, and the first thing he did was to take off his shoes and rub his feet. He'd been on the go all day, what with the President being here, his sudden departure and having to check out all the communications equipment left behind and see that it was properly labeled and shipped to the airport; this in addition to his usual rounds at four, six and eight. And then he'd had a late dinner in the kitchen of the Yacht Club, talking with Stennis, his second-in-command, about some character in a barge off the south shore. Stennis didn't like it; thought there was something funny about the barge, a reconverted Navy landing craft with a tarpaulin stretched over half its interior. Beaufort had gone to the bridge, but they hadn't seen anything and he'd figured Stennis was a little jumpy because of the President's visit. Spend any time at all with the Secret Service and you began to worry about your own grandmother.

He got a beer and padded to the desk. Hadn't even had time to look at his mail. Not that there was anything much. Magazine and ads. He flipped through the *Rifleman*, opened the first ad then discarded it. He was lifting the second ad from the pile when the phone rang.

Stennis again. He wanted permission to send the patrol boat out to cruise the south shore. 'I realize the boys are tired, Chief...'

An eager beaver, Stennis. One of the new men he'd recruited, and just what he wanted. But still, a little *too* eager after three days of double shifts.

'Why? That LC full of Russians?' He chuckled and discarded the second ad without opening it.

'Jim thinks he saw it over near the causeway a few minutes ago.'

'Thinks?'

'Well, that's what worries me. If it's there, why isn't it using running lights? And why the tarpaulin? If it's a cargo barge, it has no business in these waters. And if it's not, that tarpaulin could cover twenty men and a cannon.'

Beaufort sighed. 'If it'll make you happy, take the boat out yourself. We're a man short because of the gala.'

Stennis began to say he wanted a man with him, just in case ... then interrupted himself with, 'Hold it.' Beaufort reached for the third ad.

'A flare just went off!' Stennis said. 'We can see the barge from the bridge ... wait ... the flare's dying, but the barge is moving toward shore now! They've got men, plenty of them, we can hear the voices! They're going to try and land...'

Beaufort had hung up and was scrambling for his shoes.

After firing off the flare, Vino ran for the front of the house and the Mercedes, feeling awkward in his blue ski-suit, carrying his red face mask. As he pulled out onto Bay Drive, straining to see without the use of lights, he glanced back and noticed headlights swinging down from the bridge. He drove slowly, and reached the wooded area between houses Two and Three. By then, his rear view mirror showed another pair of lights coming from the security building.

His heart was pounding and he kept muttering, 'Christ, Christ almighty.' He'd been sweating all week, and now it was going the way it should, and he still couldn't play it cool. He was scared. He had always been honed fine before a job, but this was something else. So much riding on this one! The *last* job, if it went off. And the IF loomed large, because all the doubts he'd been pushing aside were crowding into his mind now. He was a pro and as a pro, he knew that anything this big with this many angles had to be wide open. No plan could cover it all. If you knocked over a warehouse, a jewelry store, a home, you could pretty well cover the angles, allow for most possibilities. But *this*?

He turned off the road, inching his way into a spot between the trees that he'd cased earlier. But he'd cased it in daylight and now it was night and heavily overcast; a good thing, he guessed, but still he was sweating as he inched forward.

There was a sudden and brief illumination from the bay; Bramms's spotlight. He glanced behind him, decided he was well hidden and cut the engine.

Now he could hear Bramms's tape player going; orders and answers and it sounded like an army, and that was just what Prince wanted. And still he winced, because he had always worked in silence, fearing any sound.

The voices stopped. He reached for cigarettes, and realized he couldn't use flame or take the chance that the cigarette glow would be seen.

A speedboat was approaching, its heavy, roaring sound growing louder by the second. Vino tensed for what would come next, fearing it and praying for it. And it came, the stuttering roar of a machine gun: Bramms going for the security boat. Bramms aiming at the waterline ... except that in this darkness how could he see well enough ...?

The spotlight flared again.

Bramms wasn't supposed to do that! He wasn't supposed to give his position away once ...

The machine gun stuttered again and the light went off and he realized it was something they hadn't discussed; the *speedboat's* light. Bramms had shot it out.

This was what he'd feared. Not that anything was wrong, yet. But in this, the *changes* that would begin to take place once Prince's plan was put into action, was where possible failure lay.

'Christ, Christ almighty!'

If Bramms killed any of those guards, it would be murder and if they were caught, it would mean the chair and anyway, he was a two-time loser and it would be life no matter what. He wiped at his face and tried to think how he and Sandy would spend their money, how good it would be and how he would never have to sweat again ...

'... over here! You all right, Larry?'

'Yeah,' another voice panted. 'I'm okay.'

Vino froze absolutely rigid. They were coming from the beach. Who ...?

'We have to get to Byuferd,' the first voice said, and it was coming closer. 'You got your gun?'

'You think I bothered with that? I barely made it into shore!'

They were from the security boat. Bramms had sunk it. Everything according to plan ... except that Prince hadn't figured on anyone from the boat coming ashore *here*! If they found him in the car ...

There was the sound of thrashing and a sharp, 'Goddam!' ... and it was *much* closer.

He picked up one of two guns from the seat, a long-barreled thirty-eight made even longer by a silencer extension. (Patty had managed to get them *all* silencer attachments.) He could put both guards away quietly.

But the first one ... did he have his gun? If so, what if he got off a shot? With the other guards beginning to congregate along the shore ...

And what if those other guards were on their way here, even

254

without a shot to guide them? Prince had figured on their going to a spot near or just past his house, because that was where Bramms had been aiming the LC when he'd allowed them to see him. But what if the guards overshot their mark? Or spread out thin?

'Christ almighty,' he said silently. Why had he ever gotten mixed up in this crazy scene!

The thrashing sounds seemed almost upon him. He cocked the double-action weapon for quick firing, pulled the key from the ignition and reached for the door. And remembered that the dome light would go on. He fumbled frantically along the door-post, found the switch and slid it down. Then he opened the door, crouching, got out and closed it, just to the point that it made contact.

'I got a splinter or something in my arm,' the first voice said, only feet away. 'Hurts like hell.'

'You bleeding? Maybe you caught a slug...'

'No, glass from the light, I think.'

Vino dropped flat and rolled under the car.

'What's that?' the second voice said.

'Where?'

'It's a car.' The second voice dropped, but Vino heard, '...resident maybe ... angry ...'

They were worried that a Bay Island couple had parked to make out. And so they approached carefully, and then spoke loudly to announce their presence.

'Our boat sank. We need help.'

'It's all right, we're security officers.'

He saw a pair of stockinged feet not six inches from his face.

'Anyone...?'

'It's empty.'

'What the hell?'

'Maybe they heard the firing and went down to the beach to see.'

'No key, dammit!'

'Couldn't take it anyway. C'mon, let's trot.'

'Trot, shit! I'm so pooped ...'

There was a whooshing sound and the second guard said, 'What...?' and then, 'Look, rockets!'

The explosions came. Three close together, from the direction of Prince's house; in the woods between One and Two, if

255

Bramms aimed well. Vino tensed for more.

But there were no more. There should have been a dozen.

Something had gone wrong! Bramms had been hurt, or drowned, and they'd be a man short!

The guards were running toward the road. After a while, their voices and sounds were gone and he strained to hear more rockets, to hear Bramms coming from the bay, and heard nothing.

The night seemed to change, to grow lighter. Vino stared at the ground and didn't understand it. Finally, he rolled out into the open, sat up and looked at the sky. There was light there, further east; weak, uncertain, yellowish light ... Then it grew less weak and he realized it was fire. Those rockets had set something afire! What if it was Prince's house? What if the dock burned and the boat burned?

He got back into the car and gripped the gun tightly, sweating inside his ski-suit and whispered, 'Come on, Bramms! Come *on*!'

Everything was going wrong!

It was so simple he was laughing as he lowered himself over the side of the sinking LC into the mild water. Everything just the way Prince had planned it, except that the security boat had come faster than expected and the guards on shore slower. In fact, there hadn't been any action at all from shore, so he had set off only three of his twelve rockets, and had hesitated even about those three. Still, it had turned out well, as he'd seen when the flickering lit up the darkness. A fire in the woods between Prince's and Vener's houses; something they hadn't thought of; but it would keep the security men even busier since they were also the fire department. Not that it should take them long to handle. This hadn't been a dry season and the fire should be out long before he, Fanny and the hostages were ready to leave the club and head for Prince's dock. Nothing tight about the timing there, that he could see. Looser, safer, actually, than the way they'd planned it.

Beautiful, beautiful, even if it made his swim to shore a little more dangerous, increasing the chances of his being seen from infinitesimal to slight. He compensated for this by swimming as far beneath the surface as his snorkel would allow and kicking his fins slowly so as to decrease any possible wake.

He came up once, to check his bearings, and saw that the

256

flame was now a good distance to his right as he headed straight and true for the darker area on his left that was the woods between houses Two and Three. He went under again, and for the first time in months he was calm and sure. The pleasure of this thing kept building.

He lost some of that pleasure when he came ashore, threw away his snorkel, removed his flippers and began walking into the woods. He grunted, cursing to himself, pine needles and he was barefoot.

An error. He should have carried tennis shoes; or at least have had Vino bring a pair in the car. He would have to remain barefoot all through the job.

He began walking again, clenching his teeth against occasional sharp pains. This was a dangerous time for him. He had no weapon, wouldn't get a pistol until after finding Vino, and if he ran into anyone who was armed ...

He heard something off through the trees, and saw it an instant later—a tanker fire engine; the kind that carried its own water supply, or a chemical mixture that would make short work of a small forest fire. He dropped to the ground. The tanker sped by, red swivel lights flaring, but no bell rang or siren wailed, not on *this* island. The millionaires weren't to be disturbed.

He smiled, thinking they would be disturbed anyway, once he reached that club. He lay quietly until the tanker's lights were gone, and they had showed him two things. One, he wasn't more than twenty feet from the road. And two—this subliminally—there was a shadow off to his left.

He rose and moved softly, forgetting pine needles as tension and anticipation mounted. A few steps and he saw it was a car, crouched low and continued on since it was what he had been looking for. If it was anyone but Vino, it would just be tough shit.

'Vino,' he whispered, when only a few feet away.

'Yeah! Bramms ... where...?'

Bramms ran around the front of the car. He got in and slammed the door. Vino said, 'Goddam it, you'll bring the whole security force!'

Bramms brushed at his left foot.

'Why were there only three rockets?'

'That's all we needed. Get going.'

Vino said, 'Yeah ... but I thought...' He started the car

and began backing out.

Bramms brushed his other foot, turned to the rear seat and saw the towel. He used it and asked for his mask.

'On the seat,' Vino said, 'with the gun.' Bramms found it. Vino said, 'That fire ... Jesus!' His voice shook.

Bramms looked at him as they reached the road and swung around. 'It's in the woods.'

Vino said, 'Oh,' but his face looked stark and was covered with an oily film.

'You worried about something?' Bramms murmured.

Vino barked laughter. 'Hell no! This is nothing to worry about, is it?'

Bramms said, 'Put on your lights.'

'You think I should?'

Bramms reached over, found the switch and put them on himself.

'Yeah,' Vino mumbled. 'It's all right now. We're just guests...'

'You're doing ten miles an hour,' Bramms interrupted coldly. He was beginning to enjoy this. Vino, the tough guy, the professional thief, the man who'd put the gang together, was scared shitless. Vino didn't want to get to that club.

'I'm playing it...' Vino began, then grunted and increased speed, but not by much.

'Move, dammit! The plan calls for our getting there as fast as we can and doing the job as fast as we can and getting away...'

'Don't you go giving *me* orders! I'm the one running things!'

Bramms laughed. Vino turned from the road to glare at him. Bramms picked his weapon up from the seat and cracked open the cylinder. He saw that the chambers held a full load and snapped it shut. He put it in the heavy plastic bag hanging from his belt and tightened the drawstring. Then he laughed again.

Vino muttered something unintelligible and faced the road.

Bramms thought of Prince and of that punk kid Rollins and of this frightened man beside him. And then there was the girl and the old French woman.

He leaned back, touching his revolver through the bag. He wasn't worried about who was running things, not even the little bit required to make him lose his temper. He already had

258

completed the toughest part of this job. Now it was all fun and games.

They turned off the main road. A moment later, he could see lights, cars and the club building and hear the music and voices. He checked his face mask, and slid the viewplate down over it.

'Listen,' Vino said, 'for the love of God, take it easy in there.'

Bramms leaned forward, staring at the club and the uniformed guard at the open door.

'You hear me, Bramms?'

'I hear you.'

They parked off to the right. As soon as Vino got his red ski-mask on, Bramms was out of the car. Vino whispered, 'Wait a minute!' Bramms kept going. Vino wanted to take deep breaths and talk to build up his failing courage. But Bramms cared nothing for that. He'd been waiting all his life for this. He wouldn't wait one more second!

Charley Vener had never drunk much, but tonight he'd fallen off the wagon in grand style. *Dived* off was more like it, into a gallon of martinis! And with good reason. He was unable to keep his eyes off certain people at the gala ... and all of those people were *male*.

There it was. It had finally happened. What he had fought, denied, feared like death itself. And now he was standing at the country club bar, watching a blond boy in levis and cowboy hat dancing with a lean, dark girl in harem outfit who could have been Ceecee Mortonson. One thing about these masked parties—almost impossible to tell who anyone was, unless you knew his costume in advance. And no one but Karen knew that behind the bedouin prince's robes and black mask was Charles Vener. And Karen was out there somewhere dancing with someone and Charley didn't want to think of her ... and thought of how *something* had happened between her and Bob Lacton (lovers' quarrel?). Who knew how long...

He watched the boy. He watched the boy's tight blue levis.

And no one knew that the eyes behind the bedouin's mask hungered for the boy's thick bulging crotch. And the boy was becoming excited dancing with the lean, sensuous girl. And Charley's breath came harshly and he gulped the rest of his drink, and then muttered, 'Damn,' as the boy was hidden by

259

other dancers.

He turned to the bar, telling himself he was drunk, very drunk. Being very drunk, he was acting very foolishly. When he was sober again, he wouldn't act foolishly. No real harm in just *looking* . . .

But the harm was done; he knew it, felt it. The harm was like a cancer eating into his groin and changing everything that Charles Vener of Vener Breweries valued in life.

He grunted at that, just as if he'd been struck in the pit of the stomach, when a woman said, 'Charley, are you all right?' It was Karen in her Hell's Angels mini-outfit, standing beside him.

He told himself it was the sexiest costume in the place. He told her the same thing. She smiled. He put his arm around her waist. *He'd show her who was a man and who wasn't!*

'If we were alone,' he muttered, and his eyes began sliding past her to find the boy in tight levis, and he dragged them back to Karen, his wife, his partner in life and love.

'*Let's* be alone,' Karen said.

He blinked at her.

'Just for a few minutes, Charley.'

She was begging and she looked sad, hopeful and worried, all the things she'd looked since the night of his confession. And yet he was afraid, and realizing he was afraid he tightened his arm around her waist and said, 'Yes, let's!' He would take her outside and he would put his hands under that sexy costume and she would arouse him and he would be a man and forget those sick thoughts, those insane thoughts of boys and bulging crotches.

They walked to the doors. Outside, they went a few steps to the left, along a windowless wall. And then he turned and grabbed her by the bottom. She took off her mask and he took off his mask and they clutched each other and she was sighing and moaning and he . . . he was too drunk. That had to be it because he felt nothing, nothing at all!

Her breasts. They had always excited him. Her big, fat, round German tits. He plunged his hand into her neckline.

'Oh, Charley . . . so close to the doors . . .'

He had her breast in his hand. She was rubbing against him, eyes closed, just as if they were making love in bed . . . as they hadn't for an unprecedented two weeks now. He massaged her breast . . . and it was a warm piece of meat; not exciting and not disgusting and not anything at all. *Meat*.

He stepped back from her. Hands trembling, he put on his mask.

Her eyes opened. 'Charley?'

'I'm not ... feeling well.' He turned. 'Drank too much.'

'*Charley!*'

He stopped. He waited. She knew. Goddam her, she had made him tell her and the floodgates had opened and everything had come through, washing their life together away!

She came up alongside him, fastening her mask. She said, voice tremulous, 'We have to talk later, Charley.'

He laughed to stop her. He said, acting drunker than he was, 'Goddam Prussian melodrama. Marry a good German girl, Papa said. A good German *actress*! If a man happens to drink too much ...'

She walked ahead of him. She spoke very quietly, almost under her breath, but he heard her and it branded itself on his brain.

'A *man*?'

He rushed after her. She was opening the doors, stepping inside. He reached in after her, ready to hit her; for the first time in his life, ready to smash a woman with his fist.

But then the door shut behind them and he saw who had shut it—a witch with a conical hat and a grotesque, green-rubber face. She had a gun in her hand, and he saw how frightened Karen was and it gave him a chance to regain his manhood.

He said, smiling, 'That doesn't match the costume, madam witch.'

'You will go in there, quick!'

Her accent sounded French and he smiled again and said, '*Mon ami*, is this some sort of party game?'

'Inside! Inside!' The gun leveled at his middle.

Karen gasped, 'Charley, come! She's ... please, Charley!'

He smiled and bowed a little, and followed Karen across the anteroom to the wide archway. It was much quieter now—no music and no voices—but as they entered the main room, something came over the loudspeaker system. The bandleader—a new one; the rock group had taken over—was speaking, and while his words were flip his voice shook. 'Ladies and gentlemen, all you rich people, you can see what's staring us in the face. So please do what they say. The women over against the bar, the men right here in front of the bandstand.' He stopped to listen to a man in a ski-suit who held a gun on him. Looking around, Charley could see a short man in skin diver's costume near the windows, barefoot, also with a gun. And from the way people were glancing behind them at the bar, someone with a gun was there too. 'No one'll get hurt, they tell me, if the ladies just hand over their goodies ... Yeah, okay, their jewelry. That's all they want, and since you can afford it and you can't afford a hole in the head...' The man in the ski costume shoved him. The boy in tight brown pants and leather jerkin stumbled away from the mike. The skier motioned the rock quartet down with the crowd.

Why the hell couldn't they have shown up a few minutes sooner? Charley thought. It would have saved him from that terrible scene with Karen!

All the men, including a few who made a show of muttering defiance, were moving toward the bandstand. The women began separating from them, heading for the bar, a few whimpering and one or two crying. Karen looked at him, face pale, and he smiled and said, 'Nothing to worry about. The jewelry's insured.'

She went with the women and he strolled casually toward the bandstand and the men. There must have been at least thirty-five or forty people on each side of the room. He reached the men and turned, standing right out in front, not worried because what could he lose but the few hundred dollars in his wallet and his wristwatch? He looked around, smiling a little, the alcohol fogging his mind and dulling his senses.

He could see two more thieves now—a big man in knight's costume, including simulated chain mail that hooded his head and dropped down to his waist—and a woman in clown's costume and rubber clown face. That made five, including the witch at the door, and she was now in view, halfway between the door and the archway. Five, all with guns.

'You,' the woman in clown's outfit said to the tall, slim girl in harem outfit and wispy veil who might be Ceecee Mortonson. Charley remembered her because she'd been dancing with the blond cowboy with bulging levis.

The girl was out in front of the women, the way Charley was out in front of the men. She dragged on her cigarette and looked at the clown. The clown said, 'I want you here, near me.'

'Really? And I'm not even your type.'

A man behind Charley made a small sound. Charley glanced around to see a ballet dancer. He smiled, said, 'That girl has ...'

'Be quiet there,' the skin diver said, and Charley turned to see that the man had moved up close and was looking at him.

Charley bowed a little, mockingly. Let Karen see that he was still very much a man. He wouldn't cower like the rest of them.

The skin diver continued to stare at him, eyes glinting through a black cloth weather mask and a plexiglass view plate. Charley smiled. The skin diver took a step toward him. The skier jumped down from the bandstand. 'All right! We're going to choose two men and two women to help us. No one gets hurt, *unless.*' He walked onto the dance floor, halfway between the two groups. The skin diver joined him. On the right, the knight stood ready. The clown moved to the left. Between clown and bar was the witch, watching from the anteroom.

'You, in the dancer's costume,' the skier called.

The man behind Charley walked out onto the cleared space. Another man, in white Roman toga, sandals and laurel wreath, edged into the dancer's place. He was visibly trembling. Allie Mortonson? So hard to tell with the masks ...

The skin diver had turned back to the slim harem girl. 'You were told to get over to the clown, so jump!'

The harem girl exhaled smoke, and jumped. The skin diver darted back, gun rising. The Roman behind Charley said, 'Ceecee! Do as they say!' Yes, Allie Mortonson, trying to protect his daughter.

The skin diver glanced at him. 'There's a sensible man. Come out here.'

Allie Mortonson moved slowly forward to stand beside the dancer.

The skier said, 'You two, go to the bar, one at each end, and begin collecting jewelry. Rings, bracelets, necklaces, pins, earrings ... *everything.* The skin diver will be between you. When your hands are full, drop whatever you have in his bag.'

The dancer moved quickly to the left. Allie Mortonson, bulky in his Roman toga, hesitated, then went to the right.

'Get over to the clown!' the skin diver said, once more addressing Ceecee Mortonson. She puffed on her cigarette and began to move, but very slowly. The skin diver grabbed her arm with his left hand and threw her across the room. She stumbled and fell in front of the clown, who looked down at her.

'Now that's what I call a *real* man,' Charley said, and glancing across the room saw Karen shaking her head. Pleased at her fear, he laughed sharply, insultingly.

The skin diver whirled to face him. The skier began to move between them, saying, 'Easy . . .'

Charley put his hands on his hips. He wondered if the skin diver would try to manhandle him. He almost welcomed the prospect, because it would offer proof of his courage, his manhood. He would take it without flinching . . .

A sledgehammer blow struck his chest and he fell backward. He heard screams, one of them surely Karen's. But he couldn't be hurt. Not seriously. He felt no pain, felt nothing at all. And he'd heard nothing but a dull, snapping sound. He stared at the beamed ceiling and blinked his eyes, trying to clear away a strange haze. He would get up now and keep quiet because he'd proved his mettle . . .

The lights went out. He said, or thought he said, 'Someone give me a hand.' And died.

After Bramms killed the poor fool in Arabian costume, Bucky Prince entered what could be described as a state of shock. He was aware of collecting jewelry, especially the Light of Stars from Willa Greshen. He had sufficient presence of mind to comfort the trembling old lady with a murmured, 'It'll be all right,' and was far gentler removing her necklace than with the other women, whom he stripped of their gems with numb efficiency. He was full of anger at Sandy for having chosen Ceecee as a hostage, certain she had recognized the girl and was indulging in a little feminine revenge. And he was worried about Ceecee being in the hands of that madman, Bramms, even for the few minutes of their drive to Number One where Bramms would go into the bay. But still, as he functioned and experienced on all these levels, he was in shock. For the first time since deciding to recoup his fortunes through robbery, he saw himself as a true criminal. And not just a thief but a murderer.

He was responsible for a man's death. The unknown man now covered by a tablecloth Rollins had thrown over him. The man no one dared look at.

It was a sickening, crushing thought, being responsible for that stillness under the tablecloth, and he moved, spoke; he felt a fear of numbness. Even fear was experienced from behind that veil. Fear for himself and fear for his hostages.

There were two hostages now, Rollins having chosen Karen Vener whom he'd mentioned before the robbery as a 'real important kind of woman' and whom Bucky had learned would wear a Hell's Angels costume—leather jacket, boots and micro-mini skirt. Karen had gone into brief hysterics after the shooting, but Bramms had quickly cowed her. She now stood beside Ceecee, dazed, dull eyed and absolutely silent.

Walter Bucky Prince felt fear for a great many people, and for a complex of reasons ... but especially because of his one great mistake, Curt Bramms. Vino's mistake, initially, but Bucky Prince was responsible for the whole operation. He should have taken time out to re-check the man after Rollins and Fanny made those remarks about his instability. But who could have believed he would shoot, would *kill*, for so trivial ... ?

The phone behind the bar rang. It had been quiet, dead quiet, everyone shocked by the killing, everyone quick to obey instructions out of fear of being the next victim. The sudden jangling sound made several women gasp and brought Bucky to a halt as he reached for a diamond bracelet on a tanned wrist. He glanced back at Vino. The man in ski-suit was frozen. He had forgotten to tear out the phones.

Then Rollins moved, taking the bartender and security guard from the group of men. They obeyed his murmured instructions without hesitation. No one was going to risk anything after that senseless slaying; that brutal unnecessary slaying. And Bramms stood calmly, *happily* Bucky felt, with his gun in one hand and sack in the other. Bramms held out his now-bulging sack to Allie, who made another deposit of gems, and said, 'That's the boy. Remember to be quiet while they answer the phone.' Bucky couldn't look at him, couldn't stand the sight of his stocky, swaggering figure, because it was the sight of his own folly. His entire plan had been shown up for a fairy tale. The others had known, in their talk of possible shootings and killings, what the score really was, while he had played a rich boy's game, like polo or perhaps sports car racing, thinking it entailed a slightly higher amount of risk than an ordinary sport. But across the room a man lay with a hole in his chest and other men stood away from the wide red puddle of his blood. And *that* was what Bucky Prince's plan was, what it had been from the beginning, if only he'd been able to see it.

He'd thought *Tad* a fool! At least Tad had dealt only with his *own* life. Bucky Prince's fairy-tale planning had led to an innocent man's death ... and the evening was only beginning, nothing *requiring* violence had yet occurred!

Olaf was back behind his bar with the guard and Rollins. Vino finally snapped out of his immobility, cleared his throat and jerked his gun at Bucky. Bucky went back to stripping women of their jewelry. Olaf lifted the phone and said, 'Country Club,' his normally ruddy face dead white. Rollins's gun was at his head and Rollins's ear close beside his own at the receiver. 'Oh, hi, Byuferd. Sorry ... we're busy, you know. What? Just fine; going along as always. Bailey? He's ...' Rollins pointed at the anteroom. 'He's at the door, I think. Sure, hold on. I'll send one of the waiters.' He covered the phone and looked at Rollins. Buddy-Boy suddenly began turning his head this way and that, looking around almost in panic. Bucky couldn't understand why. Rollins grabbed the phone, pressing his hand over the speaker. 'A radio!' he stage-whispered; and to Vino, 'If he hears how quiet ...'

Olaf pointed under the bar. 'Get it,' Rollins said. Olaf stepped cautiously forward, bent and brought up a small transistor. Rollins gave Olaf the phone, making sure his hand covered the speaker; then held the transistor to his ear and fiddled with the dial. A moment later dance music blared into the silent club. Rollins held the radio stretched away from the phone in his left hand, jerked his gun at Olaf and whispered, 'Say something about your hand covering the phone.'

'Hey Byuferd,' Olaf said. 'Your boy took his time, didn't he? And here I am protecting your ears with my hand covering ...' He paused. Okay, I said he's here, didn't I?' He handed the phone to the guard.

Rollins listened with the guard. Bucky's hands were full of jewelry. He turned and without looking at Bramms dropped everything into the sack. Allie Mortonson was only a few steps away, and he too dropped jewelry into the sack. They were almost finished; and the haul was tremendous.

'Yeah, Chief. No, nothing unusual.'

The music ended and an announcer began to speak. Rollins quickly turned him down, found more music, turned it up.

The guard looked at Rollins. 'No one's here who shouldn't be. I checked every invitation ...' He stopped to listen. 'You mean now? Well ... no, I'm not needed anymore, I guess.' Rollins nodded his mailed head. 'Okay, I'll be right down. The Vener house, check.' He hung up.

Rollins tore the phone from the wall and sent the guard back to the bandstand. 'Show me the other phones,' he said to Olaf. 'All of them, and no mistakes!'

Olaf said, 'There's one in the office, one in the kitchen and the two booths.'

Rollins prodded him and they went out from behind the bar and disappeared through a door near the archway.

Bucky and Allie Mortonson had met. Bucky stripped the last woman of matching emerald earrings and necklace and dropped them in Bramms's extended sack. Bramms chuckled behind his Navy mask, closed the sack's drawstrings and fastened it to his belt. Vino said, 'That's it.' He raised his voice. 'We're leaving now. We're taking three hostages ...'

There was a murmur from the crowd, and Allie Mortonson said, 'Please ...'

Vino said, 'Quiet! If anyone tries to leave, he'll be shot by our guard outside. And the hostages ... anything happens to us happens to them first. If nothing happens to us, they'll be back with their families in the morning.' He glanced at the covered body on the floor, hesitated, then said, 'Remember what can happen. Stay here just as long as you'd stay normally. Three o'clock, at least.'

No one spoke.

Vino turned to Bucky and Allie. 'You, dancer, come with us. Roman, get back with the men.'

Allie said, voice thick and shaky, 'But ... you're not taking my daughter, are you?'

'She'll be all right. Just see that no one tries anything.'

Allie said, 'But ...'

Vino waved his gun.

Allie moved slowly across the floor to the bandstand, looking at Ceecee. She stood at the right with Karen Vener, both covered by Sandy.

Rollins returned and sent Olaf back to the men. Bramms said, 'Right,' his voice full of satisfaction. He came to Bucky and shoved him toward the archway. Bucky went out as Rollins said, 'Let's have some music. Everyone go on with the party. You might as well enjoy yourselves for the next four hours.'

Bucky and Bramms went past Fanny. She followed, and as they came outside they saw they were alone. Bucky and Fanny both began to speak at the same time. Fanny said, '*Why?* There was no reason . . .'

Bucky said, 'You're insane! He was drunk . . .'

Bramms whirled, the heavy bag swinging out and thunking against his stomach. His gun rose.

They grew quiet, watching him. The little eyes behind the two masks glittered wildly. He said, 'I did what I thought best! After that, they were all good little millionaires!'

Gun or no gun, madman or no madman, Bucky couldn't control his rage and stepped toward him. Fanny grabbed his arm, whispering, 'The hostages come! Besides, it is too late to help that *pauvre*. Too late to do anything. And much depends on his . . .' She stopped as voices approached; then said, 'Take off your mask, Mr. Prince.'

Bucky had lines to say, important lines to support his role as hostage. But all he could think of was Fanny saying, 'Too late to do anything.'

Too late to go back and erase that murder. Too late to stop this thing from continuing. Too late to prevent other shootings, other killings . . .

He heard Ceecee say, 'Where are you taking us?' and he stepped toward Bramms and whispered, 'Just keep your hands off that girl!' Instantly, he was sorry he'd said it. Because Bramms hauled off and slapped him, and it was no act but rocked him back on his heels, his ears ringing. Because Bramms said, 'You were told to take off your mask, Mr. Prince!' and ripped the piece of cloth from his face. Because Bramms then turned to the hostages, even though the two masks completely hid his face, Bucky felt certain he was looking at Ceecee. He wanted to say he hadn't meant it; wanted to placate this devil . . . but the cover act had started and Vino was laughing and unmasking. 'Surprise, Mr. Prince. You'll serve *us* for a change.' And Fanny was laughing and unmasking and asking if he wanted her to prepare 'a little crow *au Brisson*'. And Rollins and Sandy unmasked the hostages and themselves and spoke their little mocking lines. Only Bramms remained masked, as only Bramms could hope to remain unidentified. He wasn't laughing and he kept looking at Ceecee.

They were moving toward the back of the crowded lot where all three cars were parked. Rollins was saying Mr. Prince would help them pick up a few more items.

He said all the prepared things about their not getting away with it and heard Karen Vener burst into tears, Ceecee trying to comfort her. But when Vino said Prince would help them or all three hostages would suffer, he followed his big hesitation scene with: 'All right, but make sure the women aren't bothered. I mean it. Or you'll never spend a penny of your money.'

Ceecee and Karen were being pushed into the back of the Caddy by Bramms and none of the three could see him for a moment. He jabbed his finger at Bramms's back. The others were startled. They looked at him and at each other, and Fanny quickly nodded as Bramms turned. Bramms said, 'All ready,' as if he'd missed the whole thing, but he looked at Bucky a long moment before getting behind the wheel. Fanny went in back with the hostages; the doors slammed; the Caddy's engine roared and it jerked forward and away. At the same time, they heard music begin in the club. Rollins grinned; and then his face tensed and his eyes slid past Bucky. 'Little cleanup job,' he muttered, and strode quickly towards the big banyan tree. They turned. A couple was strolling, arms around each other's waists, toward the club. Rollins met them, showed them his gun, hushed the girl's startled cry and shepherded them swiftly to the doors. He put them inside with much serious talk, and returned to where the others stood near the Mercedes.

'Hope there aren't any *more* of them around,' Vino muttered.

Bucky said, 'That's not what worries me. It's Bramms. If he touches those women...'

Rollins shook his head. 'He won't have time, Mr. Prince. He's going off that dock as soon as he gets to your house.' He took Bucky's arm and shoved him into the back of the Mercedes, muttering, 'Sorry, but maybe someone can see out a window.' Vino took the wheel and Sandy got in beside him. 'God,' she said. 'What he did in there! For *nothing*! Now if we're caught it's murder!'

Vino started the car and pulled slowly around the lot. 'So it happened,' he muttered. 'So maybe it helped too. No one else gave us any trouble. And we got more important things to worry about. Mortonson's safe...'

269

'Is as good as open,' Rollins interrupted. 'I've got the combination.'

Vino's eyes flashed to the rear-view. 'You've got . . .?'

Rollins laughed. 'It was simple. There was Mortonson all shook up about his daughter being a hostage . . .'

Bucky said, 'And how come you chose *her*, Sandy?'

Sandy looked innocent, but there was a definite glint in her eye. 'How'd I know *who* she was, with the veil and all? And what difference does it make anyway, *Mr.* Prince?'

He had no answer.

'Good thing you *did* choose her,' Rollins said. 'All I had to do was take Mortonson aside a minute while you people were walking out, and promise I'd look after her personally, *if* he gave me the numbers of the safe as fast as I could write them down.' He leaned over the seat and held out an open book of matches. 'No screwin' around with the stethoscope or drill, right, Vino?'

Sandy smiled at him. 'Jeez, are you ever the boy!'

Vino muttered that now Mortonson could tell the security people where they'd be. Before Rollins could give the obvious answer of Mortonson's fear for his daughter, Vino continued, 'And what if someone decides to walk out of that club? Someone who doesn't give a damn about the hostages?'

'They'll have to break down the doors,' Rollins said. 'Didn't you see me unlock and lock the front a minute ago?'

Sandy shook her head. '*Now* what'd you do?' she asked gleefully.

'Well, the bartender locks up at night, don't he? So he has to have keys, right? So I took the bartender's keys while we were ripping out the phones. And I locked the kitchen door and the garden door, and when we left I locked the front doors. All keyhole locks and no way of opening . . .'

'So what?' Vino muttered, putting on his brights as they drove along the tree-lined club road. If they decide to leave, they'll kick 'em down.'

Sandy stared at him.

They reached Bay Drive and stopped. Off in the distance, they could hear automobiles. Vino swallowed audibly. 'Christ, if they come this way!' He turned in his seat. 'Look, I say we take Mortonson's cash and forget the Greshen house.'

Bucky shrugged; but then he looked at Rollins and saw disapproval. The only good thing that had happened tonight was the emergence of a man. Buddy-Boy was supposed to be the tyro, the novice, the kid. But he was the one real man among the lot of them.

'If she still has those jeweled animals,' Bucky said, 'we could be passing up several million. It's the largest privately owned collection of its kind in the world.'

'But Beaufort's security ...'

'Turn right,' Bucky said.

Sandy said, 'C'mon, Vino! We're wasting time! You know the plan!'

'Yeah, the plan! And how many more loopholes—like forgetting about getting the combination and locking the doors— how many more like that will we run into?'

Rollins said quietly, 'Except for the shooting, everything's going beautifully. I think Mr. Prince is a genius.'

Bucky laughed a moment before Vino. But he said, 'We follow the plan. Turn right, Vino.'

Vino pointed across the road to where the lights of Mortonson's house shone, and looked around imploringly. Then he said, 'Okay! So we push our luck!' and he rocketed into a tire-squealing right turn.

'They're gone,' Vincent Drang said, coming up to Allie Mortonson, who stood with the security guard at the bar. Allie had tossed down two fast Scotches and was signaling Olaf for a third. The music pounded—rock music which had been interrupted by the robbery—and people were actually dancing, some of them quite close to the place where one of the thieves had thrown a tablecloth over Charley Vener's body.

'I said they're gone,' Drang repeated.

'How can you be sure one isn't hidden, watching the doors?' Allie asked.

Drang shook his head impatiently. 'That's not the way it works. They're counting on the hostages ...'

Allie put down his glass. 'Yes, the hostages. My daughter. Charley's wife. Walter Prince.'

'I could go out a bathroom window, a kitchen window. I could get to Byuferd ...'

Mortonson stared at him. 'I said *no*, Vince.'

Drang's face suddenly flamed. 'There are others here who've suffered, Allie. Millie's diamond pendant ...'

'*No*,' Mortonson said. 'I don't give a damn about the

271

jewelry. We're all insured. I'm sorry about Charley, but he was asking for it and there's no bringing him back. I don't give a damn about revenge. All I care about is seeing that Ceecee stays alive, Karen and Bucky Prince too.'

Drang began to reply. Allie said, voice dropping, 'Vince, I've made my decision. You'll abide by it, won't you?'

Vincent Drang was still flushed. He nodded slightly and walked away. Allie spoke to the guard. 'Bailey, stay near Mr. Drang. I'd appreciate your making sure he doesn't do anything to endanger the hostages.'

Bailey said, 'Well, how can I stop him. Mr. Mortonson?'

'Any way you want to. Beaufort would agree with me, Bailey. I brought him onto this island. Also, I won't forget your help ... or your hindrance.'

Bailey hurried away. Allie spoke to Olaf, telling him to put a waiter in the men's room, the kitchen, the anteroom, every place that had a door or window. Allie's voice grew heavy with threat and light with promise. Olaf said, 'Yessir. Right away, sir.'

Allie lit a cigar, thought and soon realized there was nothing more he could do. He then mixed with the crowd. He accepted the sympathy, encouragement and comfort of friends. He refused to consider the possibility that Ceecee wouldn't come back; that men who could kill so easily ...

He drank more. He mixed more.

Willa Dorcas Greshen had never, in all her long life, witnessed true violence. Oh, violence in sporting events, several heated arguments at board meetings and then there had been plays and movies. But her life was a special one, protected from the jolts and bruises of ordinary existence. And so the thieves with their guns and threats had shocked her badly. But nothing had ever, or would ever again, shock her the way the death of Charles Vener had.

She could remember Vener quite well ...

A woman came to the chair in the corner where she was sitting, asking if she wanted tea or juice or perhaps a little brandy. Willa shook her head, murmuring, 'No, but so kind of you ...'

And remembered looking at Charles Vener (though she hadn't known it was Vener then, just someone in Arabian robe and headdress, a man who seemed totally unafraid of the guns) as he put his hands on his hips. And then the way he had seemed to lift up and hurtle backwards, the stain on his white robe, the pathetic way he had lifted his hand and gone still and empty and what had seemed like rivers of blood.

So that was death.

Terrible. And yet ... acceptable, once it happened.

Now Charles Vener lay under a white tablecloth. And Willa Dorcas Greshen thought of him as a young man in his moment of death. And she was so old, what could *her* death mean if his meant so little? What could *anyone's* death mean?

The woman went away and someone else came to sit with her. They were all unmasked now, the party spoiled ... and yet people danced, ate and drank.

Someone told her not to worry about the Light of Stars. She smiled. Worry about that stone? After seeing death?

Of course, she hoped they recovered the necklace so that she could give it to the museum in New York. Yes, Trent had wanted it to be a memorial to him, to his wealth, power and name.

How foolish, though. Why look for memorials? Why, when the thing under the tablecloth said nothing, did nothing, needed nothing?

Imagine, a woman as old as she was who had never witnessed a death! How ... obscene!

Trent hadn't allowed her to attend her mother's final agonies; nor had she wanted to. Trent hadn't allowed her into his own sickroom the last four days and had left word he was not to be viewed after death. Addy and Marius had died in the sea and never been found. And who else would *dare* die near Willa Dorcas Greshen?

And so she had lived eighty-seven years without seeing death.

It wasn't right. An adult should see and understand death ... be prepared for it ... and she hadn't. She had *wanted* death, yes, but never allowed the wanting to be recognized.

Now she smiled at someone's kind words and wondered when they would take her home. She felt shrunken and desiccated inside the heavy satin costume, her head weary under the high-piled wig. Foolish ... foolish. She didn't belong here with all these people ... just as the man under the white tablecloth didn't belong here.

Another offer of tea, juice or brandy. Why always brandy?

She hadn't had a martini in years. Not good for her heart, kidneys, liver, whatever was left of Willa Dorcas Greshen.

'If you'd get me a martini,' she said.

The man's face expressed surprise. 'Yes, of course ...'

She sipped and shuddered a little, the chill gin and wine mixture penetrating her vitals. And yet she enjoyed the cocktail and finished it, sitting with eyes closed, smiling. Not the false smile she gave the servants. Not the foolish smile she gave to Walter Prince out of memories of long ago. But a smile of true anticipation.

Soon, she would be taken home.

Soon, she would lie down.

And soon—she was quite certain of this—she would die.

Nothing had so appealed to her in years.

Vincent Drang was stopped by Bailey as he was halfway through the men's washroom window. He lost his temper and said, 'Listen, if you want to stay healthy, get your ass ...' But then he climbed back down. Threats were no longer his bag. He tried reasoning with the man, but it wasn't any use, so he returned to Mortonson, Bailey close behind him, and put it right on the line.

'Did anyone ever think to check Prince's Dun and Bradstreet rating?'

Allie Mortonson glanced at Bailey. 'At *our* level? I wouldn't even check yours.'

Vince told himself to stay cool. Mortonson was being openly hostile now. Mortonson was reading Bailey's expression and guessing why they were here.

'Well, he has no rating! He's wiped out!'

'Welfare paid for his home, I suppose?'

'How much do you think it would take ...?'

'Where Mr. Prince keeps his money, and how he maintains himself, is *his* business.'

'But just suppose he *hasn't* any money?'

'I don't care to discuss Mr. Prince. Not with *you*, Drang.'

Vince began to answer. Mortonson turned his back. Vince had a moment of pure rage, a moment in which he thought of placing a call to New York and having a contract let on this WASP bastard. Then he grew calm. Once the details of this robbery and Prince's role in it became clear, he would know how to speak to the cops. He'd nail Prince yet, and through him, spit in Mortonson's eye ... in the eyes of the whole damned Mayflower group!

Bramms said something vile. Fanny wanted to tell him there were three women listening, but she said nothing. It wasn't wise to say anything to such a one. Besides, she had more important things on her mind. They were coming down Bay Drive toward the woods between houses One and Two, and there was the smell of smoke, a fire engine and a car were parked just off the road. She tightened her grip on her gun. No one must stop them now! In a few minutes she would know whether her plans, her prayers, would come to pass. And if not, whether she would be able to do what had to be done.

'Fire must be out,' Bramms said, as they passed without being challenged. 'Most of them are gone. Running along the shore. I'll bet, looking for us.'

The Vener woman sat between Fanny and the Mortonson girl and kept her head down and cried. The Mortonson girl sat stiffly, face pale, watching the back of Bramms's head. Bramms pulled into the driveway to Prince's house, and cursed again. 'I should be back there with the ladies. You should be driving.'

Fanny tried to placate him with a chuckle.

'I mean it! You ever try to drive with bare feet?'

'We are here.' She then said more things to add to Prince's story, his cover. And Bramms answered in the same way. And they stopped and Bramms got out, cursed the pebbled driveway and pulled the rear door open. 'Get out,' he said to the Mortonson girl.

She hesitated for just a second. Bramms began reaching in, and she said, 'Give me a chance!' and jumped out. Bramms laughed, and those masks made him look even more like a devil than his own mean face, and if he'd been coming on the boat with them Fanny would have been afraid for the women.

But he wasn't and had to get ready for his swim and then there was her call ...

The Mortonson girl made a sound of disgust. Fanny was pushing the Vener woman toward the open door, and glanced outside. Bramms laughed, standing close to the girl. 'You've got a lot more than shows,' he said. 'No wonder Prince likes you.'

That was a mistake, Fanny thought. A small one, but still a

275

mistake. Prince wasn't supposed to have discussed the hostages with them, except in a general way, when trying to protect them.

Bramms was looking at the Vener woman now. Her short leather skirt had slid all the way up as she came out of the car. He made an appreciative sound, and said, 'Too bad I'm not taking that joyride with you.'

Another mistake! And not so small this time! Where Bramms did or didn't go was an important secret! Fanny said, 'Less talk, *please*!'

He didn't answer, perhaps because he realized that last remark wasn't safe. They went around the west side of the house, moving slowly in the darkness. They had almost reached the dock, the hostages walking in front of them, when the Vener woman suddenly stopped. Where ...?

Bramms pushed her. She began to cry again, louder. Bramms slapped the back of her head. Fanny quickly said, 'There is no need to cry. We are all going on that boat. We will make Mr. Prince take us to a safe place. When we get there, you will be set free.'

They went on, and Bramms murmured, 'Where's the tank?'

Fanny said, '*Mon Dieu!* I forgot to bring it out from the storeroom!'

'Of all the stupid ...!'

'Take the women down in the boat.' She turned toward the house before he could say anything more. 'Tie them. By then I'll be back with the tank.' And she ran inside.

She went to the kitchen and, without putting on the lights, used the wall phone. She peered and dialed carefully and murmured, 'Mother Mary, *now* be with me!' The phone rang once, and the voice said, 'Beaufort.' She thanked the Holy Mother and said, 'Trouble at the Prince house, hurry!' and hung up. Then she went to the storeroom behind the kitchen and groaned as she lifted the air tank and struggled out to the dock with it, praying all the while that Beaufort wouldn't have too many guards with him. That he wouldn't take too long in coming. That Bramms wouldn't be too quick to get into the bay. That she would be able to get hold of the jewels.

So many things that could go wrong! But she had planned and prayed and everything else was working out and this would too. At the worst, she would do it herself.

Bramms wasn't on the dock. That was good. He was still

276

down in the boat with the women.

Perhaps he was bothering them?

She shrugged away her discomfort. What did it matter, compared with what would soon happen? The longer he took, the better. And so she didn't go down to help him, or interrupt him. She put down the tank near where the boat was tied and turned to look back toward Bay Drive.

She thought she heard a car.

Bramms had found and lit the shaded electric lantern Prince had hung in the cabin near the forepeak. He'd left his gun on the deck above, since he wasn't worried about handling the women down here ... except if the Mortonson girl managed to get hold of a weapon. Not at all like the Vener woman, that one. No tears and no begging. The Vener woman had said, 'Please, oh please!' just before he'd stuffed one of the gags Prince had prepared into her mouth. He'd shoved her face down on one of the two lower bunks set at right angles to each other, quickly tied her hands behind her, then turned to the Mortonson girl, sitting on the other lower bunk. She'd watched him, face pale.

He'd stuffed a gag into her mouth too and told her to lie down on her stomach. She'd been slow in obeying, trying to keep her eyes on him, so he'd helped with a shove. Back to the drawer for more rope, cut nicely to size, and he'd tied her hands behind her back.

Now he had to go back to the dock, put on the air tank ...

But he was excited; sexually excited. The killing had had its effect. That and the Vener woman's sturdy legs and tan silk pants showing from under the short leather skirt. And Prince's fear for the Mortonson girl and her long body in the white, see-through, balloon pants. And the *knowledge* that he was desirous, that he was hungering after women, white women!

He ran his hand over the Mortonson girl's buttocks. She made angry sounds and kicked her legs. He laughed and smacked her bottom.

But he had to leave now.

Instead, he went back to the drawer and the open box of hypodermics; three of them, preloaded and disposable. He would save Fanny the trouble. It would only take a minute. And instead of injecting the arm ...

He went to the Vener woman first. He pulled her pants

277

down to her knees and she wept behind her gag. He stared at her ass, and his breath came faster. Big all right. A stylish woman, but her cheeks were round and full, rosy hued in the dim light of the lantern.

She grunted as he slapped in the needle and depressed the plunger, giving her the full dose. He rubbed the spot professionally, and then not so professionally. She choked on her sobs, he liked that. She was terrified. If only he had a little more time!

He went to the Mortonson girl and sat down, shoving her against the bulkhead with his thigh. He pulled at her balloon pants, and she kicked and shouted behind her gag. He tore the muslinlike material down with one strong jerk. She wore a narrow bikini strip, and he didn't take that off because he liked it, liked the way it cut into and between her long, brown cheeks.

He gave her the needle and she stiffened. He rubbed the spot and slid his fingers under the bikini and between her legs. She tried to turn over, her shouts a muffled nothing. He laughed, but only for *her* benefit. He no longer felt like laughing. He had to have them now, both of them!

He stood up and shoved the heavy bag of jewels around behind him. He worked at the waist joining of his wet-suit, and knew it was stupid and knew he should be on the dock by now and knew Fanny might come down. But to hell with it! If she did, she could walk right out again—or watch for all he cared! He was hot for a woman, a white woman, and he hadn't been in so long and he couldn't let the opportunity pass.

He peeled down the slick, rubberized pants without removing weight belt and jewel sack. But the heavy neoprene still constrained his legs, his body, and he knew he couldn't take it off and knew he couldn't have proper intercourse. He pulled down his jock.

Both women had their heads turned to him. The Vener woman wept. The Mortonson girl shouted dimly behind her gag. He fell forward on the Mortonson girl, jamming his penis into her buttocks, rubbing in on flesh and on cloth and exulting at the incredible sensation. She screamed and jerked and kicked, it was wonderful! He approached his orgasm within seconds! But he also wanted the weeping, terrified woman with the big behind, and stopped and stumbled the two steps to her bunk. He threw himself on her and grabbed her throat and whispered, 'Hump! Hump or I'll break your neck!'

He'd judged his woman correctly. After a split second of frozen terror, her ass rose and she worked to bring him to his orgasm. He gripped her neck with both hands and groaned his ecstasy. Then he rose, dragged off her pants and used them to clean himself, exulting at his passion. Life was finally working out!

He ran up the ladder to the deck and found his gun and Prince's pair of flippers. He put on the flippers and jumped off the boat, onto the dock.

Fanny was there, standing near the tank, looking toward the house.

'Sorry I took so long,' he muttered, bending to the tank. She kept looking at the house, and said quietly, 'Not so long.' Again he put down his gun, this time for good. Fanny would take care of it when he went off the dock. He checked straps and hose and mask, then took off his view plate. He tore off his cloth mask, threw it into the water, put his glass viewer back on. 'I administered those injections for you,' he said, and straightened, swinging the tank to his back.

He was surprised when she didn't question that. She stepped behind him and began helping him with the straps. 'Anything wrong?' he asked.

'No.' Barely a whisper.

Something ... *different* about her.

Not that it bothered him. Not that *anything* could bother him now.

Fanny was suddenly running up onto the boat. 'The women,' she said, voice faint, and disappeared. He had the feeling she'd thrown herself flat on the deck, but for what reason?

When he heard the voice, he knew the reason. But why hadn't she warned him?

No time for that now. From the darkness of the house, the terrace, a voice said, 'Just hold it there. Not a move.'

He said, 'What's all this?' and smiled to himself. His foot touched his gun and he said, 'I'm Mr. Prince's guest. Anything wrong with skin diving?'

'We'll just check it out,' the voice said, and he saw a shadow move onto the dock.

'Of course,' he said, and hoped Fanny wouldn't rob him of this chance at a second major triumph. He didn't want any

279

help here; didn't *need* any. He said, 'This tank's too heavy for land use,' and chuckled and bent a little. The shadow was growing clearer now. The shadow was emerging as a proper opponent for Curt Bramms. Not like that drunken fool in the club, but a big man with a gun. A *real* triumph! Curt Bramms bent a little more, still chuckling, and said, 'I'll just slip out of this,' and his hand was inches away from the silenced revolver and when the big man took another step, *just one more step* ...

Beaufort had returned to his office at eleven thirty to be in position to direct whatever action might be necessary. He'd divided his men into two groups of four each, leaving two men on the island end of the bridge, and set them to covering every inch of the coastline on foot. He'd also made a few calls, trying to determine what, if anything, was happening, and had not yet come to any conclusion. But despite the sinking of the security patrol boat and the use of rockets to set the woods between houses One and Two on fire, he couldn't shake the feeling, the *conviction*, that it was some sort of gag. No one would be so stupid as to use a landing barge to invade Bay Island! Not if they wanted to get anything out of it.

College kids from Miami U maybe. A bunch of drunken ex-swabbies maybe. Maybe even some of the islanders or their guests in a wild and complicated prank. Dangerous as hell, yes ... but people had been known to do stupid and dangerous things, even to get *killed*, trying for a big laugh.

But professional criminals? What would they have to gain by all that rigmarole? Besides, it didn't look as if that barge had landed.

Which was why he continued to hold back on calling the Miami Beach police and asking for a patrol boat. There were too many men on the Beach force who would enjoy seeing Wesley Beaufort made to look foolish, so just as long as there was any chance it was a gag ...

He was sitting at his desk and had just thrown away a piece of junk mail. He picked up another envelope, so preoccupied he barely saw it ... and then he *did* see it. And then he cursed the mailman and tore open the Special Delivery letter. A quick skim through the five typewritten sheets made him curse again.

Three of Prince's servants were ex-cons. Only Sandy was clean, and he was sure she was tied in with them because it explained why she'd *acted* like a con. And Walter Prince had 'No apparent source of income.'

He began to rise. The phone rang. He heard, 'Trouble at the Prince house, hurry!' and no more.

A break? A diversion? Part of a continuing gag? Or some sort of trap?

It had to be one of the first three—break, diversion or part of a gag. Professionals didn't try to trap policemen. And even if they did—say because of what he'd done to Sandy—he wasn't about to let himself be trapped.

He could try and get a few of the boys, or he could go directly to Prince's place. Getting help would take time, allowing an opportunity to slip by, or playing right to the diversion tactic, draining strength from the search for the LC. As for a gag...

He shrugged. They'd laugh out of the wrong sides of their mouths if he ever caught up with them. Even residents or guests would have to answer for this sort of thing, at least with an apology.

He put the Special Delivery envelope in his breast pocket in the event of a confrontation with Prince, checked his gun in its shoulder holster and went out to his car. He didn't use lights and he drove very slowly, cutting engine noise to a minimum. He kept thinking of Prince. He hoped the man wasn't involved in anything serious. There were ways of hiding money, of having money that wasn't obvious, and so the Consolidated report didn't necessarily mean anything. But because of his servants...

He cut his engine while still on Bay Drive, coasting up to the driveway to Number One. He got out quietly and walked quietly and when he came close to the house he began stopping every few feet to listen. He didn't try the front doors, didn't try to enter any other way either, but moved east, which was to his left, so as to pass the bulk of the house and the garage. He checked windows and all were dark and it was quiet. As he came around the garage, however, he heard something from the rear. He drew his snub-nosed special and moved even more cautiously. It had taken him some time to come around the house, and took him at least as long to make the last hundred yards to the patio.

Voices? Water slapped softly under the dock and he couldn't be sure whether *that* wasn't what he heard. As for movement, Prince's boat was a dark background to whoever might be out there, and he had to step from the patio shadows and commit himself on the dock before he could be certain. It was dangerous ... but he made his decision and walked off the flagstone and onto the wooden planks. He held his gun out and high, straining to see, and called, 'Just hold it there. Not a move.' As he did he saw the man ... and coming closer saw it was a diver with tank on his back ... The diver answered and Beaufort answered him and kept coming, sighting along his snub-nosed ·38, still too far to make one shot count but coming on and flicking his eyes to that boat in case he'd have to answer to someone there too.

Now he could see that the diver was bending, still talking and laughing and just too damned cool to be legit. A real guest would be angry. A real guest ...

Beaufort hesitated just a little longer than he wanted to, because there was still a chance the man was clean ... and then he saw the quick snap upward of head and hand, and he fired. He didn't get the chance to fire again, because he felt the hole open in his stomach and he was falling and his gun was gone and he couldn't believe it, just couldn't. And then the pain was so terrible it stopped him from thinking altogether. 'God!' he said, 'Oh God, *stop*!' It didn't stop and he curled in on himself.

Fanny raised herself from the deck, looking first at where Bramms lay threshing about, moaning, and then further toward the house where Beaufort had stopped moving. She looked longest at Beaufort, and smiled a little and murmured, 'You see, Armand?' Then she flattened, once again frightened at the sharp sound the security chief's weapon had made. Not as loud as she'd thought it would be, but still louder than Bramms's silenced weapon, loud enough for someone to have heard.

She lay there. Bramms called, 'Fanny!'

She didn't answer.

'Fanny! Where the hell ...!'

She raised herself a little. He was clutching his right leg, the thigh, and pulling himself toward the edge of the dock. Too bad the monsters hadn't killed each other. Now she had to go to him and make him give up the bag of jewels.

She grasped her pistol, came erect, looked toward the bridge.

No lights coming here. They might not have heard. It must have been a small gun. Still, she wished she could remain hidden a while longer ...

'Fanny! My leg!'

She came down to the dock. 'Is it bad?'

'Just a flesh wound, but I need some help.'

'You'd better give me the bag.'

'The hell I will!' He looked up at her, and he still held his gun, and she quickly said, 'All right, if you think you can swim ...'

'I can swim. The bullet passed clean through. I'm losing a little blood, but that's all. When I get home, I'll fix it up. Give me a hand.'

She struggled to get him up and he hopped with her to the edge of the dock near the boat. 'The air mask,' he panted. She got the dangling hose and mask and brought it around to his face, and he fastened it over his mouth. He turned on the air, slid down his glass mask and nodded. She stepped away. Still holding his gun, he fell into the water. After the initial surge of bubbles and foam, all was quiet.

She turned and started toward the *diable*, to get rid of him so that if anyone came ...

She slipped, almost fell, looked down at her feet. There was a large puddle where Bramms had been lying, dripping slowly through the tight-set wooden slats. She bent, and then straightened with a gasp. Blood! To bleed so much so fast must mean a big vein, an artery, had been torn! She looked out at the bay. Could he get across? Their jewels ...

She bit her lip. Perhaps there would be enough from the houses to give them a decent cut. She felt bad. It looked as if she had cost the others their fortune. And Prince. She had grown to accept him, almost to like him, seeing how tormented a man he was, how human a man he was, not at all like the rich English back home.

Then she shrugged. It had been necessary and far more important than money.

She went to Beaufort and looked down at him. She saw his gun and kicked it off the dock; then bent, thinking to send him off too. He opened his eyes and moaned. She jumped back, clutching her gun. But he wasn't looking at her; he was rolling his head in agony.

Ah, Armand! she thought. *The Holy Mother gives us full*

283

measure!

She put the gun in her slit-pocket and bent to him and saw the bleeding from his stomach. She said, 'I heard the noise. Let me help you. We'll go to the house and call a doctor.'

He said, 'Yes ... doctor,' and rolled his head and looked at her. 'Who ...?' he asked, blood trickling from his mouth.

She didn't answer, but began struggling to help him up. He gathered his arms and legs under him, and got to his hands and knees. It took a while, and then he was leaning on her, heavily, and she was staggering around to face the house.

'Wait,' she said. 'Let me catch my breath.'

'Call Miami police,' he gasped. 'Give them ...' He fumbled inside his jacket. 'Give ...' He sobbed drily.

'You hear, Armand? You hear, Gerard?' This time she said it aloud.

He groaned terribly. 'Enough,' he said. *'Enough!'*

She took the envelope from his hand and tucked it into the slit-pocket of her witch's costume along with her gun. 'Mr. Byuferd, can you understand me?'

'Yes, get me ... to doctor!'

'I'll get you to hell, Mr. Byuferd! Do you remember Nineteen sixty-six, Mr. *Diable*? The boy killed under the bridge? My *son*, Mr. Murderer! I came here then, and an officer talked to me and another one, a guard you fired, talked to me, and they told me about the three bullets, the two in the stomach and the one in the back. Three bullets for my son, *Monsieur le Chien*: Three bullets for an eighteen-year-old boy you could have ...'

'Lescou,' he muttered. 'The cook ... the boy ...' Then he did something she hadn't thought he could do with a bullet in his stomach. He thrust her away and stumbled forward. He almost ran! If she hadn't been there, he might have reached the patio.

But she *was* there. And she bumped him with her shoulder, hard. He staggered and cried, 'Wait!' and fell. He didn't quite go over the edge of the dock, though one foot waved in air, so she bent and shoved with all her strength. Trying to clutch her and crying, 'Wait ... talk ...!' he rolled over, and in falling screamed briefly. The splash ended that. She looked down, wondering how deep it was here and whether he might not be able to stand. His arms were whipping the water to foam, but she couldn't see his head.

Then his face pushed up whitely and he gurgled something she couldn't make out. He went under again and his arms beat the water. But weaker now and not for long.

Then there were only bubbles; and after a while not even that. She crouched, waiting for some time, then rose and walked slowly back to the boat. She was tired. She could have slept. The years of hatred were over.

In the cabin, she found the women lying unconscious with their bodies exposed. She began to cover the Vener woman, and saw what was on her bottom, and quickly wet a cloth and cleaned her.

Yes, another true *diable*!

She wondered if he knew just how badly he was hurt.

At first he thought he was all right. The pain he'd felt on the dock and on first diving into the bay dulled quickly. By the time he'd kicked down about twenty feet and begun to swim toward the causeway, it was completely gone. Of course, he was uncomfortable; water was entering his suit through the bullet hole, chilling him and slowing him down. Then even *that* stopped bothering him. A little nausea, considerable weariness, but he was able to push on ... for a while. And then, when dizziness and disorientation swept over him, he told himself he would rest a moment and it would pass.

It did pass. But by then he knew something was terribly wrong. He was cold, too cold, and simply hanging in water, suspended, growing colder and weaker by the second.

He tried to look at his right leg, at the rent in his suit, but it was dark, absolutely dark, and his eyes wouldn't focus.

He began to retch. He pulled away the air mask and gagged and put the mask back on and cleared it and then retched again. He fought nausea back down. He tried to swim. He could barely move!

Up! Get up to the air, the clear night air and sky ...

He tried, feebly, to kick upward. He couldn't. The belt and heavy bag of gems held him down. He had to discard them.

Discard a fortune? Discard his triumph, his future?

But if he didn't, he would die!

Don't panic. You have a full tank of air. Just rest and it will pass; the sickness will pass.

He was sinking. He reached down to his right thigh and touched the hole and felt the outward flow of warmth. He

285

knew then. An artery.

He was sinking and he was wrapped in icy darkness and he began to scream inside the mask and flailed briefly.

Very briefly.

No strength.

Darkness and cold.

Dragged down by millions in jewels.

Dying...

Dying? When for the first time in all his bitter, twisted life he truly wanted to live?

Now he fumbled with the belt. Now he tried to free the clasp. And now he was too weak.

He touched bottom, and couldn't even kick off it. He was sinking into the muck. He was settling into the cold slime.

He lost self for a while. Then he was conscious again and was full of terror and he thought of something remembered vaguely from his uncle or was it his father or was it the pale youth who had tried to teach him when he was little? Someone ... sometime ... saying strange words...

Words to save one from the cold slime of eternity?

He pulled at his air mask. He got it partly away and spoke as water filled his lungs; spoke the words that emerged as bubbles; spoke an abortive prayer for the dying:

'*Yisgadal v'yisgadash ...*'

Curt Bramms *né* Louis Abramson fulfilled a technical requirement and all unknowing died a Jew.

Except for the tense moment when they'd been stopped by two security men, with two more standing off to the side of Bay Drive, Bucky Prince, Vino, Rollins and Sandy had experienced no trouble whatsoever in entering and robbing the Greshen and Mortonson houses. The guards had flagged them down on their way from the Greshen house. In the trunk of the Mercedes was a heavy plastic bag with Willa Greshen's jeweled animal collection, but the guards hadn't been looking for anything like that, it seemed, and both recognized Bucky, and when he asked what was wrong one said, 'Don't know yet, Mr. Prince. Some maniac in a barge shooting up our patrol boat and setting the woods on fire...'

They'd gone on, Vino continuing his steady stream of complaints (now about 'melting' in his ski-suit costume), Sandy quite pale after that minor brush with the law and Rollins as imperturbable and optimistic as ever.

Bucky had wanted to simply finish and get to the boat and assure himself that Ceecee was all right. He hadn't been able to think beyond that.

The Mortonson house had gone more or less the same as the Greshen house, though Vino was even *more* uptight, fearing that since Allie knew they were coming they would run into a trap. A logical point ... but the servants had been as easily cowed (tied and put away in locked rooms) as Mrs. Greshen's, and the safe opened promptly to the numbers Rollins provided. (Not that Mrs. Greshen's had taken much longer to open. Vino's nervousness hadn't stopped him from using his stethoscope and cracking what he termed 'a high school gym combination lock' without aid of drill or the capsule of explosive he'd brought along.) Allie's cash was there, conveniently banded into sheaves of bills and tightly packed in a brown zipper folder. Also there were three fine pieces of jewelry. There might have been further loot in the house. With the servants safely out of sight, a few verbal threats had sufficed to maintain Bucky's cover, and he'd had ample opportunity to look around. But he'd walked straight to the door, and when Rollins hurried after him and whispered, 'What about the paintings?' he'd shaken his head and murmured, 'Worthless.' Vino and Sandy had been just as glad to rush to the car, but Rollins had looked doubtful. And rightly so. Bucky guessed that the small clown in the dining room was a Picasso; and the large seascape in the hallway was definitely a Sussman. But adding a few hundred thousand no longer seemed important.

They took their places in the Mercedes, Rollins in back with Bucky, and pulled away. Then Vino glanced around and said to Buddy-Boy, 'You should've put that bag in the trunk with the other stuff! What if we're stopped again?'

Rollins shrugged, murmuring, 'So they'll say hi to Mr. Prince.' He opened the leather folder and examined the bills. 'Nothing bigger than hundreds. Lots of fifties and even twenties.' He looked up at Bucky. 'Doesn't make sense, what with credit cards and checks and all, does it, Mr. Prince?'

Bucky said no, it didn't. Vino said who the hell cared, and turned onto Bay Drive. Sandy stared through the windshield, leaning forward tensely as if to hurry Vino on his way. Rollins closed the folder. 'Funny,' he muttered. 'Like a payoff. Like he was being squeezed.' He shook his head. 'Funny.'

287

Bucky smiled a little. Idle curiosity at a time like this. If Buddy-Boy didn't end up in jail, he might yet become the Jimmy Valentine of his day. He certainly had the nerve . . .

But then he stopped smiling, tasting the depth of his despair, feeling certain they would *all* end up in jail, on death row. Or was it that he felt they—especially Bucky Prince—*deserved* to?

The feeling intensified when they met Fanny on the dock and heard about Beaufort and Bramms. 'God,' Bucky said, and lapsed into silence.

'But *why* did he come around?' Vino asked.

Fanny shook her head. 'What you call the breaks. And Bramms was hurt. Very much hurt. I don't think he could reach . . .'

'Our jewels!' Vino said, and put his hands to his face. 'Millions and millions!'

Rollins said, 'Maybe he made it. Anyway, I got to bury this other stuff, and Mr. Prince got to come with me to know just where it is.'

Sandy began to cry. 'Two of them now! We'll burn for sure if they catch . . .'

Vino suddenly whirled and slapped her, the sound a sharp crack. 'Get on the boat!'

She stopped crying instantly. She stared, and then she smiled; a savage, mocking smile. 'You,' he said. 'You lousy, yellow . . .'

Vino raised his hand again. Rollins grabbed it. 'Me and Mr. Prince got work. You have to get on the boat. If we fall apart now, we're *sure* to burn.'

Fanny took Sandy's arm. 'Come.' Sandy kept smiling. 'Sure.' They went to the boat. Vino stood there, breathing heavily. 'All for nothing,' he said. 'All that work, and killing . . .'

'Not for nothing,' Bucky finally said. He had to hold them together, had to get them safely away and see that the hostages were returned to Bay Island. Had to try and carry it off, even though there was no real hope in him; not for Walter Bucky Prince and what his life would be after tonight. 'Bramms *might* have made it; Fanny's no doctor. And besides, there's the cash and the pin collection.'

Vino began to nod. 'Yeah . . . I almost forgot. Listen, let's take it with us. Let's not risk . . .'

'If we're stopped by a patrol boat . . .' Rollins began.

'Then we're finished anyway!'

'No,' Bucky said. 'We could be stopped and still make it. Two women in costume sleeping below, and the rest of us, also in costume, all party-goers, taking a midnight sail. Nothing too unusual in Miami. No, we'll bury the items, just as we planned, because they're the only things that could *definitely* nail us.'

Vino headed for the *Spray*. Bucky and Rollins went to the patio, where Rollins stopped for a spade and rake he'd placed behind the tall urn-planting. Bucky took the cash and jewels from him; Rollins took the tools, and they went on around the east side of the house to the double row of rosebushes. Rollins dug. When two cars came screeching down Bay Drive toward the bridge. Buddy-Boy said, 'It's deep enough. Drop them in, Mr. Prince.' Bucky placed the bag and zipper folder in the wide, shallow hole. Rollins spaded in earth, tamped it down with his feet, then used the rake to make the spot identical with the rest of the cultivated ground beneath the bushes.

'Look at the garage. Mr. Prince. You can see the first window, right on a line with where the stuff's buried. Just face the garage when you're ready . . .'

'Yes, I've got it.'

Buddy-Boy sighed. 'Then we're through with this island.'

Bucky nodded. *They* were . . . but not Walter Prince. And this island was far from through with him.

Still, once on the *Spray*, his spirits began to lift. He gave soft commands to Rollins and Vino and the *Spray* caught enough breeze to heel her over and give her momentum only yards from the dock. He wanted to go below and see Ceecee and make certain she was all right, but there was no time just yet. Too many cars racing up and down Bay Drive now. Too many security men wondering where Beaufort was, no doubt. And if police boats were on their way . . .

He breathed deeply of cool salt air. He watched the main fill with wind, told Vino and Rollins to raise the jib and smiled back at Fanny and Sandy sitting on the bench behind him. 'We're away.'

Fanny answered his smile. Sandy sat sunk in gloom. Vino and Rollins stood near the mast, waiting. The breeze increased; the *Spray* heeled more sharply; everyone hung on.

When they leveled off, he checked his bearings. He had a

good half hour of straight, unobstructed sailing ahead of him; a perfect time to go below. He called Rollins, told him it was steady-as-she-goes and made his way down into the cabin.

The lantern swung, casting moving shadows. The women lay on their bunks, covered with blankets, sleeping their drugged sleep. He went to Karen Vener and she was unmarked and breathing heavily. He went to Ceecee and she too looked all right and was breathing regularly, though not as heavily as Karen.

He touched her hair, her face. He bent and put his lips to her cheek. Then he just stood there, his face tired.

He heard someone on the ladder. Fanny called, 'Mr. Prince, I forgot ...'

He met her, and took an envelope from her as she explained about Beaufort carrying it and wanting it to go to the police. She went back up, and he held the typewritten sheets close to the lantern. When he reached the one titled 'Walter Danforth Prince', his face grew even more tired. Now there was no hope at all.

How could he have thought there had *ever* been hope?

How could he have been such a blind fool!

Still, if there had been no killings, it could have worked out. He had been prepared to face such knowledge, such questions, could have carried it off with bravura ...

But there was no bravura left in him.

He looked again at Ceecee Mortonson. He understood now what he had wanted, in addition to a new start. That girl. That girl carrying what might be his child.

He tore the reports into tiny pieces, went back up on deck and threw them overboard. He took the wheel and told Sandy and Fanny they could go below and use the two upper bunks if they wished. They went, and he and Vino and Rollins sailed the *Spray*. He used his charts and he used his landmarks and he watched for other craft and their running lights since they couldn't watch for his ... he used none. He sailed, and the sky showed stars in patches and the breeze was strong and the *Spray* leaped like a joyful hound on an autumn's hunt. He sailed, his crew of two silent with each other and with him, thinking their own thoughts, tasting their own hope or despair. He sailed and the very act of sailing was enough, and he didn't think any more, neither hopeful thoughts nor despairing thoughts. He sailed. He gave fewer orders, preferring the catharsis of work. He sailed and time dissolved into landmarks and sea spray and stars and the quick run of water beneath the keel. And when they came to Vizcaya he was surprised. All the hours this past week had dragged endlessly, and now these few had flown by and he was sorry to stop sailing.

Jib and mainsail came down, and while Vino went below to get Fanny and Sandy, Bucky maneuvered between the stone breakwater and shore. He drifted handsomely in as Rollins furled sail, and then he was close enough for the youth to leap to the cracked and mossy flagstones with a bow line. The others came up from the cabin, and they all paused a moment to look at the museum-palace in cloud-dimmed moonlight.

The moment ended. Their good-byes were brief. Rollins drew the line taut as the others filed by Bucky and stepped ashore. Vino was first. 'I'll be looking for your ad,' he said. Fanny said, *'Dieu vous garde.'* Sandy came up slowly and stopped and touched his hand. 'It could've been fun,' she murmured, and hesitated as if wanting to say more, and went ashore. Rollins held the line a moment longer than necessary. The others had started up the broad span of marble stairs that would lead them to a portico and then around the palace to a spot where Vino had parked a rented car. Bucky smiled. 'Cast off, Buddy-Boy. That museum guard could come along any minute.'

Rollins said, 'Yeah, well ...' He tossed Bucky the line, bent and gave the *Spray* a powerful shove. Bucky was busy the next minute angling the bow in toward the stone breakwater. He felt a fender touch, and leaped to the damp, slippery stone with the line. Only then did he have a chance to again turn to the *palazzo.* Rollins was at the top of the stairs. He raised an arm, and was gone.

Bucky pulled the *Spray* along the shore side of the breakwater until he found a rusty metal ring. He tied up, reset his fenders and took a last look around. A snug harbor; well protected and the sky clearing and the forecast for calm weather. And still he stood and tasted the air, putting off the moment when he would drug himself; putting off the moment after that when he would awaken to face ... whatever would come.

He went down to the cabin. He took the last hypodermic of Thorazine and unbuttoned his puffed sleeve and injected himself. He rebuttoned the sleeve and went back up and walked

291

across the breakwater to the bay side. He threw the empty needle as far as he could, and went down to the cabin again.

The massive dose of drug worked quickly. He began to climb into the bunk above Ceecee's, then sat down on the floor beside her, face close to her face. It would be all right if he was found here. And he wanted to look at her, wanted to talk to her.

He took her hand. It lay limp but warm in his. He held it and put his lips to her cheek. 'It was a dream,' he whispered, feeling the numbness move like a dark, heavy cloud from his arm throughout his body. 'A dream of going back to what was. I didn't mean it to become a nightmare; didn't mean it to kill people. I didn't mean...' He sighed, growing groggy, and placed his head more comfortably on the pillow with hers. 'Didn't mean to care so much, Ceecee. For you.' He closed his eyes, and turned his lips to her ear. 'Is it my child, Ceecee?'

'Yes,' she said, voice a thick murmur.

His head came up then, not quickly because he was no longer capable of quick movement. He blinked bleary eyes at her.

She stirred, but still she slept the drugged sleep. 'Yes,' she said.

He smiled stupidly. She was speaking in her sleep, in her dream. Who knew what her 'yes' meant? He lay his head down again; talked to her again.

'It wasn't all wasted. There was Buddy-Boy. Not wasted to know...' He sighed deeply. 'And you. Not wasted ... whatever...' Again he sighed, and slid down from the bunk to the floor. 'Understand?' he murmured, cradling his head in his arms.

He wasn't sure whether he actually heard the thick, 'Yes.'

SUNDAY, MARCH 16

Voices. A woman crying. Someone shaking him.

He awoke slowly, though not completely, to the worst morning after of his life, and Walter Bucky Prince had experienced quite a few in his time. The first thing he saw was a face up close but drawing back as the man straightened. 'You all right?'

292

Bucky tried to speak but his throat was full of cotton, he tried to sit up and his body was stiff and unwieldy. The man, a City of Miami cop, helped him. Bucky said, 'What...?' Then he remembered and began to think and to watch himself.

He ached all over. Sleeping on the floor hadn't done him any good. He looked around while rubbing his neck and testing his muscles. Three or four city officers and an older man in gray —the museum guard, he guessed—and then the woman who was crying, Karen Vener, being attended to by a round little man who was probably a doctor. And Ceecee Mortonson.

Karen and Ceecee sat on their bunks. Karen was hysterical, shaking her head and sobbing and being given an injection ... as if she hadn't had enough injections. Ceecee was looking at him somberly. A cop stood between them but she had moved her head to the side and their eyes met. He smiled. At least he *hoped* he was smiling; the Thorazine hadn't had time to work itself out of his system as it had with the two women. She didn't answer his smile. She answered a question and he heard her say, '... not the entire time. I came awake a little once or twice.'

Bucky felt sick. The drug ... and what Ceecee had said. *When* had she awakened? When Fanny had come down with Beaufort's reports? When he'd sat beside her bunk and talked groggily, confessing ...?

'We'll have to take you down to the station,' the officer said. 'Are you well enough to come along now?'

Bucky said, 'I think so,' and grasped the officer's hand and rose. Things spun around for a moment, and then steadied. He looked at Ceecee again, and stepped around the officer between them. 'How are you?' he asked.

'Fine.'

'Did they bother ...?'

'I've already answered those questions,' she said, her eyes digging into his. Even though the drug was still in him, dulling his senses, he was suddenly certain that she knew. He began to turn away, nausea tickling his throat, and she said, 'I'll be over to see you when we get back home ...'

He nodded, moving now with the officer.

'Darling,' she finished.

He kept going. *Darling?*

The *Spray* had been moved over to the Vizcaya shore. There were more police there and he was helped from the boat and

293

walked between two officers who held his arms. Solicitude? Or arrest?

He tried to care; dullness and nausea made it difficult to care.

'... *when we get back home, darling.*'

Would he ever get back home to find out what she meant?

They walked for a long time, and he stopped once and retched into some flowering bushes. 'I'm sorry,' he gasped.

'Easy, Mr. Prince,' one cop said.

That didn't sound too bad. But they comforted men being led to the electric chair, didn't they?

Darling.

They drove in a patrol car. He sat in back behind the cage partition with one officer and tried not to see the heavy steel mesh. Prison. Walter Prince would die in prison. Or, if he was lucky, he'd get a chance to die *before* prison.

Tad had died before things had been able to close in on him. His brother could do the same.

Drugged thoughts. Nothing had happened yet.

Easy, Mr. Prince.

Darling.

Biscayne Boulevard. Other streets. An old street with old buildings—old for sun-washed Miami, that is—and the patrol car stopping and the door opening. He got out by himself, but on the street the officers were there, one on each side, and even though they didn't take his arms now he was walked between them into an old building, an old police station.

He had never been in a police station before. Never in all his life. It smelled bad. He hated it. He had to go to the bathroom and vomit. One of the officers went with him and stood there and said, 'Easy ... easy ...' And then, when he was washing his face at the grimy little sink, 'What was it they shot into you, Mr. Prince?'

He almost answered, 'Thorazine'. But how could he know? He was one of the hostages, wasn't he? That question ... was it an attempt to trap him? Was this the beginning of hours and days and weeks of attempts to trap him?

He said, 'Don't know, but whatever it was it's still working.' (They had to tell him that he had the right of counsel, didn't they? They had to warn him that anything he said could be taken down in evidence and used against him. The Supreme Court ...)

The officer said, 'You're lucky you're alive. All three of you hostages. You saw what they did to one of the party guests, didn't you? As cold-blooded a killing as I've heard of, and in my business I hear of plenty.' He shook his head, a ruddy, middle-aged man who seemed genuinely pained. 'Did you know Charles Vener, Mr. Prince?'

Bucky froze. He'd avoided thinking of whom Bramms had killed; actively avoided it.

And yet, Karen's hysteria ... the man's voice...

He turned back to the sink and was sick again.

The cop said, 'You know about that security man on Bay Island?'

Bucky used his hands to cup and sip cold water. He drank slowly and thought slowly. Traps again? He said, 'I heard them talking, the thieves I mean, while I was sailing them to Vizcaya. I think they shot him.'

'Killed him. Well, let's go now. The D.A.'s waiting.' He grinned. 'Big time, Mr. Prince.'

They went out into the hall and the other cop was gone. And he wondered if the washroom had been bugged and whether wherever he went in here people would be listening to him.

Think! Think before you speak!

The room was surprisingly cheerful; pale green walls, a neat desk and three windows with bright sunlight pouring in. A young man in turtle-shell glasses and a good summer weight suit sat at the desk and an officer with gold braid on his shoulders sat on the right side. Bucky was given a chair at the left side of the desk. The young man introduced himself as Assistant District Attorney Geller. He said, 'If you're not well enough, Mr. Prince...'

'It's all right.'

The cop standing beside him said solicitously (or was it part of the trap?), 'He threw up a few times.'

The D.A. looked at him. Bucky repeated, 'It's all right.' They were treating him as a rich man from Bay Island. Or *playing* at treating him as a rich man from Bay Island.

He was tired and he was sick. He was afraid.

Darling.

He said, 'Are the others—the two women, I mean—are they all right?'

The D.A. looked at the officer in gold braid. The officer in

295

gold braid looked at the cop. The cop said, 'The doctor said one was in shock, but otherwise all right. The one whose husband was killed. And then there was something about a sex crime...'

Bucky stiffened.

'Minor thing, Mr. Prince,' the cop said quickly. 'The other one, your fiancée, she's fine. Real strong gal.'

The D.A. frowned. The cop cleared his throat. 'Both all right, Mr. Prince.'

His fiancée?

Darling?

'Good,' Bucky said. 'Now what can I tell you?'

The D.A. said to start at the beginning.

The cop in gold braid said, voice quiet, 'At about the time you hired those servants.'

And so here it was, one of the weak points. But without murder, with strength and panache...

'Rather foolish of me, I suppose,' he began, 'but when I got a call from a man purporting to be an employment agent ... this was when I was in Philadelphia setting up the purchase of my Bay Island home ... well, I arranged to meet Charles DeVino. He struck me as an experienced butler, and when he offered to hire the rest of my staff, what with servants so hard to find...'

He went on to his stay on Bay Island and his total lack of suspicion, or *reason* for suspicion, that his servants were anything but what they said they were, and his shock when they showed up at the gala and took him and the two women...

He told of being forced to help them in the country club, and of being taken along to gain them entrance to the two houses. He told of trying to protect the women by doing exactly as he was ordered.

'Understandable enough,' the D.A. murmured, 'when your own fiancée was one of them. A clever plan, Mr. Prince.'

'Yes,' Bucky said, trying not to read anything into that.

'When did they inject you?' the cop in gold braid asked.

'After we docked at Vizcaya.'

'Then how did the boat get to the stone jetty?'

But this he had planned for. This was easy.

'I mean they injected me when we docked at the *jetty* at Vizcaya. How they got across to the mainland I don't know. It's not much of a swim—maybe twenty feet.'

'It's shallow enough to *walk*,' the cop said.

The officer in gold braid cleared his throat. The D.A. fiddled first with his glasses and then with a pencil. Bucky tried to draw a deep breath unobtrusively. Now the picking away, the *real* questioning, would start. He wondered just how long he could stand up under it. Two murders ... The phone rang. The D.A. picked it up and said, 'No. Geller. But he's right here.' He handed it to the officer in gold braid. The officer listened and said, 'Drang? He's in our files, isn't he?' He listened for quite a while. Bucky managed his deep breath. 'Well, take it down. Just be careful, Frank. Remember where you are. No ...' His eyes found Bucky. Bucky was exhaling carefully. It was all he could do; breathe in and out and wait for whatever would come. 'At the Mortonson house, right. Say an hour.' He hung up. 'Suppose you give us names and descriptions of your servants, Mr. Prince.'

Bucky mentioned their security cards. The officer nodded. 'Yes, but those little pictures ...'

Bucky described them fully. It was part of the plan not to hold back, not to risk any suspicion. There was enough suspicion already.

He finished and waited for questions. There were no questions. The officer with gold braid rose abruptly. Bucky was surprised at his height; at least six three. 'I'll drive you home, Mr. Prince.' Bucky looked at the D.A. Geller put out his hand. 'Thank you, Mr. Prince. Get some rest now. Maybe you'd better see your doctor.' An almost imperceptible pause. 'Just what was it they shot into you people?'

Bucky shrugged. 'Something to make us sleep. Except that I didn't get enough sleep, having received my shot hours after the women.'

He was thinking about that reference to Vincent Drang.

And were they *really* allowing him to leave? Or was he on a short leash, to be yanked back here when his defences were down, say this evening?

He stood up. 'Could you tell me how much they got away with?'

'Not too much,' the D.A. said. 'The skin diver ... did you know they gave most of their take to a diver?'

Bucky said, 'He collected it in the club. I don't know what he did after he left us.'

'The skin diver was shot. We found him at seven this morning, about an hour before finding you. Not too far from your dock. The jewels were on him. Bled to death, did he, Margeson?'

The officer in gold braid said, 'Death by drowning goes on the coroner's report.'

Bucky said, with absolute honesty, 'He deserved it. He killed without reason.'

'Ten, twelve million is reason enough,' the D.A. said, then smiled. 'At least for most of us, Mr. Prince.'

Bucky was too tired now to try and analyze that smile. He said, 'I guess so. My own feeling is that nothing, not all the money in the world, is worth a human life.'

'I wish the rest of our customers felt the same.'

Bucky nodded and turned to follow Margeson. He was going to thank the cop for his help, but didn't. Bay Island millionaires didn't notice such services, did they?

He wasn't sure any more. He wasn't a Bay Island millionaire and hadn't been for years.

If he got out of this, it was back to Chicago, to P.R. and back to the bottle. Yes, back to the bottle to forget what could have been and what *had* been.

A rosy future. He smiled thinly as they walked out. Margeson said, 'Did you think of something that could help us, Mr. Prince?'

Bucky said, 'Geller was under the impression that ten or twelve million isn't a lot of money to me. It is, you know. I'm a very poor millionaire.'

They were walking down the narrow, gloomy hall toward the front doors. Margeson said nothing and Bucky wondered if he'd made a mistake. But they'd find out sooner or later, wouldn't they? The Consolidated Investigations report would have to come to light again, wouldn't it? Speaking up now might take some of the curse off the revelation...

Margeson opened the door for him, and said, 'So I've heard. But your fiancée is something else again, Mr. Prince.'

Bucky nodded. 'Yes, something else again.'

They rode in an unmarked car, and this time he sat up front and there was no wire cage. But he felt the cage anyway. It was there, waiting to close in around him.

Margeson talked. He was a captain with sixteen years' service in Miami and this was the first time he'd ever had anything to do with Bay Island. And only because the *Spray* had been docked in the City of Miami. 'Man in charge is a Beach

298

Lieutenant. My man will step out of it, unless asked to help. You'll probably meet them...'

Bucky nodded and kept his eyes on the sunny streets. He didn't try to read the captain's face or voice or words: 'You'll probably meet them...' Riding in the car was bringing back nausea and all he wanted was a few hours alone at home. A few hours of peace.

He got a few minutes, ten to be exact. Margeson took him to his door and said, 'Better lie down, Mr. Prince.' He drove away and Bucky turned to watch. The captain didn't go back over the bridge; he drove west along Bay Drive. The Mortonson house was there, and the two policemen Bucky would probably meet.

He went around back to the dock, and saw the uneven circles chalked around the dark stains. He went in through the patio doors and directly to the bar and poured a highball glass full of straight bourbon. He took a long sip, and his stomach turned over and the room spun and he sat down. He closed his eyes. He knew he should eat something but the thought was repellent. He sat. And his ten minutes were up.

There was a knock at the door and a voice in the hall, and he opened his eyes and rose. Ceecee came into the study. 'There you are,' she said.

'You left out "darling".'

'There you are, darling.'

'Darling fiancé, isn't it?'

'Yes, my darling fiancé. You look awful, my darling fiancé.'

He turned from her, because she looked marvelous. She was wearing a light yellow mini-suit and matching shoes and her hair was tied back into twin ponytails with yellow ribbon. She was young and she was beautiful. He said, 'And you look rather well.'

'Rather well is a triumph after having a murderer cornhole me.'

'Please,' he muttered, picking his drink up from the bar.

'Is it the facts or the poetry in which I couch the facts?'

'Both.' He drank, taking a small sip this time. It still tried to come up.

'You're very sensitive,' she said, 'for an accessary to murder. That's how they say it in the old Perry Mason shows, don't they? Accessary to murder?'

He stood there with the glass in his hand. He laughed, but he didn't turn.

'You want to play games?' she said. 'You want to pretend it isn't so?'

When he felt he'd gained control of his face and voice, he turned. 'Look, Ceecee, will you please explain that fiancé business ... and then leave? I've had a trying night. Perhaps more so than you.'

'Despite my being cornholed by a madman?'

He shook his head, not at her but at the image of Bramms and her. He said, voice weak, 'I'm going upstairs to sleep now.'

She went to the black leather couch facing the windows and sat down. She crossed her legs and reached into a small white handbag and came out with a cigarette case. He said, 'Don't smoke those things here. I have enough trouble as it is.'

'If you mean pot, I threw it in the bay half an hour ago. I feel that a married woman and soon to be mother has no business with drugs. We don't want our child popping pills in the crib ...'

'*Our* child?'

'I told you that last night, didn't I?'

He tried to look puzzled.

'I was awake on and off,' she said. 'I guess you didn't get full value for your money, or else different individuals react differently, since Karen was completely out until that museum guard woke us.'

'I don't know what you're talking about.' He was sick again, the nausea rising again, and he couldn't look at her and he couldn't leave her.

Her face changed. Her voice changed. 'Bucky, Vincent Drang was at my house talking to the police, trying to make them believe that you're broke ...'

'I *am* broke.'

'Yes, I decided you would have to be in order to do such an insane thing.'

'What insane thing?'

'Stop it!' She was standing and she was angry. 'If it wasn't for my telling Allie about our child and that we've been secretly engaged for a month—which I doubt he believes but which he'll *act* as if he believes—Drang might have turned things against you. If it wasn't for Allie ordering him out of the house in front of those policemen, and my saying you snubbed him and that's why he's trying to hurt you, and that I

300

heard your servants threatening you *on the boat* when no one was supposedly able to hear them, and my father explaining that you'll be marrying forty million dollars, *minimum*, and could have no possible motive, even if you were broke, which he said is foolish since he personally knows of hidden assets . . .'

'Yes, you've both been very helpful and I thank you. But I really must lie down now.' He had to get her out of here, right now! He was going to be sick again . . . and he was already; very sick—of himself. He tried to drink and gagged and rushed headlong from the study to the little bathroom off the foyer. He vomited until there was nothing left to vomit. And felt her hand cool on the back of his neck and was humiliated and said, 'Go out, *please*!' She went out. He washed, and when he stepped into the foyer, she was waiting.

'The police will come,' she said.

He nodded. 'And when they learn we're *not* going to be married . . .'

'But we are.'

'I believe I have something to say about that.'

'Only if you say yes. Because my child needs a father. Later, if you decide we can't make it . . .'

He returned to the study and his drink. She followed. He said, 'You'll just have to forgive me. I can't talk now. That injection . . .'

'We haven't much time, Bucky.' She came close. 'I want you free and clear, not rotting in jail.'

'Even if I deserve jail?'

'Even if you deserve it, and I don't feel you do.'

'Crime and punishment go together, don't they?'

'Only for the helpless, the poor and those who get caught.'

'I'll remember that, in case I ever consider a life of crime. But in the meantime . . .'

She interrupted. 'Tell me, how did that diver know just where to find the gags and ropes on *your* boat?'

He smiled faintly. He hadn't thought of that. Bramms should have fumbled around, as Fanny would have done, acting as if he were searching.

'How did he know just where to find the hypodermics? And what were they doing on your boat anyway?'

He grasped an answer. '*They* put them there . . . just before coming to the gala.'

'Took you a moment to think of that, didn't it? Well, try to think your way out of this. I *heard* you last night. Half asleep or half awake or what, I heard you say things and I know you were part of it.'

He drank and was able to hold it down.

'And thinking back, to that time I visited your house ... I knew then something was wrong.' She came close and touched his hand. 'I *know*, Bucky, and I don't care.'

He put his drink down carefully on the bar and nodded. 'Yes, I'm sorry, I never wanted you to be part of it. But now there are two murders...'

'Not you,' she said firmly. 'If you want to play guilt-ridden neurotic, please pack it into the rest of this week. By next week, when we get married, I want a rational male.'

He didn't have time to discuss it. A broad man in plain clothes came in and introduced himself as Lieutenant Vestry. He wasn't very friendly and he didn't try to hide it. He asked if his men could search the house and grounds.

'Of course,' Bucky said, remembering what was buried under the rosebushes.

The lieutenant went outside a moment and they heard voices and then he returned. He didn't talk about the robbery, but asked when 'the happy event' would take place.

Ceecee said, 'Late next week.' Vestry nodded glumly. Ceecee said, 'Don't you approve, Lieutenant?'

Vestry seemed to remember with whom he was dealing. He said, 'Of course,' and made a smile. Ceecee answered the smile and Vestry looked at Bucky and Bucky asked, 'Is there anything bothering you, Lieutenant?'

Vestry was an honest cop. Vestry said something he was probably afraid of saying and obviously had to say. 'If it wasn't you people. If it wasn't the marriage to forty million—excuse me, Miss Mortonson. If it was anywhere else, Mr. Prince, you'd have motive and we'd have circumstantial evidence and maybe it wouldn't get to court and maybe it would. But I'd sure try.'

Bucky nodded. Ceecee nodded. Vestry looked down at his hands. The voices from outside came inside. Vestry said, 'I'll see that everything's kept straight,' and went out.

'Crime and punishment,' Ceecee murmured.

Bucky turned to the bar for his drink. She said, 'I gave up *my* monkey.'

'Monkey? This?' He laughed; and suddenly *saw* the huge

302

drink and was embarrassed and put it down. He said, 'I'm clear now ... you heard him. We can have a public quarrel and call off the marriage. You need a richer, safer man.'

She wasn't impressed. 'Money's *your* hang up, not mine. I blow my mind for the Cream, Mozart and Bucky Prince.'

He shook his head. 'Ceecee, I *mean* it!'

'Money. There must be something wrong with our country if it makes people forget Francis Chichester and emulate Clyde Barrow. Must be something terribly wrong to drive them to money, money, always money.'

'You're not listening! I've *done* this thing! And not only that, but I'm much older than you ...'

'Of course,' she continued, 'with forty million of my own, I can afford to be a moral little black girl.'

'If not for the child, I'm sure you wouldn't want ...'

She put a finger on his lips. She murmured, 'Love you, Bucky, yes, just a little, for now.

There was no arguing with that, with the memory and the urgency of that. He kissed her finger, and then her hand, and then her face and mouth. A Beach cop came in and muttered, 'Oops,' and went out. She said, 'You haven't brushed your teeth.'

He kissed her again.

This time *two* cops came in, and Vestry behind them. The lieutenant said, 'This is the last room.'

They went outside and walked. Bucky told her what was buried near the rosebushes. She said, 'We'll find it some day. We'll bring it to the police and Mrs. Greshen will have her toys and my father will have two hundred and fifty million again instead of a mere two hundred and forty-nine. Meanwhile, who cares?'

He didn't say so but *he* cared. He cared about Buddy-Boy; about Sandy and Fanny and Vino. He couldn't do anything about the pin collection, but the cash ... Allie would stay a million poorer ... He'd wait three or four months ... There was some risk, but it was a matter of responsibility ...

They walked. The police left. Ceecee made him a boiled egg and instant coffee. He brushed his teeth. They went to his room and she said, 'Love you, Bucky, yes, just a little, for now.'

Only when she slept, huddling into his drained, exhausted body, did he think of that forty million dollars. She was buying a husband as he had always refused to buy a wife. But he would ransom himself. In ten years, perhaps less, he would double that forty million and be his own man. Prince Mining was still viable . . .

He planned, planned, but she stirred and sighed and he stopped planning; as he would always stop doing things other than those connected with loving her when she was there to be loved. He waited for her to speak, to say something to reduce the intensity of his feelings, to give him back his dreams of making money.

But she didn't.

'Take me sailing,' she said. 'Take me and my belly sailing.'

They drove to Miami Beach and rented a little Coronado 15 and sailed. She worked for him and sat with him, and he revised that ten years to fifteen, maybe twenty. He wasn't sure just how much mind and heart he would have for business from now on.

EPILOGUE

On a hot, gray day in early July, Walter Bucky Prince walked up to the circular information booth on the main floor of New York's Grand Central Station. In his right hand he carried a black attaché case. In his left he held a thin cigar, raising it to his mouth as he examined a rack of timetables. A pretty girl gave him and his fine clothes an approving, and inviting, glance as she too examined the rack. He paid her absolutely no attention. After another glance, she drifted off.

A lean, ferret-faced man in gray slacks and blue polo shirt ambled up on Prince's right and looked at the rack. Bucky Prince put down his attaché case and picked out a timetable. He fought to keep his eyes there, but had to turn to Charles DeVino, just once. The ferret-faced man was lighting a cigarette; then he stooped, straightened and walked away.

Bucky Prince remained at the rack a little while longer. He would have liked to have said a few words to Vino; asked if he knew anything about Sandy, Fanny and Buddy-Boy; told him about his marriage and Mrs. Greshen's death and the buried jewels remaining buried—Vincent Drang being forced to sell by the Bay Island committee and the opening of a Prince Mining Company office in Manhattan...

Many things. Much to tell and much to find out. But of course, they didn't know each other, he and the ferret-faced man who had walked off with his attaché case.

He left the station, walking quickly to lose the sad feeling, the inexplicably sad feeling.

Three days later, a Sunday morning, Vino was at Washington Square Park, having taken a bus from his shabby room in the west seventies. It was bright and pleasantly breezy. Vino strolled past the benches, looking at the summer students from N.Y.U., smiling to himself at some of the haircuts, whistling to himself at some of the girls. He couldn't wait to see Sandy! Almost four months since they'd split up in Miami. They were all here in New York, that was the plan, but he'd never run into any of them. Not surprising in a city of nine million. Still, he'd always looked for Sandy. Not that he'd have risked trying to contact her before the payoff, but if they'd just happened to meet...

He sat down on an empty bench. He was early. He kept the attaché case close beside him. Inside were three large manila envelopes. Two hundred fifty thousand dollars for Fanny, a hundred twenty-five thousand each for Sandy and Rollins.

He hummed, lit a cigarette and quickly put his free hand back on the case. There'd been a typewritten note with the money when he'd opened the case Thursday afternoon.

'The jewelry is lost. An even division would be right.'

He smoked and smiled. Even division hell! Prince couldn't run things any more. Old Vino was the boss now, and he was taking the boss's share. Anyway, who was Prince to talk about even divisions? Who knew what he'd *really* done with the Greshen pins?

At least that was the way he rationalized it. Actually, he trusted Prince right down the line, felt the man had made it somewhere else and that's why he'd handed over the whole million.

Half of that million now belonged to Vino.

Sandy would want to join him for that, and for what they'd had together before the Bay Island job. He was sure that after a drink or two, a few soft words...

A shadow fell over him; his head jerked up; Buddy-Boy Rollins, looking much like one of the long-haired students in blue chinos, open-necked shirt and scruffy buckskin shoes, was sitting down. Vino opened the case and took out an envelope marked 'Rollins'. Buddy-Boy took it and said, 'How's Prince?'

'I didn't ask. You got a hundred twenty-five G's in there.'

Buddy-Boy smiled. 'He look all right?'

'Rich, baby. Man like that always comes out on top. *Born* on top.'

Rollins nodded. 'A good guy.'

Vino shrugged ... and saw Sandy coming around the arch. College kids looked at her. She was something to look at, in her tight, white stretch pants and black blouse. His heart started to pound, and he murmured, 'No use hanging around, Buddy-Boy.'

'Want to say hello. We're out in the open anyway, right?'

Sandy began to smile while still some distance from the bench. Vino rose to greet her, but then he realized she was

306

smiling at Rollins, not at him, and he sat down. 'Hey, man,' she said, 'you're looking cool.'

'We rich people always look cool,' Rollins said.

'Then I should be frozen stiff,' Vino said, not able to help it. He opened the case, and she finally looked at him. 'How's the boy, Vino?' He nodded and gave her the envelope. 'A hundred twenty-five,' he said.

'Crazy! Now I can get outa this sick town. You like New York, Buddy-Boy?'

'Not me. I'm off west somewhere.'

'Like Vegas maybe?'

'Maybe.'

Vino said, 'How about a little further west than that? Like L.A., and then Honolulu?'

She nodded. 'Bet you'll be able to *buy* those towns, if I know you.'

He shrugged. 'I got the big cut, sure. But that's the way we agreed.'

'*How* big?'

She and Buddy-Boy were both looking at him. He figured what the hell and told them. They'd know anyway, if Fanny showed up before they left. It was simple arithmetic, adding their three cuts and subtracting from a million.

Sandy nodded, and now her smile was the same as it had been on Prince's boat; tight and nasty. He said, voice low, 'Let's you and me have a drink. After Fanny comes, I mean. Let's talk, baby.'

'About money?'

'All right. About money.'

She shook her head. 'Uh-uh. I've got enough money.' She turned to Buddy-Boy. 'Haven't we, honey?'

He grinned. 'I'm small time. Plenty for me.'

'A hundred twenty-five and a hundred twenty-five makes a quarter of a million,' she said. 'We're quarter of a millionaires, Buddy-Boy!'

'You mean *together*.'

'Let's walk together and see how it feels.'

They were grinning at each other, and Vino was burning and trying to think how to reach her, and then Buddy-Boy got up and they began to walk away. He started to follow, calling, 'Stick around a while, will you?'

Sandy looked back. 'Maybe we'd better. To make sure you

wait for Fanny.'

'I was waiting for you, wasn't I?'

'Easy,' Rollins murmured, and Vino realized he'd raised his voice. Dammit, he didn't want that kid telling him what to do! Didn't want to remember March fifteenth and how he'd lost his nerve and how Rollins had been so cool and sure...

'There she is,' Sandy said.

'She looks bad,' Rollins said.

Vino turned his head. Fanny was walking away from a cab near the college side of the square. She *did* look bad. She wore a black dress like an Italian widow's. She looked thinner and more dried out than ever. She walked quickly, with jerky steps; a skinny little crow. When she reached them, she didn't say hello or anything, just 'My money. The cab waits.'

'Sure,' Vino said, taking out the envelope. 'Two hundred fifty G's, Fanny. Not too bad...'

She grabbed the envelope. 'Yes, I have to go. My husband...' She shook her head. 'Very bad. I could not be in New York, but the paper I bought every day. I fly back in an hour. Toronto. Very bad.' She looked at Buddy-Boy. 'Be careful, *mon cher.*' And she rushed away.

'That's Fanny for you,' Vino said, and chuckled.

'It *must* be bad,' Rollins muttered, watching the black-clad figure enter the cab. 'Her face ... her eyes...'

'Now we can go,' Sandy said, and took his arm.

'You mean you and me,' he said, smiling at her, 'or you and my envelope?'

Vino said, 'Let's all have a drink,' and knew it wasn't any good and couldn't help remembering and couldn't help begging. 'Sandy, c'mon, the three of us.'

Rollins nodded, but Sandy said, 'You want to talk about March fifteenth, Vino?'

'If you want to.'

She smiled. She tugged Rollins's arm and they walked away. Rollins looked back and waved his envelope. Vino cursed him. Then he walked toward Greenwich Village, thinking he'd have a few drinks and find a broad. There were broads all over the city...

Except he wasn't going to bother with this city. He was heading for L.A. at nine tonight. He had his reservation—*two* of them, but he'd cancel one and to hell with Sandy!

He changed his mind about the drink. He hailed a cab. No

308

more buses and no more running scared. A few days to swing in L.A., and then Hawaii, and later maybe Japan. And then ... Christ, he had half a million! Half a million dollars and he could go anywhere he wanted to and do anything he wanted to!

Broads? He laughed aloud and the cabby glanced at him in the rear view and he didn't give a damn. A guy with half a million could find all the broads he needed. More than he needed. All the broads he could stand!

He tipped heavy outside the dingy brownstone and went upstairs and packed. He had a few drinks from a bottle of blend and smoked and paced up and down and tried not to think of the good years with Sandy; of her body throbbing in his arms and her lips against his chest ...

He dressed in his new tan summerweight and grabbed a cab and was taken to Kennedy. It was hours before his flight, but maybe he'd be able to pick up a cancellation. He couldn't wait to split this scene!

The girl at the American desk suggested he try the TWA desk. There he landed a first class on a five thirty flight. He was paying when he felt someone looking at him. He glanced to his left, it was a cop. He froze for a second, but then he told himself not to be stupid; he'd been walking around this town for close to four months and nothing had happened. He didn't hurry. He talked to the girl, put his ticket in his breast pocket and picked up his suitcase. He walked right past the cop, uptight and sweating, yet not really expecting anything, feeling it was his lousy nerves, his nerves that had started to go bad on Bay Island. Then the cop said, 'Just a minute,' and he almost laughed.

He kept going. The cop started after him. He laughed, really laughed, and said to himself, 'He's not talking to you.'

He saw a woman in front of him look startled, and the man beside her yank her out of the way. He looked back, and that cop was beginning to run! That cop had his hand on his gun and was calling, 'Just a minute, please!'

Please! It was nothing! If he stopped he would find out it was nothing. Like a movie where a guy runs from a cop and there's a chase and then he's caught and he thinks he's had it and it turns out the cop wanted to give him something, his wallet or ticket or something.

Except he had his wallet and his ticket and the cop was

pulling at his gun and Vino was running; he hadn't realized it but he was running; must have started running right away. He couldn't be stopped now! He had half a million in his suitcase and he was almost home free!

ALMOST! ALMOST!

He saw the escalator leading down to the baggage section, and headed there.

'Halt!' the voice called, and there weren't any people near the escalator and he realized he should have stayed with the crowd, with the people, so the cop couldn't fire.

Instinct and professionalism told Charles DeVino to stop. A Colt ·25 in his pocket—he'd have dumped it in a washroom before taking off—and half a million in his bag, and the knowledge that he was a two time loser and one more time could be life and accessary to murder made it *sure* to be life ... all this made him run.

That escalator was a thousand miles long! He'd be trapped in a narrow shooting gallery!

He stopped, digging at his Colt, and began to turn. At the same time he was shouting, 'What the hell *is* it! What...'

He never heard the cop's gun. He caught a bullet above the left ear. He never found out *why* he died. And it was something so simple, so very simple, the *old* Vino, the thief with all the nerve in the world, might have laughed.

Airports aren't like city streets. Police at airports *examine* people. The wanted posters are remembered at airports, because that's where the wanted, the hunted, are likely to be seen.

Charles DeVino had simply had the bad luck to run into a cop with a good memory.

Buddy-Boy Rollins had this old Ford. Sandy wanted him to buy a new car, but he said no, paying that much cash would be dangerous. Besides, he was pretty good with engines and the heap really moved.

They went west and he kept avoiding the big towns, saying he'd had enough of them for a while. Besides, big town cops were tough.

She wanted to buy things everyplace they stopped. He wouldn't let her. He said it was dangerous.

'Then what good's all this dough!' she asked, one night in a motel off Route 66. 'We might as well be broke!'

She had her envelope out and bundles of greenbacks spread over the bed. His own envelope was under the Ford's rear seat; he carried some cash in his wallet and had some more stuck away in the glove compartment; and while he didn't say so, that was another reason for a beat-up old heap. No one was likely to steal it.

He said they had to wait a while; let things cool off.

'It's been five months, hasn't it? Things are stone cold dead!'

He went to the bed and put his hand on her arm. She shook him off angrily. 'I'm getting sick and tired ...!'

He sat down beside her and began putting the money away. He told her to save it for later. He was paying for everything, even if 'everything' wasn't much—gas and food and liquor and motel rooms. She was worth it. But he was beginning to feel oppressed. She complained too much. She looked at other guys too much. One night she'd left their room for a bucket of ice, and hadn't come back until dawn.

He hadn't said anything. But when he was with a girl, he felt she should be with him. Not forever. He certainly didn't want *that*. Not yet anyway, and not with Sandy. But still, she was too much.

They drove to Las Vegas, even though he felt it was the wrong town for them. Lots of smart people in Vegas. Lots of people with connections. And cops with big town action.

She'd begged. She'd always wanted to see the casinos. 'Only for two, three days, baby,' she'd said, the night he'd had to make the decision. 'Just to look around. Just to wear some good clothes and see a few shows.' And she'd worked on him, in bed, and he'd said all right.

They stayed at a small place north of town, even though she screamed blue murder, wanting a big hotel. They dressed. She looked at his gray suit, made a face and said he had to buy some sharp threads. He had to admit that next to her he wasn't much. She wore a cocktail gown, yea-high at the bottom and yea-low at the top and everything showed just right. He admired it so much he tried to pull it off, but even though she laughed she wouldn't go for it.

At the Sands Hotel, he lost her. One minute she was at the table with him, and the next minute she wasn't. 'Got to see the man,' she'd said, but she never came back.

Okay. That was her bag. He lost twenty bucks in the casino

311

and returned to the motel and watched TV. At two a.m. he
went to sleep.

She wasn't there in the morning. Still okay. Her big time
out.

But then he thought of something. She'd been carrying a
black purse; a pretty big purse for just make up and tissues.

He went to the dresser where she'd put her envelope. He
counted, and she was twenty thousand short.

Twenty thousand!

If she spread *that* much around...

He went to the dining room, had breakfast and sat looking
out at flat, ugly country. He made his decision. He went to the
desk and said he was leaving but that his wife was staying on a
while. He paid a full week in advance, just to make sure her
envelope would be safe. If she stayed away longer than that,
she'd either be dead or in jail. Probably in jail.

He packed and left a note on the dresser:

'It was great. Take care. Everything's where it ought to
be.'

Then he put her envelope under some blouses.

The minute he pulled onto the highway, something heavy
lifted from his shoulders. Cheez, he'd been sweating every inch
of the way with her and hadn't known it! How *good* it felt to
get away, even if he knew he would miss her at night.

He didn't have any place in mind. He just drove. He ended
up in Albuquerque, New Mexico, and after taking a room in a
nice motel, he drove around town. At first he just hit main
streets, like he did whenever he looked over a new place. But
then he suddenly decided he *liked* it here. It was a city, yes, but
it wasn't old and rotten and tall and crowded. More like a
small town, or a lot of small towns put together, and the air
was cool and clean.

He got a city map and began covering ground, a lot of
ground. He had dinner at a diner near the motel and there was
this dark-haired girl serving and she began kidding him a little
and he played her game and when he left he had her number.
Well, there were always girls. This one was nice though; a little
shy; not the Sandy type.

The next morning he drove to the section where all the
streets were northeast. There were these brown hills right off at
the end of some streets, and then he came to three big green-
houses and a sign reading 'FOR SALE. PRINCIPALS ONLY'. He

312

drove by and U-turned and drove by again. He parked and went inside the office.

Two hours later he returned to the diner and the dark-haired girl was there and he talked to her more seriously, asking how she liked this town and whether she thought *he* would like it. She kept kidding though. She said, 'Sure, you'll *love* it, if you use my phone number.'

Well, she couldn't help him anyway. He had to make up his own mind. But he knew he was going to do it. They wanted a hundred thousand for that greenhouse business. He could make it pay; and better than the old man with his two work-men. He could just about do all the work himself, maybe with one part-time helper, a high school kid say.

But he couldn't pay that hundred thousand all at once; even though he had it, and twenty-four grand to spare. No, he had to put some down and get a bank loan and little by little work it off and save the heist money for other things, feeding it into his profits so there was no way for anyone to see it.

That heist money would last him the rest of his life, in extras.

He went back to the motel and took paper and an envelope from the desk. He did something he'd been wanting to do ever since leaving New York. He knew Fanny's Toronto address; she'd given it to him when they'd split up in Miami ... 'In case you come to Canada, *mon cher,* and want good food.'

He just wanted to tell her he was okay and thinking about her. She was a nice old girl. He also wanted to tell her he was going to have a greenhouse and work with flowers and make his life here and that he hoped her husband felt better and hoped she felt better.

So that's what he did tell her, writing slowly, painfully, and then writing it over again because he didn't want to send her a messy letter. He finished with: 'I miss your cooking. Love, Buddy-Boy.' He looked at that 'Love', surprised. He considered writing the letter again, but a *third* draft was beyond his literary capacity.

He mailed it at the desk and went back to the diner. The dark-haired girl got off at nine. It was a quarter to. He drank coffee and they left together and she looked at the old Ford and said, 'Hey, this is some sports car you got.'

He grinned. He took her to a drive-in movie. She didn't mind the 'sports car' after a while.

313

Fanny Lescou was alone in the small apartment on Robert Street. It was August and the college girls had been gone since May and Armand had been gone since July twenty fifth. He'd suffered, her *pauvre*. It had been a blessing when he'd died.

Now she had to get up and move. She'd been saying it for two weeks. 'Get up and *do* something, Lescou!'

She had spent as much money on Armand as she could, but what could you buy a dying man? She had almost all the money; more money than she would ever need. Imagine, a quarter of a million dollars! And to think they had planned on so much more! What would she have done with more?

What could she do with *this*?

Well, of course she would live on it. No more working for *beeg* bosses. She would get another apartment, a little smaller but in a nicer section.

Maybe move to Montreal?

What about a visit to France? She had always wanted...

No, not she. Armand. He was the one who'd spoken of France as if it were home. To her, Canada was home.

Or was it? To her, where Armand and Gerard had been was home. Now...

She sat at the kitchen table, drinking coffee. She had to go out. She had to do something. She had to...

To what?

She sat. She drank coffee. The future was something not to be looked at; empty and gray.

She didn't even weep. She had wept so much these two weeks, there were no more tears left in her.

Or so she thought... until she went down to check the mail, something she did each day without hope because who was left to write to her? Only advertisements came now...

There was a letter. Above the printed return address was scrawled, 'B.B. Rollins'.

B.B. Rollins! She was torn between joy and fear. Joy at hearing from him. Fear at his being so foolish as to write openly to another member of the gang.

What if the police had put a watch on her ... or him?

She walked out and sat down on the front step and looked around. She opened the letter.

It was short. Much too short for her needs. But the emptiness weakened, the grayness lifted. She read it again, and again. He was well. He was going to work with growing things.

314

He missed her cooking. And 'Love, Buddy-Boy'.

A word. They used it carelessly nowadays.

But it was the only word that could save her and she went down the street to the small grocery, got change and entered the phone booth and placed a call to Mr. B.B. Rollins at the Waysider Motel in Albuquerque. It was eight thirty there. Perhaps he would be in.

He was, and he was surprised to hear from her. She didn't mince words. 'You are not going to *stay* at that motel?'

'I been looking at places. There's apartments ... even a small house on Bellamah Avenue.'

'You will need a cook and housekeeper, a *beeg* boss like you, not so?'

He laughed.

'How will you have time for the business and the girls, always trying to make meals, or eating out? How will you grow...?'

He laughed again. 'I'm through growing, Fanny.'

She had said all she could. He said nothing. And then she felt she was a foolish old woman and why would he want her around, getting in the way...

He said, 'Listen, do you mean it? You want to come out here?'

'Yes.'

'Well then ... sure, c'mon. I'll take the house.'

'Good, it will be a few days, and then I will see you.' She was proud at how steady her voice was. And she was proud at how she held herself together until she was back in the apartment.

Oh, she had tears and tears left in her! But these tears were *good*.

On March first, Sandra Blake had to move from her twelve hundred dollar a month hotel suite into an apartment motel on the outskirts of Las Vegas. She also had to accept a job as cigarette girl in the Diabolo Casino where only last month she'd lost over ten thousand dollars. Not that she was broke; far from it. Her *cash* was gone, yes, but what the hell, nothing lasts forever. She had three closets full of clothes—suits, pants-suits, dresses, gowns, four mink stoles, two mink jackets, two full-length mink coats. She also had a diamond bracelet and matching earrings and a few good pins, just like those rich

315

bitches on Bay Island. (She just wished she could wear them, and the minks, for Bucky Prince! God, how she wished . . .)

Not that she'd bought them all herself. There were always a few big time spenders around, and wouldn't the Hollywood gossip writers love to know what famous singer and what famous comic had paid for some of little Sandy's goodies! But of course she wouldn't say anything, because there were some very rough customers in this town and they might not like having their friends embarrassed and Sandy didn't think she'd enjoy having her face messed up and being put into some backwoods cat house.

Oh, she could take care of herself all right. She knew which end was up, and when to *put* it up. And she was happy enough, even with the dough running out. Though how had it gone so fast? My God, a hundred twenty-five thousand since August! Eight months, and she'd thought it would last eight *years*! But then again, she'd had that bad run of luck after doing so well at blackjack, and she'd *never* been able to make it at roulette or craps.

Still, she was doing all right. So she'd be walking around the Diabolo in that satin bikini instead of the mini-gowns she'd worn before. And she'd be making dates for before and after working hours instead of before and after gambling hours. Not much difference. It still came down to banging, banging, banging all the time with as many different men as appealed to her. Maybe now she'd take on a few older men with fat guts and fat wallets, where before she was kinda picky.

Only a few times had she run into anything nasty. One guy, not at all bad looking, had turned out to be a real pig and tried to use a belt on her. 'Kneel and kiss it, baby,' and crap like that. Reminded her of Beaufort (roasting, she hoped, for all eternity!) and she'd screamed the roof off the place. Boy, had *he* run! And that quiet German who'd said he was a professor of psychology and then started putting things into her. And *what* things! A little fun and games, all right, but stuffed animal pricks? That time *she'd* done the running!

Mostly, however, it was kicks. Men came to Las Vegas for fun. Sandy *lived* for that kind of fun.

Then came March fourteenth and she finished her tour at the Diabolo and came home with a dancer from the floor show and while he didn't have a quarter he made up for it by doing everything he could. *She* played the kneel-and-kiss-it-baby

316

game and as long as it lasted she didn't think how tomorrow was the first anniversary of the Bay Island job. But the dancer didn't want to stay all night, didn't want to sleep with her, and for once she really needed someone to sleep with her. He left and she got to thinking, and then to drinking. The next afternoon she was so hung over that only a full head of hair of the dog that bit her got her to work and kept her going.

She went home early the night of the fifteenth, saying she was sick. Sal said okay in that cold way of his, but she knew she'd better not try it too often. He got a cut of her take. The syndicate, as they called the mob here, got a cut of *everything* except the Howard Hughes setup.

She wished she knew Howard Hughes. Maybe he was like Bucky Prince ... though she didn't think *anyone* was like Bucky Prince; not for her.

So there she went again. And it being a year ago tonight made it worse. She let go, sat in her room and thought and thought and drank Jack Daniels. (The drinking was getting to be a big thing with her, and she worried about it a little, but hell she was young yet, only twenty-seven and it couldn't hurt her, not for a long time.)

She took a hot bath and afterward she came out nude and looked at herself in the full-length closet mirror and turned and it was still all there, maybe a little more than last year but still prime, grade A, top-notch hookie, as Sal had said when he came over last month for another kind of cut.

Bucky Prince wouldn't turn it down again; not after a year. She sort of watched for him. Maybe he'd come to Vegas one day and they'd meet and she'd play it cool, as if she still hadn't forgiven him for what he'd done when she came to his room that night, and then he'd grow hot and she'd say maybe and they'd come here and then, and then ...

'Bucky,' she whispered, staring at her nude body. 'Bucky, baby.'

She wanted him. Maybe if she had him for a while, a month or two as a steady, she could kick the hang up. Say a year. *Then*, maybe ...

She turned from the mirror without believing it. She felt ... she felt something for him she couldn't kick, ever. Never had felt it before and never had felt it since.

God, she didn't want to think of him!

But she thought of him. She went to the closet and took out

317

her silver mink and put it on. She went back to the mirror and turned and posed and said, 'Why, Mr. *Prince*! What are *you* doing in Las Vegas?'

He would see how beautiful she was.

If he came *this* year. Next year she might not be as beautiful, what with the booze and the crazy hours and all. She didn't like the way her eyes looked lately. And her belly had grown...

That always frightened her. She had to stay young and beautiful. How could she live if she wasn't young and beautiful and the men always after her?

The phone rang. She went to the bedside table, happy that she would have a date tonight, because it was always some *guy* who called—she didn't even know any women here—and heard, 'Sandra Blake?' She stopped breathing, and then thought, *No, it can't be, it's just a voice like his.* She said, 'Yes.' He said, 'Very dangerous of you to keep that name, Sandy.'

'Bucky! It's you!'

'Just passing through, and I always check the telephone directories. Do you know what tonight is?'

She said, 'Yes,' and, 'Where can we meet?' and her heart was pounding and she thought that everything she'd played at in front of the mirror would come true!

He didn't answer. She said, 'Bucky?'

'I'm sorry. I'm with my wife and son.'

'Wife and...'

'Is there anything you need? Money?'

She laughed as hard as she could. 'I've got so much ... ran it up at the casinos and what with the rich men out here ...'

She went on a while that way, letting him know that she didn't need anything from *him*, thank you!

He finally cut in with, 'Must go now.'

She quieted. 'Thanks for calling. Hear anything about the others?'

'Only Vino.' He paused. 'I'm afraid he's dead.'

'Oh.' She didn't ask how, and they said good-bye, and she hung up as if he were just another guy.

What else was there to do?

She had a long drink and thought of Vino. *Screw him, dead or alive!*

The phone rang again. It was a guy she'd met early this

evening; one of the fat ones with the fat wallets.

'Oh, yes, *Ron*. Well, I *was* feeling sick, but now ...'

He'd meet her in the lobby in half an hour. She dressed. She examined herself critically in the mirror. As she touched on mascara, one small tear slid from the corner of her left eye. She watched it, allowing it to travel down her cheek. Then she wiped it away, all traces of it away, and swung out the door.